THE
TW|NS
OF TRIBECA

THE TWINS OF TRIBECA

RACHEL PINE

miramax books

HYPERION

NEW YORK

Copyright © 2006 Rachel Pine

All rights reserved. No part of this book may be used or reproduced in any manner whatsoever without the written permission of the Publisher. Printed in the United States of America. For information address Hyperion, 77 West 66th Street, New York, NY 10023-6298.

ISBN 1-4013-6000-9

First Paperback Edition
10 9 8 7 6 5 4 3 2 1

For Adam, who looks after my heart;

For the exquisite Sabrina Rose Lane;

And mostly, for my family—
My mother, who is so proud,
My father, who would have been,
And my brother, who cheered for me at every step.

THE
TW|NS
OF TRIBECA

SUNSET BOULEVARD

It was the shove that got me thinking. This was no just-passing-by accidental bump—it was a swift and vicious push clearly meant to get me out of the way. More interesting than the shove, though, was its source: a ponytailed action star who was supposedly some kind of lama incarnate. I must have been blocking his path to enlightenment, because when I politely told him that he had more guests than we could accommodate, his only response was to hit and run. One quick shove and I was gone, all five feet of me, reeling backward in my heels as he dashed down the red carpet with his gang. Only the obscene thickness of that carpet kept me vertical; otherwise, I would have landed on my butt. Still recovering from my brush with greatness, I heard my earpiece squeal.

"Karen, Jesus, what are you doing up there? He's got too many people—why did you let them in?" It was Vivian Henry, the executive vice president of publicity at Glorious Pictures. Not my boss, directly, but one of the twenty-five or so people who had attained a position in the Glorious hierarchy that entitled them to yell at me.

"Vivian, I tried. He just shoved me and they all ran past!" I said.

"Forget it. Forget it. You're useless," she snapped. "I'll take care of it on my end."

I turned and peered at the entrance. Vivian was "taking care of it" by enthusiastically ushering my assailant and his flock inside. He tossed off a dismissive wave in my direction with one of his gigantic hands before ducking through the mosquito net covering the doorway. My heart still pounding from the shock of the encounter, I tried to slow down my pulse to its normal rate and concentrate on greeting the other, less violent celebrity guests as they arrived at our gala. After an arduous Oscar campaign—ordered by Phil and Tony Waxman, the fraternal twin brothers who'd founded Glorious Pictures, and carried out by everyone who worked at the company—we'd achieved our goal: *The Foreign Pilot* had won the Academy Award for Best Picture.

The Foreign Pilot had all the ingredients of a Glorious Pictures legend from the start. Rescued from the trash heap of a major studio, it starred marvelously talented (though previously unknown) European actors and had been adapted from a novel by a literary genius who'd escaped his country's brutally oppressive regime with the manuscript stuffed inside his shoes. As Phil had said nearly a year earlier in a meeting with the entire publicity department, "If that's not enough of a story for you people to work with, you might as well shoot yourselves in the head." This was Phil's characteristically subtle way of letting his staff know that *The Foreign Pilot* had better be a big picture. A Best Picture. Or else. That meeting took place about nine months before my arrival at Glorious, but it had been recounted by my colleagues so often and in such detail that I felt as if I'd actually been there. By the time I started in the publicity department in February, saying the place was exceptionally tense would have won Best Understatement.

And so I'd stumbled like a toddler on unsteady legs into a world of bleary midnights and head-splitting sunrises spent in the service of *The Foreign Pilot*'s corps. We'd made thousands of phone calls to Academy members, cheerily asking them if they'd enjoyed *The Foreign Pilot*. We'd dialed until our fingers cramped. We'd stayed up all night to reach voters in every single time zone. We'd manned those phones with the fervor of televangelists offering Heaven for just three easy payments. How skilled the leading actor's performance! How deft the direction! How breathtaking the scenery! The score! The costumes! We'd brayed our praises at the members who deigned to take our calls and then, because so many of them were elderly and hard of hearing, we'd brayed even louder. We'd meticulously executed a brilliant awards campaign that mimicked the tactical plans of the nation's finest political strategists. (We knew this to be true because when the president's congratulatory telegram arrived at the party, he told us so himself.) Now it was ten o'clock, the ceremonies were over, the Glorious party was in full swing, and we were awaiting the arrival of our victorious leaders.

In L.A. for five days and awake for most of the past three, I'd helped to mount our assault from the elegant confines of the Four Seasons, and my experience of Hollywood so far had proved both glamorous and humiliating. My room was beautiful but I hadn't had time to enjoy its amenities, most noticeably the multipillowed, elegantly duveted chariot of sleep for which this hotel was famous. For the right price, those beds could be shipped directly to one's home, high-thread-count shams and all, and rumor had it they were responsible for more than a few celebrity spawn. Now, as I choked down a room-service breakfast, I eyed mine wistfully, noticing that I'd barely made a dent in the dainty white coverlet during my three-hour snooze after our all-night party-logistics meeting. My Frosted Flakes had arrived with all the pomp and circumstance of a grand feast, surrounded by silver bowls of berries, yogurt, and bananas, but I had no time to contemplate the views from the flower-bedecked balcony on which the table had been set—I had an eight o'clock appointment at the Glorious hair and makeup suite. Lapping up the last drops of sweetened milk and taking a few gulps from my third cup of coffee, I grabbed my loaned designer gown and headed down to the second floor.

I stepped inside and immediately felt a hand on my back. The hand belonged to Marlene MacFarlane, the senior vice president of publicity, who had been placed in charge of the department's "look" for the event. She propelled me toward the hairdressers' room, noting, "Your hair will certainly be the most labor-intensive." There was no denying that most of the time my hair defied all styling products and betrayed a casual disregard for the laws of gravity. Still, this remark stung coming from Marlene, who wore her usual unflattering pageboy, although she'd stuck on some kind of glittery headband in deference to the day. I was seated in a salon chair specially installed for the occasion, while two stylists tag-teamed me. Gradually, I saw a glossy light brown mane evolving in the mirror. Glancing from side to side, trying not to move my head, I could see that we were all becoming shinier, sharper, more polished versions of ourselves: it was like that scene in *The Wizard of Oz* when Dorothy and her fellow travelers get spruced up before they go to meet the wizard.

Next up was the dressmaker, who pinned and basted and then swapped me a robe for my gown, so that she could make the needed alterations. While I waited for the dress, a makeup artist applied multiple layers of cosmetics to my face. "Now, I gif you new undervear," the seamstress said, in a vaguely Baltic accent. She handed me two paper ovals that looked alarmingly like mailing labels, right down to their peel-off backings. Seeing my confusion, she said, "It ees the bra. You steeck it on. Panties you leaf here." After maneuvering the stickers into place, taking care to create some cleavage, I stepped into the gown, marveling at its perfect fit and lack of distracting lines. I might be a little chilly tonight, but it would be worth it. She put a tiny vial of liquid in my hand. "For later. Eet dissolves zee glue." I tucked it into my evening bag.

Looking in the mirror again, I barely recognized myself. My hair gleamed, my skin looked bronzed and healthy, I had a curvy figure, and everything about me glowed, sparkled, shone, or did these things in combination. I felt like I was starring in the *E! True Hollywood Story* of my own life, the good part, where the narrator's voice would contain just a hint of warning as to the downfall sure to follow the commercial. For now, I turned slowly, submitting myself to Marlene's inspection, so that she could decide if I had achieved a sufficiently glamorous faux finish. After receiving her begrudging approval—"You're as good as you're ever going to get"—I dashed over to the Hotel Modigliani to begin rehearsing for my role as VIP doorstopper.

My actual boss, Allegra Orecchi, president of publicity for Glorious Pictures, was standing on the curb in front of the hotel, clipboard in hand, looking impatiently imperious—which was how I believed her face had frozen many years earlier.

"Sorry I'm late. My alterations took a while," I said, self-consciously running a hand through my now-luxuriant length of hair.

"Line!" Allegra whispered fiercely, by way of a salutation. The previous day, Allegra had suddenly developed serious doubts about my ability to greet the evening's guests.

I snapped to attention. "Welcome, Big Star. Thank you for coming." This was my single line, no ad-libbing allowed. I'd been reciting it over and over, trying out different inflections, cadences, and volumes, but nothing worked for Allegra.

"No, Karen, that's *still* not it," she frowned. "You need to accentuate the 'you.' You're thanking *each* person for coming. These are some of the most famous people in the world and you're *representing Glorious*," she said, as if training me in the Method. Trying to arrange my expression into the proper blend of politeness mixed with awe, I tried again.

"Welcome, Big Star. Thank *you* for coming."

She tilted her head and sighed. "No, no, that's still wrong." Allegra's cell phone rang and she stepped away, as if to prevent me from overhearing her conversation. This was merely a symbolic gesture; Allegra was generally inaudible even when standing uncomfortably close. I stood and waited for her to return, unpleasantly aware that the straps of my sandals were already beginning to pinch my insteps. She finished the call, spun around, and frowned. "You were *supposed* to keep practicing, Karen. Just because I'm on the phone doesn't mean that I'm not still working with you. I really don't feel like you're *trying*."

While in charge of a party for two thousand and supervising a staff of forty full-time publicity staffers and twenty freelancers, Allegra had curiously fixated on her invention of my inability to say seven words. The pressure was excruciating. Now she was inviting other people to add their comments. She had me rehearse a few more times and then brought over Matt Vincent, the vice chairman of marketing. Matt ranked just a hair above Allegra in the Glorious hierarchy and she was always turning handsprings in her attempts to impress him. Most of the time he ignored her.

"Welcome, Matt Vincent. Thank *you* for coming."

Matt was one of the people I liked best at the company. He seemed to have weathered six years of Glorious drama with his sense of humor intact. Just a few days before we'd flown out for the Oscars he'd climbed up on a milk crate in our TriBeCa office and delivered a hilarious rendition of Tony's acceptance speech, flawlessly imitating the raspy Bronx growl we all feared. For the last forty-eight hours, however, he'd been run ragged, putting together a tremendous ad campaign touting *The Foreign Pilot*'s Oscar win as well as a contingency plan should the unthinkable happen. Harassed and sleep-deprived, he looked like a different person. Now he listened to the line, looked at me distractedly, and said, "Well, there's no one else we can stick out here, so I guess she'll have to do." Then he left to get dressed for the evening.

Dissatisfied that I hadn't received a negative review from anyone else, Allegra couldn't restrain herself from one last mumbled barb before she left me. "Karen, don't move your hands when you greet people. They might think you're trying to touch them." Finally alone, I marveled at Allegra's ability to make me feel insufficiently welcoming yet intrusive at the same time. I reminded myself that Matt and Allegra had a way of bringing out the worst in each other. There was a lot riding on tonight's awards, not the least of which was their jobs. Post-Oscar housecleaning was not uncommon in the industry, and Glorious was no exception.

It was just after one in the afternoon, and while guests wouldn't be arriving for the viewing for about three hours, I had to hold my post in case anyone showed up early. The viewing party, where guests would watch the awards on a huge screen in the hotel's ballroom, was for people who hadn't been invited to the actual awards ceremony, like the author of *The Foreign Pilot*. (The Oscars are about screenplays, not novels.) The rest of the crowd would be mostly Glorious "friends and family"—industry executives and stars on the decline. They would need to be directed to the regular, non-VIP entrance. The viewing party was going to be small, but we described it as "intimate." The actual Oscar party would be enormous, and Glorious had rented the hotel's entire lobby, its three restaurants, the pool area with its two outside bars, as well as a penthouse suite on the fifteenth floor to serve as a VVIP room.

Behind me, a construction crew put the final touches on the red carpet entrance. It had been designed to look as if a biplane had crashed into the building, with just half the cockpit, the tail, and a piece of wing jutting out. The huge lobby doors had been replaced by large swaths of mosquito netting, and tremendous potted palms were being rolled into place to line the walkways. From where I was stationed I could hear Marlene barking orders at florists, bartenders, hotel employees, and anyone else who she thought might not be up to his or her given task, which was everyone. Several men unloaded tables and chairs from a truck and one of them offered me a seat, which I gratefully accepted.

At two-thirty Dagney Bloom, who made up the other half of Allegra's assistant team, arrived with Robert Kojima and Clark Garland, two of our colleagues from the New York office. Dagney was in a terrible mood. In the weeks leading up to the Oscars, she'd lobbied nonstop for an "inside" position. "That way, I'll get to see everything," she'd told me authoritatively at the desk we shared in New York. Marlene, who didn't really care for any of us but liked Dagney even less, had acquiesced to her repeated requests by awarding her the job of VIP elevator operator. Dagney would spend the entire evening in a tiny service lift, shuttling only the most "V of the VIP's" to and from the penthouse suite. "I can't believe that I'm going to be in that shoebox for six hours!" she hissed at me.

"At least you'll see all the stars up close," I replied coolly. I was still annoyed at Dagney for skipping off yesterday to shop on Melrose, leaving me at Allegra's beck and call for eight interminable hours while I covered for her. She and I got along about as well as could be expected for two people who shared both a crowded desk and a boss who was maddeningly vague about what she wanted from us.

As Robert handed me my headset and showed me how it worked, six delivery men arrived with the red carpet and began to painstakingly unspool it behind us. Seconds after they finished, Marlene materialized by my side and interrupted Robert's instructions. "Karen, why didn't you call me when the carpet arrived?"

"The guys just got out and unrolled it."

"Can't you see that it's all wrong?"

Clark, Robert, Dagney, and I all stared down the carpet's length. It stretched out like a wide red ribbon from where we were standing and ended right at the entrance. None of us said a word.

Marlene shook her head and frowned, as if I was trying her patience. She tapped one of the carpet deliverymen on the shoulder and began shouting, and soon the entire crew was struggling to drag fifty yards of red carpet an inch and a half to the left.

"As I was saying," Robert said, "this little part fits right in your ear and then you adjust this microphone so that it's not too close to your mouth. All of us with 'outside' jobs will be on channel three tonight." He and Clark got wired up and then we tested to make sure we could hear one another.

Twenty minutes later, Marlene came back up, looked at the carpet critically, then nodded. "That's much better. At least people will know where they're going," she said, before striding off to torture a hapless caterer.

When we were positive that the radios were working, Clark and Robert took their places on Sunset Boulevard. I was alone at the top of the carpet, shivers of excitement running through me. It was five o'clock, the ceremony was beginning, and guests would start arriving soon. I watched people in gowns and tuxedos stream into the viewing party through the regular entrance.

Clark had explained to me earlier that even though the awards wouldn't be over until about nine, celebrities would start trickling in about half an hour after the first Oscar was handed out.

"You mean they don't stay and watch the show?"

"If they win, they go backstage for media spots, and if they lose, they usually just want to get out of there. If they're only presenting, they basically bolt after the envelope's been opened."

It seemed strange to me. A billion viewers around the world watched the show on television, dreaming of being there. The people who were couldn't wait to leave.

Clark said that for the most part, the stars would arrive in little clusters throughout, with the big crush taking place about an hour after the conclusion.

True to what he'd told me, the first couple of hours were easy. There were only a few minor celebrity guests, none of whom needed to be formally announced. I just greeted them casually and pointed them toward the entrance.

When it came time to finally say my line, I had the mike of my headset turned on so that my like-wired colleagues could hear the name of each arriving celebrity. The first person to spring into action was Bill, a publicity manager in our L.A. office. Bill was stationed in the press pen amid the thick swarm of reporters and photographers who lined the main walkway. The journalists were separated from the red carpet by an iron barricade that was low enough to photograph over, but too high to jump. There was also a barrier behind them, so all the press, not unlike livestock, were collected into a chute. Each time I said my line, Bill would announce the celeb's name to them, and they'd start yelling and snapping pictures. It went like this:

Me (enunciating, hands at sides): "Welcome, David (pause) Spade. Thank *you* for coming."

Bill (loudly): "Oh my God, you guys! DAVID SPADE is here!"

Press (in unison): "David! David! Over here! Over here!"

Depending on the level of fame of the celeb currently walking the carpet, coupled with how interested the press was, Bill and I would figure out how to time the next one. Bill would ask me who was on deck and then say either, "Hold her a minute, he's still working them" or "Yeah, send her down, he's wearing a hole in the carpet."

Sometimes the shout would change right in the middle of someone's name, as the press would see the on-deck celeb beginning her descent. "Dav . . . ELIZABETH! ELIZABETH! Over here!"

When things really started to get rolling on the red carpet, I was almost too busy to take note of the myriad of celebrities I was greeting but not touching. The entire cast of *The Foreign Pilot* arrived, opting to walk down together. Four out of the five Best Actress nominees, all of the Best Supporting Actors, and, in a strange coincidence, the Best Supporting Actresses of the last four years, showed up in the order in which they had won. The gowns were magnificent and the jewelry absolutely eye-popping. Many of the women were wearing upward of a million dollars' worth of borrowed gems. The jewels were generally accompanied by bodyguards who would see the wearers safely inside, where the in-house security team would take over minding them.

Before people could get into the party, they first had to get out of their cars. Years of experience had taught the Glorious publicity staff that the best way to deter gate-crashers was to make sure that anyone who wasn't invited couldn't even get close to the curb. To this end, Robert and Clark were assigned to be "on cars." Stationed four blocks east and west of the hotel, respectively, they would stick their head into each limo, assess the situation, and then surreptitiously press a sticker onto the car's front bumper. There were three different levels of stickers. The first was an open red circle, which meant that you could come to the party with one guest, via the regular entrance. The second was the standard red circle with a slash through it. This meant that you hadn't been invited and we weren't even going to let you waste our energy arguing about it. The valets, who acted as our private Marine Corps, didn't allow those slash-stickered limos to maneuver over to the curb to disgorge their passengers. Some of the drivers circled the block twenty times before they figured it out. A few of the uninvited thought they could get out of their cars a couple of blocks away and simply walk into the party. In Los Angeles this is about as inconspicuous as setting your hair on fire.

The third-level sticker had a star on it, signaling "Star in the Car." Cars bearing stars were waved into the correct lane so that their occupants could be deposited at the top of the red carpet, where Bill and I started up the dog-and-pony show again. Before the star sticker was even placed, though, our car guys checked out the limo's passengers and made sure that each invited star had brought the legal limit of only one guest. How had the shover gotten around this? I wondered, making a mental note to ask Clark and Robert about it later. Robert had invented the sticker system a couple of years ago and was extremely proud of its success. If there was a loophole, he'd definitely want to seal it immediately.

"One guest per person" had been our mantra in the week leading up to the awards. Splitting up the evening's nearly one thousand RSVPs, we'd phoned each invitee, or their representative, and reminded them of the one-guest limit. We then put an asterisk next to the name of anyone who seemed likely to disobey the rule so that they could be monitored closely upon arrival. One of the people on that list was Ted Roddy, a publisher of pornographic magazines. Ordinarily he wouldn't have been invited, but this year, as the subject of a much-nominated biopic, he'd gotten the nod. When I called, his assistant said that Ted would be bringing his wife as his guest and that he traveled with a security guard and a man who pushed his wheelchair. I immediately walked over to Vivian, the designated point person for these situations. "I just spoke to Ted Roddy's assistant," I said. "Ted needs his bodyguard, a guy to push his wheelchair, and he's bringing his wife."

"Bodyguard? Why does Ted Roddy need a bodyguard?" she sniffed. In fact, everyone knew that Ted was wheelchair-bound due to an assassination attempt; it seemed wiser, however, not to bring this up, so I simply shrugged. "Probably just paranoia."

"Look," Vivian said. "Call the assistant back. The wife pushes the chair and watches his ass. One guest. End of story."

I took a deep breath, called the assistant, and relayed the information. "The man is paralyzed," he said. "Can't you make an exception?"

"No," I said. "I'm sorry, but I can't."

"There is something so *wrong* with you people," he sputtered, his voice full of disgust.

"Look," I said, as a wave of shame washed over me. "It's Ted plus one. One wife or one bodyguard or one chair-pusher. I don't care who he brings as long as it's only one of them." Vivian nodded approvingly as I hung up the phone, stunned by what had just come out of my mouth. I moved on to the next call with a bad feeling. Not only had the man at the right hand of the world's most famous pornographer just questioned my integrity, he'd been entirely correct.

Now, three days later, Ted Roddy was rolling up to the red carpet. Resplendent in a white tux and his famous golden wheelchair, he was being pushed by none other than Freddy Allen, the very actor who portrayed him in the film. Freddy had opted to give his "plus one" to Ted's very large and completely intimidating bodyguard. There was no doubt this guy could block bullets using his body mass alone. Ted's wife walked beside them, in a diamond necklace that started up near her chin and ended somewhere inside her impressive décolletage. I noticed the bodyguard was slightly wall-eyed, all the better to keep one eye on Ted and the other on his wife's jewels at the same time. Their presence assuaged my guilty conscience.

"Welcome, Ted Roddy," I said, flashing him my warmest smile. "Thank *you* for coming."

Right after Ted's arrival, I heard over my headset that *The Foreign Pilot* had just won Best Picture. Simultaneously, everyone inside the party started cheering and applauding. A thrill ran through me, and I looked around for someone to celebrate with. I caught Bill's eye, crammed in the press area though he was, and he blew on his index fingers, as if they were a pair of six-guns. We'd known that *The Foreign Pilot* was the film to beat, but that wasn't the same as having the award in hand.

I couldn't wait to start celebrating. Maybe now the difficult moods of my bosses and colleagues would simply melt away, leaving us to enjoy the victory we'd pulled off together, basking in Phil and Tony's pride.

The Waxman twins were the ultimate outsiders in an insider's business. For the last twenty years, their mix of edgy films and take-no-prisoners deal-making had been knocking the industry on its ear and then kicking it in the ass for good measure. An Oscar for Best Picture, however, had always eluded them. Phil and Tony didn't believe "it was an honor just to be nominated." They believed in Winner Take All. Tonight, with *The Foreign Pilot,* they had finally done just that. Not only had the film tied a decades-old record for the number of Oscars awarded to a single picture, but Glorious's overall tally had set a new one for wins by a single studio.

Suddenly the commotion on Sunset Boulevard increased and it became clear that Phil and Tony Waxman were about to make their entrance; through my headset I could hear Robert and Clark working with the LAPD to hold back the traffic in both directions. The moment that had long been dreamed of and meticulously choreographed had finally arrived. The only thing left to chance was which brother would be holding the trophy as they left the car.

As the limousine glided to a stop at the curb a klieg light was switched on, and the helicopters hovered so low that the churned-up air from the rotors blew back my hair and plastered my gown against my body. The driver got out, then paused with his glove on the handle before opening the rear door with a flourish. A million flashes went off as Phil and Tony burst out of the limo, together lifting their Oscar skyward.

They were an unlikely duo. Phil was huge—six four, with the immense shoulders and chest of an offensive lineman. He had a tremendous head with a fleshy face and a pair of small, fierce eyes that didn't miss a trick. His tie was unknotted and his shirt collar opened to make room for his enormous neck, his bulk clearly straining the seams of his custom-made tuxedo. Tony was a slender six feet tall with pleasant-enough features completely ruined by his hair. Light brown and frizzy, it gave the distinct impression that something might be living in it. Tonight, however, in a Valentino tux, he looked pretty good, at least from the forehead down. Gloria Waxman exited the limo last and waited at the top of the carpet, beaming motherly love at her boys. In her beaded Escada gown and Blackglama mink stole she was every inch the elegant matriarch. With her hair frosted especially to complement the golden statue she'd never once doubted her sons would win, she proudly looked on, a Jewish Rose Kennedy in couture.

Gloria Waxman, her sons' inspiration and the studio's namesake, reveled in telling stories about the twins' difficult birth. During her emergency C-section there was one terrifying moment when the obstetrician thought that Phil and Tony were conjoined.

Instead, it turned out that each infant was tightly grasping the other around the neck. Now, some forty-eight years later, they'd only slightly loosened the hold. The Waxmans fought like a pair of ghetto pit bulls and were incredibly jealous of one another. Although they shared producers' credit on all of Glorious's films, in reality a picture was either a "Tony" or a "Phil." If one had a film that was doing well in theaters, the other would deride his brother's next project mercilessly. What was breaking box-office records for Tony "sucked" compared with what Phil had just "wrapped." The soundtrack album accompanying Tony's next film "rocked," while Phil's newly acquired script "had straight-to-video written all over it." Tony's marketing campaign was "goddamn hilarious," while Phil's casting of Hollywood's It-est It Girl in an upcoming film was "purely your dick talking, not that I blame you." And on and on it went. Phil and Tony, Tony and Phil, beating the crap out of each other for fame and fortune, which they ultimately split down the middle and shared.

The twins hammed it up for the cameras—first pretending to tussle with the award, then cradling it like a swaddled infant. Even Tony, who generally shunned the spotlight, looked like he was enjoying the adulation. They practically danced on the red carpet as they made their way to the victory gala. At one point, Tony jumped on Phil's shoulders and held the award aloft, the three of them resembling a bizarre Hollywood totem pole of Fat Phil, Fit Tony, and their gleaming baby Oscar. That image would become one of the year's most famous photographs. Then they motioned their mother over and handed her the trophy. Although she was seventy, and quite small, its heft didn't faze her one bit. She pumped it over her head with one hand while waving with the back of the other in a sort of half-Rocky, half-royal pose that was 100 percent Gloria Waxman.

After twenty minutes of antics, the Waxmans disappeared into the party. I found out via my headset that Robert and Clark had been called inside to coordinate a champagne toast for the cast and crew of *The Foreign Pilot,* and I felt slightly deflated; there was no sign that any of us would get a break to join in the festivities. For the next couple of hours, it was business as usual on my little piece of sidewalk—greeting celebrities and sending them down the carpet, listening to the shouts from the press pen, and routinely hearing Vivian or Marlene on the walkie-talkie upbraid me or one of my colleagues for a horrible faux pas that had undoubtedly ruined the evening. I heard Robert tell Clark that Tony said to cut off Gloria's Mai Tais. I smiled, imagining Gloria teetering on her heels, holding up her empty glass as Clark handed her a rumless refill.

Looking up at the hotel, I could make out dozens of faces in the windows facing Sunset. For the people staying in the Hotel Modigliani, our party had become something of a nightmare, turning them into frustrated voyeurs paying through the nose for the privilege to stare. They were not permitted access to the lobby or the pool, and they had to enter and leave the building through an underground garage in elevators programmed not to stop on any of "our" floors. Many of them watched the spectacle of the arrivals with a wistful air. One man even shinnied down a rope made of knotted together sheets only to be met by an irate Marlene the moment his feet touched the ground. After about thirty seconds of being shrieked at, he scrambled back up to the safety of his room.

It was 3 A.M., the time of night when people started showing up with strange stories, including two men who each claimed to be a certain William Morris agent who had arrived two hours earlier and a heavily made-up woman in a tattered squirrel coat carrying a counterfeit Oscar that she said she'd just won. For what, Best Fabrication? I thought unkindly.

Then a man walked over to me, lingering at the top of the carpet without trying to come in. He had gray hair and his face was heavily lined. His hands shook a bit, and they had brown spots on them, but he had the air of someone much younger than he appeared. His suit was worn but sharply pressed and his striped tie was done up in a double Windsor knot. "Do you know how many people are inside?" he asked.

"I'm not sure," I answered, thinking he might be working undercover for the fire department, which had been threatening to end our party if we went over capacity.

"Anyone interesting in there?"

"Sure, half of Hollywood," I said, deciding that he was probably just some eccentric out for a predawn stroll on Sunset Boulevard.

"And the Waxmans? Are they at the party?"

I nodded.

"Well, what about Ted Roddy?"

"He's here, as far as I know." From where I was standing, I could see only arrivals, not departures.

"Interesting, having a guy like him around. What's he like?"

"I didn't meet him. I only saw him for about two seconds when he came in with his wife and the others."

"He brought a lot of people?"

"Actually, it was unusual because we'd told everyone that they could have only one guest—even Ted, who usually has a bodyguard and a wheelchair attendant, and of course, his wife along with him." I was so tired that I was rambling to this complete stranger.

"So only Ted was allowed to have extra guests?"

"No, he wasn't. But apparently Freddy Allen made Ted's bodyguard his guest, and pushed the chair himself."

"Really. How noble of Mr. Allen."

"That's what I thought. I mean, the guy's in a wheelchair. We could have at least cut him some slack." My thoughts were skipping the part of my brain that made decisions and going straight for my tongue. "Excuse me," I said, walking a few yards down the carpet.

"Marlene," I whispered into the mike. "There's a guy up here who's really strange. He's asking me an awful lot of questions."

"Thanks, Karen. I had no idea that there was anyone weird walking around Hollywood in the middle of the night. Can you please try not to waste my time with this utter nonsense?"

The radio went dead and I glanced back up at where the man had been standing just a minute before. He was gone. I immediately regretted having bothered Marlene, thereby giving her yet another opportunity to insult me. This, I knew, was how people at my company spoke to each other. This was how they spoke to their friends and their coworkers and their children's nannies and their husbands and their wives and their boyfriends and their parents, although knowing this didn't make me feel much better at the moment.

From my very first day at Glorious, I had to keep reminding myself that everyone was under enormous pressure. The fact that we were so close to finally winning Best Picture had driven everyone to work at a backbreaking pace. Tempers were short, expectations were high, and emotions were on a razor's edge. It was natural to snap at those nearest and dearest, I had rationalized, especially with so much hanging in the balance. So why now, when we had accomplished our goal, was there no sense of relief?

At about a quarter to five in the morning, all of us who had outside jobs were allowed, finally, to come into the hotel, and the people who had been given inside stations could abandon their posts. We all collapsed onto the couches and overstuffed chairs in the lobby. Within five minutes, Tony strode by, glanced at us, and barked through clenched teeth, "Don't any of you ever do anything? Do you think you're here on some kind of goddamn paid vacation?" Allegra then materialized and added her two cents. "You guys are an embarrassment. You make us all look like a bunch of lazy incompetents." I looked around the room. The place was nearly empty, save for a few catering employees who were folding up tables and stacking wooden chairs. I felt anger convulse through the group, but no one said a word. We were too damn tired.

Best Picture had been safely in the Waxmans' hands for several hours now, yet the venomous tone had already crept back in. In those predawn hours following the awards, I began to grasp the error of my logic: At Glorious Pictures, push would always come to shove.

Realizing that it was better to return to the hotel than stick around and wait to see who would scold me next, I hitched a ride back to the Four Seasons with Clark. As we rode up in the elevator he tried to cheer me up. "Glorious tradition. Noon, at the pool, we've got the two best cabanas reserved. We'll have mimosas, we'll get some massages, facials, the works—and tonight will be a nasty little memory before you know it. Get some sleep and I'll see you later." He patted me lightly on the head as if I were a child.

Carrying my shoes, I limped off to my room, hitting the mattress in full black-tie attire.

EYES WIDE SHUT

I t's not as if I went into this with my eyes closed. Glorious was famous for being a difficult place to work. I'd heard rumors that there was even a twelve-step program for former employees that met somewhere in the suburbs of New Jersey. GlorAnon was either truly anonymous or purely fictional, because later, when I asked around, no one was ever able to confirm its existence. Still, tales abounded of bright young things who went to work at Glorious and left barely capable of asking, "Will that be to stay or to go?" such was their emotional state. I chose to focus, though, on the stories with better endings: the twenty-four-year-old executive vice presidents with staffs and salaries to match their impressive titles; the assistant who wrote glowing coverage of her own pseudonymous screenplay and saw it green-lighted within weeks; the receptionist who so impressed a visiting director with her unsolicited commentary that she was promoted to production executive. My own stint at Glorious, however, had been instigated less by blind ambition than by art and science conspiring against me.

Before Glorious, I'd spent nearly four years working in the advertising research department of CNN. Most recently, I'd put together a study to show the percentage of CNN viewers statistically likely to have "persistent or recurring" heartburn now or in the future. The money was okay, the people were nice, my semiannual reviews were excellent, and my future there seemed assured, despite the fact that I had persistent and recurring doubts that I'd ever feel fulfilled in this type of role. But if the work was dull, the evenings and weekends more than made up for it—my social calendar was in the hands of my best friend, Arabella, a struggling actress, and my boyfriend, Gabe, a struggling painter, and they kept it extremely full. Arabella was always dragging me off at odd hours to the Film Forum or the Walter Reade, and Gabe considered it a point of honor that we attended as many gallery openings as was humanly possible. Gabe, Arabella, and I (along with whomever Arabella was dating at the moment) ran around the city in our own little gang of four, checking out everything from James Bond–inspired opera to "forensics as art" slide shows to a performance of *Equus* by a seventh grade class in one of the more "progressive" private schools. Together we feasted on whatever New York offered us, as long as it was free or reasonably cheap.

Arabella Thompson had been my best friend since our freshman year at UMass Amherst. (Her name's really Abby, but after sophomore year she'd refused to answer to it.) She'd majored in drama and I was a political science wonk, so our paths might never have crossed if we hadn't ended up on opposing panels for a debate about "truth in the movies" following a screening of *All the President's Men*. That evening we discovered that it was more fun arguing with each other than agreeing with anyone else, and we soon became inseparable. An insatiable movie buff, Arabella knew everything about nearly every movie ever made, not to mention celebrities, directors, and producers, and she was a veritable Who's Who with regard to film industry executives. Unfortunately, she also came from a long line of doctors—three generations so far—and all of them, even the long-deceased, it appeared, were putting intense pressure on her to go into the family business. She'd been accepted at the Johns Hopkins School of Medicine, the Thompson alma mater, but had deferred admission several times so that she could continue taking acting classes and auditioning in New York. Finally, she'd reluctantly concluded that while she could certainly become a doctor, she would never play one on TV. And so she moved to Baltimore, where she would act like a medical student for the next twenty years—or at least that's what it felt like to me.

We'd promised to spend at least one weekend a month together, either in Maryland or New York, but pretty soon the rigors of anatomy, physiology, and histology made that impossible. By mid-autumn it was clear that we were lucky to speak on the phone once a week, and her conversations were now littered with medical jargon and gruesome updates on the dissection of Lloyd, her cadaver, instead of the cinematic nuggets she used to discuss obsessively. She had also become Abby again, the saddest part of all.

Then Gabe and I had a horrible fight over Thanksgiving weekend. Both Gabe's talent and his inability to successfully market himself were considerable; though he longed for a place in the downtown galleries and SoHo lofts of would-be patrons, he was supporting himself with a succession of temp jobs. The most recent one was at Christie's auction house, where he'd hoped to network with the art crowd; instead, he'd found himself on the loading dock, carrying antique furniture in and out of moving vans. After a week he quit in disgust, saying he was sick of his boss's acting as though the Chippendale chests were more valuable than his back. Instead of pointing out that his suspicion was probably true, I suggested that it might be time to consider making his living in some other way, perhaps in the commercial arts. Gabe took this as a sign that I'd never believed in his painting in the first place and announced that he was moving to eastern Kentucky, where he could live with his great-uncle for almost nothing and "create without distractions." Although the accepted remedy for heartache is to stay busy, I had no one to stay busy *with*, and I felt both abandoned and bored out of my mind. Given that Gabe and Arabella had suddenly been removed from my orbit, I decided to examine parts of my own life that might benefit from a change. "Career" was the slide currently under the microscope.

All through school I'd burned with ambition, wanting to take my degree and run with it, although where to had never been perfectly clear. I'd had a few different entry-level jobs, and had fallen into my current position at CNN through a friend of a friend, staying much longer than I'd ever intended. Somehow four years had gone by. While Abby had given up her dream, her plan B was hardly a losing proposition. And Gabe had decided to keep moving forward with his painting, ultimately choosing it over our relationship. The irony didn't escape me—they each knew what they wanted, while I, the one with the twice-a-month paycheck, the health insurance, and the maxed-out 401(k) hadn't a clue.

All of this was on my mind as I trudged through the January dark one evening to join the rest of my department at Itchy's Taco Heaven, our customary Thursday night gathering spot. As the blinking neon chili pepper became visible through the gloom, I grew hopeful, anticipating a strong margarita in my immediate future; these Thursday evenings had become the high point of my week.

At least I was getting to know my colleagues a bit better, I thought, elbowing my way through the midtown crowd of commuters and secretaries with my first drink, searching for our table.

As I angled into an empty seat, I saw that an unfamiliar face had joined our group. "Karen, this is Clark Garland," said Pete, our department's head statistician. "We went to school together. I don't see him too much these days, since he's always slaving away for Glorious."

Had I heard correctly? This guy worked at Glorious Pictures? Abby wouldn't believe it. Of all the millions of movies we'd seen together, the ones from Glorious were her favorites. She had a complete fixation on the twin brothers who ran it, especially Tony Waxman, the shorter of the two. The media tended to portray them as either greedy slobs or brilliant artistes, depending on which day of the week it was, and some of the stories she told me about the company were as compelling as the movies themselves.

I jumped up, eagerness causing me to nearly knock over my drink. "Karen Jacobs, nice to meet you," I said breathlessly, extending my hand. "I love Glorious's movies. I cried so much at *Teatro Incantato* that I was afraid the ushers were going to ask me to leave." I realized that I was still pumping Clark's arm up and down and, mortified, I stopped abruptly, causing him to spill some of his martini. He gallantly pretended nothing had happened, while Pete gave me a puzzled look. He sat only two cubes away from me in the office, and I'd probably just said more to Clark than I'd said to him in the entire time we'd worked together.

Clark was about six feet tall, and his patrician good looks combined with his rangy, athletic physique gave him the appearance of someone who played a lot of squash. His dark brown hair was thinning in a couple of places, but he had the most confident smile I'd ever seen. While my colleagues and I looked like corpses at a wake, due to our company's incredibly stiff dress code, Clark was fashionably dressed down, and everything he was wearing—the investment-quality denims, the black cashmere crewneck sweater, the broken-in Gucci loafers—had a warm, lived-in look to it.

"I liked that film, too," Clark said. "There are some great new ones coming out in the next couple of months—if I live that long," he said, smiling.

I nodded solemnly. "I've heard it's a tough place to work. What do you do there?"

"I'm in the publicity department, which is the craziest part of the whole crazy place. But I absolutely love my job."

He loved it! I couldn't wait to call Abby and tell her that I'd met an actual Glorious Pictures publicist, and that he loved it, and that it was just as fun and insane as we'd imagined it would be. For the rest of the evening, I followed Clark around like a hungry little spaniel, pestering him with questions, eager for any Glorious morsel he might drop before me. Pete, trying to get a word in edgewise with his friend, asked if it was true that the Waxmans argued a lot.

"Argue? That's not even the word for it. It's more like hand-to-hand combat," Clark said. "There are days when I just can't believe what goes on."

"Like what?" I asked, excited to get some inside information to pass along to Abby.

"Tony's constantly complaining about Phil's diet—which, admittedly, is terrible. The other day Tony walked in while Phil was eating a foot-long Philly cheese steak, put his face right in Phil's, and screamed, 'Keep it up—you'll die and I'll get everything!' On the other hand, Tony works out a lot, especially when he's stressed, which is, of course, always. He comes to work every day dressed in this whole seventies work-out look—you know, nylon running suits with terrycloth head-and wristbands. Anyway, last week he was skipping rope during a meeting with the director of *The Raven II: Nevermore* and he accidentally lassoed Phil. Needless to say, Phil was not pleased. I think his exact words were, 'Get that fucking thing off my goddamn neck, Tonto.'"

"He said *Tonto?*" Pete and I looked at each other with raised eyebrows. We'd attended a company-sponsored diversity training workshop last month and learned to avoid that particular word at all costs. Apparently it offended not only indigenous peoples but Spanish-speakers as well because "Tonto" translates idiomatically into "stupid" in Spanish. "Isn't that considered extremely politically incorrect these days?" Pete asked.

"Guilty as charged," Clark said. "It's just that kind of place."

After a couple more rounds of drinks, I started to say good night to everyone.

"Karen, it was great to meet you," Clark said, still smiling that great smile. "How do I get ahold of you? There might be something else you and I can discuss." Not sure what he wanted, I gave him my card. I had the distinct impression that Clark was gay—although it was getting rather hard to tell in New York these days—but I hoped I was wrong. A movie date with a Glorious employee would undoubtedly lift my spirits.

The next afternoon, just after I'd discovered that 57 percent of our viewers liked to eat gelatin, and of those, 85 percent listed "blue" as their favorite flavor, Clark called. "Hey Karen, there was something I wanted to tell you last night, but I didn't want to mention it in front of everyone," he said. "Our president of publicity needs a new assistant. You know so much about our films and you're so enthusiastic. Would you consider interviewing for it? I think you'd be terrific."

"Wow. Thanks so much for thinking of me." Adrenaline began to pump through my body, causing my phone hand to perspire. Switching hands and trying to maintain a modicum of composure, I listened as Clark told me what I had to do to officially apply. He said that once my résumé was received, I'd get called to come in for an interview. Within minutes of hanging up the phone, I had reviewed my CV, e-mailed it to Clark, and phoned Abby.

"Hey Karen, I'm studying for an exam in the anatomy of obstetrics. Did you know that when a woman is pregnant her appendix moves over to the left side?"

"No, I didn't. That's bizarre. Did you know that I'm applying for a job at Glorious Pictures?"

Abby shrieked into the phone. "Really? *The* Glorious? With the Waxmans?"

"Yup, that's the one." I gave her the rundown on how I'd met Clark.

"Karen, I'm off to the lab, but I'm going to cross my fingers for you. I'm even going to cross Lloyd's fingers for you."

"Can you do that?" I asked, trying not to think of Lloyd's pruney, rigor-mortised hands.

"Definitely," she said. "He's incredibly cooperative."

I spent the rest of the afternoon trying to continue the gelatin research, but my mind kept drifting back to my conversation with Clark. In the past couple of years, Abby, Gabe, and I had seen some terrific Glorious films together—*A Crying Shame, Perp Friction, Fortune's Fork,* and *Whisper of a Girl,* to mention a few— which more often than not had led to spirited discussions at the Turkish kebab joint where we frequently ended our evenings. Sometimes other diners would weigh in with their opinions; one evening two radical feminists almost attacked Gabe with their skewers after overhearing his comments on the mutilation scene in *The Oboe.* I knew that all of Glorious's movies didn't elicit such passionate responses, but year after year, the company's bottom line increased, and its success was discussed not just in the entertainment press but in the *Wall Street Journal* as well. The place had become proof that money could be made with risky, artistic endeavors; you just had to pick the right ones. Even as an assistant, I'd be in close proximity to some of the world's brightest, most innovative filmmaking talent. And who knew? If there was one place that proved the sky was the limit, Glorious Pictures was it. It had been a long time since I'd been so excited by possibility, and it was a truly magnificent feeling.

"Karen?" It was Pete, tapping my computer monitor with his pencil and wearing a slightly peeved expression. How long had he been standing there? "Do you have the gelatin comparisons for me?" I handed him a printout. "No, I need the part about powdered versus prepared," he said. "It's due in an hour."

"I'm sorry, Pete. Just give me twenty minutes, and I'll bring it by for you." I'd completely forgotten he'd asked me for those figures earlier in the day and I felt suddenly mortified that this was how I spent most of my time. Powdered versus prepared? I just had to get out of here.

Two weeks later I was at my desk, reworking the heartburn data; now the potential advertiser wanted to know what percentage of our viewers experienced heartburn at least three times a week. This fascinating endeavor was interrupted by a telephone call from a woman with a mezzo-soprano voice who identified herself as Geraldine Waters, head of human resources at Glorious. "I was hoping you could come in and speak with me," she said. "Can you be here in an hour?"

An hour? I'd assumed that I'd have at least a day's notice so that I could put together an outfit that looked reasonably trendy—now I'd have to go in my CNN dress-for-success look, with its regulation no-more-than-two-inches-above-the-knee skirt and no-higher-than-two-inch-heeled pumps; and mine were in desperate need of a shine. Not to mention the fact that I was supposed to present the new heartburn information at a four o'clock meeting.

"Sure, I'll be there," I said, hanging up, already planning my exit strategy.

I stuck my head into my boss's office. "I'm really sorry. I completely forgot that I had an appointment with my gastroenterologist today at two." It was no wonder that I'd selected that particular alibi—my stomach was doing the mambo. "I've e-mailed you the document with the heartburn numbers and I'll rush back as soon as I can," I said, trying to sound just harried enough to avoid additional questions. Then I took off at a run down the hall to the ladies' room. Once inside, I shut myself in one of the stalls, carefully balanced my compact on top of the toilet paper dispenser, and put on some lipstick, mascara, and blush. With a wayward barrette coughed up from the depths of my purse I attempted to trap one particularly difficult section of hair into a neat little wave. I stepped out of the stall, and prayed that I looked better than the greenish pearl-wearing Stepford wife staring back at me in the mirror. I opened the bathroom door and peeked out right and left to make sure no one was in the hallway. Then I walked briskly to the elevator, zipped through the lobby, and jogged to the next corner before hailing the cab that would take me to Glorious. It wasn't until I got in and closed the door that I was able to fully exhale. I gave the driver the address and he looked back at me. "Where?"

"Greenwich Street."

"You must mean Greenwich Avenue."

"No, I'm sure it's Greenwich Street. Why don't you just head downtown on the west side and I can try to figure it out on the way," I said, kicking myself for not having gotten more specific directions. TriBeCa—which had gotten its name from being the Triangle Below Canal Street—is tucked into the lower left-hand corner of Manhattan, beyond the reach of the numbered streets, and it was easy to get lost there. The area had been the city's manufacturing hub in the late 1800s; now, a century later, it had been rediscovered because it had the one thing that could bring wealthy New Yorkers to their knees—space. The abandoned warehouses and factories were quickly being converted into luxury lofts large enough to entertain a couple of hundred people, house an impressive art collection, and provide the kind of high-ceilinged theatricality that celebrities, moguls, and successful creative types crave. But while investment banks and other white-collar industries were moving in, it was New York's independent film community that had really put TriBeCa on the map—even if most cabbies still needed one to find it.

My cab took a sharp left turn that tossed me sideways as the driver located Greenwich Street about ten feet too late and decided to go for it anyway. Spotting the building, a low red-brick affair with Lincoln Town Cars parked three deep in front of it, I alerted the driver, who jammed on the brakes with gusto. I went inside, got a visitor's pass from security, and rode the elevator up to the floor that housed Glorious.

After I introduced myself, the receptionist said that Geraldine was running "just a teensy bit behind." I waited, looking around the reception area at the numerous movie posters, award statuettes, and plaques that filled the space, which was otherwise somewhat shabbily furnished with a stained old couch and well-worn carpeting. I'd been sitting for about five minutes when four deliverymen got off the elevator, each carrying a bag bearing the Second Avenue Deli's distinctive logo and an enormous tray loaded with delicatessen sandwiches. Even through the plastic wrap, the smell of cured meats and mustard was utterly mouth-watering. This, I decided, was a good omen. My father insisted on making a pilgrimage to the Second Avenue Deli every time he came to visit, and I'd happily accompany him for their monstrous pastrami sandwiches on rye that melted in your mouth, only to reassemble, like a brick, later in your stomach. The receptionist picked up a phone and said, "Phil's lunch is here," before directing the men toward a door. How many of those sandwiches, I couldn't help wondering, could Phil Waxman actually consume?

After ninety minutes of waiting, I started to obsess over the fact that I was extremely ill-prepared for this interview. True, Abby had been e-mailing me quizzes on the history of Glorious, and on the phone made me practice answering questions like "What value will you bring to our organization?" and "How do you handle intense pressure?" But there was no getting around the fact that my background was in advertising and research, and I had absolutely no publicity experience whatsoever. I felt my hands go clammy and my mouth dry up. Besides Clark's recommendation, what did I actually have to offer? I stretched my neck and moved my shoulders around, trying to relax, regretting all the times I'd refused to try one of Abby's yoga classes. As I twisted my head from side to side as far as it could go, I noted a very large painting dominating the entire wall behind me. It consisted chiefly of red blobs sprouting clusters of what appeared to be plastic string. I turned around completely to read the card:

My Heart's Desire
Oil on Canvas with Fishing Line and Scotch Tape
Trudi Waxman

This, I thought, was a real testament to blood being thicker than water. Too bad Gabe wasn't related to the Waxmans. I thought of him now, somewhere in rural Kentucky, probably wearing overalls and creating wonderful art without my negativity around to discourage him. For the hundredth time that week, I debated whether or not I should break down and call him. I wasn't sure if it would be more like a knife wound than a peace offering for either of us. Just then, a tall woman appeared, hand outstretched. Her hair, eyebrows, fingernails, lipstick, and pantsuit were all the same shade of carrot orange. "You must be Karen," she said, grasping my hand firmly. Her handshake clearly said, "I'm in charge." I tried to make my grip just as firm, but then she added some more muscle and I finally had to let my hand go limp in self-defense.

I followed her around a series of hallways and then into her office, where I took a seat on the other side of the desk. As I reached down to get my résumé I noticed an adorable miniature dachshund in the corner. "Hey there," I said, attempting to pat the dog on the head. He growled, baring his teeth.

"That's just Harvey," Geraldine said. "He can be a real monster sometimes, but he doesn't usually bite." She didn't sound very convincing, and I stealthily repositioned my briefcase so it was between me and the dog. Harvey responded by showing me all of his teeth in a sort of angry grimace.

"I don't think I've ever seen a dog with such white teeth," I said, casting about for something nice to say about her nasty little weasel.

"I'm so glad you noticed," Geraldine said, looking over at Harvey with adoration. She gave him a cutesy little wave and he moved his tail about an inch. She beamed as he yawned and inspected a paw. "Harvey's smile just wasn't what it should be, so I took him to the doggie dentist and had his teeth bleached." Geraldine said everything very quickly, as if she was in a rush to get it all out. I looked over at the dog again, who was still displaying his cosmetic dental work, although his expression now resembled more of a scowl. He could have been a hostile Osmond brother.

"Clark Garland told me about you," she said. "He thinks you'd do well in the Allegra position." The Allegra position? Was this related to the Heimlich maneuver or Kegel exercises? Apparently not—Geraldine went on to explain that Allegra Orecchi was Glorious's president of publicity and that she had two assistants to help her with the day-to-day running of her office as well as with larger, more interesting projects, such as planning premieres and providing support at out-of-town events like the Sundance Film Festival and the Academy Awards.

"You'd be her second," Geraldine said, meaning second assistant, "but her first just started a few months ago, so you'll be pretty even, in terms of seniority. It's a very high-profile position—you'll spend a lot of time interacting with Phil and Tony Waxman, as well as with the actors and filmmakers."

I kept waiting for my chance to mention my knowledge of the company—Glorious's Oscar track record, box office figures on their last two years of releases, the films they currently had in production—but the moment never came. Mostly, Geraldine spoke while I nodded and listened. When she finally did have a question, though, she asked it with great gravitas. "The age thing, are you okay with that?"

I hadn't the slightest idea what she was talking about. When I didn't answer, she spelled it out for me. "I can see from the year that you graduated that you're about twenty-nine."

"Twenty-eight," I corrected.

"Yes, well, either way you're going to run into a lot of executives here who are quite senior to you, but are at least a couple of years younger. Some of the older assistants have had problems with that."

Did Geraldine think I was already washed up? "No, that's fine. I think that the opportunity to learn from such incredibly talented people will be a privilege," I said brightly, finally using some of the job-interview-speak I'd rehearsed.

"Well, that's all then. I'll be in touch." She stood to walk me out. I watched Harvey carefully as I picked up my briefcase and coat. I didn't want my hands anywhere near those sharp, shining teeth.

After two weeks I'd heard nothing from Glorious and was close to giving up hope. The Academy nominations were announced and Glorious's film *The Foreign Pilot* had been nominated in a dozen categories, including Best Picture, Best Director, Best This, Best That, while I continued to do my Best Impression of a person trying to stay sane. Then, three days after the nominations were announced, while sitting at my desk, diligently working out the correlation between cable news watchers and floor wax users, my phone rang. "Karen? Geraldine. You've got the job."

"That's great! Thank you so much!" I couldn't wait to tell Abby that she could uncross poor Lloyd's fingers, if they were still intact. This was amazing—I wouldn't ever have to deal with Jell-O or heartburn or stuffy dress codes again. I was heading for bigger and better things. I was . . .

Completely swept away by my euphoria, I almost didn't hear Geraldine repeat herself.

"I said, we'd like you to start on Monday."

It was 4 P.M. on Friday. I couldn't just walk out of here and never come back. That would be completely unprofessional. I took a deep breath. "I'd like to finish up what I'm doing here, give two weeks' notice, but yes, I'm definitely interested in the position."

"Karen, the job starts Monday. Will we be seeing you Monday at nine?"

This was a once-in-a-lifetime opportunity. Could I afford to pass it up over two weeks' notice? After all, this was Glorious Pictures and they wanted what they wanted. Right now it was me, on Monday, at nine. "I'll be there."

That evening I breathlessly stumbled into the apartment I shared with my cousin Ellen. Four years older than I, Ellen had split up with her husband a couple of years earlier. Ever since then, we'd shared her apartment. It was almost as if we were back in Providence, Rhode Island, where we'd grown up on the same block. On Friday nights, Ellen usually made dinner, and before Gabe's and Abby's disappearances, I would eat the leftovers for lunch on Saturday. Now, though, I was happy to have someone to hang around with on the weekends, although I worried that the two of us might grow old in this apartment—blue-haired spinster cousins. Sure enough, I found Ellen in the kitchen washing lettuce, the unmistakable scent of lasagna wafting out of the oven. A Pinot Noir was open on the counter beside her.

"Ellen, you'll never believe it!" I said, not even stopping to take off my coat. She turned.

"You got the job at Glorious."

"I start on Monday. I'm going to be the second assistant to the president of publicity!" I said, still excited. I took off my coat and poured two glasses of wine, handing one to Ellen.

"You start on Monday? When did you find out? You have to give notice, don't you?"

Like a heat-seeking missile, my cousin had found exactly what was making me uncomfortable.

"Yeah, well, there was no time for notice. They called me to-day and said that I had to start on Monday, or they couldn't give me the job."

She shook her head and sighed, not saying anything. My cousin was a tax attorney who did everything strictly by the rules and was mistrustful of anyone who didn't.

"Ellen, you don't understand. I am *dying* to work at this place. I may never get another opportunity like this."

"Okay, but if this doesn't work out, you may have burned some bridges."

Quitting with no notice *was* horrible. But then I thought about Phil and Tony Waxman, and how when they wanted something, they damned the torpedoes and went for it. Suddenly, I felt like a different person. A Glorious person. Someone who thought outside the box, broke the rules, shook things up a little. Ellen would never understand. Once when we were kids she walked half a mile to return an extra nickel the supermarket cashier had accidentally added to her change. "It's about much more than the five cents," she'd said, at the age of eleven already a person of deep convictions.

"I have to try this, or I'll never forgive myself."

"Just promise me you'll be careful. Everyone knows that Glorious Pictures is a tough place to work."

I was surprised that she had heard this. Rumors had to travel pretty far to get to Ellen, who spent much of her life with her nose in ledgers and audit documents. I was grateful for her concern, though. As a child, I had been the one who would rush headlong into anything, including traffic, and more than once Ellen's steadying hand had saved me. While I didn't always understand why she would always choose the tried-and-true over the new-and-improved, I loved her dearly and knew without question that she was only trying to look out for me.

"How about this?" I suggested, wanting to offer up some kind of deal that would both pacify Ellen and ensure that I didn't get stuck again. "I'll give Glorious one year. In three hundred sixty-five days we'll reconvene to discuss how it's going. If I'm unhappy, I'm out of there."

Ellen made a big red "X" in Monday's box on our kitchen calendar. "You're on." I clinked my glass with hers to seal the deal.

On Sunday afternoon, by some bizarre coincidence, or perhaps kismet, Lifetime ran an *Intimate Portrait* called "Mothers of Moguls" with a segment on none other than the indefatigable Gloria Waxman. The show recounted the story of how she'd raised her sons by herself in a one-bedroom apartment in the Bronx. The twins' father had abandoned the family shortly after their second birthday, and if Gloria missed him, she never let on. Instead, she focused her considerable energy on her boys. Phil and Tony would lack for nothing, Gloria decided, even if she practically had to sleep on her feet.

I'd heard this before, from one of Abby's recitations on the Waxmans. She'd insisted that there was a Waxman family rule that their father's name was never to be spoken. There seemed to be evidence of this in the way Gloria glossed over that part of their history, as if he'd been just a bit player in the overall scheme of things.

The narrator's voice gave way to Gloria's own, telling about the beauty parlor she'd run out of her kitchen, and how women in the neighborhood flocked to her apartment with requests like "Gloria, I want you should make me look like Lana Turner." Or "Gloria, can you do me like Rita Hayworth? Her my husband likes." Gloria transformed her neighbors into their favorite screen goddesses, "which, believe me, wasn't so simple," she said, laughing guiltily.

The show was full of Waxman family photos, including one of Phil and Tony playing in a sandbox, or, more accurately, Phil burying Tony in a sandbox. The next one showed Tony feeding Phil from a bag of concrete mix.

"They were always each other's best friend," Gloria said, looking fondly at the pictures. The narrator noted that after a few years, Gloria had saved enough money to open a small salon. Gloria's Gorgeous was never a gold mine, but it paid the rent, put food on the table, and, most important, left enough over for admission to the movies. Every Sunday, Gloria would make sandwiches and the three of them would picnic at the pictures.

"We'd go to double features, triple features—whatever was playing," Gloria said. "Phil loved the real epics, you know, *Lawrence of Arabia* and *Doctor Zhivago*. My Tony, he was more interested in Westerns and comedies—I think we saw *How the West was Won* five times. Me? I looked at the hairstyles so my customers always had the very latest."

When the narrator spoke about the Waxmans' romantic lives, the camera cut to Gloria giggling before saying that both her sons had always had quite the eye. "For Tony, there was only Natalie Wood. He used to write her name on all his notebooks like she was a girl from the neighborhood." She sat back for a moment, before continuing, "And Phil, always with the Europeans. He was madly in love with Sophia Loren and Audrey Hepburn. I used to say, 'Phil, you have to pick one.' And he would always answer, 'Ma, who could make a choice like that?'" Gloria beamed at the memory.

There was a commercial for an upcoming Glorious release, *A Crushing Blow*, and then the show came back with a montage of photos starting with Phil and Tony as infants and ending in the awkward adolescent stage during which their current features had apparently formed. Then Gloria said solemnly, "I promised them on their sixteenth birthday, I'm going to get you two to Hollywood—even if I have to give a million permanents."

The program had me completely fascinated. Of course I'd heard the story of the twins' mother, her fierce devotion, and how they'd named their studio after her. But I hadn't known just how humbly they'd grown up, or how much their mother had sacrificed for them. It was a whole new perspective on the company and the people who ran it that made me more excited than ever.

That evening I took a long bath to relax, attempting to focus on what tomorrow might bring. Then I went through my wardrobe, trying to figure out what to wear for my first day of work for the Waxmans. I needed to look businesslike but not uptight; casual without being sloppy. I finally settled on a funky black dress and boots that had formerly served as my "performance-art-happening" outfit. As I ironed and snipped loose threads, I daydreamed about what my Glorious future would hold. I was in the middle of enjoying myself at a party on a yacht in Cannes when Ellen knocked on my door and handed me a copy of *Variety* she'd picked up for me on her way home from the gym. The page-one above-the-fold headline read: GLORIOUS HIJACKS B.O. FOR 17TH STRAIGHT WEEK. I couldn't wait to get started.

FIRST BLOOD

When I stepped into Geraldine's office on Monday morning, she jumped up from her desk and hurriedly looked me up and down. "Karen, good morning. I'm so relieved," she said.

"I don't understand. Did you think I wasn't coming?" I wasn't sure what she meant. Geraldine shook her head impatiently.

"I had no doubt you'd be here. I'm relieved about your clothes. When you came for your interview you were wearing a *twinset*," she reminded me. I could feel my face burn as I stammered something about the dress code at my former job. Geraldine nodded vaguely and suggested that we get started with a quick tour of the office—"quick" proving to be the operative word.

The building, which had formerly been a spool factory, was incomparably hipper than my previous office, with the kind of exposed-brick, high-ceilinged, industrial look I'd seen only in architectural magazines. Moving at warp speed, Geraldine whisked me through a bewildering warren of temporary work stations, briskly pointing out Phil and Tony's suite; the areas that housed production, development, and marketing; and some other points of interest, including the bathrooms and freight elevator. I was practically jogging in my attempt to keep up, and when Geraldine whipped around the corner that separated the storage room from the door leading to the publicity department, I misjudged and swung wide, grazing my knuckles on the brick wall. Instinctively, I brought my hand to my mouth and tasted blood.

Slowing her pace just a hair, Geraldine gestured as we entered the maze of cubicles and desks that comprised my new department. "Counting assistants, interns, and temps, on any given day there are about forty-five or so people working here," she said. How could so much hype be generated in such a small space? I don't know what I'd imagined but a chicken coop had never come to mind. Each cube had two or three chairs in it, shoved together arm-to-arm; some partitions leaned at precarious angles while gigantic filing cabinets lined the other side of the hallway, making the thoroughfare extremely narrow. Power strips sprouting many extension cords and multiheaded adapters snaked from every available outlet. It looked like those overcrowded factories in third-world countries where children toil for pennies an hour, except that this place had phones.

Geraldine skidded to a halt in front of a young woman seated at an L-shaped desk wedged between a cabinet and a bookcase brimming with videotapes. Crowding the desk were two computers, a wheezing fax machine, a printer, several cell phone batteries being charged, and a haphazardly stacked tower that appeared to contain every newspaper and magazine published in the United States. Papers that could no longer be accommodated on the desk had migrated to the floor, which was littered with memos, correspondence, press clippings, and even more periodicals. Geraldine nodded at the chaos, as if reacquainting herself with it. "This is it," she announced. "Karen Jacobs, Dagney Bloom, Allegra's 'first.'

Now, I'll just let you ladies get to know each other," she finished, and sprinted down the hall.

Dagney extended her hand, but I pointed to my bleeding knuckles. "I had a little run-in with the wall," I said, smiling weakly.

"Fucking brick," Dagney observed, sliding open a drawer and handing me a couple of Band-Aids.

Tall and model-thin, Dagney was dressed completely in what I recognized as Dolce & Gabbana, from her lacy black top and pleather mini to her over-the-knee, grommeted boots. Shiny, waist-length auburn hair worn in a loose ponytail framed a face with perfectly clear skin and delicate, fine features. Standing next to her, I felt distinctly hobbitesque: Dagney had the kind of pulled-together style that made you keep checking to see if there was toilet paper on your shoe.

"This is a pretty crazy time to be starting, because we're dealing with the Oscars on top of everything else. Allegra is trying to make sure that all of Glorious's nominees are attending—plus the celebrities from our upcoming films who are presenting—and we need to get their hotels, airplanes, and cars figured out as soon as possible. We've also gotten totally slammed with Academy calls. I'm glad you're finally here. I've had some temps and interns," she said dryly, "but there's only so much they can do. It's just been . . ." She paused and made a small, hopeless gesture at the mess surrounding the desk.

"The first thing is to get you set up. You'll be sitting in this chair, to my left. Allegra is in there," she added, nodding to the closed door behind us; Allegra's office, I noted, was the only one in the department that had a door and walls that went all the way to the ceiling. Dagney then handed me a headset that plugged into the telephone, which I recognized from TV and films as the must-have accessory for all entertainment-industry assistants.

"We need Systems Alejandro to get your computer up and running and give you an e-mail account," Dagney said.

"Systems Alejandro?"

"Alejandro Salazar. Call reception at zero and ask for him. We have a directory here—somewhere"—Dagney's glance darted among the various piles of paper under the desk—"but people come and go so fast that it's always out of date." I put on my headset, dialed, and asked to be put through.

"Systems, Alejandro," a pleasant voice answered, and I had to bite my tongue not to laugh.

"Hi, this is Karen Jacobs, Allegra Orecchi's new assistant. Can you help me get set up on the server?"

"Sure, I'll be around in five minutes."

While I was on the phone, Allegra's line rang and Dagney answered it on the first ring: "Allegra Orecchi's office. Yes, she's in. May I tell her who's calling?" She put the call on hold, waited a moment, picked it up and said, "I'm sorry, Allegra's in a meeting. She'll have to call you back."

Dagney showed me the phone log, explaining that once my computer was set up and password-protected, I'd have access to it as well. I watched her type in the latest message—a producer from *Extra* wanted to know if his crew could have an inside position at the Glorious Oscar party. Dagney shook her head as she typed. "Never going to happen," she said. "We're not allowing any inside press, although I'm not going to tell him that yet. Allegra's going to have me call all the media back the day before the party and tell them they'll have to be outside. That way they won't spend the next five weeks begging us to change our minds."

"Are you going to the Oscars?"

Dagney nodded, trying to be nonchalant, but I could tell she was excited. "Yeah, it's part of my job."

I almost asked if it would it be part of my job, too, but didn't want to seem too eager.

An incredibly good-looking guy appeared at my side. "Karen?"

"Yes," I gulped.

"Alejandro," he said, reaching over to shake my now-bandaged hand. "Just give me a little while and we'll have you set up." I gave Systems Alejandro my chair and stood between him and Dagney.

While he worked on my computer, Dagney asked if I was hungry, explaining that the company paid for our breakfasts and lunches as long as we ate them while working. If we stayed in the office past seven, we could order dinner, also on Glorious. This was a nice surprise. "Whatever you're having is fine. When will I meet Allegra?" I added nervously, glancing at the closed door behind us.

Dagney shrugged. "Probably when she needs you for something. I wouldn't worry about it."

By ten o'clock most of the publicity department had arrived and the entire area came alive with ringing phones, faxes rolling continually out of the squeaky machine, and the constant pinging of new e-mail messages. Dagney introduced me to whoever walked by our desk as "Allegra's new second," which made me feel like a chipped vase at a rummage sale.

"Of course, you'll need to meet everyone," she said. "It's just that we are absolutely, positively never to leave the phones. If I walked you around, it would be the end of both of us." She went on to explain that we would even need to coordinate going to the bathroom. I wondered how she'd managed before my arrival. "Isn't there voice mail?" I asked.

"Sure. But Allegra freaks if a call goes into it. You have four rings and then"—she mimed a throat-slashing gesture.

Dagney answered three more calls, each time putting the

caller on hold, returning with the information that Allegra was in a meeting, and then adding the message to the log.

"Okay, Karen," Systems Alejandro said. "I need you to enter a password." Abby would definitely appreciate Systems Alejandro, I thought. In honor of her burgeoning medical school career, I keyed in "LLOYD" and hit "Enter."

"It needs to be six or more characters."

I entered "LLOYDISDEAD."

"You're all set," he said. "Call me if anything's not working right." He turned back to flash me a reassuring smile, nearly colliding with a small blond woman in a huge goose-down coat whose right shoulder sagged under the weight of an enormous tote bag brimming with notebooks, papers, and file folders: She looked as if she were wearing her duvet and carrying her night table. Without even pausing to acknowledge us, she charged straight into Allegra's office. I expected to hear some sort of shout of protest erupt from within, but instead Dagney simply leapt up, grabbed the latest printout of the phone log, and followed, calling back over her shoulder, "I'll go see what she needs. Answer the phones?"

This was my new boss? I'd assumed that Allegra had been on the premises for hours. She hadn't even looked in my direction and I couldn't tell if she'd actually registered my presence. Maybe Dagney would introduce me to her later. While she was in with Allegra, I surveyed my new habitat. There wasn't a free square inch left on that desk; when my breakfast arrived, there wouldn't be any place to put it. In addition, twenty-five new faxes had come in within the past hour and a huge stack of mail had been delivered. Soon, I told myself, this would all be different; I prided myself on being neat and organized. My first order of business would be to get this stuff off the floor and desk and up where we could actually see it. Allegra's phone rang, and I answered it per Dagney's instructions.

"This is Marlene MacFarlane, the senior vice president of publicity," said a woman with a grating nasal voice. "I need Allegra." I asked her to hold while I saw if Allegra was available. Another line rang with a caller inquiring about a photo credential for the Glorious Oscar party. I put him on hold, too. Another line rang, and I asked that caller to hold before asking who it was. A fourth line rang and I picked it up. "Allegra Orecchi's office, please hold." A man sighed. "Sure, all right." The fifth line rang and I grabbed that, only to hear Marlene say, "I'm waiting." Her voice seemed to be coming through in stereo; I later realized that this was because her cube was only ten feet from my desk. I was so frazzled that within two minutes I'd lost all the other calls and had Marlene on three different lines. I took her message—"Have Allegra call me"—and hoped that the people I'd accidentally disconnected would call back. Rattled from the experience, a tap on the shoulder startled me. It was the delivery man with our breakfast. With a shaky hand, I signed the receipt and dug through the bag until I came up with a cup of coffee. In the middle of my first sip the phone rang again.

"Allegra Orecchi's office." A gruff voice shouted, "Tony!" Realizing that it was Tony Waxman, I nearly choked. "Yes, I'll put her on the line." I got up and ran toward Allegra's office, lightly tapping on the open door. "Allegra? It's Tony." She didn't look up, just nodded at Dagney and picked up the phone. Dagney followed me out of the office and unwrapped the rest of the food.

"I don't understand," I whispered nervously to Dagney. "Why did you tell all those people who called that Allegra was in a meeting?"

"We always say Allegra's in, no matter where she is. If it's someone important, we put the call through to her office or conference them in to her cell or her apartment. Otherwise, we say she's in a meeting or on another call. But she is never, ever 'not in.'"

"How do you know which calls to put through?" I asked, slightly alarmed at the idea that I might have already screwed this up.

"Usually it's pretty obvious. Phil and Tony, of course. Talent calling on their own—but no agents, managers, or personal publicists. Reporters from the top-ten newspapers," she motioned to another list lying on a different patch of floor. "Also the gossip columnists, but only the actuals—no assistants. Matt Vincent, the vice chairman of marketing. Executives from this department, but only if it's an emergency. The idea is to make it seem as if she's always at her desk. I had Tony on the line once and she was in the shower but took the call anyway. She just turned off the water and started talking to him, as if it were the most normal thing in the world. Two weeks ago, when I had to call her at six in the morning because of a really nasty item about Phil in the *L.A. Times*, I heard her boyfriend in the background, begging her to come back to bed, but she acted as if she couldn't hear him. I heard the door slam— he probably couldn't take it anymore. I don't even think they're still together."

"I guess she's really crucial to the company or they wouldn't need her to be perpetually on call."

"Phil and Tony will call Allegra to find out what time it is—just because they know she'll always get on the line. Phil has six assistants and Tony has two, so it's not as if they can't get anything done without her. I think they enjoy the fact that she'll always jump for them. Eat now, it's safe," Dagney added. "If she's on with Tony, she won't take another call, unless it's Phil. Just keep one eye on the phone so we know they're still talking."

Enthusiastically, I dug into an egg-white omelet stuffed with tomatoes and peppers, taking care as it rested precariously on my keyboard. Then I washed it down with freshly squeezed orange juice. Dagney had ordered well: at CNN, my morning meal had usually consisted of coffee and a suspicious-looking cruller from a cart I passed between the subway and the office. Between bites, I told her about my phone encounter with Marlene. Dagney responded with a combination head-shake/eye-roll—a look I would get to know well in the coming months. "Now she's going to call us back at least ten times to make sure we actually gave Allegra the message. Allegra gets so sick of Marlene's constant whining that she takes her time calling her back. Needless to say, this makes it much worse for us."

"But why would Marlene have called back five times in a minute and a half to leave a nonmessage?"

"Because she didn't want to tell you the real reason for her call. Marlene's big on secrecy, which is a complete joke." Dagney swallowed before continuing. "There's nothing that goes on around here that you won't know." She pointed dramatically to a small button on the side of the volume-control box between the headset and the phone. "There it is. The mute button—better known as the key to this particular kingdom. You can listen in whenever you like, and you won't believe what you'll hear. They're always planning, strategizing, figuring out what to do to whom and when. Last week I heard Phil tell Allegra that the new Buddy Friedman movie—you know, the one about the beekeeper?—is a total disaster and needs to be pushed back by at least six months so that it can be completely reedited."

That was some major dish. Buddy Friedman's new film, which, like all of his movies, had a closely guarded plotline, was already generating tons of anticipatory buzz. The movie had become the subject of much media speculation, especially after some of the bees escaped the film's Central Park location shoot and swarmed a building on Fifth Avenue, causing as many stings as threats of legal action. Phil Waxman responded by sending a care package of calamine lotion and honey to each tenant, along with the promise of a private screening. This, according to a *New York Times* article Abby had e-mailed me, had ended all talk of lawsuits. "I've been reading about the film, but I hadn't heard there were problems with it, besides that bee situation."

Dagney grinned. "Yeah, well, that means we're doing our job, right? The gossip columnists and trade reporters sniff around Glorious all the time, but Allegra's usually pretty good at controlling them, feeding them some line, or telling them just part of the story. Once in a while, though, they'll try to get to people who might let something slip—like interns—or new assistants," she added, looking at me meaningfully.

"I'm not going to say anything."

"Just be careful. Especially of Elliott Solnick, the guy who writes for Page Six. You can be talking to him about nothing at all, like the weather, or what you had for dinner, and somehow he'll manage to work it into a piece he's doing on some celeb. He's never asking a question just to be friendly. There's always something else going on."

That was interesting. Abby was always reading me juicy tidbits from that column and it was full of just the kind of details Dagney was describing: so small as to seem inconsequential out of context, but once in print, vivid enough to convince you that they definitely had the goods. I resolved to watch my step with this guy.

"There's one other thing you need to know about it," Dagney said, draining her grapefruit juice. "George Hanratty. He's an old reporter who used to be at the *Daily News*. He's supposedly writing a biography of the Waxmans—completely unauthorized of course."

"Supposedly?"

"That's the rumor, but he's such a lush no one here thinks he can actually get it done. Not that we're taking any chances. He's already tried to get into a couple of premieres, and called Clark a few times, asking random questions about Phil and Tony, or trying to find out if they're in town." She pointed to a tiny, yellowed piece of newsprint taped to the side of her monitor. "That's a picture of him, from when he used to have a column. It's at least ten years old." I leaned over and took a look—I could just about make out two eyes, a nose, and a mouth.

"So if I run into him?"

"Don't say anything, but put it on Allegra's phone sheet. She's watching to see if there's any spike in Hanratty activity. So far, I haven't seen him or spoken to him, but we keep track of anyone else in the department who has."

Even the phones here are dangerous, I thought, noticing that my Band-Aid had started to peel off. This job was going to be an exercise in extreme caution.

Just then my own extension rang. My first Glorious call! I answered it, trying my best to convey competent professionalism. "Publicity, Karen Jacobs," I said. "It's Robert Kojima," said a quiet, steady voice. "We haven't met," he continued, interrupting my frantic mental search. "I'm a publicist in this department. You have Pepto-Bismol in your bag—I saw it and I need some. I'm going to come by and borrow it." He hung up and within three seconds a slender, Asian man about my age was standing in front of me. Wordlessly, he put out his hand and I placed the bottle in it. Robert poured an inch of the pink liquid into a paper cup he'd brought over, handed the medicine back, and then turned on his heel, disappearing back into the maze. Did all of my new colleagues need to know that my nerves were hard-wired directly into my stomach?

"What's his story?" I asked Dagney.

"Robert's worked here for just under three years, is completely anal-retentive, not to mention nosy, and in case you're interested, he's got a fiancée in the Peace Corps in Bora-Bora."

"Pago Pago" came Robert's voice from somewhere on the floor. This open-plan office would take some getting used to.

Suddenly, I heard a voice blasting from inside one of the cubes. "Wonderful, that's great. *Muy bien. Sí, sí. Gracias. Adios.*"

A moment later the voice was back. "This makes me *tan feliz.* You can't imagine." While the voice was loud, the Spanish words received special emphasis.

I turned to Dagney for enlightenment.

"That's Vivian Henry, the executive vice president of this department," she said. "The story goes that she started as a temp in Phil's office, and on her third day she overheard him shouting at a journalist who'd found out about some difficulties on the set of a Glorious picture. Anyway, Vivian took it upon herself to call the reporter back and calm him down. She told him that if he didn't publish the story, she'd make sure that he could have an exclusive first look at Larry Roman's directorial debut."

"Larry Roman, the former child star whose parents took all his money?" I asked. "I didn't know he became a director."

"He didn't," Dagney said. "But it was enough to throw the guy off the trail. Phil hired Viv on the spot and now the only person above her in this department is Allegra."

"I can't believe she pulled that off," I said, doubting that in two days' time I'd be displaying that kind of initiative.

"It was a big gamble, but she's been here ever since—eleven years." Dagney took a long sip of coffee before continuing. "As for the Spanish, I don't think half the people she's speaking with know what she's saying. Just ignore it. And her, too, whenever possible."

I wondered why Dagney was so quick to dismiss Vivian. She certainly seemed to have the right stuff for this place.

"So we don't work with her at all?"

"Vivian does pretty much everything herself. To ask anyone for help would be an admission of weakness."

"But if she's an EVP, she must be extremely busy."

"She is. Most of the time she's here until midnight, at least."

"She doesn't have any help at all?"

"She has an assistant, Kimberly, but Vivian hasn't trusted her ever since she misspelled Johnny Lucchese's name on his invitation to the *Perp Friction* premiere. Kim's out right now at the health food store, getting Vivian's organic spelt. When she comes back, she'll get started on the soup list, and after that, she'll pretty much wait around until Viv gives her something else to do."

"The S.O.U.P. list?" I assumed this was an acronym of some sort. Stars of Upcoming Projects? Screenings of Unreleased Pictures?

"Vivian only eats soup for lunch. Every day, Kimberly calls all the restaurants that deliver in TriBeCa and finds out what the soups are for the day. She gives Viv the list, then e-mails it to the rest of us. You'll see."

"WHERE IS ALLEGRA?" a voice boomed in my ear. This, I realized, must be Vivian in the flesh. The woman was a knockout—tall and slender with wavy dark hair and intense green eyes.

"She's on with Tony," I said. "I'll add you to the phone list."

"MAKE SURE YOU DO THAT," she thundered, before walking away.

Dagney plucked a copy of *Rolling Stone* from the stack of periodicals on our desk. "Whenever we have a spare moment, we skim these and pull out any articles that mention Glorious. I'll show you what to do with them later. Just tear out whatever you think is relevant. If you're not sure if a film is ours or not, look on this list." She reached down and tugged a piece of paper out from under one of the wheels of her chair. "It would be great if you could get through a bunch of them—I've fallen way behind because of all of the Academy work," she said, standing and reaching for her coat. "I'm going out for a cigarette. Allegra's got a stack of stuff she's working on in there, and if she asks you to call anyone, all the information's in Outlook."

I spent most of the afternoon going through magazines, sorting faxes, and trying to familiarize myself with the various lists, directories, and memos that were on or under the desk. The phone rang several times but no one from Dagney's list called—it was mostly media with questions and requests about the Glorious Oscar bash and a couple of publicists wanting to know if their clients could attend. I took all the information down and carefully recorded it on the log. This party was certainly causing a stir, even though it was over a month away. Pulling a few more magazines from the stack, managing not to topple it, I continued skimming. It seemed that everything from *U.S. News and World Report* to *Utne Reader* to *Guideposts* mentioned Glorious Pictures at least once. I had to be careful and make sure I searched the entire publication for mentions, because they turned up everywhere: in letters to the editor, in the crossword, and even in interviews with business leaders, who often cited scenes from Glorious films like *Perp Friction* and *Mullets Under Manhattan* as inspiration for their boardroom behavior. I was finally feeling more at ease. By the time Dagney returned I'd accumulated a nice-sized pile of press clippings and a wastebasket full of disemboweled magazines. I stood up to stretch and was pleased to realize that it was now possible to see over the stack.

Allegra walked past us with her coat on. After she left, Dagney told me that she'd gone to an outside meeting, although I hadn't heard her say anything. I excused myself to search for the ladies' room, breathing a sigh of relief when I found it on my own.

The day was going okay so far, I thought, looking at my reflection over the sink. People here are a bit different than what I'm used to, but I can't expect the staff of Glorious Pictures to be like everyone else, I reasoned. I was sure Allegra would have some kind of welcoming chat with me within the next day or two, and once I got to know Vivian and Marlene I would undoubtedly learn a tremendous amount from them. But it was clear that I'd have to keep my eyes and ears open and be extremely careful of what I said. Turning on the taps, I held my hand under the soap dispenser and pulled the lever. Nothing. I tried the ones next to the three other sinks but they didn't work either. I cased the bathroom. The jubilation that accompanied the discovery of a supply closet quickly turned to disappointment: it was stocked top to bottom with reams of photocopy paper and the world's largest collection of rubber bands. I lingered for a few minutes, figuring I'd follow the lead of the next person, but no one came in. Finally, I simply rinsed my hands and went back to my desk.

"Hey!" I turned and saw Clark behind me. He bent down and gave me a quick kiss on the cheek. "Love that dress. Prada?"

"No, Banana Republic, but I'll take the upgrade." What had I been thinking? He was definitely gay, and completely full of it.

"How's your first day been?"

"Great, but I'm still mostly learning how to answer the phone without making some kind of career-ending error."

"I'm sure you're fine. Have you met everyone?"

"Just Dagney and Vivian, and Allegra, sort of. Oh, and Robert," I added hastily, as Robert himself appeared around the corner. Technically, almost none of these encounters counted as introductions in the usual sense. "I also spoke to Marlene on the phone," I said, without elaborating.

Clark opened his mouth to say something, but shut it like a fish as Robert began, "Glorious people come in categories, and it's much easier to navigate this place once you figure out who's in which group."

"Categories?"

"Yeah. The first two are the big divisions—Golden Child and Work Horse. The Golden Children show up late, leave early, and get most of the credit for everything. Then you have the Work Horses. They're buried under stacks of paper, are here at all hours, and no one thinks twice about asking them to do some more."

"Oh, come on, Robert, you're going to scare Karen away. It's only her first day!" Clark said. "Give her a chance to see for herself."

Undeterred, Robert glanced significantly at Clark before continuing. "The strange part is that it's usually the Golden Children who burn out first."

"Why is that?" I asked.

"Because stealing credit is extremely exhausting. Clark, you see, was anointed a Golden Child years ago," Robert added, "while I keep trudging along, hoping someone will throw me a sugar cube every now and then." He whinnied.

"Who decides which one you are?" I asked.

Robert shrugged. "I don't know. You fall into one category or the other. And once you're there, baby, there's no changing it."

"Are there any other categories?" I asked.

"Well, there's sort of a subcategory of Golden Children known as Tony's Tryouts, which is made up of Tony's ex-girlfriends. Once he's through dating them, they get a guaranteed job for life," Robert said.

"Are there a lot of them?"

"Hard to know. Some of them deny it, some of them claim they used to date Tony but *he* denies it, and then there are a few who are in the e-mail directory and have offices here, but no one's ever seen them."

"How *Peyton Place*," I mused.

"Well, there is Delilah Billings in Promotions," Dagney said. "She comes to work every day."

"I've never been able to find out if she actually dated Tony or not," Clark said.

"Maybe it's not your business," Robert answered.

"This from the man who inspects everyone's belongings," Clark said, shaking his head before asking me, "How are things going with Allegra?"

"I don't know. She hasn't spoken to me yet."

Robert suddenly looked very serious. "Are you absolutely sure?"

"I don't understand."

"Allegra is completely and utterly inaudible," Clark interjected. "She either speaks so quietly that you can't hear her, or mumbles so you can't understand."

"So how do you know what she wants?" I asked, fear raising my voice a couple of octaves.

"It *is* kind of like charades," Clark admitted, putting his index finger on his nose.

"I can read lips," Robert said smugly.

"I just do what I think she's asked, and if I'm wrong, she lets me know—although she's much happier when I manage to figure it out the first time," Dagney said.

"She definitely uses it to her advantage," Clark said, "When Phil's in a screaming rage she speaks into his ear and he settles right down. It's why she's known as 'the Phil Whisperer.'"

"Well, I guess I'll just have to use my bionic hearing," I said, brightly. I was more than a little unnerved by this inaudible boss thing, not to mention my nosy colleagues, the fire trap office, and the caste system. My Glorious experience was off to a wonderful start. How was I ever going to face Ellen?

"Don't you two have anything to do?" Dagney asked Robert and Clark. "If you're going to continue lurking, at least help us go through these."

The threat of more work sent them packing immediately, Clark pausing just long enough to snatch the new *Details*.

Dagney picked up *New York*. "Interesting, they gave three and a half stars to *Feeling Fine in Phoenix When You're Fried*. That should make Phil moderately happy. And when Phil's happy, Allegra's happy, which means there's hope for us yet." She tore out the page with a satisfied flourish.

Feeling Fine starred three character actors who were often in search of a role, and from what I'd read so far today, the good review in *New York* was definitely against the grain. I hadn't seen the movie, but it sounded extremely violent—"blood and guts standing in for plot and narrative," according to *Premiere,* which I'd read earlier in the afternoon.

I continued making my way through the stack. *Maxim* had given a rave to an upcoming film called *She Swings Both Ways,* which I'd heard of because Gabe was a huge fan of the director's. *Bazaar* had a fashion spread on *The Foreign Pilot*'s costumes, and *Mother Jones* had inexplicably included *The Oboe* in its list, "Fifty Films the Far Right Needs to See." We continued reading and ripping late into the afternoon, when I realized that I needed to use the bathroom again.

"Hey, Dag," I began hesitantly. "In the bathroom. Where's the soap?"

"There isn't any." She slid open a drawer, revealing a bottle of liquid Ivory. "You can use mine until you buy your own," she added.

"No soap? Of course there's soap," said Robert, popping up once more. Was there anything this guy didn't overhear? "There's just no soap for *us*." When celebrities came to the office, he assured me, a bottle of L'Occitane's verbena-scented gel would appear in the appropriate bathroom, only to be removed and placed in a locked drawer as soon as they left. "Geraldine wears the key on a lanyard around her neck," he finished. "But I refuse to participate in these discriminatory practices." He reached over and snagged Dagney's bottle from the drawer. "Soap is a right, not a privilege," he said, raising his fist in the air as he walked quickly toward the men's room.

"He won't buy his own damn soap," Dagney translated. "And pretty soon I'm going to wring his neck." Dagney began to fill me in on some more information that I'd need to know—how often to give Allegra an updated phone sheet (once an hour or whenever she asked, whichever was more frequent); how to rent a private jet (dial 1-800-4-PLANES and say, "I'm from Glorious and I need a plane"); and how to get the Sunday *New York Times Magazine* section on Wednesday (from an elderly *Times* copy editor who'd been secretly on the Glorious payroll for years).

"Is there some kind of handbook?" I said, even though I instinctively knew the answer.

"A handbook?" Dagney said. "I thought I told you. They don't even update the phone list. By the time you get added, you probably won't even work here anymore. If you have a question, just ask around until someone gives you the answer you want and use that one."

I thought wistfully of CNN, where we'd each been given a binder with sections on policies, procedures, and information about everything from how to submit a health insurance form to what to do in case of ingesting poison. The HR department continually sent around updates, conveniently three-hole punched, which we'd made fun of incessantly. Now I was longing for a Glorious equivalent—ideally, one with a Spanish phrasebook, a floor map showing where the fire extinguishers were located, and some kind of nondenominational prayer.

SHE'S GOTTA HAVE IT

Over the next few days I learned the many ways in which everyone contributed to the care and feeding of the Waxmans. In addition to juggling their many requests, the senior executives seemed to be constantly hatching schemes with which to impress them. I would answer Allegra's phone and hear "Phil needs the op-ed from last week's *Washington Post*, I'm not sure which one, though, you should know," or "Tony wants to get this video into Prince Charles's hands." The assumption was that no matter what was needed, Publicity could get it done. Allegra prided herself on the department's ability to pull off the undoable, the unthinkable, and the damn near impossible, even though she was never the one actually doing it. The completion of these tasks determined whether or not the Earth could continue to rotate on its axis; contrary to everything I'd learned in science class, it spun purely by staying in the good graces of the Waxmans, just as did everything else in the world of Glorious Pictures.

As I finished my carrot ginger bisque on Thursday, I tallied up the failures of my first four days. My attempts to organize the area had flopped completely. Stuff still littered the floor—I'd lobbied for a bulletin board, but given that our desk faced a brick wall, there was no way to hang one without drilling into it, which we couldn't do because the space was rented. The cube people could use tacks, pins, and tape on their fabric-covered walls, but nothing stuck to that brick, which explained Dagney's floor-level filing system. We had to keep often-used documents nearby and were now both ankle-deep in paper, with no letup in sight. People dropped memos on our chairs and left documents on top of our printer and fax machine, ignoring the wire in-boxes we'd placed on the bookcase in a vain effort to keep what was new separate from what had already been dumped on us. The phones were insatiable, shrieking like hungry infants and demanding the full attention of at least one of us all the time. Allegra's schedule was always in flux, which had us constantly reprioritizing or just scrambling to get everything done.

The only dependable thing was Kimberly's soup list, which pinged into our e-mail boxes at precisely 11:30 each morning. It listed the daily soup offerings of about fifteen restaurants with annotations next to many of them—a "c" if it contained cream, "m" if it had meat, "p" for puree, and "nr" if it had been tried before and was not recommended. TriBeCa's fantastic apartments and high-net-worth denizens had been followed by some of the world's most formidable chefs, so our in-office meals were often quite extraordinary, especially when there was time to chew before swallowing. Soup was a favorite, however, because it required no utensils and only one hand. I also had the distinct impression that I'd already sown my oats as a Work Horse. Since that first omelet, I'd eaten every single meal at my desk and would have gladly paid for the most deluxe lunch in exchange for the privilege of eating it elsewhere. Underrested and overstimulated, I was counting the hours until Friday night.

This morning had begun badly even before I was in the office. Robert got out of the subway just ahead of me. "Hey there," I called out, noticing that he looked lost in thought.

"Oh, hey," he answered.

"Do you live on the Upper West Side, too?" I asked.

"No, the Lower East. I had to run up to Madison Square Garden and pick up some Knicks tickets for Tony. Courtside. Right next to Spike Lee," he grinned. "Robert Kojima hits the three-pointer!"

"And the crowd goes wild," I added. We stopped to get coffee.

"Hey Robert, when's that girlfriend of yours visiting again?" the guy behind the counter asked.

"She was just here at Christmas so she won't be back for a while. But thanks for asking," Robert said, as we turned to leave.

"That must be hard," I said, "having her so far away. I give you a lot of credit." Gabe hadn't even been willing to try a domestic long-distance relationship, something I'd suggested during one of our last conversations.

"It can be. Especially now, during the banana harvest. I'll be lucky to get even an e-mail or a phone call for the next month."

We walked into the lobby together. There, just about to get on the elevator ahead of us, was Eddie Di Silva. An Oscar-winning actor known for his ability to undergo unbelievable physical transformations for his roles and brilliantly portray the deepest, most alarming aspects of the human character, Eddie had also made a killing in the TriBeCa real estate market. In fact, he owned this very building, making him Glorious's landlord. Abby had informed me of this fact right after I'd interviewed for the job and now she said, "Are you talkin' to me?" every time I called her in Baltimore. Mentally, I was already on the phone with her—"Guess who I rode the elevator with?"—when Robert pulled me back gently, motioning for me to stop. Eddie got in the elevator alone and once the door closed, Robert explained that the legend had a strict rule that no one was allowed to ride with him.

"Never?" I said, feeling slightly indignant.

"He got sick of being trapped while strangers pitched him ideas." Robert saw my crestfallen face and added, "Cheer up. At this place, you'll see more celebrities than you ever thought possible. You'll get jaded. I promise." I didn't believe him, but I felt mildly consoled nonetheless.

My second and third gaffes came in quick succession. As I was sorting the morning mail, I found an envelope for Allegra with "Confidential" written across it in red ink. I placed it on the stack designated "Most Crucial."

Then the phone rang, and, as Dagney was on one call with another two holding, I answered it. "Allegra Orecchi's office."

"Is she in?"

"Yes. May I tell her who's calling?"

"Mackie Moran," said an impatient-sounding woman. I pressed the hold button, counted to ten, picked up the phone and said, "I'm sorry, but she's in a meeting. May I have your number so that she can call you back?"

"She has it." The woman clicked off and I recorded the information on the log, finding the phone number and listing it for reference, before going back to the mail.

"Open it," Dagney said, hanging up and pointing to the "Confidential" envelope.

"Do you think we should?"

"Definitely. If anyone needed to tell her a secret, they wouldn't put it in her in-box. Just open it." She turned to answer another ringing phone.

The envelope held a memo from Marlene on which she'd copied Phil and Tony along with Geraldine. It was a complaint, and the problem was me:

RE: Your New Hire

Karen Jacobs, your new second, put me on hold for an *interminable* amount of time when I *desperately* needed to reach you. When she *finally* allowed me to leave a message, the situation had deteriorated *exponentially*. I am *gravely* concerned about her ability to function in this role.

Marlene's italics danced in front of my eyes like nasty, finger-pointing kids in a schoolyard. She hadn't been on hold for more than two minutes, I was sure, even counting the time she spent waiting while I had placed her on hold because I had to answer her calling on the other lines. Why had she copied the head of HR and both Waxmans on her memo? It had been only the second hour of my first day—did this need to become a major incident?

I was embarrassed and, not wanting Dagney to see the note, I hurriedly placed it in the middle of the stack, before stuffing the whole pile into Allegra's special red folder and bringing it into her office, leaving it in the customary space next to her desk. I slunk back out, nagged by the certainty that the next time my phone rang, it would be someone telling me to get my things and go.

"Keep moving," I told myself, trying to get caught up in the ebb and flow of messages and let Marlene's memo recede into the background. Dagney got up to bring Allegra a new printout of the phone log, and when she walked out of the office her mouth was set in a grim line. I was sure this was it.

"Haven't you ever heard of Mackie Moran?"

"She called Allegra a little while ago."

"I mean, you didn't recognize her name?"

"Should I have?"

"She's the hottest interior decorator going. I guess I thought everyone knew that." Dagney grimaced in frustration before continuing, "Anyway, Mackie's one of the people who needs to get put through to Allegra no matter what."

"Can't we just call her back?"

"Mackie's in the middle of redoing Allegra's loft and when she calls, it means she's having a brainstorm and she needs Allegra while she's 'still in the moment.' Otherwise, she forgets about it."

Allegra's decorator was some kind of creative genius who couldn't bother with a notebook and pencil, and this was my fault?

"Anyway, we can't do anything about it now. Allegra said she'd talk to you about it later." Then Dagney left to go out for a cigarette, leaving me alone with my dark thoughts and cold soup. I was sure that my spot in the unemployment line was secure.

As I carefully balanced the container on top of the overflowing wastebasket, Allegra appeared at my side. "Karen," she said, uttering—well, whispering—my name for the first time. I stared at her mouth, willing all the office noise away so that I might hear what she was saying. "When Dagney gets back, take this to Phil's office." It was a copy of the next issue of *Entertainment Weekly*, the cover emblazoned with photos from *The Foreign Pilot* arrayed around an Oscar, with a headline reading, "WILL THE WAXMANS FINALLY WIN?" "Make sure you put it in his hands," she said, before walking away.

"Okay," I said, to no one.

After Dagney's return I began my mission to bring the magazine to Phil. If I put it in his hands, would that count as meeting him? I walked to the other side of the floor and paused to collect myself at the entrance to the chairmen's office suite—a dead end in the hallway. A small sign to my right read, "MR. TONY WAXMAN." The unmarked door on the left had to lead to Phil. I pushed it open, revealing a long counter on one side and three cubes on the other, all of which were empty. On top of the counter were huge crates with handwritten signs: "PHIL SCRIPTS," "PHIL MAIL,"

"PHIL PHONES," "PHIL NEEDS TO SIGN," and one that made me feel strangely welcome: "PHIL PUBLICITY." At the end of the counter was another door, which was slightly ajar. I could hear the low hum of conversation and a buzzing noise coming from inside. I heard a voice I guessed to be Phil's say, "No fucking way." There were more murmurs, and then a loud, "Crap," followed by, "He can just go to hell." The magazine was getting damp from my hands. I'd sweated through the "E" in *Entertainment Weekly*. The buzzing got louder and I wondered if Buddy Friedman's bees were nearby. To advance or to retreat seemed equally perilous. Clearly, I couldn't afford another mistake today, so I stood there for a moment, deciding what to do, before gently tapping on the door. Something sounding vaguely like "Come in," came out of there and I walked inside, holding the magazine in front of me as if for protection.

Completely dominating the surprisingly small space was Phil Waxman, hunched over a desk strewn with papers. He was eating an enormous omelet with his hands while a barber shaved his neck with an electric razor. As Phil looked up at me, a mushroom fell out of his mouth, but he caught it before it hit the plate and shoved it back in. Then he said something that could have been, "Leave it," and I gingerly placed the magazine on the edge of the desk. Turning to go, I saw Vivian and two other people I didn't recognize wedged onto a tiny couch against the opposite wall. Vivian's eyes were saucer-round and her eyebrows threatened to join her hairline. I hurried out, back to the relative safety of my desk, and grabbed a ringing phone, taking a message from a newspaper reporter who wanted to interview Tony for a feature about "the current explosion of the horror genre." Given my day I felt uniquely qualified to speak to that point.

"Karen. Karen. Karen." Well, Vivian knew my name after all. She loomed over me. "You are never to do that again," she said.

"Never." This is the sort of opening line that makes one's colleagues sit up and take notice; I heard the sound of phones being put down in syncopated rhythm all around us. Kimberly looked up from her *TV Guide* crossword and I could see Clark in my peripheral vision, standing just close enough to hear and see what was happening.

"You just barged into Phil's office as if you belonged there," she continued, while all I could think of was how excruciatingly timid I'd been, and how the whole thing had lasted fewer than ten seconds. "What were you thinking? Can you please tell me that?"

I tried to answer her but Dagney stepped in. "She was bringing Phil the new *EW* because Allegra wanted him to have it."

"Fine, that's fine, but doesn't she know how to behave in an office?" Viv continued. I felt like someone trapped under a car waiting for the Jaws of Life to extricate them. "Phil has assistants that you give things to," she said, hissing on every "s" in "assistants." "That's what they're for."

"But no one was there and—"

Viv cut me off. "If no one is there, you come back later when someone is. But you do not walk into the chairman's office unless you have been expressly invited to do so."

I nodded, afraid that if I spoke I would cry.

"Can you promise me that you'll never do that again?"

I nodded again, more vigorously this time. When I was finally able to bring myself to look up, Vivian had vanished and everyone else was studiously avoiding my eye. My phone rang and I composed my voice enough to answer it.

"Hey, it's Clark. Let's go talk on the roof. I'll meet you at the stairway."

"I need some air," I stammered to Dagney while buttoning up my coat.

At the bottom of the stairs Clark motioned me ahead of him.

We climbed four flights and then he opened a door and we were outside, with a stunning view of downtown and the winter sun setting in front of us. Clark sat with his back against the parapet and I joined him. He lit a cigarette and offered me the pack, which I waved away. Clark squeezed my shoulder and I started to cry. Not the huge, heaving sobs I thought would come, but more of a soundless, big-teared weeping, which was actually better because it allowed me to talk and cry at the same time.

"You can't let Vivian get to you. She's got this alpha-bitch complex going on. Now that she's publicly shamed you, she'll leave you alone."

"She will?" I sniffled.

"Absolutely. She's done what she needed to do. You should have seen what she did to Kimberly last year."

"Dagney mentioned it, but I didn't hear the whole story. What happened?"

"Vivian was in charge of the *Perp Friction* premiere. And Kim was in charge of addressing the envelopes. Next thing you know, Phil's office gets a message from Johnny Lucchese—'If Phil wants me to come to his party, he should learn how to spell my name right.' It turned out that Kim had misspelled 'Lucchese.'"

I cringed at the scene that had undoubtedly followed. "Was Phil really angry?"

"He never knew about it—one of his assistants handled it with Viv. But Vivian made Kimberly write 'Johnny Lucchese' five hundred times on the back of a *Perp Friction* poster and then send it with a note of apology to Johnny himself."

"Wow. That's pretty harsh" was all I could think to say. I was still crying, but I started to laugh a little, too.

"Do you know what Tony called Vivian once?" Clark asked.

"What?"

"The Mussolini with the Botticelli face."

"He really called her that?"

"Uh-huh," Clark said. "He meant it as a compliment."

"Wow," I said again, suddenly not crying. "While we're on the subject of crimes and misdemeanors, I'm in huge trouble with Marlene." I told him all about the phones, and the memo, and Clark gasped in make-believe shock.

"You've just been moaned," he said.

"Moaned?"

"Yeah. We call those memos Marlene's Moanings. She sends them out about once or twice a month. No one takes them seriously but we all get them because Sabrina in Phil's office makes photocopies for us. Phil and Tony don't ever see them, and even Geraldine told me that she stopped reading them two years ago."

"And Allegra?"

"Allegra will send her an e-mail saying that she'll look into it. Then she'll file it away somewhere, but I promise, you will never hear about it."

I felt better, and then remembered my Mackie Moran mistake.

"Mackie Moran gets inspiration from the cracks in the sidewalks, or the achingly lonely howl of a car alarm at dawn. She'll call again; she probably has already. Are we done now?" Clark huffed in mock annoyance. I smiled. "Good." He offered me his arm, and we went back inside.

Dagney was waiting for me, looking slightly guilty.

"Can you do me a favor?"

"What do you need?" I asked, a bit warily, thinking that the best place for me was at home, where I couldn't do any more damage.

"On Thursday nights one of Allegra's assistants has to go to the *New York Times* printing plant in Queens to get Friday's paper because it has the reviews," she said. "But it's my blowout night with Felix, and I've missed three weeks in a row. He's going to cancel me if I don't come and I'll never get back in."

Felix Acosta was one of New York's top hairdressers, a man whom mere mortals waited six months to see. I'd read about him in beauty magazines; his highlights graced the heads of dozens of actresses and supermodels.

"Sure, I'm happy to do it, but can't we just get it on the Internet?"

Dagney explained that while the paper was published online at about midnight, Allegra was concerned that the web edition might omit a crucial, quotable line from the print edition, so only the physical newspaper would do. She went on to tell me that the paper came out at about eleven, and that I would take a Town Car with a driver to the plant. "Usually, we fax it to Phil, but he's not somewhere that he can get a fax tonight, so you'll call his assistant and he'll patch you through and you'll read the review to him. Tonight should be a breeze; it's that Iranian movie everyone likes."

Dagney had already printed out directions for me, which included how to call a Town Car, the address of the printing plant, and several cell phone numbers for the assistant who was "covering" Phil for the evening.

"Oh yeah, you'll also need this," she said, handing me a brand-new cell phone. "Geraldine brought it by today. It's yours for as long as you work here. Just keep it switched on all the time."

Later that night, as the Town Car zipped over the Brooklyn Bridge on the way to the *New York Times*'s printing plant, I realized that the dog-tiredness of this afternoon had been replaced by exhilaration. The driver parked outside the plant and I checked with a security guard who told me that it would be about half an hour until the first papers rolled off the press. Part of me wanted to call

Abby and tell her everything, but another part of me was just busy re-creating the day. Surviving the ordeal had given me a dose of supreme self-confidence, and I was reveling in it.

At 11:15 a man came out and placed some newspapers in the machine outside, and I ran into the lobby and purchased two. Back in the car, I quickly located the review and dialed the first cell phone number on my list. The assistant answered and asked me to hold while he patched in Phil. "He's on the line," the assistant said. "Phil, this is Karen Jacobs from Allegra's office. I have the *New York Times* review of *The Sparrow in the Olive Tree* for you."

"Go ahead."

I read the review, taking care to speak slowly and clearly, the way I'd read book reports aloud in class as a child. It was a very good review, full of phrases like "elaborate in its simplicity," "a gentle, yet utterly compelling film," and "a powerful understatement of the filmmaker's plea for peace."

At the same time the thought "I'm sitting in the backseat of a car in Queens, reading by maplight to Phil Waxman!" kept running through my head like a looped soundtrack. Occasionally Phil would ask me to reread a sentence, or say something like "Right" or "Got it," and I could hear his breath whistle slightly on the other end of the phone. It was oddly intimate, as if we were having late-night pillow talk in the dark—well, I was in the dark, anyway; he was off somewhere exotic, unreachable via fax.

I finished reading, and Phil said, "Thank you," and then the assistant who had been voyeuristically listening in the whole time asked me to please put a copy of the review on his own desk in the morning. I said good night and fell into a deep sleep that lasted all the way home.

THE SECRET OF
MY SUCCESS

Four weeks later, at 6:30 on a Thursday morning, I was zipping down the West Side Highway toward TriBeCa in a Town Car. After my first few weeks at Glorious, I had proof that the company's insanity wasn't exclusively bad-crazy. Sometimes it was the good kind.

The plan had always been that eventually Dagney and I would alternate the early mornings, with the person who came in first able to leave the office sometime before the beginning of Jay Leno's monologue. The previous week, after three nights straight of Oscar-lobbying until two in the morning, Dagney had decided that I was ready to handle the 7 A.M. shift alone, starting immediately. I emerged from the subway station near the office that first day to find nine messages from Allegra on my cell phone, each one a more panic-stricken but otherwise identical version of the last: "Where are you?"

I dialed her at home immediately. "Sorry—I was on the train."

"For how long?"

"About half an hour."

"Half an hour on the subway? Where do you live?"

I told her that I lived at 112th Street and Broadway and heard her sigh. "They didn't tell me you commuted," she said reproachfully.

As soon as she arrived in the office, Allegra had me put her through to Phil. I hit the mute button to learn what was up, and was horrified to discover that she was, in fact, talking about me. "Phil, she lives all the way uptown—practically in the Bronx. If you factor in the potential for delay, she could be out of range for up to ninety minutes a day. I don't need to tell you that this poses a direct threat to my entire operation." My heart froze for a moment, before Allegra continued, "We're going to have to get her a car."

A *car?*

Phil seemed to be reading my mind. "You're telling me that we have to get your goddamned assistant a fucking car?"

"Anything could happen while she's down there. The alternative is just too risky. Remember the morning we found out that Buddy Friedman had moved in with his step-niece? I couldn't start dealing with it until nearly eight o'clock. By then it was *everywhere*, remember?"

Phil paused for a moment, and only the sound of chewing could be heard as Allegra and I waited in suspense. "Okay," he said grudgingly, "but it's coming out of your budget." Allegra sighed and agreed. This was the first time I'd witnessed Allegra's spinning technique in motion, and I had to admit, the woman was talented. In the worst-case estimate it would take me forty-five minutes to get to work by subway, but generally the trip took only thirty. I was fascinated that a woman tough enough to go toe-to-toe with Phil Waxman couldn't bear the thought of having an assistant underground while she dialed into thin air.

In truth, I might have preferred the extra half hour of privacy, but decided instead to take the car as a hopeful sign. Would Allegra have gone to so much trouble and expense if she didn't think I was a good investment? The use of a car and driver was normally reserved for senior vice presidents and above, so the exception raised some eyebrows and put some noses out of joint. As I dropped my health insurance forms off in Geraldine's office, she remarked, "West 112th Street? I hope you keep Mace in your purse." In my neighborhood, the greatest danger I faced was being hit on by an earnest Columbia philosophy major in the West End Tavern, but I kept this to myself.

When Dagney, who lived in Greenwich Village and walked to work, heard about my transportation arrangements she was furious. "That's the most unfair thing I've ever heard," she declared, stamping her stiletto-heeled, python-skinned boot for emphasis. Faced with a twenty-five-year-old whose parents had bought her a duplex on Jane Street, I had no difficulty keeping my pity in check. Ever since then, though, our tiny work area—in which we were both spending up to fourteen hours a day—had positively brimmed with negative energy.

This morning, however, I was in high spirits as I hunched down in the car's roomy back seat with scissors, Post-its, and highlighters at the ready, scavenging the major newspapers for Glorious mentions that would be circulated around the office later. The company itself, its films, Phil or Tony, Glorious's corporate parent, information on competitors, all of the gossip columns and FYIs—anything that might be of interest to someone on the Glorious Pictures staff was my prey. The driver already had the *New York Times*, the *Post*, the *Daily News*, and the *Wall Street Journal* on board when he picked me up so that I could get a jump on the news and have everything in front of me in the likely event my boss called.

Allegra's dedication to media-gathering was, in reality, closer to a full-blown obsession. She spent all of her waking hours presenting Glorious's best face to the world, and was nothing less than fanatical about retrieving and analyzing every word that was printed or broadcast about the company. She thought that as long as she saw everything first she could control its impact. When anything questionable was reported about Glorious, Allegra would have a carefully scripted rationalization ready—usually before anyone else had even heard about it

For Dagney and me, this meant continuously gathering newspapers, magazines, broadcast transcripts, and tapes, and conducting multitudes of online searches to provide real-time media analysis for our boss. We had an Associated Press wire specially configured to sound an alert when anything regarding Glorious had been filed. It was like some kind of alternate universe news desk where, instead of publishing information, we captured it. We got the news so early that I wondered if one day I might inadvertently stumble across my own obituary.

So far, I noted, as we sped by Chelsea Piers, today's papers had pretty much the usual stuff—Oscar prediction articles, interviews with actors from upcoming Glorious films, and news and rumors about movies in preproduction. Had I found anything troubling or off-key, I would have called Allegra immediately and read her the questionable article. If it was an offense against Phil, I'd find him and connect the call so that she could ease him into what had been written. Tony, however, wasn't interested in being spun by Allegra. He wanted to punish the journalist involved, something at which she was equally adept.

She'd take care of this, too, starting with editors or producers and working her way up to publishers and even network heads if Tony was in an unusually bad mood or the transgression was particularly egregious.

After pulling off the highway at Canal Street we would stop at a newsstand on Hudson that was run by an Irish woman named

Belinda. Each morning, she would hand me a stack of all the newly published magazines and weekly newspapers, along with the L.A. *Times*, the *Washington Post*, *USA Today*, *Daily Variety*, and *The Hollywood Reporter*. Belinda was my secret weapon. Often she had already flagged items for me. She was a huge fan of Glorious Pictures with an encyclopedic knowledge of film, and she routinely caught things I might have missed otherwise, especially during my first few months at the company. As acting den mother to the neighborhood's film crowd, which regularly congregated in her small store, Belinda was plugged into all types of show business news and gossip. And since Dagney had the papers delivered to the office on "her" days, refusing to carry anything that was not a fashion accessory, Belinda's assistance was all mine.

Papers in hand, I jumped back in the car and rode the final two blocks to Glorious, where I used the security code to let myself in, disabled the alarm system, and flipped on the lights. Almost as soon as I'd put down my papers, the phone rang, and I felt a queasy feeling in the pit of my stomach. I picked it up warily. "Allegra Orecchi's office."

"Is she in?" a man's voice asked.

"Yes, she is. May I tell her who's calling?"

The caller hung up. I glanced nervously out the window at the low rooftops adjacent to our building. This had happened every morning I'd been in early over the past two weeks, and it gave me the creeps. At this hour, I was the only one in the office; maybe the only one in the building. When it first started to happen I'd thought it was just Hanratty, the phantom biographer, but Clark had told me that at this time of the morning he would definitely be sleeping one off, certainly not in any condition to be calling.

I'd pressed Clark for all he knew about Hanratty, and I still wasn't satisfied. To hear Clark tell it, Hanratty had been a huge supporter of the Waxmans in the early days of Glorious, and at first they'd responded in kind, giving him exclusive access and inviting him to all of their parties and events. But as Phil and Tony grew more successful, they relied on him less and less, until they barely acknowledged his existence. When a rival paper's Glorious scoop caused Hanratty's dismissal and neither brother would take his phone call to help him out, George Hanratty had sunk into a dismal and vengeful existence. About five years ago the story about the biography had begun floating around, but many people dismissed it as an alcohol-fueled fantasy.

"If he helped them out at the beginning, why were they so awful to him later?" I asked.

Clark shrugged. "Because they could be, I guess."

"But to cut him off completely? That just doesn't sound right, even for the Waxmans."

"Maybe there was something else," Clark agreed, "but I have no idea what it could be. All I know is, Hanratty's career is over, and he's become too much of a drunk to resurrect it. It's really a shame—I read some of his early work and it was terrific. He was incredibly talented."

"What a waste," I'd said.

After this morning's hang-up, I wished it *were* Hanratty, given the alternatives I was currently trying to push out of my mind. Could a sniper be watching me through our huge former-spool-factory windows? Or perhaps it was some psycho who was actually inside the building, armed with God knows what plus the knowledge that I was all alone? And, in a bizarre twist that would result in screaming tabloid headlines, he'd act out the script from one of Tony's horror movies—all too many of which I'd actually seen. The empty, echoing building, coupled with my general lack of sleep and this eerie hang-up thing, had me way too paranoid. I wanted to ask Dagney if the same thing happened to her, but I was hesitant to bring it up with things so rocky between us.

My next caller was, as usual, Allegra. She always phoned at exactly 7:45 so that I could give her a brief rundown of the day's news while she lay in bed, pretending she wasn't. She then, as she did each day, had me read all of Page Six aloud before faxing it to her at home. That column had a mysterious hold over her, and she studied it with the intensity of a Talmudic scholar. She seemed to believe there was a deeply nuanced and perhaps even encoded meaning buried within its boldfaced mentions.

The day before, however, there'd been a blind item on Page Six that even a novice like me had had no trouble decoding:

Just Asking?
Which stuttering studio head has to keep his ex-wife's artistic endeavors in full view to satisfy his divorce judgment? Staffers describe the work as "painful to look at."

So this explained that awful painting hanging in reception. I'd heard Phil speak and he didn't stutter, but I'd noticed that Tony's communications were limited to barked near-monosyllables. Trudi Waxman must be the former Mrs. Tony.

As soon as I reached the office, I dialed Allegra's home number and read the item aloud. "Karen, you didn't need to wake me up for this," she replied coldly, but I could hear her feet hit the floor. "I'm sure this is about Caleb Daniels at Warner." Then she hung up.

Half an hour later, the phone rang. "This is Elliott Solnick from Page Six. I'm returning Allegra's call."

"I'll put you through," I said, my suspicions confirmed.

"Wait, before you do that, did I see you at the screening of *She Swings Both Ways* last Wednesday?"

"You might have." I'd been there, but we certainly hadn't been introduced.

"Long light brown hair, black suede mid-calf boots, size six and a half?" he persisted.

"That's me," I said, flattered that he'd noticed those particular boots, since they'd cost nearly what I earned in a week. But he was the first person I'd ever come across who could accurately guess a shoe size.

"Who are you, 'Me'?" he said, laughing.

"Karen Jacobs."

"It's nice to meet you, Karen. I'll be speaking with you again soon," he said, in a self-assured manner that I found undeniably attractive. Then I remembered Dagney's warning.

"Let me put you through," I said, trying to sound more businesslike.

I rang Allegra. "I have Elliott Solnick from Page Six for you."

"I don't know what he wants from me this early. Tell him I'm in a meeting."

I began to relay this to Elliott but was interrupted by the sound of another phone ringing in his office. Elliott put me on hold and then returned a moment later, saying, "You don't have to leave a message; I have Allegra on the other line."

I smirked as I entered Elliott's information onto the phone sheet anyway, and wondered when I'd get the chance to chat with him again.

Today, however, the morning was off to a calmer start. After finishing my first call with Allegra, I picked up the waiting stack of faxes from the monitoring service and scanned them while ordering three cups of coffee and a chocolate croissant from the neighborhood's best patisserie. Glorious utilized a company that had people watching every channel in every city across the country, twenty-four hours a day. I could picture them—a pajama-clad, Doritos-eating, insomniac army of television addicts—each one the envy of their friends: "You get *paid* to watch TV?" They took notes on what was shown and discussed, and every morning a fax machine full of summaries awaited us; if we wanted more information, tapes and transcripts were available. The whole thing was similar to a wire-tapping operation. If an affiliate in Topeka trashed our latest release, we knew about it immediately. By lunchtime, the station's entertainment producer would have been not-so-gently reminded of the access our junkets provided—access that would certainly be enjoyed by a competing station in their market. The next morning's report would generally show another, better review.

As I continued to gather together the "Hits"—a collection of all the articles and television transcripts that had been published or aired since the previous day—I put through calls for Allegra, leaving messages for people she knew wouldn't be in, but who could nevertheless now be crossed off her phone log. Today's Hits were average, coming in at around 150 pages. At nine, an intern arrived to photocopy and deliver the packets to the more than sixty-five people on the distribution list. Then, at about ten, the Glorious staff started to drift in—many of whom proceeded to toss the Hits directly into the trash. It was hard for me not to feel a little protective, so after a couple of weeks on the job I'd sent around an e-mail asking if anyone would prefer not to receive them. Marlene promptly informed Allegra of this latest lapse in judgment, insisting that my polite communiqué would have undoubtedly offended many of its recipients, as, indeed, it had offended her. Allegra immediately had me send another e-mail, this one under her name, apologizing profusely for my error and citing my "recent hire" status and "lack of familiarity with the importance of media distribution." Apparently it was considered a privilege at Glorious to throw out the Hits—one that many people were loath to give up. Clark subsequently explained that a person could be added to the Hits distribution list only with Allegra's written permission. Interested parties had to describe in detail why they deserved to receive them and Allegra would consider it for a few weeks before handing down her decision, which ran about three to one against.

Dagney arrived at 10:30, settling into her chair without saying a word. Clearly the cold war between us was still on, although its exact temperature changed frequently. The Hits finished, I turned to a far more frustrating task: my attempt to transport Sean Raines, the star of *The Foreign Pilot* and nominee for Best Actor, from New Zealand to Sydney to Los Angeles. The moment the Academy campaigning had subsided, at midnight on the last day that ballots could be mailed, all kinds of last-minute demands and headaches associated with the Oscars had begun cropping up. Sean—who insisted his name be pronounced "Sheen"—was proving to be famously difficult even in this virtual sea of famous and difficult individuals. Currently he was on location in New Zealand; on Monday, his publicist had called Allegra and told her that he required a private plane to bring him from New Zealand to Los Angeles. Phil would approve this only if Sean first flew to Sydney and did a press day to support the film's Australian opening. He would need to fly to Sydney commercially, in first class, and after he'd fulfilled his media obligations there, a private jet would fly him to Los Angeles. Sean sulked about it but eventually agreed, as long as he would be able to rest adequately during the long flight.

Allegra had delegated the jet-chartering to me, and using Dagney's instructions, I set out to rent one. I looked at fax after fax of interiors that had been converted into boardrooms and bedrooms and chic little apartments, trying to select one that would guarantee "adequate rest." By lunch on Tuesday I'd chosen a plane that had been laid out to include a master bedroom suite and a fully-equipped media room. After e-mailing the information to Sean's publicist, I immediately received a response saying that Sean would require some "additional services" for his single day in Sydney; the remainder of the afternoon was therefore spent trying to find him a "Cordon Bleu–trained but Tuscan-leaning" chef as well as reserving him a car and driver. I was amazed that Allegra okayed this, but Robert explained that it was a matter of protecting the studio's investment—without them, Sean would most certainly be petulant and morose with the Australian media, and the entire stopover would be useless.

Wednesday brought with it a more exotic challenge—Sean's publicist informed me that he wouldn't show up at the Wellington airport without an actual ticket. Three years ago he'd had "a harrowing experience" with a missing plane ticket in Marrakech. An e-ticket wouldn't work, as Sean didn't "believe" in the Internet. The only acceptable method of transport was to have his ticket hand-delivered to him in the remote village where he was currently shooting. I'd found a messenger service willing to do the job, but now Allegra wanted everyone reassured that Sean had the ticket in his possession and would be in Sydney and Los Angeles as planned. Unfortunately, the time difference and lack of cellular coverage in the tiny outpost where he was staying meant that I hadn't yet been able to confirm that the hand-off had taken place.

I told Dagney I was going to get a glass of water, and detoured into Robert's cube, where I moved into the corner so no one else could see me.

"Who behaves like this?" I asked. "Can you please tell me what kind of adult carries on about this kind of complete nonsense?"

"One who can," he answered. "One who knows that he'll be

passed around and rocked and coddled until he gets what he wants."

"And that publicist of his. What a witch! She's called three times already today to see if he'd gotten the ticket."

"Don't worry about it. And definitely don't take it personally."

"How can I not take it personally? They're all yelling at me. Personally." I said, and Robert smiled.

"It's not worth it. When the messenger in New Zealand hands Sean the ticket, his publicist is going to call him up and describe in great detail how she got it all done. Because, really, when you think about it, Sean hired her, so if he doesn't get what he wants, it's her neck on the line, not yours, *parenthesis*, no matter how much she will definitely blame you should anything go wrong, *close parens*," he said. I had to laugh, while envying Robert's ability to maintain an even keel.

"Thanks, I think I get it."

"So did he get the ticket yet?" Robert asked in a whiny voice, needling me as I walked out.

"I'll have to get back to you," I said in an altogether snotty fashion, tilting my nose in the air.

"There you go. You're a champ."

At our desk, Dagney was working on plans for the L.A. premiere of *She Swings Both Ways,* an event that was scheduled to take place two days after the Oscars. The film marked the debut of Ivan-Melissa Pell, an actress who had renamed herself "in honor of her paternal grandparents," according to her official biography. "Always address Ms. Pell as 'Ivan-Melissa,' never 'Ivan'" was number nineteen on the long list of instructions we'd been given with regard to the ingénue's maintenance. I thought the name made her sound like a pre-op segueing between genders as well as films; given that I was currently unsuccessfully tracking Maori messengers through the antipodean bush, however, I was probably not the go-to girl for career advice.

Ivan-Melissa, on the other hand, had proved herself one thoroughly savvy hyphenate. First she'd let it slip that she was "secretly" dating Bob Metuchen, the director of the film; then, although it was supposedly her character who swung both ways, she'd coyly suggested in the accompanying round of interviews that there was some real-life basis for her casting. Faster than you can say "girl on girl," Ivan-Melissa Pell was officially in demand.

Dagney was in charge of booking all the hotels, limos, and bartenders needed for the party. As with most Glorious premieres, though, there was no catering budget. Food cost money, and besides—the Waxmans had learned that their parties generated much more ink when the guests drank on empty stomachs.

I was in the reception area, picking up my lunch from the deliveryman, when I spied a foil-covered china platter that smelled amazing. "Mmm, what is that?" I asked the receptionist.

"Brisket," she said. "Gloria makes Phil and Tony her special brisket every Thursday—it's been their family tradition since the two of them first got teeth."

"Can I take a peek?" I asked. "It just smells so great—I need to see it." She nodded and I lifted off the foil, revealing a beautiful roast. The tray was a gorgeous Royal Doulton platter in a pattern I remembered seeing when I'd gone with Ellen to register for her wedding gifts.

"Thanks, have you ever tasted it?"

"Nope. As far as I know, they've never shared it. I do know that Tony's half is rare and Phil's half is well done—something that, if you ask my grandmother, is not physically possible."

"Does she ever miss a week?" I asked, carefully tucking the foil back in place. I was strangely compelled by this brisket.

"If Gloria can't make it, the brisket comes alone in her Jaguar—with her driver, of course."

"How nice for it," I said, taking my sandwich back to my desk.

Shortly after lunch and my seventeenth conversation with the dispatcher at the New Zealand messenger service, the phone rang. "Allegra! Now!" was followed immediately by the slamming down of the receiver. Both of Tony's assistants often adopted their boss's gruff manner when making calls on his behalf. I couldn't decide whether this was a case of imitation being the sincerest form of flattery, or if they just liked being able to act like assholes without fear of retribution. As soon as I relayed the message, Allegra gathered up a pile of folders, clippings, and videotapes, grabbed a newly charged cell phone battery from my desk, and disappeared in the direction of Phil and Tony's office suite.

Two minutes after Allegra's departure, Dagney announced, "I need a cigarette," to no one in particular, then stalked down the corridor. While Dagney smoked and Allegra met with Tony, I answered the phone and dealt with Allegra's e-mail. Allegra didn't seem to grasp the significance of the "e" in "e-mail" and insisted that Dagney and I print out the contents of her in-box hourly. She then wrote her reply on each piece of paper and we typed and sent them. It was extra work, but between listening in on phone calls and reading e-mail I had an all-access pass to the show at Glorious. Besides, Allegra's stinginess in sharing information was matched only by her frustration when we didn't know something she hadn't told us, so Dagney and I needed to use every available method to keep ourselves informed. We discussed it, and decided that anything that was not under lock and key was within our purview.

Now, reading through her in-box, I learned some of the

strategy behind the L.A. premiere that Dagney was working on. Bob Metuchen was a boy-wonder director whom Tony had discovered at Sundance several years earlier, and the film—which I'd apparently watched in the dark with Elliott Solnick the week before—was smart and edgy. It was said to be Bob's best work so far, and Tony was betting heavily on it. Scanning the entire thread, which had begun long before my Glorious arrival, I realized that Allegra's post-Oscar timing of this premiere was a way of strategically demonstrating that the company's indie cred was very much intact. Bob was the company poster child—the kid who was always smiling and proclaiming the good fortune that had befallen him, thanks to Glorious. His movies didn't earn lots of money, but they didn't cost much to make, either. Most important, everything about them shouted "Indie!" loudly enough to be heard on both coasts. And, as always, in maintaining the delicate balance between the Waxmans, *She Swings Both Ways* was a Tony to Phil's *The Foreign Pilot*.

At home, earlier in the week, feeling the need to brag a little about my new job, I'd told Ellen about all the access I had—from the e-mail to the mute button to the ability to overhear nearly any conversation taking place on the premises.

"It's like having sex with a dog in the room," she'd said.

"What?"

"You know, people have sex while their dog is in the room because it doesn't matter what he sees or hears."

I couldn't believe how mean she was acting. "Ellen, how can you say that? It's because they *trust* me."

"Okay, so they trust you. I'm sorry. But please, watch your back at that place."

I swore that I would, and was thinking of her analogy now, while printing out more of Allegra's e-mails and writing down highly sensitive phone messages.

I printed out twenty-two new e-mails and was entering some calls onto the phone sheet when Robert appeared. "Soap?" he said. I handed him my Dial super-antibacterial liquid. Given our soap-less status, the hours we were all keeping, and the fact that, if you sneezed, there were at least fifteen people close enough to say "Bless you" (not that anyone ever did), I wasn't taking any chances on getting sick.

"Karen. Karen. Karen. I have to see Allegra. Where is she?"

No matter how many times I heard it, Vivian's patented triplicate name shout never failed to send adrenaline racing through my body like the sound of a starter's pistol. She would triple-name me in exactly the same tone whether she was reprimanding me for having missed a two-line item about a film not yet on our release schedule or—if others were present—telling me that I had lipstick on my teeth. "She's in with Tony."

"Is she *in* with Tony or is she sitting on that little bench outside Tony's office?" she asked. Absolute specificity was another Vivian Henry trademark.

"As far as I know, she's inside Tony's office, meeting with him. I'll put you on the phone sheet." I added Vivian's name to the list, and noted the time, which was 3:45 P.M. I also noted that Dagney had been gone for nearly an hour and I really needed to use the bathroom.

Vivian walked into her cube, made a quick call, then walked back out and three-named me again—her voice loud enough to be heard for blocks. "She's *outside* Tony's office, on the bench," she announced triumphantly, as if she'd caught me in a lie. "He's working with his Pilates trainer now."

"I'll make sure to give her the message," I repeated. "Because as far as I know, she's in with Tony," I said, trying to give Vivian a conspiratorial smile, which she returned with a glare.

Vivian was in charge of pre-Oscar press for *The Foreign Pilot.*

While the complex media schedule involving talent and journalists on five continents was a perfect match for her mania for logistics and detail, the gargantuan scope of the project had worn her thin patience down to virtual transparency. Still, she refused to delegate so much as the licking of a single envelope. Vivian retreated to her cube, listing out loud everything she needed to do in the next two hours, as if for my benefit. I felt like calling over the divider, "Yes, you are the busiest of them all, Vivian!" but instead I put in another unsuccessful call to New Zealand.

Dagney came back stinking of cigarettes, but in a much better mood. "Allegra's meeting with Tony—or, according to Viv, sitting on the bench outside Tony's office," I said, trying to match Dagney's breezy nonchalance.

She rolled her eyes. "When one of the brothers calls Allegra, they usually keep her waiting for at least a couple of hours before they see her." She explained that Allegra insisted on keeping up the pretense that she was actually meeting with them for the entire time. "She doesn't even want *us* to know that she's not actually in the meeting, which is why she dials her own calls while she's waiting."

"Why would she sit on a bench pretending to be in a meeting?" I asked.

"It's a mindfuck," Dagney said, using a tone that suggested I knew nothing of the business world. She said that Allegra's game plan was to make the other Glorious executives think she got more face time with the twins than anyone else did: In fact, Allegra rarely spent more than fifteen minutes with either brother. "Phil and Tony have more important things to do than try to hear Allegra," she finished, flipping through the latest *Vibe*.

Right now, the most important thing I had to do was to reach the bathroom without being waylaid, always a difficult exercise. Allegra's office had been purposely placed at the opposite end of the corridor from the restrooms so that she wouldn't have to endure a steady stream of people passing by her always-closed office door. Dagney and I walked a veritable gantlet every time we had to pee, obstructed and harassed by various members of the department who needed something from our boss. Allegra's rule over Publicity was absolute and her explicit approval was required for everything from okaying flights for nominees' extra family members to signing off on the exact shape of the Oscar-shaped chocolates that would be in the Glorious gift bags. She was maddeningly slow to answer their queries, often leaving the staff unable to move forward. With the Oscars less than two weeks away, the entire department was in a logjam.

Our attempts to reach the bathroom were constantly interrupted with reminders to have Allegra call or e-mail other publicity staffers. Dagney and I, though powerless, were at least audible and visible, and therefore frequent targets for their exasperation. I didn't have time for one of those conversations right now. I strode purposefully, head down, and slammed right into Marlene. "Owww, that was my bad elbow," she said. I apologized and tried to make my way around her, but she wouldn't let me pass.

"Marlene, I really have to go," I said, shaking my soap bottle for emphasis. "I'll stop by on the way back."

"I *have* to talk to Allegra," she said, rubbing her elbow meaningfully and flexing her fingers as if testing for any nerve damage I might have inflicted. "Can you make sure I'm the next one she sees?"

"I'll put you on her phone list."

"But I have to be next," Marlene whined. "It's about Buddy Friedman. He's saying he won't come to the Oscars unless we fly his parents in from Miami *and* get them tickets to the Awards."

I sidestepped her and sprinted down the hall, calling behind me, "Buddy's parents will still be in Miami when I get back from the bathroom." No doubt this would earn me another memo—it was a clear case of reckless endangerment with a side order of insubordination, but by now I knew that Marlene was someone who only had to be tolerated, not feared.

Marlene was indispensable to Glorious because she ran the press junkets that took place nearly every weekend. It was a difficult job that involved looking after emotionally needy celebrities and their "people" while making sure the 250 or so journalists in attendance were also reasonably happy. When presiding over a junket weekend Marlene was truly in her element, and she performed her duties flawlessly; it was the rest of the week that posed a problem. From Monday morning to midday Wednesday, she would complain about what had gone wrong over the previous weekend. Then, after breaking for lunch on Wednesday, she began predicting what might go wrong the following Saturday and Sunday. But her junket management skills, coupled with her willingness to give up virtually all of her weekends for the greater good of Glorious, had apparently exempted her from having to follow even the most rudimentary rules of socialization.

When I got back to my desk, Allegra had returned and Marlene and Vivian were pacing in circles outside her closed office door like caged tigers, with Dagney halfheartedly trying to fend them off. "But I need her now," Marlene was saying, as Vivian stated, "I must see Allegra this instant."

"She's on a call, and she knows you're waiting," Dagney said, studying her manicure intently. "I'll get you when she's off the phone."

"But who is she going to see first?" Marlene asked.

Dagney looked at me and raised her eyebrows ever so slightly. It was hard to stay truly angry with each other—only we could fully understand our situation. This scenario repeated itself at least once a day and was impossible to mediate. The single thing that united Marlene and Vivian was how much they hated answering to Allegra, and the fact that Allegra had been installed over their heads just three years earlier, even though they were both Glorious veterans, added fuel to the fire. The situation was close to blowing up entirely, but then it always was; our department existed in a perpetual state of near-hysteria.

Unable to take it any longer, Marlene charged into Allegra's office, Vivian close on her heels. Allegra was on the phone, cuddling the receiver between her cheek and shoulder as she murmured soundlessly into the mouthpiece. Startled by the interlopers, her eyes grew wide as she waved one hand in alarm, while the other grabbed a pen and scribbled, "ON W/OPRAH" on a Post-it. She thrust the note at them as her wave changed to a shooing motion.

Dagney and I watched this mini-drama unfold from our desk with considerable amusement. We knew she wasn't talking to Oprah. Mackie Moran had seen the Chrysler Building this morning "with brand-new eyes," and it had opened up a "world of possibilities" for Allegra's foyer.

Vivian and Marlene slunk away, defeated. There was no competing with Oprah, even an imaginary Oprah, and they both knew it. "I'm going out for a cigarette," I said to Dagney as I slipped into my coat. "But you don't smoke," she said sulkily to my departing back, as if now I would be competing with her in yet another area.

I went to the Korean deli on the corner to assemble my faux-smoking arsenal and picked out a bright blue Bic lighter. Having never bought cigarettes before, I looked at all the choices behind the counter for a while before deciding on Marlboros, because that was what Clark smoked. "I'll take the soft pack," I added, grabbing a tin of Altoids to imitate a smoker's minty post-cigarette breath.

Once outside, I opened the pack and lit up, then set off to kill fifteen minutes or so window shopping. Unaccustomed to my new habit, however, I kept forgetting that I was holding a lit cigarette. After being asked to leave both the health food store and a fancy rug shop, I decided to sit on a bench and call Abby on my new Glorious cell phone.

"Karen! I was just thinking of you," she said, when she answered.

"You were?" I asked, wary of her enthusiasm. Lately everything Abby talked about had to do with mysterious illnesses that were usually diagnosed too late. "How much time do you think I have left?" I asked.

"It's nothing like that. I'm done with the module on fatal reactions."

"Is that what they called it?"

"Of course not. The official name was Commonly Misdiagnosed Diseases of the Endocrine System, and I'm really glad it's over. Although I'd recognize one in the dark, if need be. The worst part was that on our last day the resident who taught us said we'd be lucky if we saw any of these even once in our careers."

"Well, you'd be luckier than the patient."

"True. Anyway, how are you? How's Glorious?"

"I'm finally getting the hang of the job itself, but the people are a whole other story. On paper, I work for my boss, Allegra, but in reality I also answer to Vivian, the EVP, and Marlene, the SVP, and they're really kind of difficult."

"How so?"

"Not only are they constantly hostile for no reason, they're competitive to the point where it's not healthy. Vivian's just a touch more senior than Marlene, and Allegra's over both of them, so it always feels as if a catfight's about to break out."

"Sounds like a great work environment."

"The part I can't figure out is that, even though they can be unbelievably bitchy, they're smart, they're great at what they do, and they have really exciting jobs. I'd admire them, if they'd just let me." I laughed, trying to hide my frustration.

"Maybe it's the kind of situation where you can learn what they do well, without picking up their bad habits."

"I'm trying," I said, eyeing the long ash on my cigarette before accidentally flicking it onto my coat. "Promise you'll let me know if I start exhibiting any shrewlike tendencies?"

"Never a problem. But don't let them shove you around, either. You have to promise me that."

I agreed, said good-bye, and made my way back to the office. Abby knew that I had a history of letting things get out of hand, and we'd had endless conversations about it. I'd stayed way too long at my last job just because it was easy, and hadn't confronted Gabe about his need to have a real source of income until it was too late. It had just always seemed simpler to avoid conflict, and it was something I was going to start working on immediately. Otherwise, I'd be eaten alive.

In front of the building, I daintily ground out the cigarette with my shoe, and, ever the citizen smoker, picked up the butt and deposited it in the trash before going inside.

As I approached the desk I could see Dagney's grim face from down the hall. The emotional temperature of our work area had changed again since I'd left, but fresh from my conversation with Abby, I wasn't about to assume it had something to do with me. "What happened?"

"Oh, you know, phone stuff," she said, staring at her computer screen. It was obvious that she didn't want to elaborate.

In an office where the phone rang upward of one hundred times a day and the phone sheet was, in reality, twenty pages printed out on an hourly basis, it was inevitable that a small percentage of calls and callers got lost in the shuffle. Even so, I was glad that this time it was Dagney who had screwed up. This was turning out to be the first day at Glorious during which I hadn't gotten into some kind of trouble, and I wanted to keep the rest of it unblemished.

It had taken me over an hour last Sunday to adequately describe Glorious's phone rites and rituals to Ellen in a way that a right-thinking individual could understand. She said it sounded more complex than the new rules governing dividend income from offshore corporations. I didn't tell her that the consequences of an error were, in this place, possibly more catastrophic than a trip to the federal penitentiary. After all, the telephone formed the nexus of the company's hierarchical culture, and its power struggles were played out on the phones in ways that would have had Alexander Graham Bell wondering if his invention might actually be a tool of the devil.

Allegra's style was classic old-school Hollywood. If she initiated a communication, it was up to the recipient to call her back. She would not call again until the other party had attempted to reach her. An office destroyed by fire, a long absence due to illness—neither of these were reasons to repeat a phone call. If someone called her first, the decision about when or if to call him back was based on an algorithm she'd invented that factored in how important the caller was and then multiplied and divided by what she needed from him now, what she might need in the future, any currently unsettled disagreements, and maybe even an old grudge that the caller thought was long-forgiven. Each time Dagney or I printed out a phone sheet, Allegra strategized anew, handing us back a fully annotated document. The numeral "2" meant she would call them back in two days. An asterisk indicated there was a memo or clipping she needed to have on hand as a footnote to her conversation. "CAS-NO" denoted that one of us was to Call and say "NO" to the caller's query—there was no "CAS-YES." "POT-V" stood for Pass this call over to Vivian or Marlene or Clark or whomever the initial indicated. "LATER" meant that they wouldn't be hearing back from her anytime soon.

Phil's phone style wasn't really a style at all, but more of an escalating harangue. If someone didn't call him back promptly after he'd left word, his assistants had instructions to leave five to ten messages every hour until the conversation actually took place. Tony's calls, on the other hand, were delivered only once, with the precision of a mob hit. Inside the company it was just "Tony!" Outside it was "Tony! Wax! Man!" The recipient had two choices—pick up the phone and deal with an angry Tony now, or call back and speak to an enraged Tony later on.

Marlene, I'd already learned, called frequently to say nothing, whereas Vivian's phone messages bristled with explicit details and had to be read back to her at least twice to convince her that we'd written it down correctly. Nine times out of ten, she sent an e-mail with the identical information. In short, the phones were like a high-wire act, and as with most things at Glorious, there was no net. With that in mind I handled each call, ingoing or outgoing, as carefully as a member of the bomb squad would a suspicious package.

At about four, I looked at my watch and realized that I needed to find out where Phil and Allegra would be later, so that I could get them the *New York Times* review of *Feeling Fine in Phoenix When You're Fried*, which was opening the next day.

Newspapers publish reviews on the day a film opens—usually Friday—but Glorious went to extraordinary lengths in its attempts to anticipate the reviewers' reactions so that any necessary damage control could begin as early as possible. This meant that whenever Glorious screened a film for critics, publicity assistants and interns took up positions around the room, furiously scribbling notes in the dark describing every hiccup, posture change, nose scratch, and throat clearing exhibited by the reviewers in attendance. The watchers were being closely watched.

They were also, whenever possible, being manipulated by the power of suggestion. If the film being screened was a comedy or action flick, Glorious would fill the audience with teenagers who would laugh uproariously or stand up and cheer at the slightest provocation, making it difficult for the critics not to get caught up in the emotion. We had cultivated relationships with several of the city's rowdiest high schools, knowing that their exhausted administrators would happily send their most discipline-challenged students on a field trip whenever one was offered. By loading the deck and keeping an eye on all of the players, Glorious could usually get a general sense of the overall journalistic reaction to a particular film.

The reviewers from the *New York Times*, however, did their best to remain absolutely inscrutable. They had learned to sit in their seats with a preternatural calm, as if they had sent in their wax-body doubles to view the film. If we were going to watch them watch a movie, they weren't going to give away any clues. Not even a roomful of screaming kids could sway them. It was a stalemate. Therefore, as a rule, no one outside the newspaper had any idea what the *Times* would say in their critique. When their fact-checkers called, Dagney and I would try to wring some meaning out of their questions, but they were usually just checking the spellings of characters' names and film locales. "But *how* did they ask you to spell 'Bob Anderson?'" Allegra would ask in a whispered plea.

"I think he wanted to know if it was an 'o' or an 'e' in Anderson," Dagney said.

"Did he sound as though he *liked* Bob Anderson?"

"He sounded as though he wanted to know how to spell his name." Dagney savored Allegra's rare displays of apprehension.

Ever since that first Thursday a few weeks earlier, when I'd read Phil the critique of *The Sparrow in the Olive Tree*, Dagney had decided that review nights were my permanent job. Usually, review nights involved more than just reading to Phil, and I'd created a system to make the process move efficiently. At around eleven I'd head out to Queens in a Town Car. The plant would appear completely dark and deserted until, all at once, rows of garage doors would open and dozens of *New York Times* trucks filled with the next day's papers would emerge. I'd dash into the building's lobby, buy two, jump back in the car, and immediately phone Allegra to read the article aloud as the driver sped to the nearest Kinko's, where I would fax it to Allegra, Phil, and Tony. Even with the fax, Allegra often had me phone Phil to read it to him directly. Sometimes, Phil had me reread a sentence or paragraph. He was also interested in the reviews of competing films that were opening the same day. Two weeks before, I'd read Phil half the Weekend section and some NBA scores.

A stellar review or an out-and-out pan meant that I would get home quickly, but anything in between meant I'd be up nearly all night connecting Phil and Allegra to each other as they tried to figure out the exact percentage of the review that was very good and how they would downplay the portions that were less favorable. The *Times* doesn't use the "star" rating that most other papers do, so the two of them would try to ascertain how many stars it would have received had it appeared in a paper that awarded stars. I stayed in the car outside Kinko's because I might be asked to fax the review to more people involved with the film. I never knew who would be invited to these late-night phone summits or how long they might last, but I got to see firsthand how hard the highest level of executives at Glorious were willing to work to spin a story, and exactly how they went about doing it.

On the previous Friday Allegra had remarked in passing, "Phil said you read well." Normally I wouldn't have considered this a huge compliment, as I'd been reading for the past twenty-five years, but I was secretly pleased that Phil had noticed me. Dagney, however, was less so. Today, after I made my customary call to Sabrina, the assistant who handled Phil's schedule, Dagney piped up, "I'm going to do the reviews tonight, Karen. You've done them for four weeks in a row."

"Don't you have Felix tonight?" I asked.

"I swapped with my mother; she's been going to him for years."

"I'm going, Dagney. It's as simple as that."

"We're supposed to alternate," she said, practically spitting out the words.

"Yes, we are. But you haven't been. And you can't change your mind just because Phil paid me a compliment."

"Fine. Be my guest," she said angrily. "It's not like you have anything better to do." She flounced away.

The next morning began well: A production assistant on Sean's set confirmed that the ticket had finally arrived. According to him, the messenger had driven three hours and trekked the final twenty kilometers on foot. Sean had reciprocated by refusing to sign for the delivery until the on-set masseuse had left his trailer.

I put the message on Allegra's phone list, and a short while later she asked me to come into her office. She was seated at her desk, surrounded by folders, writing answers on e-mail printouts. "Phil suggested that you might be a good choice to announce the celebrity arrivals at the Oscar party," Allegra whispered in the direction of her pen, not bothering to make eye contact. "You fly on Wednesday morning." At this point her glance drifted from the desk to the window, signaling that the conversation had ended, but I was far too ecstatic to be insulted. Dashing out to the desk, I called Robert and then Clark to tell them. Dagney overheard and when I put down the phone she said, "You're coming to L.A. with us? You only just started."

"Allegra said that Phil specifically asked for me to be there," I said, enjoying every syllable. Clark came over immediately. "This calls for the Bubble Lounge tonight. You'll love it," he announced. I was dialing like a madwoman—my parents, Ellen, Abby—leaving voice mail hither and yon: I was Oscar-nominated, L.A.-bound, headed for Hollywood! Who cared if Marlene and Vivian and Allegra and Dagney were coming with me?

That evening, as Robert, Clark, and I approached the Bubble Lounge's discreet awning on West Broadway, I was so wrapped up in the things I needed to do to get ready that I walked right past the entrance. Clark ran out and retrieved me. "Cinderella, the ball's not for a week and a half!" he said, shaking me and laughing. After carefully surveying our various seating options—upholstered settees, antique love seats, and some tasseled ottomans—we chose a spot near the back on a long velvet couch plentifully appointed with throw pillows. A waitress came over and presented Clark with the champagne list—there were more than three hundred from which to select. Clark chose quickly and handed the menu back. I settled into the cushions, the knowledge that I was going to L.A. with everyone else emboldening me. I had accumulated lots of questions since I had started at Glorious—now I finally had the courage to ask them.

"What's the story with Phil's office?" I'd always imagined it would be some kind of vast, uninterrupted space, like Gordon Gekko's in *Wall Street*.

"Phil can have any office he wants," Clark nodded knowingly. "But that little room provides tactical supremacy."

"Does it? I thought he'd want something that reflected his

success a little more. It's really tight in there." I could still see the barber in my mind's eye, squished into the tiny space between Phil's head and the wall.

"Precisely right. That's exactly how he wants it," Clark said. "A nice, tight squeeze," he said, pressing the palms of his hands together.

I still didn't understand.

"Okay. Imagine you want something from Phil," he started. "And he wants something from you. You're negotiating."

"Okay."

"As soon as you step into that office, he gains a supreme psychological advantage. It's small, he's big, you're trapped on that little couch. When he starts yelling, you can practically see his tonsils."

"Hmm." I was beginning to get the picture. "So, Phil can kind of put the screws to whoever's in there with him."

"There you have it, dear," Clark said. "Claustrophia and Fear— Phil's trusted associates."

Just then our bottle came, and the waitress performed one of those fancy popless openings before pouring the champagne into our glasses.

"Here's to Karen," Clark said.

"To your first month at Glorious; it will never be this hard again," Robert added, clinking my flute.

"To the two of you, who helped me keep it together," I replied. We nodded ceremoniously and drank. This didn't taste like any champagne I'd ever had. "What *is* this, Clark?" I asked, taking care not to drain my glass too quickly.

"It's a 1973 Bollinger RD, one of my favorites. But you're definitely worth it." He and Robert grinned at each other.

"So what exactly am I worth?"

"Oh, about four hundred fifty bucks." The number nearly

popped the bubbles cheerily dancing around in my glass. There was no way I could afford my third of this. Seeing my worried face, Clark added, "Of course, this is business, so it's on the Glorious expense account."

"Can you just do that?"

"Golden Child," Robert grinned, taking another sip.

Clark ignored him. "We'll just say you're a magazine journalist, and this was where Ivan-Melissa insisted on holding the interview," Clark said, laughing. "So, how did you get your very unusual name, Ivan?" he leaned forward and intoned in a BBC accent.

"It's Ivan-*Melissa*." I shot back. "Didn't those losers at Glorious tell you anything?"

Pretty soon we'd finished the first bottle and Clark ordered another, equally expensive one to replace it.

"So how are things going with Dagney?" Clark asked.

"Well, aside from the smoking breaks, hissy fits, and protracted sulks, she's actually not so bad."

"Oh, but she's more Machiavellian than she looks," Robert cautioned. "Watch. The more competent you become, the more she'll slack off. She even writes down the most devious Glorious schemes in a little book she keeps in that Tod's tote of hers."

"How do you know that?"

"Routine fact-finding mission," Robert said, trying to pull an innocent face. "I needed some Advil."

"Robert! When are you going to stop going through everyone's stuff?" I protested, even though I was glad to know that Dagney was armed and dangerous.

"Probably never," Robert said. "But I am something of an information hunter-gatherer. It's useful. Ask me anything." Clark rolled his eyes.

"Okay, why does Allegra always tell me to put things directly into Phil's and Tony's hands? Vivian almost murdered me that first week."

"That's easy. For the same reason she says she's on with Oprah, or in with Phil when she's on the bench. It's just her way of reminding herself how important she is. And how you are to think of yourself as a physical extension of her."

I shook my head. I was her assistant, not a pair of robotic arms. "Next?"

"What happened to the person who had the job before me?"

"I think her name was Cecelia," Robert said, "She wasn't here for very long."

"What happened? Did she run screaming from the building?"

"Not exactly." He and Clark exchanged glances.

"You've heard of Marvin Fischell, right?" Robert said.

"Of course I have." Marvin had been in many of Johnny Lucchese's early films, and had a role in the movie that had helped make Eddie Di Silva so famous. His career had been a bit uneven for a while, but after a breakthrough performance in Glorious's *The Oboe* he'd become hot again.

"Marvin has an office in our building," Robert continued. "He's doing a lot of producing these days." Clark shot him a warning look, but Robert went on. "Anyway, Cecelia was really busty. And Marvin is crazy about large-breasted women. He's completely harmless, not touchy-feely; just likes to be around women who look like they could be lingerie models. He saw her get off the elevator on our floor, and an hour later called Phil and asked if he could hire her to work for him."

"Just like that?"

"Yeah, exactly like that. Well, what happened next is duly noted in Dagney's little book. Phil said okay, but only if Marvin agreed to do three extra press days for his next Glorious project.

So now Cecelia is Marvin's D-girl." He sat back and took a long sip of champagne. Then both he and Clark reflexively looked at my chest, complete with its very small breasts.

I was stunned. In an instant, a lot of things became clear— Clark's initial interest, the lack of questions during my interview with Geraldine, the need to start immediately. It was to replace my well-endowed predecessor who'd clearly been meant for bigger things.

"Is this why you asked me to send my résumé, Clark?"

Clark looked down at his shoes and didn't answer. Of all the things in the world I'd thought could open doors for me, I never in a million years would have thought it would be this—I'd been hired because of my tits. I felt angry for about five seconds. Then I began to laugh hysterically, and soon Robert and Clark had joined in. After all, I'd survived my first five weeks. I was running up a bar tab that rivaled my rent and I wasn't paying for it. I was going to the Oscars. And I hadn't even needed to take my shirt off.

DOWN AND OUT IN
BEVERLY HILLS

It was the morning after the Oscars and my head was ringing. No, it was the alarm clock that I'd set for noon. Could it be twelve already? No, it was the phone that was ringing. I stared at it, uncomprehending, then looked at the clock and saw that it was eight A.M. And the phone was ringing. The phone was ringing at eight A.M. and I'd gone to sleep at six. "Hello?"

"Karen, you're working on the *She Swings Both Ways* premiere today. The L.A. office needed an extra body and I told them you would be there."

Allegra's choice of words couldn't have been more accurate. I was, in fact, little more than a body at the moment. "You really need to be there almost immediately," she continued, as I tuned back into the conversation. "But first, can you bring my earrings back to Sandy Schwartz?" she asked, as if there were more than one possible answer. "You're going down Wilshire anyway."

"That's fine."

"They're waiting for you at the front desk with the address. Once you get to our office, someone will be there to supervise you. You won't need to call me again." Before Allegra clicked off, I heard the rustle of sheets. Waking me up had clearly been enough work for her at this hour. I had thought that the morning after the Oscars would be clear of obligations, but I was wrong. Ever since deplaning at LAX I'd been wrong. It was becoming a theme.

In my room, the heavy drapes were drawn and it was pitch black. The precision thermostat held the atmosphere at a perfect temperature for slumber. I switched on the bedside lamp, swung my legs over the side of the bed, stood up, and immediately came crashing to the floor. The lower half of my gown had twisted around me while I slept, entrapping my legs and rendering me a virtual mummy. I untwisted it enough to push up to a kneeling position and stood. I took a step and felt a searing pain in my foot as the upended heel of my slingback dug into my arch. "Fuck!" I yelled, limping pathetically. The dress was so twisted that I was unable to properly hop around the room in pain.

I got to the bathroom and leaned on the door frame for support as I hit the light switch. Carnage. The oversized three-way mirror above the sink provided a triple view of the devastation. Makeup was smeared everywhere, and I looked like a cartoon villain peering out of his hiding place—just a couple of blinking white circles enveloped in blackness. The straps of my gown had cut into my shoulders, leaving deep red marks that swelled up as soon as I tugged it off. My hair, sleek and lustrous the night before, had hardened into a tangled mess of hair spray clumps. As I started to wash my face, I saw that my skin had broken out with a force unseen since puberty. I didn't know where to start and wondered if I could just call in ugly. After all, I was in Los Angeles.

As I looked up from the sink, I saw that my breasts were still in the fully upright and locked position. My stick-on bra was exactly where I'd stuck it nearly twenty-four hours earlier—what the hell was this glue made of, anyway? I found my evening purse slung over a chair and turned it upside down, searching for the dressmaker's dissolving fluid. Extra headset batteries, lip gloss, a couple of crumpled twenty-dollar bills, a valet ticket, and a stale cookie fell onto the vanity, but no little vial. I pulled the lining of the bag inside out, hoping it might be stuck in one of the corners, but it had vanished; dissolved, perhaps, leaving me with a stuck-on stick-on bra that wouldn't budge a millimeter. I tested the left side cautiously, to see if there might be a way to peel it off, but had no success. I certainly couldn't bring myself to do one of those "pull it off fast" maneuvers: This was clearly not an ordinary adhesive, and I had no idea what might come off with it.

I stepped into the shower and let the hot water sting my shoulders and sore foot, not to mention my residual party blisters. I reached out and groped around for the bottle of Advil I'd left near the sink, gulping down four with the water right out of the showerhead. After ten minutes of full-frontal immersion, both sides of the bra were transparent. I noticed one of the ends curl up a little, like a sign, and then they both slid off easily. Quickly, I tossed them from the shower onto the bathroom floor, afraid they might somehow reattach to another part of my body. Then I turned my attention to my hair, which began to feel real again only after I'd gone through six tiny bottles of shampoo and conditioner. Turning off the water, I stepped out and gingerly pulled on a fluffy hotel bathrobe.

Rummaging among the clothes I'd brought for an outfit that wouldn't bind, chafe, or squeeze, I gave some serious consideration to the robe, but only with a different belt. After gently easing on a jean skirt and a loose button-up sleeveless top, I weighed my footwear options, settling on the ankle socks and sneakers I'd packed while under the delusion that I would get to use the hotel gym during my stay. The outfit wasn't fashionable but, when paired with my plethora of zits and the huge dark circles under my eyes, I told myself that I'd pulled off a semi-convincing stab at heroin chic. I picked up my purse, rental-car keys, and sunglasses, and left the room, not permitting myself to look back at that gorgeous bed.

At the concierge desk I was handed a crumpled, ripped envelope with "Karen" scrawled across it and an address for Sandy Schwartz on Wilshire Boulevard. The company had made sure that everybody working on Oscar night looked their best for the occasion: our gowns had been rounded up from various designers by a stylist who was looking for more Glorious assignments, and the same people who wouldn't pay for bathroom soap in New York proved willing to shell out thousands of dollars for top hair and makeup professionals, even for those of us who were only pushing elevator buttons or directing cars. Allegra, however, had also insisted on borrowing jewels—a privilege generally reserved for stars and their spouses. Dagney and I had spent the last two weeks in New York calling Beverly Hills jewelers and then listening in as Allegra spun a tale about the amount of exposure she was bound to get on Oscar night with celebrities and industry executives alike, not to mention the bountiful camera time she'd undoubtedly have on the red carpet, given the plethora of Glorious nominees she'd be escorting. The idea of Allegra having access to borrowed gems irked Dagney to no end. "She's pretending to be something she's not," Dagney complained. "Does she think someone's going to mistake her for some famous silent movie star?" Sandy Schwartz, the seventh jeweler who took her call, caved only when Allegra promised he'd be given first shot at the neck, ears, arms, and fingers of Ivan-Melissa Pell for her red-carpet sashay at the *She Swings Both Ways* premiere.

Once in the car, I opened the envelope and looked at the earrings. I hadn't seen them last night, obscured as they were by Allegra's last-minute decision to wear her hair down. I couldn't believe she'd woken me up to hand deliver these. Was this

Sandy's idea of a joke? The earrings resembled tin potato gnocchi inlaid with bits of orange, pink, and purple colored glass. Then again, Allegra wouldn't have bothered to borrow them if they were as cheap as they looked, I reasoned, so they must be worth something. When valued against an extra half hour of sleep, however, the earrings would have had to be far more special to placate me. I needed to stop dwelling on this and get going, so I dropped the earrings into the car's cup holder and made my way out to Wilshire Boulevard.

Only after making sure I was headed the right way for Sandy's place did I realize that it was in the opposite direction of our L.A. office—the addresses were more than five thousand numbers apart. And Wilshire was completely jammed. I craved a vat of coffee and craned my neck looking for somewhere decent to stop, but found none. Finally I pulled into a gas station with a Quik Mart where I loaded up on every type of junk food imaginable, plus some muddy brew that smelled as though it might have been sitting around for a day or two. I hadn't eaten anything since those Frosted Flakes and I needed it all—carbs, salt, sugar, chocolate, and several sources of caffeine. I looked in my basket and decided that I hadn't been generous enough with myself, so I added a couple of brightly colored Gatorades and a package of Hostess Sno Balls—green from St. Patrick's Day—and who knew what else. Then I rang it all up on my Glorious credit card. Satisfied, I continued driving toward Sandy Schwartz's store. The earrings were taking up valuable cup holder space needed for the coffee and Gatorade, so I tossed them onto the passenger seat.

I fiddled with the radio and resumed my four-miles-per-hour journey. I was singing along with Donna Summer, my mouth full of Pringles, when I noticed a great-looking guy in an Aston Martin alongside me. He took it all in—the maroon Ford Taurus, the pimply woman inhaling chips while keeping time on the steering wheel—and gave a slight shake of his head before zigzagging two cars ahead of me, guaranteeing I'd never be in his line of sight again. I felt conspicuously atrocious.

Creeping along, I reflected on my Oscar experience. The most difficult thing to deal with had been the endless demands of the celebrities and their "handlers." Each notable was there because they were a nominee, a presenter, or just wanted to do a little red-carpet rumbaing. Yet most of them acted as if they were doing us a tremendous favor by showing up, and woe to anyone who forgot that even for a moment. No request was too small, and no one could imagine doing anything for themselves. What had started in New York as a flurry of activity had snowballed into a blizzard of gimmes, get-mes, and full-on tantrums. "Please" and "thank you" had been temporarily suspended from the English language, and I wasn't feeling confident about their return. The Sean Raines affair, as I'd taken to thinking of it, had blown up in my face two days before the Oscars when a rep from the charter company called to tell me that the plane was in Sydney, but Sean wasn't there to meet it. Heart palpitating, I phoned his publicist. "Oh, I forgot to tell you, I've been so busy," she said. "Sean ran into Tom Cruise in Sydney and Tom invited him to fly on his 727, so he doesn't need the plane after all. I meant to forward you the e-mail he sent. You need to set up a limo to meet Tom's plane when it lands at LAX. Sean doesn't like waiting, so make sure the car's on time."

Just thinking about it made me angry all over again. It had cost a fortune—more than six times my annual Glorious salary—to charter that plane, only for it to be cast aside with no more thought than if it had been a used Kleenex. Not to mention the fact that a guy who didn't believe in the Internet sent e-mails when faced with the possibility that he might have to hail himself a cab. Vivian, of course, had questioned me closely. She seemed to think I could have prevented Sean from thumbing a ride with Tom Cruise—or that I should have foreseen their inevitable meeting in the lobby of the InterContinental Sydney and suggested in advance that they fly together. "But I didn't know they knew each other," I'd said, pleading my case.

"Haven't you figured it out yet? They *all* know each other." Then she turned her back on me to go over hair and makeup schedules with Dagney.

I heard a car horn honk and as I swerved to avoid it, Allegra's earrings bounced onto the floor. I left them there, glad to have them out of sight. The traffic was so slow that it felt as if all the cars had sunk to the bottom of the ocean—the really deep part, where the fish move their fins about once a day. The red light afforded me the opportunity to wipe the fingerprints off my new designer sunglasses. Putting them back on, I smiled at my reflection in the rearview mirror. Certainly, they were the best perk I'd received all week.

When I'd returned to the hotel the previous Friday, I'd found a huge gift basket in my room. The accompanying card read, "Hope your night's a golden one, from your friends at *InStyle*." I'd eagerly checked out the contents and found it stuffed with expensive cosmetics and lotions, a couple of best sellers, Belgian chocolates, sugar cookie Oscars, the special "Style Academy" issue of *InStyle*, and a pair of designer panties, size "S" (as if anyone could be another size). There was also a card inviting me to a preview suite to receive a free pair of next season's sunglasses from Malcolm Leonard, he of the eponymous couture, cosmetics, home décor, and denim. "Let us grace you with the perfect ocular complement to your features," the card read.

With five minutes left before I was due to start my shift in the office we'd set up in the hotel, I'd dashed up to the Malcolm

Leonard suite to claim my pair. As I left a near-mutiny had broken out when some of the celebrities demanded extra pairs and the staff, unable to accommodate them due to a limited supply, had refused.

"I may be haunted by the wailing of movie stars denied for the rest of my life," I'd said later, telling Robert about the scene.

"Just think," he'd deadpanned, "you'll always be able to say that you got your sunglasses during the famous Malcolm Leonard Oscar riots."

Since the moment I'd set foot in Los Angeles, I'd become more and more aware of the vast amount of loot on offer to the famous and potentially famous during Oscar week. The nominees were feted at gala events thrown by sponsors who asked only that their humble offerings be accepted. Bejeweled cell phones. Loans of luxury automobiles. Televisions nearly as large as movie screens with all the accompanying accessories. Week-long stays at the world's most exclusive resorts—or two weeks, if that suited you better. Cosmetics housed in platinum compacts. Stereo systems guaranteed to impress your rock star friends. Limited edition sneakers with low serial numbers. Lotions, creams, and elixirs guaranteeing that youth and beauty would remain intact. Plastic surgery "consultations" in case they didn't. Magnums of champagne. Certificates for massages, facials, and anything else that can be legally done to a person in the confines of a spa. Crates of caviar. Luggage. Pharaohs were buried with less, fully confident they'd enjoy a stylish eternity.

While many people were gracious in accepting these goods, others weren't ashamed to go for more, even though they asked us to demand the extras on their behalf. For the most part, the gift-givers acquiesced because they desperately wanted their company and its products to be popular with the Hollywood set. Clark told me that most of it would be regifted to various relatives and staff, who were sure to be left breathless by their benefactor's generosity.

The light turned green and I gunned the Taurus, enjoying the open expanse the intersection provided. Scanning the street signs, I saw that I'd be at Sandy Schwartz's store soon and brightened at the prospect of getting out of the car. The address Allegra had given me was for an exclusive-looking high-rise building—there was no jeweler in sight. I inquired with the valet, who assured me that Sandy was indeed here, in Penthouse C. I turned the ignition off and leaned over to get the earrings from the floor. I didn't see them and couldn't believe I might have lost those ugly lumps that I'd driven all this way to deliver. They had to be here. I got out of the car and walked around to the other side. Opening the passenger door, I knelt on the pavement and angrily started to tear through the candy bar wrappers, cups, and other garbage wedged in and around the seat. Suddenly, I saw a glint of metal and found the earrings stuck to the bottom of a half-eaten Sno Ball. There was some coconut and marshmallow on them, but they were otherwise in fine shape. I handed the keys to the valet, put the earrings in my pocket, and got into a mahogany-paneled elevator.

The door opened into an all-white aerie—white carpet, white walls, even a couple of white-framed white canvases—in the center of which sat a man playing a white concert grand piano. I detected the faintest scent of vanilla. "My "dirty girl" ensemble jarred with the purity of the décor and I thought I might smudge something if I looked at it for too long. Instead, I focused on the man at the piano. Dressed in jeans and a white silk shirt, he was playing a Mozart concerto with his eyes closed; he appeared completely peaceful, sharing his serenity with a large, white bird that was perched on his shoulder. He hadn't yet realized I was there. Then he opened his eyes, smiled at me, and launched into some jazz. "Good morning," he said cheerily, tossing in some Ray Charles-style stride. "What brings you here so early?"

"Earrings. Hi, um, I have Allegra Orecchi's earrings for you. From Glorious?" I said lamely.

"Wonderful. The first return of the day," he said, rising from the piano bench. He was short, almost petite for a man, and I noticed that his feet were bare. I covertly gave the earrings a final wipe and handed them over. "Wanda," he called. "Come in with Allegra's form, please."

A small Latina woman appeared, also in blue jeans, a white silk shirt, and bare feet, carrying an empty velvet tray and a clipboard.

"Manners! I'm Sandy Schwartz," he said, still smiling. "This is Wanda Carillo, my assistant," he continued, rolling the "r" in "Carillo."

"Karen Jacobs," I said, holding out my hand, which they both shook, appearing not to notice that it was sticky. "And this," he said, smoothing the feathers at the nape of the bird's neck, "is Estella."

"Is that a mynah bird?" I asked. Estella was looking at the earrings with keen interest.

"I'll take those from you, dear," Wanda said quickly.

"Yes," Sandy answered. "She's an albino mynah from Singapore. And she would gladly spirit those earrings back to her cage if we let her."

I placed the earrings on Wanda's tray and she handed me a receipt to sign. I picked up the pen and was about to scribble my name when I noticed something that stopped me cold. The earrings Allegra had left at the hotel in a torn envelope, the earrings I'd tossed into the cup holder of my unlocked car at the gas station, the earrings that had nearly been lost in a pile of crumbs and candy bar wrappers, the earrings that looked as if they were made of scrap metal—were worth $85,000. "Is this right? Eighty-five thousand?"

"Oh yes, that's exactly what they're worth," Sandy said, handing me a jeweler's loupe and putting the earrings on a light box. "Let me show you."

What would have happened to me if I had lost these? My hand trembling, I put the loupe to my eye and bent down to look.

"Do you see those pink stones? They're pink rubies from Burma. The orange? Orange sapphires from Tanzania. Lavender jade from Pula. Lapis from Afghanistan." The colors resembled much of the food I'd inhaled in the car on the way over, and a wave of nausea washed over me. "They have perfectly matched pairs of each stone, and they've been set in hand-sculpted platinum seashells."

"They're incredible" was all I could think to say.

"I think so," he said. "Colored gemstones aren't very popular with Americans, but my Middle Eastern clients really enjoy them. As a matter of fact, two called this morning, asking about these earrings. They spotted them when Allegra tucked her hair behind her ear while walking Phil and Tony down the red carpet. There's a jet waiting at LAX to take them to Dubai."

I had a sudden urge to sit down and, as if by magic, a furry white ottoman appeared right behind my knees.

"Stay as long as you like," Sandy said. "We're going to spend the rest of the day begging people to return the jewelry that they borrowed from us. You'd never believe what we have to go through to get it all back."

"Or the number of people who suddenly forget the difference between 'lending' and 'giving,'" Wanda added, shaking her head.

"Actually, I would," I said, suddenly laughing in spite of myself. "But I really do need to go." They were the first people who had been civil to me in days and I was reluctant to leave their kind haven. "Thank you again," I said.

"Give my best to Allegra," Sandy said, "And please tell her that I've got no hard feelings about the Ivan-Melissa Pell thing."

"What about Ivan-Melissa Pell?"

"She's decided to go with a puka bead theme for the premiere," he said, smiling. "Puka's never been my thing." I said good-bye to both of them, and slipped into the elevator.

Back in the Wilshire traffic lineup, my mood soured once more, and the farther I got from Sandy's the worse it became. I was crashing from too much sugar and too little sleep, not to mention Allegra's complete lack of respect. How dare she let me carry those earrings around without knowing how valuable they were? I was thinking of all the unpleasant things I'd like to say to her when I noticed a large newsstand on the corner where I was idling, waiting for the light to change. From the driver's seat it was easy to spot six different Roddy publications on the rack, even with the lower three-quarters of each cover obscured. I'd felt so good when he'd come in, his wife in her unborrowed jewelry, their gargantuan bodyguard and the actor steering him. I remembered how happy I'd been that he'd outwitted Vivian's "one guest per person" rule the night before.

Then I had an awful thought. Why in the world had I told that strange man that Glorious refused to okay a bodyguard or an aide for him? What if he was George Hanratty and I'd given him some information about the company's inner workings to use in the book he was supposedly writing? My superiors would definitely know it came from me—Vivian never forgot anything, and I'd been the one involved with Ted Roddy's RSVP. I tried to remember what that teeny picture on Dag's computer looked like, and in my mind the pixels rearranged themselves into a mirror image of his face. If it was Hanratty, I'd lose my job for sure. I replayed the momentary lapse in my mind about a hundred times before finally pulling my car into the garage underneath Glorious's West Coast office, shoving the gear handle into Park.

I stomped up the stairs and found Kellie, one of the L.A.-based Glorious publicists. The office was empty except for the two of us. She was on the phone, but as I approached her she slammed it down. "Damn," she said. "Sorry. Hi. Thanks for pitching in. We've got no one coming tomorrow night and I'm at the end of my rope." Kellie was operating on as little sleep as I was but somehow managed to look none the worse for it. A blond-haired, blue-eyed, Rose Bowl Queen type, she appeared daisy-fresh in surfer baggies, a halter top, and chunky flip-flops. I tried to hide my horrible outfit behind the desk, hunching down low while Kellie explained the game plan to me.

We were calling the various PR firms to see who, among their glittering roster of representees, would attend tomorrow night's event. We hadn't anticipated that this would be difficult, given that we were still basking in the glow of our Best Picture win. Wouldn't all of young Hollywood want to be seen by the Waxmans? Apparently not. "I just spoke with OMG," she said, referring to the industry's leading star factory. OMG "owned" nearly everyone, and Kellie had just ended a complicated negotiation with them. "They tried to make us take two *writers* just to pass along our invitation to Francesca Davis, with no guarantee that she'll come. It's just not worth it."

I agreed. Writers don't give good red carpet. We needed to deliver some real star power to this party. Glorious had figured that "everyone" would be in town and that this premiere would be like an extra victory lap for them.

Just then my cell rang. It was Clark. "Honey, when are you going to come outside and play with us? Gloria's here, and she's cheating—I mean beating—me at canasta. I'm going to have to go to the ATM pretty soon if she keeps it up."

"I'm in the office."

"You're where?"

"Allegra called me this morning and said I needed to work on the premiere."

"You're working in the L.A. office?" I heard Robert's whispered, "What the . . ." in the background.

"Yup. I've been up since eight."

"Well, try to hurry back. We're all just lounging around. The cabana boys brought ice buckets for our feet. It feels divine." I could just see them on the striped poolside furniture, calf-deep in ice cubes, downing cool, tropical drinks while the inexhaustible Gloria dealt hand after hand.

"It's not looking good."

I hung up and called the next name on Kellie's list, launching into the whole *She Swings Both Ways* spiel, adding that Ivan-Melissa and Bob Metuchen would be "arriving" together, and that the rest of the cast would be present as well. The movie also featured Will Herrick and Ed Bailey, two actors who would go on to win an Oscar for cowriting a screenplay. The authenticity of their claim was always in question, and they became the film industry's very own Milli Vanilli, although they were never stripped of their award.

The first publicist I reached, who represented the star of a popular television show, told me that her client couldn't attend due to an early call time the morning after the premiere. Then a record-label rep for a singer whose latest single was topping the charts told me that the songbird was out of town, even though I'd seen a poster advertising her "meet and greet" at the Virgin Megastore the following afternoon. The personal assistant to a young male star who had a lead in an upcoming Tony film told me that he couldn't come to the premiere because he was "completely burned out from five consecutive nights of partying."

"I don't get it," I said to Kellie. "All of a sudden no one's around, they're too tired, they're working too hard. Since when don't stars like to come to these things?"

Kellie sighed. "Since Ivan-Melissa started to look like a threat," she said. "They usually love to come to premieres, but they have to like the people involved—and Ivan-Melissa's not anyone's favorite these days."

"She's not even famous enough to be hated yet," I said.

"That's where you're wrong. On paper, Ivan-Melissa has it all—the director boyfriend, the wacky name, the kinky sex," Kellie replied, standing up to make her proclamation. "But even though most of them would do exactly the same thing if they had the opportunity, she's made it look too calculated. None of these people want to help make her big night even bigger."

Now I understood. Making Ivan-Melissa sit alone in the lunchroom was the best revenge the other celebrities could mete out. The media, on the other hand, loved her. They couldn't get enough of her weird, raspy voice and penchant for saying anything that came into her head. Ivan-Melissa's newly minted star status would only make it worse. We were going to have dozens of press in attendance, all of whom would definitely report on the lackluster turnout.

Kellie was having her own problems. "Well, if he comes, Amy Ortega's going to cancel and I'd rather have her than him, so the answer is no," I heard her tell someone. I wasn't sure how to deal with the politics of who could attend and whose attendance would cause another's disappearance. "Don't worry," Kellie said, when I admitted my uncertainty about a couple of the people I'd invited. "We can always call back and disinvite."

This was very different from how we worked in New York. For last month's *Prunyak* premiere we'd had written invitations. The list of invitees had been proposed, edited, approved, seconded, Allegra'd, and the invitations finally hand-delivered.

By four o'clock we were despairing of having even one real star at the event. All we had to show for our efforts were a couple of former *Baywatch* girls, a Laker on the DL, a backup singer from one of the boy bands, and a few other not-very-notables. Tony would go ballistic. This premiere was on the heels of the veritable Philfest that had overtaken the town just forty-eight hours prior, and he would demand that the same homage be paid him.

"Let's just call it quits for today," Kellie said, smarting from her most recent snub. I was surprised that she was advocating that the two of us give up without having secured at least one major star, although I'd heard that the L.A. office was much more relaxed than ours. Of course, this was hardly a fair comparison—the staff here didn't have Phil and Tony breathing down their necks.

We agreed to return tomorrow; in the meantime, I would try to wrangle the celebrities still staying at the Four Seasons. Unfortunately, most of Glorious's nominees had flown out this morning, including Sean, who went uncomplainingly on a commercial flight. He seemed to have a bit less of a sheen to him after his Oscar loss and appeared eager to return to New Zealand, even carrying his own luggage out of the hotel when no bellman was available.

There were a couple of hours of daylight left, and I hoped that Clark and the others would still be poolside, or in the hotel bar. I felt I'd earned at least a couple of umbrella drinks.

Dagney would probably be gone by now; she was taking a few days' vacation in Laguna Beach to recover from her post-Oscar exhaustion. I grabbed a stack of premiere invitations and headed for my car.

As I was pulling out of the garage, Allegra called. I could tell immediately from her arctic whisper that she was aware of our failure to confirm any newsworthy guests. "I had Dagney book you on tonight's red-eye. You'll be more useful in the main office while I straighten out this premiere. Besides, the Hits haven't gone around in three days and no one in New York knows what's going on."

The red-eye. I had just enough time to get back to the hotel, break camp, and make it to the airport for my flight. Angrily, I tossed the premiere invitations out of the car window, hoping that every homeless person and Sunset Strip sex-worker would consider themselves invited. My flight would land just in time for me to go straight to the office and put the Hits together so that they could be thrown in the recycling pile by the ever-appreciative Glorious staff. At least I could sleep on the plane.

I arrived at LAX, checked my luggage, and headed for the gate. Halfway there, I realized that in the rush to get to the airport, I'd forgotten to put a few goodies in my carry-on for the gate agents and flight attendants. An Academy screener, a T-shirt, and a soundtrack or two were usually all it took for a bump up to first; Robert had taught me this trick, and I'd used it on the way over. Clark once spent half of his flight in the cockpit after giving the pilot and copilot Glorious baseball caps. I settled into the middle seat that Dagney had undoubtedly selected especially for me, arranged the blanket and pillow, and tried to fall asleep before takeoff.

Half an hour into the flight, I felt a tap on my shoulder. I'd been dozing, but snapped to immediately.

"Karen Jacobs?" the flight attendant said. "Please follow me."

She led me to first class and an empty seat next to a grinning Robert. "I heard a rumor that you were on this flight."

"Thanks for rescuing me."

"No problem, but these flight attendants are getting greedy. Must have to do with how many film people have been flying this route lately. It took seven *Foreign Pilots*, two chocolate Oscars, and my Malcolm Leonard panties to get you up here."

"Sorry about your panties, Robert, but I have something for you that may make up for it." I reached into my bag and pulled out a dozen hotel-sized bottles of soap. "For the masses."

"Thanks. This is so thoughtful." He put them into his carry-on and looked as if he were thinking about something else.

I told him about the bad turnout expected for the *She Swings Both Ways* premiere. "Figures," he said. "Sometimes they just don't know when enough is enough. Anyway, we've got worse problems now. Gretzky died this morning."

"Wayne Gretzky died?" I nearly shouted. Twenty first-class heads swiveled in our direction.

"Shhhh. Not Wayne Gretzky." He turned to the other passengers and stage-whispered "Not Wayne Gretzky" before turning back to me. "Gretzky, the Alaskan Husky from *Block That Pup*. I'm going back early to find an identical dog to do his press tour. We've already got *Today*, *Live*, *Letterman*, and *The View* locked in for him. No one can know he's dead. We need a sub."

"Can't one of the actors go on instead?"

"There isn't really anyone those shows would want. Gretzky was the star of that film."

Block That Pup was a sappy story about a kid who moves to a new town and gains popularity due to his dog's incredible ability to play hockey. "How are you going to find a dog that looks like

Gretzky? Weren't his eyes different colors, and didn't he have that big brown spot on his coat?"

"We'll find one. It's just going to take some doing," Robert said, as if dog-matching was something he did every day. "*Block That Pup* is Tony's movie." He didn't need to elaborate. A suitable replacement would be found. "*Or else!*" as Tony was fond of saying.

I told Robert how tired I'd gotten of all the nonsense around the Oscars, and he told me that he'd had his fill as well. "On Saturday I tried to explain to Rebecca Ripley that I couldn't just call Prada and tell them she'd lost the purse they'd given her—she had it right in her hand. Rebecca had a fit and I got chewed out by Marlene for ten minutes."

"So what happened?" I asked. Rebecca Ripley had a small role in an upcoming Glorious picture, but was better known for her former career as a procurer of "dates" for high-powered Hollywood executives.

"I called Prada and they thought it meant she wanted to wear the purse to the awards, so they sent another over. And then she wore Tod's," he said.

"That's just obnoxious," I said. "Did you hear about Nolan O'Leary, the cinematographer?"

"He wanted something weird last year, but I don't remember what it was."

"Before he arrived, his assistant called and said that Nolan's room had to face north because that was the light 'to which Mr. O'Leary was accustomed to waking,'" I said, finger quoting and imitating the assistant's precise manner of speech.

"This is going to be just great, I can tell."

"When O'Leary checked in, he took out a compass and started to carry on because the room was ten degrees short of true north. The assistant screamed at me about the 'exact instructions that had been given,' before throwing in some lovely four-letter words for emphasis."

"Did you tell her that there wouldn't be any rooms facing in any direction four days before the Oscars?"

"No. I mentioned that the Best Western on South Sepulveda was rumored to be the only hotel in all of California to be built exactly on a north/south axis. And that was the last I heard from her."

"Best Western, excellent!" Robert said, trying not to laugh. "The next best thing to Valium."

"Seriously, Robert, by Friday, I was saying the nastiest things as if they just came naturally," I said, shaking my head. "It was as if I'd turned into mini-Marlene or something."

"You either do it, or you catch hell for your incompetence," he said, solemnly. "The important thing is to be conscious of what you're doing, and remember that this is not how you act in the regular world."

I desperately wanted to tell Robert about my possible Hanratty encounter, but I was too ashamed. He would think I was an absolute idiot for babbling on about company business to a complete stranger.

Noting the troubled look on my face, he said, "Listen, did you hear what finally happened with Nikolaj?" I rolled my eyes. Even eight-year-old Nikolaj Tiborescu, star of *Prunyak*, the Romanian entry for Best Foreign Language Film, had fallen victim to the bad behavior epidemic.

He'd arrived on Thursday with his mother, neither of them speaking English. We'd had their itineraries translated into Romanian and had arranged free Valentino for both, because Nikolaj's manager had informed us there was nothing Oscar-worthy in even the finest shops of downtown Transylvania. At first, Nikolaj was thrilled to be in California, and excited about going for a swim in the hotel pool—at least, that's what he seemed to be indicating during our half-sign-language, half-charades exchange. I'd felt so hopeful that he would be the little boy who showed us the True Meaning of Oscar.

"Yeah, I thought he'd be different, too," Robert said. "But Nikolaj adapted like one of Darwin's damn turtles. I should have filmed it for a documentary."

Robert was right. Nikolaj had barely figured out how to push the correct elevator button for his floor when he'd simultaneously realized that if he couldn't speak the language, he couldn't get the stuff. He quickly mastered some key phrases to assist him in his quest and started collecting freebies like an experienced Oscar-goer.

The last time I'd seen him, he was trailed by two bellmen laden with packages who'd looked startled when the boy snapped his fingers and shouted, "Being careful! Is belongs to Nikolaj!" I related the story to Robert, who said, "That kid figured out Hollywood English like no one's business. He called me that same afternoon to tell me I needed to get him another driver, and later to say that he and his mother needed a larger room."

"So what did you do?"

"I tried to explain to him that he needed to keep this driver and this room, but he started to yell at me. Finally, I had him put his mother on the phone, and told her that if her son continued to behave this way, they'd be on the next plane home."

"Did she understand you?"

"'Romania,' and 'now' were pretty loud and clear. I never heard from them again."

Robert and I talked through most of the flight, reliving the injustices and petty demands we'd been subjected to over the last six days. The bullying. The begging. The inability to comprehend even the simplest of instructions. After a few hours, we'd gotten it all out of our respective systems. I resolved that going forward I'd learn how to let it slide off me, the way Clark did, and then I fell asleep. When the plane landed at JFK, I awoke, mortified to find that my head was on Robert's shoulder. "I'm so sorry," I said, red-faced.

"The soap has absolved you," he said solemnly. We stumbled off the plane and headed in different directions; I, to the office, and he, to a kennel in Westchester.

PAYBACK

Two weeks after everyone had returned from Los Angeles, work began on the release of *The Gravedigger*, a movie billed as "the blackest of comedies." A veritable circle jerk of obligations, its talent included Harry Spindler, a television actor–turned–director, Harry's college roommate–turned–screenwriter, and assorted supporting players from the Glorious stable. It also featured Juliet Bartlett, an actress just a blond-hairsbreadth away from major stardom, in a small though pivotal role. Juliet had wrapped several Glorious films that had yet to be released, but word of her exceptional performances preceded them. That buzz, combined with her stunning looks and romantic attachment to an A-list actor, rocketed her to a level of fame usually reserved for those who could lay claim to at least a nomination or a major scandal.

The entire publicity department watched *The Gravedigger* together in the company screening room, except for Dagney, who was manning Allegra's phones in case Oprah called, and Robert, who'd gone to New Jersey to follow up a hot tip on a Husky that was a dead ringer for Gretzky. The owner had e-mailed photos of his dog from all angles, and he definitely looked like the One, if not the Great One.

We usually screened films on Thursdays, and Gloria often joined us after she'd made the brisket drop-off; everyone tried to sit near her because she always brought boxes of Raisinets in her huge Louis Vuitton doctor bag. The screening room was much better than an actual theater—the seats were large and covered in velvet, and each one had a perfect view of the screen. There was enough space between the rows to stretch your legs out all the way and not touch the chair in front of you. The plush surroundings could make a good film seem great and ease the discomfort of the less-satisfying ones. After the first twenty minutes of *The Gravedigger*, however, I realized that it was possibly one of the worst movies ever made, by Glorious or anyone else. When it was over, I pulled Clark aside and asked him how we'd gone so quickly from *The Foreign Pilot* to this mess.

"Phil and Tony have stacks of IOUs and piles of favors to call in," Clark explained. "They promise something to someone; someone promises them. They even make deals with each other. Every once in a while they tally up who's owed what and pull it all into one movie. It opens, it closes, and the slate's clean for a while."

"I guess it's better than having to spread them all out, and ruin a lot of movies."

"I'm proud of you, Grasshopper."

In this case, the trail of favors was easy to track, stinking as badly as it did. Harry Spindler was a member of the ensemble cast of *Fuckbuddies*, a massive sitcom hit whose actors were as famous for their haircuts as they were for their iron-fisted salary-negotiation skills. While the other five had already appeared on the big screen, consistently delivering their enthusiastic fan base to the box office, Harry was more selective than his friends. Highly original in his ambitions, what he really wanted to do was direct.

Phil signed Harry to a multipicture deal that included a single stint in the director's chair. He also accommodated Harry's promise to his college roommate that someday he would direct one of his screenplays. To Phil and Tony, *The Gravedigger* was something to be fast-forwarded and faster forgotten so that the most certainly bankable Harry could be part of other Glorious projects—in front of the camera.

Juliet Bartlett, on the other hand, had agreed to appear in *The Gravedigger* as a trade-off in order to be cast in the roles she truly desired—important literary heroines like Emma Bovary and Dorothea Brooke; substantive parts that would broaden her ever-expanding range. In their column, Rush & Molloy of the *Daily News* reported that Juliet had told her hairdresser that she'd been "totally Phil'd into doing this completely *shite* movie."

"So Phil and Tony know the movie sucks? And they're releasing it anyway?"

Clark smiled. "The audience isn't part of the favor chain."

Neither were the critics. They wouldn't be allowed to see the film until after it had opened on Friday, ensuring that the earliest a review could possibly appear would be on Saturday, the least-read day of the week. *The Gravedigger*'s box office would be protected for its all-important opening weekend.

The following week, on the night of the premiere, I stood outside the building, assisting the crew from E! TV by making sure that every celebrity in attendance appeared on camera for the *Gravedigger* special they were taping. E!'s broadcast would show the celebrities chattering enthusiastically about Harry and how excited they were to see his movie, interwoven with clips from the film which had been selected with extreme care by Phil himself. I held each actor on deck and explained the drill. Each person was to offer Harry well-wishes and then briefly discuss their current projects. They were all happy to comply, providing the channel not only with sound bites for this broadcast but miles of film for all kinds of future programs. The footage E! shot here would be spliced, diced, and edited to be used repeatedly for years to come on shows like *It's Good to Be . . .* and *Fashion Police*. The RSVPs for tonight were exceptional, and I was working feverishly to keep up with the steady stream of stars.

"Hello Mrs. Spindler," I said, as Harry's mother walked up to the entrance. She was nearly as recognizable as Harry, as she was frequently interviewed with him.

"I need seven extra seats, all together," she said. "My son, the director"—she paused here for effect—"told me to bring as many guests as I liked."

Assuring her that this wouldn't be a problem, I urged Mrs. Spindler to go enjoy the party. She hadn't seen the film yet and I wanted her to get as much pleasure as possible before the inevitable happened. Using her edict as an excuse, I decided to check out what was going on inside.

Allegra had planned the event as an upside-down premiere—the party would take place before the screening. We were in an old movie theater in Chelsea with an adjacent ballroom rapidly filling up with actors from the film, their guests, and dozens of celebrities, including all of Harry's television cast mates. Absolutely no press had been invited, however—they could attend only the arrivals outside. Gloria was there with her mah-jongg ladies. Tony was escorting Délica-C, the beautiful lead singer of the new R&B group Love Child Bride, who was wearing something that looked almost long enough to be a dress and a pair of six-inch-heeled over-the-knee boots that made her tower above him. Bacardi rum had invented a specialty cocktail for the occasion, and Phil made repeated toasts—"Lift your glass high to Harry!"—presumably hoping that if people were drunk enough the film would go down much more easily. The Graveswigger was basically a Long Island Iced Tea with double the rum, made opaque by the addition of an inky food coloring. Scooping one up from a waiter's tray, I took a couple of sips and started to sway a little, so I left it on the edge of a bar, pocketing the tiny plastic headstone as a souvenir for Abby. Stopping in the bathroom for a lipstick touch-up, I saw that the drink had turned my tongue black.

Two minutes after I'd started to rearrange some of the RESERVED signs to accommodate the Spindler group, Harry's younger sister appeared at my elbow and curtly informed me that her mother would be conducting an inspection in five minutes. There was more than an hour left before the movie was scheduled to start, but when I mentioned this, she began to berate me, bringing Mrs. Spindler flying into the theater, lungs at full blast. "This is my *son's movie!*" she bellowed, projecting like Ethel Merman. "What kind of morons does Phil Waxman hire?" My question exactly, Mrs. Spindler, I thought without saying.

She started moving from the back of the theater toward where I was standing in the fifth row, tearing off the RESERVED signs and throwing them to the floor as she went. I watched her approach with trepidation. She was only two rows away from me when Clark appeared out of nowhere and deftly intercepted her.

"Mrs. Spindler, CNN's outside and they'd love to talk to you about Harry."

Instantaneously, Mrs. Spindler's mouth untwisted. Turning, she summoned her daughter. "My makeup," she said, waving an imperious hand.

"Do you think they want to talk to me?" the sister asked, revealing a shy smile.

"Absolutely," Clark said, winking at me as he ushered them out of the theater.

About half an hour later, just as the crew from E! had decided to pack it in, a limousine pulled up to the curb, prompting a roar from the assorted paparazzi lining the sidewalk. When the door opened, Juliet Bartlett stepped out, a slinky sequined dress clinging to her nearly six-foot frame.

"And *that*," said Robert, who was suddenly standing next to me on the sidewalk, "is a woman with perfect timing."

Even from a distance it was easy to see why Juliet was making such an impression on the worlds of film and fashion. She waved to the photographers and then posed for them, calling out, "The magnificent Mr. Armani," when asked who she was wearing, and smiling impishly without answering when they yelled, "Where's Zac?" referring to the actor rumored to be her boyfriend.

As she approached the E! area, I asked her if she would appear on camera for the special. She smiled as if there was nothing she'd rather do, then spoke for several moments about how thrilled she was to be a participant in Harry's directorial debut. While her character—a woman so alluring that men slipped her their phone numbers at a funeral—was one of the film's few bright spots, Juliet heaped mountains of praise upon her costars, mentioning them each by name. If she had been bribed or Phil'd or anything elsed into participating in *The Gravedigger*, nobody watching her tonight could have guessed it. The performance Juliet gave for E! was surely Oscar-worthy. As she walked up the stairs, turning around for the tenth time to pose for the photographers begging "Juliet, just one more," I scanned the crowd for anyone who might be George Hanratty. I was still too unnerved to tell anyone about my conversation with the stranger in L.A., but had upped my level of vigilance. It was no use tonight—the place was so mobbed that I couldn't get much of an overview, and besides, I wasn't even sure who I was looking for.

Clark took my elbow. "Let me guess, Karen," he said, as I stopped squinting for a moment to refocus my eyes. "You're on Hanratty patrol." I squirmed with embarrassment. "Trust me, you'd be more likely to spot Dagney in a Wal-Mart."

"I know you keep saying that I shouldn't worry, but with my luck he'll show up while I'm at the door, and I won't even know who he is."

"Karen, you have nothing to be concerned about. None of us would recognize him unless we were close enough to smell his breath—and tonight, that might not tip us off. Let's go inside and see who falls asleep during the film, per Phil's best intentions."

Clark and I entered the party, now in full swing, and I had to acknowledge Allegra's brilliance: by the time the evening was over, E! and the rest of the press would be long gone, aware only of the excited reaction from the multitude of celebrities on their way into the movie. No potential ticket buyer would know that seeing *The Gravedigger* was enough to make you long to be put out of your misery.

Monday's papers showed that the American public had cooperated in the Glorious scheme—*The Gravedigger* had finished in second place at the box office, earning slightly more than it cost to make. Now it could sink into blessed obscurity, allowing everyone involved to reap the rewards their participation had earned them.

For Harry, this meant that he'd go back to work on his sitcom and wait for Phil or Tony to extract their pound of flesh during his next hiatus. For Harry's screenwriting former roommate, it meant that he'd most probably never hear from Harry again. For

Juliet Bartlett, however, the merciful death of *The Gravedigger* meant that she could focus on the wealth of other opportunities coming her way.

"If they knew her, they'd see that she's really not all that," scoffed Dagney, as she scanned a stack of fashion magazines, each of which had Juliet's glowing face on its cover. Dagney had attended the same boarding school as Juliet, and the discrepancy between their career paths was causing her more than a little grief. "She was Nora in *A Doll's House* sophomore year, and she blew half her lines. It was the worst production ever. And at our school," she added, "people knew a good Nora when they saw one. Of course, when your family donates most of the money to build the new theater, they *have* to give you the leads."

Unfortunately for Dagney, if things went according to Phil's grand plan, Juliet Bartlett would soon be one of the most sought-after actresses in the business. I thought she was a pretty good pick, and far less obnoxious than most of the other starlets I'd had dealings with in my Glorious career—although none of this was information I could share with Dag. True, international fame is not the destiny that usually befalls one's chem lab partner, but my colleague acted as though it were simply a random bit of bad luck that had catapulted Juliet to stardom while she toiled obscurely in media servitude. Phil's insistence that Allegra make Juliet a top priority only exacerbated her envy. The two of us spent considerable chunks of time confirming flight reservations, booking five-star hotels, securing hair and makeup artists, and hiring cars to bring Juliet to the fittings, photo shoots, and interviews that filled her days when she wasn't in rehearsals or taking meetings with producers.

The next Juliet film slated for release was *Circle of Eight*, in which she portrayed a 1920s-era American writer. An art house movie with a strong ensemble cast, Allegra thought that *Circle* provided an ideal way to introduce Juliet to the legitimate film journalists. She would participate in interviews with the rest of the cast, enabling her to discuss the film as part of the group, instead of as the It Girl she was quickly becoming. Juliet had told Allegra that she would gladly do whatever she could on behalf of this film in particular.

A problem arose on Wednesday when Juliet phoned Allegra and insisted that she couldn't fly to Los Angeles as originally planned. "She always behaved like a spoiled brat," Dagney said, while typing an e-mail from Allegra to Phil, explaining that instead of one first-class airfare to Los Angeles for Juliet, seven would now be needed to transport the rest of the cast to New York. "Phil is going to freak when he sees this," she predicted gleefully. Then she called a bunch of her friends, filling them in on what she deemed Juliet's diva-like behavior. Dagney was palpably disappointed when an e-mail pinged back from Phil fifteen minutes later. "Have already okayed. Make sure she stays on message."

Within an hour, Elliott Solnick was on the phone. "Is it true that Juliet's gone prima on you guys? And that Phil's beyond pissed off?"

This was the handiwork of someone in Dag's inner circle, I was sure, and Allegra would know that the only place this information could have originated was from our desk. The last thing I needed was to be held responsible for spreading a nasty rumor about Juliet Bartlett via Page Six, of all places.

"I'm sorry, Allegra's in a meeting, and she'll have to call you back."

"Oh, come on, Karen," Elliott cajoled. "You must know something. Juliet is Phil's top priority, Allegra's the president of publicity, and you're her assistant."

"Thank you for pinpointing my exact spot in the universe," I said. "Where do you come up with this stuff, anyway?" I asked, but in true journalistic fashion, Elliott wouldn't reveal his sources, other than to say he'd heard it "around." I enjoyed talking to Elliott, no matter what the circumstances, which only made it harder for me to stick to the company line.

"I need to go," I said reluctantly, "but I'll make sure Allegra gets back to you."

"Yeah, that's fine. One more thing—would you let me buy you a drink sometime? I promise I won't try to get any Glorious news out of you."

I decided to say yes immediately—and worry about how to keep it a secret later.

After hanging up, I confronted Dagney. "Page Six is already on the story. I know that you can't stand Juliet, but please, don't get us both fired. She's not worth it," I said, knowing that this wasn't the time to try to explain that Juliet was far more important to Glorious than the two of us combined. Dagney turned her back on me and picked up the phone to inform her friends that Juliet's insatiable lust for power would be reported in the papers. There was no stopping her, but now my mind was on other things: Elliott Solnick wanted to meet me.

I returned from a press screening of *Circle* the following morning to find Dagney missing and the phones ringing off the hook. Our desk looked as if we'd been burglarized, but Allegra was "in with Phil" and unaware of the destruction. While righting chairs, restacking magazines, and bullying the fax machine into working again, I noticed the new *People* on the floor under Dagney's half of the desk. Glancing down at the cover, the cause of the blowup was immediately obvious. Juliet and "Sexiest Man Alive" Zac Grundle gazed dreamily into each other's eyes over a coverline that read, "ZAC: I'VE FOUND MY ANGEL."

When Dagney returned, she spent the rest of the day making phone calls to her old school chums and comparing notes on Juliet's alleged teenaged rap sheet, which apparently included boyfriend-stealing, curfew-breaking, chewing gum in Latin class, and—most nefarious of all—having been named "Most Beautiful," "Most Popular," and "Star of the Future" in the yearbook. To hear Dagney tell it, Juliet had actually spent most of her boarding school years brownnosing the faculty and getting excused from calculus to attend play rehearsal. I offered to take some of the Juliet-related work off her hands, but she flatly refused.

Knowing that Allegra would want Phil to see his new favorite on the cover of *People*, I decided to bring the magazine to his office. Just before I entered the Waxmans' office suite, I saw Matt Vincent, the vice chairman of marketing, sitting on the bench, reading the *Hollywood Reporter*. Much to Allegra's chagrin, he'd been continually cited in industry articles as the driving force behind *The Foreign Pilot*'s triumph. Matt sightings were a rarity these days, as, right after returning from Los Angeles, he'd insisted that his department be relocated, due to what he called the "corrosive and disruptive environment" of the main office. He was probably the only Glorious executive who could do this without being told by Phil or Tony to take a flying fuck. Now Matt and his team worked out of a cluster of offices in a building a couple of blocks away and remained there as much as possible. I'd seen him only a few times since the Oscars, and had attributed his behavior in L.A. to nerves wound tight as guitar strings—he'd been back to his usual pleasant and polite self ever since.

"Hey Matt. How's everything?" I asked.

"Better than expected," he said, smiling. "I'm here for a meeting with Phil and Tony and a really hot new interactive company to finally launch a Glorious Web site." He went on to tell me that he planned for the site to go live in mid-May, barely a month from now.

"That's going to be a huge help—fans are constantly calling about release dates and rumors. The switchboard sends all the calls to us."

"Well, now they'll be able to send them to www dot Glorious Pictures dot com," he said, hitting an imaginary ENTER button.

"They've waited a while—I think we're the only studio without a site."

"We are," he agreed. "Not that I haven't been trying to convince them for about two years. You must spend a lot of time online," he said. "I'm sure your boss, in particular, wants to know exactly what's out there."

"Allegra thinks that I can actually monitor the entire Internet for Glorious mentions," I said, "I surf around enough to give her the impression that we've got cyberspace under control."

"That figures," he said. "Allegra may not fully understand that it's a rather large media outlet."

"True," I agreed. "But it's amazing how fast rumors go around online. I learn more about Glorious on the Web than I do in the office." I laughed.

Matt thought for a moment before saying, "When the site goes up, it's going to need a ton of content to start off with. Cheryl, Kenny, and I don't have the time to pull it all together." Cheryl and Kenny were the two vice presidents in his department. The three of them operated Glorious's hyper-efficient marketing machine. "Do you think you could lend us a hand?"

"I'd definitely like to work on that."

He said that he'd send me an e-mail about what types of things he needed. "It's mostly going to be short descriptions of films and some photo captions, but there could be more, depending on how it goes." I was trying not to show how thrilled I was. Matt was about to say something else when Sabrina stepped out and waved him into Phil's office. I gave her the magazine. "I'm handing this directly to Phil," I said, as she tossed it onto an overflowing pile of memos. She gave me a thumbs-up as I walked away.

At my desk, I e-mailed Abby to tell her that not only did I have a pending drinks date with an actual gossip columnist, but I was also going to be writing for the Glorious Web site. I couldn't wait to tell my cousin, either. I wasn't even three months into the year I'd allotted myself, and things were taking a decidedly positive turn. Writing for the site would be a little tough to juggle time-wise, but intuition told me that it was a good idea to get some experience in another area of Glorious.

Dagney needed to be left out of the loop, on both counts. If she knew that I was planning to meet Elliott, she could pin every subsequent Glorious leak on me, leaving her free to spread rumors as she pleased. And if she learned I was working for Matt she would only feel more threatened. Juliet Barlett's success was gnawing away at Dagney; her behavior had become completely erratic.

When I ran into Robert the following day while sneaking a faux-smoke behind the building, we discussed it. "She spends hours on the phone, feeding her friends all kinds of information about Juliet. It's as if nothing else is more important than giving them their fix. She's become a gossip junkie."

"Well, frankly, it's beginning to show," Robert replied.

I knew exactly what he meant. Incredibly stylish and groomed to perfection when I'd first met her, ever since her return from California, Dagney had resembled a "before" picture in a beauty magazine. Way before. Her face looked worn. Her eyes were dull; her skin was oily and blemished. Dag's designer wardrobe had been replaced by worn jeans, baggy sweaters, and a beat-up pair of L.L.Bean moccasins. She'd abruptly given up on all the manicures, pedicures, blowouts, and facials that she'd once considered crucial to her existence; now hangnails dotted her chewed-up fingers, and her hair, which had been so beautiful, now looked dry and lifeless. It was as if Juliet's rise to stardom had drained Dagney of her will to live—or, at least, of her will to live beautifully.

"We have to cut her some slack," Robert said. "How would you feel if the girl you sat next to in homeroom became the Next Big Thing while you made sure her driver was on time at Heathrow?"

I took his point, and as we rode back upstairs I resolved to shield Dag from recent Juliet developments, like the article in the latest *Us Weekly* detailing Juliet's deplorable closet situation. So many designers had showered her with clothing that she'd been forced to turn her bedroom into a wardrobe and was currently sleeping on her couch while looking for a larger place. At my desk, I neatly removed the pages from the magazine with an Exacto knife, hoping to spare Dagney some additional grief.

But by the end of the day Dag had heard about it from someone else, and she was awash in righteous indignation. "With all the hungry people in the world, don't you think Juliet could think about someone besides herself for once?" she asked. I couldn't quite make the connection, but Dagney, who had a limitless supply of cash and had rarely repeated an outfit back in the days when she cared, obviously believed that Juliet's acceptance of free finery was a barrier to social progress. As Dagney reached for the phone to pontificate on this latest affront, I decided to ignore her and started on the first draft of my *Circle of Eight* description for the Web site.

When Elliott called half an hour later trying to confirm a different, unflattering story about Juliet, I felt completely flustered and on edge. Last night my cousin had read me the riot act about agreeing to go out with him, and even though I'd defended myself—swearing that there was no way I was going to give him any information that I shouldn't, that there was nothing intrinsically wrong with our seeing each other, etc.—I had a nagging sense that she might be right. We hadn't even gone out yet but Elliott could get me into serious trouble if he didn't let go of this Juliet bone.

Tersely, I asked him to hold for Allegra. "Don't worry, Karen," he interrupted, "I'll make sure she knows that I didn't hear it from you, promise."

"Thanks," I said, only slightly relieved. I still wasn't sure if our boss knew where Dagney ended and I began.

As it turned out, she did. Immediately after taking Elliott's call, Allegra beeped Dagney to come into her office. Allegra had recently had electronic messages boxes installed on our desks and a corresponding one placed on hers. I'd programmed it with a bunch of her favorite phrases, including, "LATER," "HOLD or call back," "FIND Phil," "GET Tony," "TRY Oprah," "NO!!!" and the one that was currently flashing, "IN HERE!" With its single finger operation and customized functionality, Allegra had finally found a technology she enjoyed using. She was trigger-happy with that thing, but at least we knew what she wanted from us.

Dagney went in, closing the door behind her. I tried to listen from the other side but could hear only Dagney. "But I was just . . ."

"It didn't seem like such a big deal, I mean, I just thought it was kind of funny."

"I do want this job," followed by a sniffle.

I moved away from the door so that Dagney wouldn't suspect I'd been eavesdropping. She walked out of Allegra's office, her eyes red-rimmed. "What are you looking at?" she snapped. Then she grabbed my cigarettes, which had gotten slightly crushed in the bottom of my purse, and shook her head in disgust. "Why are these all bent?" But she took them anyway, courteously handing me back the crumpled, empty pack when she returned.

The week's end brought Dagney a reprieve from her Juliet surveillance as a new development began to unfold. In a feature titled

"The Moms Behind the Men" in the previous month's *Ladies' Home Journal*, Gloria had said that it made her sad that Phil and Tony hadn't collaborated on a film since the early days of the company. The accompanying photograph was a grainy snapshot of the twins in their playpen. It looked as if one had the other's head in a toy vise. The bolded quote on the facing page read: "There isn't anything I'd like to see more than my sons working together, side by side, just like Jack and Bobby."

The twins had responded with uncharacteristic sheepishness, agreeing to team up on a movie for their mother's upcoming seventieth birthday, but so far this filial gesture had failed to bring them any closer to a decision. For weeks Phil and Tony spent every morning fighting in their office suite, unable to agree on a project. They argued. They threatened. They slammed doors and threw things at each other.

Phil wanted to make more of what he loved—perhaps a dramatization of a literary work, and certainly a film full of costumes, accents, and upholstery—whereas Tony, who had become completely fascinated by hip-hop culture, wanted something with guns, bling, and a certified-platinum soundtrack. He'd been spending a lot of time with rap stars and African American comedians, and was convinced that bringing the flava would bode well for Glorious's financial future; his growing appreciation of bootylicious women could also be served by such a project. Every couple of days a reporter would call our office to ask about the "Untitled Phil and Tony Project." We'd issue the usual "no comment" and note the call on Allegra's phone log.

But this week, after a particularly fruitful guided-meditation session, Tony had a eureka idea that Phil endorsed enthusiastically. Instead of one of them having to compromise, they could blend together what they each loved and create something brand

new. *Air Jane,* a hip-hop retelling of *Jane Eyre,* would be in the-
atres this time next year.

Needless to say, this would involve some minor alterations to
the plot—Lowood would now be a reform school, Rochester a
former NBA star, and the Reed family residents of a Chicago
housing project. Dagney and I faxed out thousands of copies of
the official Glorious press release, which read in part, "What
West Side Story did for Shakespeare, we plan to do for this nine-
teenth-century classic."

The news immediately generated a frenzy of media response,
ranging from the laudatory to the incredulous to those who predicted that *Air Jane* would mark the beginning of Glorious's
downfall.

I also e-mailed Matt with the idea of posting the *Air Jane*
release on the site when it went live, and he agreed, asking me to
flesh it out with some additional information. He'd also liked the
plot summaries I'd written for the company's next five films, and
told me to keep going and write the next six months' worth.

Elliott called, first thanking me for the fax, which I'd made
sure he'd gotten first thing, before saying, "Do you want to get
that drink on Thursday?"

I banished all thoughts of Ellen from my mind and decided to
give Dagney back the *Times* run as I said, "That sounds perfect."

THE IDOLMAKER

The surge in media activity around the *Air Jane* announcement kept Dagney and me so busy that she forgot about Juliet Bartlett and decided to rejoin the Glorious workforce. Monday found her with freshly highlighted hair and everything else back to its previous level of extreme high maintenance. Choosing not to mention her lapse into scruffiness, I paid tribute to her new Versace blouse and we quickly settled back into our old routine.

I filled Robert in on Dagney's renewed work ethic as the two of us walked around the block. More precisely, we were walking Mo around the block, the Husky that had finally been chosen to masquerade as Gretzky in the upcoming television bookings for *Block That Pup*. Mo's owner, a biker type named Charlie, had driven down from his home in Harrisburg, Pennsylvania that morning so that Tony could make a final decision. According to Robert, who'd spent the entire three weeks since the Oscars looking for a suitable replacement for the late dog star, Mo was the only Husky on the East Coast who possessed "Gretzky's essence." As soon as they'd entered Tony's office, Robert recounted, Mo stepped between

Tony and Charlie and stayed there. "It works!" Tony pronounced, and that was that. Our whole department breathed a collective sigh of relief. "Gretzky" was slated to start his media tour Friday with an appearance on the *Today* show.

Now Charlie was having a burger at the Pig & Whistle while Robert and I spent some quality time with his dog. Gretzky had always had a trainer at his appearances, but we'd decided it was a safer bet for the two of us to work with Mo; a professional handler might be concerned with the ethics of our doggie switcheroo. Ordinarily, I would have been, too, but on balance it seemed innocent enough, or so I kept telling myself. I'd volunteered to help with the *Block That Pup* media tour because I wanted to see how Robert was going to pull this off. Watching him in action had become my best Glorious learning tool by far.

I finally felt confident enough to discuss my Oscar misstep with Robert. "The problem is, I don't know if that guy was Hanratty or not, but I was just so tired and annoyed that I wasn't thinking clearly. I even told him that we refused to let Ted Roddy have his bodyguard or wheelchair attendant at the party, which really makes us look terrible."

Robert thought this over. "True, it wasn't the smartest thing for you to say, but it wasn't a personal directive from Phil or Tony, after all. The best Hanratty could do with that information is use it as an example of the fanaticism of the Glorious staff—how we carry out every order to the letter, regardless of whether or not it really makes sense," Robert gently tugged on Mo's leash, urging the dog away from a glassblower's studio. "Which isn't exactly news, anyway. Whenever one of the Waxmans says something, everyone turns somersaults to do it and then dresses it up in some way, and the worst offenders are in our department."

"What do you think drives them to be like that?"

"They spin things for a living, and I'm not completely convinced they can stop," Robert said, shaking his head. A couple of teenagers approached and patted Mo, who lifted up his head and offered them the soft underside of his neck.

"So what do you think's going to happen—I mean, with Hanratty?"

"I have no idea. Everyone here discounts him, but he was a highly respected journalist in his day. I don't know why he'd tell people he's writing this biography if he wasn't actually planning on doing it."

"It seems easier to do it the other way around—to not raise anyone's suspicions and just write the book."

"I agree. There must be something that we're missing," Robert said. "Mo. Drop," he said firmly, as the dog picked up an empty Budweiser bottle.

I laughed as the dog looked confused, then carefully put the bottle down. "Looks like he's been schooled in the finer points of beer retrieval."

By the time we got to the tavern where Charlie was eating lunch, Mo was heeling next to Robert like a Westminster champion. Robert ducked inside to retrieve Mo's owner while I waited outside with the dog. When Charlie came out, Mo greeted him with three short barks. Robert took Mo's leash from me and the dog immediately heeled as we walked down the street together. "How'd you get him to walk like that?" Charlie asked.

"All well-trained dogs heel," Robert said, and upon hearing the word "heel" again, Mo moved a half-step closer to Robert.

"Man, I can't believe that. He pulls like crazy when I walk him."

"Have you trained him at all? Does he fetch or play ball or anything like that?" Robert asked.

"Nah, I never bothered with that stuff. I was really happy when he learned how to crap outside."

"Right."

"You know, he does do one thing," Charlie said. He stopped, knelt in front of Mo and said, "Nice to meet you, man." Mo responded by giving Charlie one of his large paws.

"That's great," Robert said. "I can work with that." Robert and I said good-bye to Charlie and Mo in front of our building.

"Just bring him here on Thursday and then we'll go to your hotel," Robert said, speaking slowly and clearly for Charlie's sake. "We'll have a groomer there. And remember, don't tell anyone what you're doing. Loose lips, you know . . ."

"Right, man." Charlie made a zipping motion across his mouth.

Robert and I walked into the building. "Robert, what are we going to do? Gretzky played right wing. This dog can barely shake paws."

"Nice to meet you, man," Robert said, drily. "Don't worry."

Things were pretty much back to normal after that—actually better than normal, as Dagney had resolved that the only thing keeping her from success on Juliet's level was a sense of commitment. To this end she was suddenly grabbing work out of my hands. My own resolution was to enjoy it.

Her new attitude was tested when a fresh rumor swirled our way: Juliet Bartlett had her heart set on playing Jane. Tony, who was already envisioning Jane and Rochester grinding on the roof of a burned-out tenement, wasn't confident that Juliet would be convincing as the tough-talking, hard-rhyming heroine he had in mind; furthermore, he certainly hadn't imagined *Air Jane* as a blonde. And so Juliet, who was dying for a chance to play against her already-established good-girl type, set out to prove him wrong. She hired a consultant—a "hip-hoperator" who called himself LeVine the Fine—to help turn her into a gangsta princess and convince Tony that she wasn't the über-WASP everyone assumed.

On Thursday afternoon, Robert and I were standing outside our office, reassuring Charlie that it was fine to leave Mo with us as we took him on Gretzky's appointed television rounds. Even though Charlie would be staying nearby at the Royalton and we'd promised to check in with him frequently, he was having a stage-mother moment of his own. "What if the two of you lose him? What if someone takes him?" Charlie's babbling was cut short when a white Lincoln Navigator zoomed up to the curb, bouncing on its shocks as the driver hit the brakes. The car had gold chrome, pinstriped detailing zigzagging into oblivion, and a thumping bass from inside that shook the sidewalk. I'd seen tinted windows before, but these were so dark that I didn't see how navigating the Navigator was even possible.

A door opened and Juliet Bartlett jumped down from the passenger seat, ready to put her new bad self to the test. She had the fingers on each hand splayed pinky/ring-middle-index/thumb and strode toward the building with a man I realized must be LeVine the Fine, and two other men in full hip-hop regalia in tow. Before she got inside, though, she ran into Geraldine, who was taking Harvey for a walk. Juliet immediately dropped to the ground to play with him and he rolled over so she could tickle his belly. Even Harvey, the evil little ferret, was charmed by Juliet.

"You my dawg, Harvey, ain't ya, baby?" she cooed. Harvey wriggled joyfully.

"Jools!" LeVine the Fine intoned. "That's a dog!"

"Yeah, you my little dawg," she said, still cuddling Harvey.

"A dog is not a dawg!"

"It's not?"

"And that's barely even a dog!" Everything that LeVine the Fine said came out as a command. *"That,"* LeVine said, pointing at

Mo and nodding his approval, "is a dog!" Charlie waved back, but LeVine ignored him.

Juliet gave Harvey one final pat before getting up. Harvey whimpered in complaint as Geraldine pulled him away.

Before getting into the elevator, Juliet and her posse exchanged a series of complicated handshakes with the man at the security desk.

"Knuckle to knuckle comes first?" Juliet asked, chewing her lip in concentration.

"Second! Elbow bump is first!"

"Right. Elbow bump to knuckle to knuckle . . ."

"It's like this!" LeVine the Fine slowly demonstrated a five-part handshake with one of the other guys.

"Thank you, LeVine."

"Thank you LeVine THE FINE!"

They rode up in the elevator and arrived at reception. "Who may I say is here?" the receptionist said.

"It's me, Juliet," she said, removing her Kangol hat and very large, gold-framed sunglasses.

"Oh, I'm so sorry. I didn't recognize you."

"I didn't recognize you," mimicked LeVine the Fine in a falsetto. "What's that shit on the wall?"

"It's a piece of art."

"It's a piece of shit!"

"Okay, it's a piece of shit, you made me say it," the receptionist replied, trying hard not to laugh. "I'll tell Tony you're here, Juliet."

"Yes, tell him I've brought LeVine the Fine and his posse, and we don't like to be kept waiting?" She ended the statement as if it were a question.

"Word!"

The receptionist relayed the message and soon Tony himself came out to greet them. Tony gave LeVine the Fine a handshake that had different choreography than the earlier one downstairs. This one ended in a sort of reciprocal chest thump. The other two repeated the gestures and Juliet gave it a try, getting as far as the third movement, a palm to palm slide. The four of them followed Tony into a conference room, and the last thing anyone heard before the door slammed shut was LeVine the Fine saying, "This is how it is!"

A couple of hours later I was in the bathroom, getting ready to meet Elliott for drinks. Washing my hands, enjoying the feel of the pricey lather that was in there for Juliet's benefit, I heard someone say, "Hey, girlfriend, help a sister out?" In the mirror I saw Juliet exiting one of the stalls.

"Does this look okay?" She was trying to adjust her oversized jeans so that they fell just right over her navy blue Timberland boots. The pants were huge, and she was so slender that even zipped up, and with the support of a gigantic leather belt that had "JOOLS" spelled out in crystals on the buckle, they threatened to fall off her completely.

"I think you need to tighten the belt a little more."

"Yeah, I think you're right." She tightened it, but then the buckle was over her right hip. "How is it now?"

"Too far to the right."

She adjusted it and straightened up. "Thanks. I'm having a hard time getting used to these clothes. They fit so differently from what I usually wear."

She had on a baseball jersey with the word "METS" outlined in multicolored rhinestones and a thick gold chain around her neck, with a round, diamond-encrusted medallion hanging from it engraved with what looked like an insignia. Her earrings were gigantic gold "J"s that dipped beneath her chin. "Better now?" she asked.

I nodded, astonished that I'd just given Juliet Bartlett fashion advice. I was still trying to finish my makeup as Dagney walked in.

"Juliet. So nice to see you," she said, coolly.

"Hi?" Juliet said.

"It's Dagney, Dagney Bloom?"

Juliet was clearly drawing a blank.

"You know, from Mr. Cadwallader's chemistry class?" Dagney began to turn a deep shade of red.

"Oh, right," Juliet said, still sounding unsure. "You went to Foxfoot Academy?"

"Is that our school crest?" Dagney latched onto Juliet's medallion.

"Yeah, I couldn't think of what else to put on it, and my guy said I should have one," she said.

"Are you talking about Zac?" Dagney asked, her eyes glittering.

"No, someone who's helping me out." I left the bathroom as Juliet, while extricating her necklace from Dagney's grasp, explained about LeVine the Fine.

I was shutting down my computer when Dagney returned. She immediately picked up the phone, not wanting to lose a second, having either forgotten or temporarily suspended her new pledge.

"You are not going to believe this. *She* was just in the office. She *hugged* me, like we were best friends. She wants to be in this rap movie, so she's dressed like some kind of person from MTV!"

I didn't want to hear any more and left to see Elliott.

We were meeting in a Greenwich Village bar where it was reasonably certain we wouldn't run into anyone from Glorious. I wasn't going to give him any information about the company, but it was still best not to be spotted. He'd called late in the afternoon to confirm and to ask what type of shoes I was wearing.

"Tall black boots that end just below the knee. How will I know you?"

"I know you, remember?"

"Can't I have an idea?" I hated the idea of just standing there waiting to be recognized.

"I'll find you," he said, hanging up.

I walked over to the bar, wanting to have some time to get Glorious out of my head before meeting Elliott. I hadn't been on a date with anyone since Gabe and wasn't sure I remembered how to do the whole small talk/laugh in the right places/does he want to see me again thing. The fact that I was meeting Elliott Solnick only made it more confusing because of the intimacy of reading his column each morning. It was as if he were someone I chatted with over coffee, but in fact I had no idea what he was really like.

I arrived at the bar and paused a second before going in, using the reflection from the neighboring store window to give myself a final once-over, frustrated that I couldn't get a good look at my boots. Fluffing up my hair and pushing the door open, I was no more than five feet inside when I heard a familiar voice say, "Karen, it's so nice to meet you." Elliott wasn't tall, but he was exactly the right height for me, with slightly wavy dark brown hair and nice, broad shoulders. As he drew me toward him and kissed me on the cheek, I could see that his eyes were a warm hazel.

The hostess seated us at an anonymous table in the back. Elliott ordered a Scotch and for some reason I said, "I'll have the same," which was odd, since I couldn't remember the last time I'd had Scotch or wanted any. But I vaguely remembered something about it being a good source of courage.

"So, how are the brothers Art and Commerce treating you so far?" he asked, which made me laugh. By the time I'd finished my drink I felt perfectly comfortable; after the second round, I was confident that I could speak about Glorious without saying something I shouldn't. Pretty soon the conversation turned to Juliet Bartlett.

"So, what do you think, Karen? Are Phil and Tony going to let her be Air Jane? What's the story?"

I told him that I didn't know, but that Juliet was working hard to convince them that she would make a believable Jane, and that I found her efforts impressive. After the third Scotch, I filled him in on some—well, most—of the details of her transformation: LeVine the Fine, the Navigator, the diamond-encrusted school crest, and the rest of the stuff that Juliet was doing to try to become a believable Jane. I also mentioned that Juliet's success had caused one of my coworkers to come briefly unglued, and I had to bite my tongue to keep from giggling.

"Juliet has that effect on a lot of women, especially in New York," he said. "Every day someone tells me another nasty story about her, and it never checks out, like that stuff I was calling Allegra about last week."

"Why do you think that is?"

"Well, the girls here are extremely competitive," he said. "They have a hard time when they see someone they perceive as being just like them suddenly become a huge star."

The sheer ferocity of Dagney's reaction still didn't make sense to me, and I told him so.

"Karen, let me try to explain." Elliott had stealthily hooked my ankle with his own, and was pulling my foot toward him. I tried to concentrate on the conversation. "Let me guess, this Dagney, she's from New York, has rich parents, went to a fancy school." My foot continued its journey as I nodded. "Well, girls like that, and I know because I grew up here, but in Brooklyn, where it's not so insane"—now my foot was on the edge of his chair, and he had his hand around my ankle—"anyway, these girls have lots of money, a bunch of homes—they have all this *stuff*. But when it comes to the things that money can't buy . . ." Now my foot was in his lap, and he was kneading my ankle emphatically. "That's where they just fall apart. They love a good hard-luck story—you know, an actress who had to pull herself out of poverty, parents were migrant workers, survived a terrible disease—they'll embrace her. But a girl like them? Not allowed."

This was all very interesting—both Elliott's explanation of Juliet's effect on women from her social class, and the way his fingers felt on the outside of my boot, where they were currently massaging that spot right on the front of my ankle where the foot joins the leg. I'd have to ask Abby what it was called, exactly. For now, I was calling it the Elliott spot.

"Juliet's going to be around for a while, they're going to have to get used to it," I said, thinking how I could get used to this.

He nodded. "Phil's got huge plans for her, but for every good Glorious picture he puts her in, she's going to have to be in one dog, at least. That's the Waxmans' new math."

Dog! I had to be at the Royalton at five A.M. to meet Robert and take Mo to the *Today* show. I pulled my foot back so quickly that Elliott looked alarmed.

"I have to take a guest to *Today* at five," I said, apologetically. "You just reminded me."

"I'd really like to see you and your little feet again."

I told him I'd like that, too.

"Listen, Karen, I have a little secret to tell you." Elliott leaned forward and whispered into my hair, "Juliet as Air Jane is a done deal. Phil and Tony are just letting her run around town looking like a rapper to get the buzz started on the movie. Oh, and the reason Juliet couldn't go to L.A.? Her grandmother is really ill and she doesn't want to be away from her."

Then he kissed me, quickly, on the mouth and murmured, "Next time, no boots."

At 5:15 in the morning Robert and I, coffees in hand, rode the Royalton's wood-paneled elevator to the eleventh floor to pick up Mo. We knocked on the door and heard Charlie say, "Come on in, I'm decent."

Robert shook his head before pushing the door open. Mo, looking soft and silky from his trip to the groomer the day before, was lying across the king-size bed with various plates of room service food in front of him. As we entered, he was snuffling down a rasher of bacon while eyeing a plate of sausage links. "Look at him go, eating all that fancy food and stuff," Charlie said. "Mo was born to be a star."

Charlie was sitting in a wing chair, hoovering a plate of corned beef hash with a fried egg on top. "I love this hotel—they said they'd make me whatever I wanted for breakfast," he said, happily dipping a fry into a ramekin of ketchup. "It's my boy's big day." Charlie beamed at Mo, who had swallowed the sausages and was now wolfing down a stack of blueberry pancakes.

"Is that good for him?" I asked.

"He ordered it," Charlie said.

I exchanged a sharp glance with Robert.

"Nah, I just wanted to see if he'd like it while I could order it for free. He'll be fine. Won't you Mo?"

Mo wasn't slated to be on air until the 8:30 segment, but we were supposed to report to the studio at Rockefeller Plaza no later than six. The *Today* show liked to have everyone captive and accounted for in the greenroom at least a couple of hours before they were scheduled to go on. We hung around in Charlie's hotel room while Mo finished eating. Robert pulled a special dog groomer's mitt out of his briefcase and wiped Mo's face. "Nice to meet you, man," he said, and the dog immediately put his large paw in Robert's hand. Robert produced a small treat from his pocket and Mo swallowed it whole.

At 6:02 Robert's cell phone rang. "Hi, we're on our way. We'll see you in four, no, three minutes," he said.

"Let me get you his stuff," Charlie said.

"That's okay. I've brought a gift for him," Robert said, displaying a beautifully hand-sewn leather collar and matching leash. Each bore a small brass plate with the word "Gretzky" etched into it.

Robert put the collar on Mo and clipped on the leash. "Heel, Mo," he said, and the dog went to his side. Charlie knelt on the floor in front of his dog, giving him a little pep talk.

"He'll be on between eight thirty and nine," I said. "It's channel 4 here. We'll see you later."

Robert and I left the room and got in the elevator. I hit L and Robert hit 7.

"What are you doing?" I said. "We're going to be late!"

"We're fine Karen, it's only six twenty-five." Robert's phone rang again, but he didn't answer it. On the seventh floor Robert pulled out a room key and the three of us went inside. Robert said, "What are the chances Katie Couric will say, 'Nice to meet you, man'?"

He told the dog to sit and Mo sat instantly. Robert gave him another treat. Then he got down to business teaching Mo several new commands, each of which would result in the necessary paw offering. Within half an hour, Mo was shaking on "Hello," "Welcome," "Hi, Gretzky," "Thank you," and "Thanks." At 7 A.M., I switched on the television to watch the beginning of the show. Robert's phone had been ringing incessantly but he didn't pick it up. Instead, he called one of the producers and said, "This is

Robert Kojima and I'm here with Gretzky. He needed some last minute prep. We'll be there shortly." He hung up before they could respond.

"Oh, no," I said. On the screen the camera was panning the Rockefeller Center rink, which had been made over for roller hockey with a goal net and chalk circles. "Coming up," Katie Couric said, "Matt hits the rink with Gretzky, the canine star of *Block That Pup.*"

Robert was going over Mo with the grooming mitt, and some kind of spray that made his coat even shinier. "Don't worry about it. It's all under control."

At 7:45 we left the room and briskly walked the five blocks to the studio, passing the rink on the way. Prop people were adjusting the goals and putting out hockey sticks and pucks.

My stomach was sinking. "Robert, they think he's going to play hockey with Matt Lauer. What are we going to do?"

"We're fine," he said.

We got through NBC's security at 8:05 and rode the elevator up to where we were supposed to have been more than two hours ago. On a monitor overhead I could see Matt taking a preliminary skate, outfitted in protective gear and wearing the *Block That Pup* promotional hockey sweater we'd sent over the day before.

A frazzled producer met us. "You're finally here. What happened? We have to get you out there immediately," she said.

Robert shook his head. "Gretzky won't be playing hockey today."

"Of course he will. That's why he's here. Matt's out there already, warming up," she said, pointing up at the monitor.

I heard Katie's cheery voice say, "And after the weather, we'll see if Matt can *Block That Pup* as he goes one-on-one with Gretzky."

It was 8:10.

"Would you ask Catherine Zeta-Jones to catch a Frisbee in her mouth?" Robert asked.

The producer looked confused. "What?"

"Would you?"

"Of course not. What kind of a question is that?"

"Why wouldn't you?" My mouth was dry with panic as I wondered where in the world Robert was going with this.

"Because she's an actress. A really big star. What the hell does this have to do with anything?" the woman said, looking at her watch and twirling her hair nervously.

"Precisely. And so is Gretzky. He doesn't have to do some stunt. He'll be on the couch with the hosts." Robert handed her a tape. "This is the clip that Tony Waxman sent over."

The woman took it and started to speak into her headset. On another monitor I saw Matt Lauer skate over to the nearest exit, drop his stick, and roll right into the building.

Robert, Mo, and I were escorted to the green room, where there were pastries, fruit, and coffee on a low table, along with two monitors, one with the show on and the other with a live feed of the set. Matt dashed by our open door while pulling off the sweater and putting on a suit jacket. He'd had his shirt and tie on underneath the whole time. On the monitor we watched Today's weatherman high-fiving and shaking hands with the crowd of people on the plaza, who were waving homemade signs and cheering wildly.

Suddenly, a small, wiry man pushed his way to the front. He had a bullhorn and carried a sign that read, "NOT THE REAL GRETZKY" and had a picture of Gretzky on it. He started to speak into the bullhorn, "The dog you are about to see is not Gretzky from Block That Pup! Gretzky is dead! Don't believe the imposter!" He repeated "Gretzky is dead" over and over while brandishing his sign in full-camera view. The segment producer appeared on the monitor beside him, flashing her credential and hustling him off-camera.

"This is not good," Robert said. The two of us sat there, transfixed.

A minute later, the producer entered the green room, this time with the agitated protester in tow. "You'll see, this dog won't even know me," he said. Mo, who had been napping, opened one eye, glanced in the man's direction, and went back to sleep. The man was still holding his sign, and now that he was up close I could see his jacket was covered with oversized Gretzky photo buttons.

"You Glorious people!" he shouted. "You don't even respect the dignity of my dead dog. You think it's okay to take some other animal and pretend he's Gretzky," he said, pointing at Mo, now awake from all the shouting. "Gretzky had more talent in one ear than that hairy beast has in his whole body."

"Is this the truth?" the producer asked.

Robert and I both looked down, not answering.

"Well is it?"

"Gretzky died and we were trying to keep the booking," Robert said, quietly.

"I can't believe you thought another dog would be as good as Gretzky," the man said, putting his face a little too close to Robert's.

"Will the two of you just leave?" The producer said hurriedly, before proceeding to explain to someone on the other end of her walkie-talkie that the segment planned for one and a half minutes from now had been scrapped. Robert and I ran out of the studio with Mo bounding along next to us. We left through an exit on the other side of the building, away from the horde of *Today* fans who would undoubtedly turn into a hanging mob if they caught sight of the liars who'd tried to dupe Matt and Katie.

The three of us kept up our rapid pace all the way back to the Royalton, where we returned a panting Mo to Charlie. "I watched the show, but he wasn't on," Charlie said.

"We got outed by the real Gretzky's owner," Robert said.

"I'm afraid we won't need Mo anymore," I added, "but we'll mail your check."

Charlie looked confused. "We were really psyched for this."

"I know"—I patted Mo sadly—"but it just isn't happening."

As Robert held the door open for me, he turned back to the unexpectedly demoted dog and his disconsolate owner. "Feel free to order more blueberry pancakes, or whatever else you'd like," he said to Charlie. "But please don't let Mo eat trash from the street. I've almost broken him of that."

On the way back downtown in the cab, Robert and I tried to figure out what to do about Tony.

"We should just tell him what happened," I said. "It wasn't our fault."

"It doesn't matter. Tony didn't get what he wanted, and that's what counts."

"Maybe we can just tell Allegra?"

"She'll say we should have thought it through more carefully."

"But we did. You did. You thought of everything. The Gretzky leash, the extra training, Catherine Zeta-Jones . . ." I trailed off, knowing that this wouldn't convince him.

The cab pulled up in front of Glorious. We went inside. I glanced around, fervently hoping to see Eddie Di Silva so that he could lock us out of the elevator for a while and postpone the inevitable. No such luck. We rode up in silence and returned to our desks.

I held my breath, waiting for the summons.

Robert walked over and tapped me on the shoulder. One of Tony's assistants had called and told him to "bring the girl, too."

We walked into Tony's office, me hanging half a step behind Robert. It was a huge space, equipped with a gym's worth of the very latest exercise equipment, and I smelled some kind of incense burning.

Tony, barefoot in shorts and a tank top, was standing on one foot on a mat in the corner, with his arms over his head in a prayer position. He looked the two of us up and down without moving his head. His yoga teacher, a slender dark-haired man, made small adjustments to the pose.

"You fucked up!" he screamed, still balanced on one foot.

"And when you're ready, slowly enter the Crow Pose," the teacher said softly.

Tony bent over and put both hands on the floor. Then he crouched down and lifted his knees up onto his elbows, bringing the heels of his feet near his ass. "You fucked up," he said again, but this time it was more of a snarl.

"I'm sorry," Robert said, but Tony interrupted him. "The dog you found couldn't play hockey. Gretzky's owner found out. What the fuck do I pay you for?" In the Crow Pose, Tony somehow managed to look harmonious and threatening all at once.

"Listen to the sound of your breath," the yoga teacher said.

"Can you hear my fucking breath now?" Tony said, still holding the pose.

"I'm sorry," Robert repeated. "I guess the owner saw the promos earlier in the week."

"You're sorry? You guess?" Tony put his head down on his intertwined hands and unfolded first his right leg and then his left straight in the air. Unfortunately, his facial expression, although upside down, was still fully visible. "I'm standing on my fucking head," he said, as if we hadn't noticed.

Robert and I nodded.

"I'm standing on my fucking head and you got kicked off the *Today* show."

I was missing something. The yoga teacher tried to intercede. "Anger is unhelpful," he said.

"I'll tell you what's unhelpful," Tony said, legs straight as lampposts in the air.

The teacher asked him to breathe again. Tony ignored him. "Fuck!" he shouted. "I made the fucking movie. I'm standing on my fucking head. I just needed you to find a fucking dog that played hockey and looked like the one in my fucking movie and you couldn't even do that."

"You might use this as an opportunity to let go," the teacher said. I wholeheartedly agreed. Then the teacher added, "And in your own time, slowly make your way into the Compass Pose."

Tony glared, then folded both of his legs down, not even wobbling for a second as he eased into a sitting position. From there, he stretched his right leg out straight to the side and picked his left foot up with his right hand, holding it behind his head, which rested on his left leg, while he turned his head to the right. He looked as if he were literally trying to pull himself apart.

"Remember to breathe," the teacher said.

"Remember to breathe? If I had to pay someone to remind me to breathe, do you think I'd own this fucking studio?"

"I'm sorry." This time, I said it. Robert and I were both staring at our feet, and I had this horrifying premonition that if we looked at each other we would burst out laughing.

"Get the fuck out of my office," Tony said. "The next time I need something done, I'll find someone who can fucking do it."

Robert and I bolted out of there, heads down, and ran straight for the stairwell, where we then ran down two flights of stairs so that we were not yet in the lobby, but safely away from our company's floor. The second we met each other's eyes we exploded; we were laughing so hard that tears were running down Robert's cheeks and I started hiccupping, which just made us laugh even more. Every time we started to pull ourselves together, Robert would say, "I'm standing on my fucking head," sending us into another round of hysterics. Finally catching my breath I asked, with a hiccup, "Robert, are we in so much trouble?"

He looked serious for a moment. "Not *so* much. Just enough," he said, and it was so utterly hopeless that we both cracked up again.

I returned to my desk just in time to relieve Dagney, who was dying for a cigarette break. I spotted the *New York Post* on the floor and quickly flipped to Page Six to see what Elliott was up to. The first item had a photo of Juliet in her "Jools" attire. "HIP-HOP MIXED-RACE REMIX" was the headline. In addition to having the scoop on Juliet as Jane, the item noted that Q. Didley and Nefertiti had been cast as Rochester and Mrs. Reed, respectively. Phil was quoted as saying, "It's time for a literary classic to knock boots with another kind of culture."

I was certain I wouldn't be here when it opened.

RAGING BULL

id-July in New York City is always hot and humid, but it
was ten degrees warmer inside the Glorious offices than
it was out on the street—something to do with the building's faulty circulation system, according to Geraldine. Every
time one of us tried to switch on a fan it overloaded the already-
taxed electrical wiring and caused a temporary blackout, shutting down our computers and laying waste to our documents,
phone logs, and e-mails. At first I felt sorry that Geraldine was
getting the brunt of everyone's overheated frustration, but when
she told me that she'd sent Harvey to stay at a friend's house in
East Hampton, my compassion evaporated.

Our situation in Publicity had been made more uncomfortable still by the arrival of the summer interns. While we needed
the extra help, there was no place to put them, so it felt like an
infestation—interns sprawling on the floor, perching atop file
cabinets, and squeezing into any available sliver of space. There
didn't seem to be enough oxygen to go around.

Sweatshop conditions notwithstanding, an internship at

Glorious was highly coveted, especially by wealthy New York parents looking for a place to park their offspring for the summer. When the Waxmans needed to offer extra incentive to extract a contribution to their favorite political cause, they'd dangle an internship for the child of the decision-impaired. A check would be produced quickly. Often these kids had already completed a White House internship. Their parents thought it would add a one-two punch to their budding résumés: Washington? Bam! Hollywood? Pow!

We also had interns from NYU—film students burning up to do anything that might put them in the proximity of one of their heroes. They'd prowl the hallways, holding up their hands to frame the action on the way to and from the photocopy machine. They often tried to secure their internship through some creative device, such as making a short film, or writing their cover letter in screenplay form:

An Intern's Tale
INT. GLORIOUS PICTURES PUBLICITY
DEPARTMENT—MORNING.

Through the window we see Dudley Fenster, intern extraordinaire. Dudley looks left, then right, then straight ahead. We hear a ringing phone, which Dudley picks up.

DUDLEY
(bristling with professionalism)
Glorious Pictures, how may I help you?

PHIL
(voiceover)
Who is this? I don't recognize your voice.

DUDLEY
(proudly)
Why, I'm Dudley Fenster, a new intern in the publicity
department.

PHIL
Will you do anything to help this company succeed?

DUDLEY
(standing even straighter)
Why, yes, sir. Anything at all.

PHIL
Dudley, this is Phil Waxman. Come to my office at three
today.
Kid, we're going to go places!

In short, the intern program mirrored exactly the Golden Child/Work Horse paradigm in which we all existed.

When I found out by reading Allegra's e-mail that Tony wanted someone to watch a nearly finished horror movie repeatedly throughout a day of audience testing, I jumped at the chance to spend time in an air-conditioned theater. The film was called *Imitator*, although a better title would have been *The Thing That Chewed up My Oscar and Spat It Out*, because that's exactly what it did to its star. She'd won Best Supporting Actress a couple of years earlier in a Buddy Friedman film and now she was sharing the screen with a different, although equally familiar, New Yorker— *Periplaneta americana*, the common cockroach. Granted, the one in *Imitator* stood eight feet tall and had a voracious libido, but it didn't seem like anything a phone call to a reputable exterminator couldn't solve.

Imitator's director, a Costa Rican who wore his beard in a long braid, was completely fixated on a scene that took place exactly two minutes and forty-three seconds into the film. Apparently, he'd infected Tony with his belief that if the audience was not completely terrified at the crucial two minutes and forty-three seconds mark, the movie would suffer a gruesome death at the box office.

At ten in the morning I took my place in the back of the darkened, deliciously cool theater armed with a stopwatch and Oliver Burton, one of our interns. The place was jammed to capacity with five hundred kids from the Parks Department's summer enrichment program, and they started to scream even before the lights went down.

At the exact moment the film began, I hit the button on the watch. Oliver stood, notebook and pen at the ready. In the opening scene, the actress, portraying a biologist in search of a cure for the Ebola virus, moves confidently about the lab. She is unaware of anything except her petri dishes and the body-hugging fit of her white coat, the length of which she smooths several times. The camera pans from the clock above her that reads 11:30 to the room's one small window, which frames a full moon. The director has now successfully established that this is a creepy laboratory. I glanced down at the stopwatch and saw that we were at 2:37. "Damn!" says the actress, as one of her sleeves accidentally sweeps a beaker off the table. It falls in slow motion, tumbling over and over until it hits the floor, smashing into thousands of pieces. She bends down to survey the mess and suddenly sees—*it!* 2:43. The theater erupted in screams, gasps, shouts, and a bit of nervous laughter. Oliver and I ran outside to construct our report.

"How many do you think screamed?" I asked.

"Probably half," he said.

"Write that down. And gasped?"

"Around a third? Maybe a quarter."

"Put twenty-nine percent. And around fifteen percent shouted, I think."

"And only a few laughed. Most of them seemed pretty freaked."

I added in my head. "Six percent, then, and we're good to go." Oliver went down the block to get us a couple of iced coffees while I phoned in the report. Tony wanted the statistics immediately, but of course it wasn't as simple as just calling his office. Allegra had to tell him herself. I called Dagney to start the ball rolling, and, for the first time ever, heard Allegra's voice mail pick up. Having no idea what had possessed Dagney to leave the phones, but with no time to worry about it, I dialed around to find someone else who could bring Allegra this crucial data. Clark didn't answer, so I tried Robert, before remembering that the two of them were at the airport picking up Jimmy Chin, the Asian action-film star. *I Eat Dragons for Lunch,* Jimmy's first film dubbed into English, would be released in three weeks, and he was embarking on an intensive press tour to promote it. Jimmy was the biggest star in China, and in Phil's words, "A billion of those people can't be wrong."

Still needing to get those scream/gasp/shout/laugh percentages to Allegra, ASAP, I dialed Vivian's number, steeling myself for a conversation with Kimberly, who could be counted on to tell me that *Imitator* wasn't "Vivian's movie" and whatever other excuse she could muster for why what I needed wasn't part of her job. I was pleasantly surprised when a crisp, professional voice answered. "Vivian Henry's office. This is Trisha."

"Hey, Trisha. It's Karen. I have the numbers from the *Imitator* screening that just started. They need to go to Allegra right away."

"Sure, just give me the information."

After I read her our findings, Trisha read them back quickly and said, "I'll walk this into Allegra's office right away—consider it done."

Trisha Sadowsky was the best intern we'd had since I'd started. Eager, bright, and thoroughly competent, she was spending the summer working for Vivian without pay. Robert, who was in charge of interns, had assigned the bright sophomore to this trial by fire and so far she was handling it beautifully. I had no doubt that the message was already in Allegra's hands and on its way to Tony.

Oliver reappeared at my side. "Here's your coffee, babe." Oliver Burton's parents owned an oceanfront home on Nantucket where the First Family frequently houseguested. At twenty-three, Oliver was a little older than our other interns, but he'd only just graduated from one of the East Coast's "Frisbee schools," so he fit in just fine. He had light blue eyes and dark brown hair, and dressed in a sort of groovy seventies style—open-collar shirts, pants that were tight on top and flared at the bottom, and boots with heels. Whenever he walked by, I always imagined a Barry White song emanating from somewhere deep within him, as if he had a personal soundtrack. Oliver called everyone "babe." The combination of his wealth, his face, and the fact that he shared a SoHo triplex with the lead singer of the hippie jam band Ziplock allowed him to work this look without a hint of irony. He was "dreamy" in the mold of David Cassidy.

The next screening of *Imitator* didn't start until noon, but instead of going back to the stifling office, Oliver and I decided to hang around near the theater, where there was a small park with some benches and shade trees. Oliver stretched out on the bench across from me, his cell phone resting on his slightly rounded belly. I dialed Clark's cell to see if Jimmy had arrived.

"I'm in the British Airways office," he said, sounding unusually stressed. "They've lost Jimmy's luggage and I'm filling out forms so they can track it. He checked two bags, but we found only one on this end."

"His luggage got lost on the Concorde?" This made no sense. "It only fits about one hundred twenty-five people."

"I know, I know. But they think that someone else took his luggage by mistake, so it may still show up."

"What a mess. How's he taking it?"

"He's perfectly calm. If this happened to me, I'd be screaming my head off, but he's been incredibly understanding about it. He's waiting in the car with Robert now and as soon as I'm finished here we're going to drop him at the Sherry-Netherland," Clark said. "I swear, if I ever get to fly on this thing I'm bringing my old Samsonite softsider. Every bag that came off was Louis Vuitton—that big trunk piece, which, of course, is what Jimmy had. What are you doing besides sweating right now?"

"I'm at the *Imitator* screening, getting reactions for Tony."

"Oh, yeah, the director wants to make sure everyone screams at two minutes and forty-eight seconds."

"Two forty-three," I corrected him. "I'll see you later."

I glanced over at Oliver. "The Concorde lost Jimmy Chin's luggage," I said. "Can you believe that?"

"Was it Louis Vuitton—the one that looks like a trunk?" he asked, opening one eye.

I nodded.

"Figures," he said, in a world-weary voice. "Last time I flew on it Juliet Bartlett took mine by accident."

"She did?"

"Yeah, but we figured it out. She stopped by my place to drop it off and we got a drink. No harm, no foul."

"Really?" Oliver's phone rang.

"Yeah, she's sweet, but not really my type," he explained, flipping open his phone.

His incredible web of connections never failed to amaze me. What would have sounded like boorish name-dropping from anyone else was completely authentic in his case.

After half-napping on the bench for a while, eavesdropping on Oliver's calls, I saw that it was a quarter to twelve, time to head back to the theater. "We need to go watch the beginning again," I said to Oliver.

"Karen, you don't mind if I take off now, do you? One of my friends really needs me. He's in the middle of this really heavy situation."

"That's fine." This was certainly something I could handle on my own; besides, denying Oliver's request would not be expedient, judging from the treatment he received around the office. On his first day, we were all shocked when a smiling Phil brought him up to our floor and introduced him to Allegra, who in turn audibly welcomed him to the department. Dagney and I sat there open-mouthed as Allegra fussed over Oliver, asking after his parents and telling him amusing anecdotes about a costume party she had attended with his father, Phil, and the president, who'd been dressed as the Three Amigos. It was as if Allegra had been replaced by a normal human being with an actual personality—not to mention a voice you could hear. A few minutes later Robert, on Allegra's gushing instructions, was escorting Oliver to the much-coveted empty cubicle. So many of us were after that cube that Allegra had turned it into a "guest office," which was really her way of saying that no one could have it.

"Guest" was a good term for what Oliver had been so far this summer. It wasn't that he didn't want to help out, it was just that his lifestyle frequently prevented him from showing up. Hanging out with the velvet-rope crowd, chasing models, and occasionally accompanying his roommate on tour didn't leave a lot of time for faxing and filing at Glorious, and the weirdest thing was that no one resented him. It just wouldn't have been fair to make him choose Glorious Pictures over his own glorious life, and everyone took it in stride. The best thing Oliver did was to offer me his cube—"For when you need to get away from things, babe." From then on, whenever I needed an escape and didn't feel like pretending to smoke, Oliver's "work crib" was where I could be found. I'd read a book, or daydream while staring at the J. Crew catalog–looking snapshots he'd thumbtacked to the wall. The pictures showed him splashing in the surf with the president's Labrador. No stiff formal portraits of Oliver with the commander in chief— everyone had those.

At the noon *Imitator* screening, I got nearly the same results— the gasp percentage went up a little bit but was evened out by a drop in shouts. Nervous laughter held steady at six percent. I phoned it all in to Trisha and returned to my bench, loving the fact that I had nothing to do until two. I called Abby. We'd always spent a lot of time together in the summers, hanging out at the beach and going to rooftop parties and taking the occasional long weekend at her grandparents' house in Watch Hill. I'd been eagerly looking forward to her return—she was going to stay with Ellen and me for July and August—but at the end of June she'd been selected to participate in a prestigious research project, and was spending the summer in what I was sure was a decidedly uncreepy laboratory on campus. We'd left dozens of messages for each other and dashed off a bunch of e-mails, but it had been nearly two months since we'd had an actual conversation.

"Karen!" She answered the phone on the first ring.

"This place," I started.

"I know—I've been completely swamped, too," she said.

That was the best thing about Abby—we could always just

pick up where we'd left off, and we started chattering right off the bat.

"My intern, Oliver Burton, of the Nantucket-pals-with-the-president Burtons, just ditched me because he had something better to do," I said, laughing. "Dagney has a huge crush on him, so she's always walking by his cube, hoping that he'll see her, but of course he hardly comes into the office."

"Are you enjoying it, though? This is just about the halfway point in your deal with Ellen, isn't it? Do you think you'll last the year?"

"It's about five months," I said, realizing that I hadn't thought about this in a while. "It's hard to say. The spaces between humiliating reprimands are getting longer, so that's an improvement, and I've been doing more and more work for the marketing department, which is great. The site's up now and the feedback's been good. Of course, no one in Publicity knows I have anything to do with it. They're unbelievably territorial."

"Wow, you're really in the middle of it," she said.

"Actually I feel like I'm always just outside," I said, admitting it aloud for the first time. "It's confirmed—I'm a Work Horse."

"Cheer up. You could be spending your summer in a lab."

"I think I might already be. This is obviously some kind of experiment in human endurance."

I considered telling her about Elliott but decided against it. He'd called a couple of times saying he wanted to see me again but he'd been vague, always coupling it with a query about a Glorious rumor he'd heard. I wasn't sure what to think, and the fact that I found him highly desirable further complicated matters. I didn't want to drive myself crazy with hypotheticals.

Abby and I hung up, promising to speak again very soon.

The two screenings I'd seen so far today had been Tony's version; the afternoon ones would be the director's cut. Shortly before

two, a pair of Town Cars pulled up, disgorging Tony and the director. They didn't look at each other as they entered the theater.
When I pulled out the stopwatch, they took positions on either
side of me, clearly agitated.

"Now we will see who is correct," the director said, practically
spitting out the words.

"You bet we'll see who's fucking correct," Tony answered.
Both sets of eyes were glued to the stopwatch in my hand, which
threatened to spasm at any moment. I had to will myself not to
hit the button too early.

The film started and at the crucial moment, 75 percent of the
audience screamed—screamed bloody murder as a matter of fact,
while the rest either gasped or shouted. Not a soul laughed. The
director gave Tony a triumphant look, aggressively flipping his
braided beard in Tony's direction in what was clearly meant as an
"up yours" gesture. Something was slightly different about the film,
but I couldn't figure out exactly what had changed. Tony looked
annoyed. "Fucking fluke. We'll see what happens next time."

The last screening wouldn't start until four. I got a smoothie
and reclaimed my real estate on the shaded bench. Just being
away from the office was relaxing, although the *Imitator*'s opening scene was doing nothing to allay my fear about being alone in
the office in the morning. Those hang-up calls had increased dramatically in frequency and were now occurring almost every day,
spooking whichever one of us was on the early shift. Dagney and
I had started a log, noting each call on a piece of paper we kept
in a place of honor on the floor, listing the date and exact time of
each one. I insisted on doing this so that someday the FBI could
nab the perpetrator. Dagney had rolled her eyes at me when I'd
first suggested we keep track, but after a couple of mornings
alone she'd begun to add to the list as well. The calls always came
in between 7:15 and 7:30, and although the caller seemed to

have a different voice each time, the exchange was always the same: "Is Allegra Orecchi in?"

"Yes, may I say who's calling?"

Click.

Geraldine, displaying her characteristic interest in our welfare, turned a deaf ear when I asked if she could alert the police so that they might be able to tap the phone, or even come in and listen—the precinct was right around the corner from our office.

"Really Karen, I'm sure it's nothing. If you're that worried, just stay low when you're near the windows."

I still believed that the calls just might be connected to Hanratty, although what he wanted with Allegra was beyond me. No one in Publicity had seen or heard from him in months, and it appeared likely that he'd given up the effort, as most of the Glorious people had predicted he would. The whole story was intriguing—a puzzle that I needed to figure out. Why would he have helped Phil and Tony in the beginning, only to be shunned by them, then vow to tell everyone the truth but not carry out the threat? I would have loved to read a biography of the Waxmans, and was willing to bet that a lot of other people would, too.

My reverie was interrupted by a phone call from Robert. "How are you, man?" he said, in a dead-on impression of Charlie. I started to laugh.

"What are you up to?"

"I'm pulling together the Jimmy Chin event we're putting on at Planet Hollywood next week. It's going to be tremendous."

"Do you think anyone here has heard of him?"

"No, and that's the whole point of the event. It's going to be a sort of ceremony welcoming Jimmy into the society of action stars."

"How does that work?" I was totally lost.

"Like you said, not too many people in the U.S. know Jimmy Chin. But they certainly know Ronald Ululater and Fly Faccione.

And if Ronald and Fly present Jimmy as one of their own, he's in like Chin," Robert said, clearly pleased with himself.

I saw how the event would be an exceptionally astute way to bring instant street cred to Jimmy. Frederick "Fly" Faccione had risen to considerable fame and fortune first for his portrayal of an underdog boxer who won the hearts of a nation, and later as a vigilante Vietnam vet. Ronald Ululater, a European former body-builder, had immigrated to the United States and appeared to be checking off boxes on a vast to-do list specifically geared toward making him wealthy, famous, and powerful. He'd starred in countless movies as the force with which others had to reckon. For the action movie crowd, Jimmy's induction into this elite club would be a momentous occasion, on par with the day Superman and Batman invited the Flash to join the Justice League.

Using established actors and directors to anoint one another was a method that Phil Waxman had honed into a razor-sharp tool, cutting out the tiresome and often costly process of building new talent film by film. In this way, movie audiences could take the word of people they already admired, and Phil could attach some very big names to much smaller projects in which they ordinarily never would have been involved.

"But what about the premiere guests? Are they going to want to turn out for Jimmy?" The glittering crowd who attended our New York premieres seemed unlikely to give an unknown star much of a chance. They had dragons for hors d'oeuvres, then turned their skin into expensive handbags.

"We're not even bothering with them. It's going to be all radio contest winners, Morning Zoo DJs and the kinds of people who'll be excited about going to a party like this."

"Robert, you amaze me."

"Where are you?" he asked. "I thought maybe you and Oliver had run away together."

"I couldn't do that to Dagney," I said. "And besides, Oliver ditched me hours ago. I'm at the *Imitator* test. We just screened the director's cut. It's almost identical to Tony's, but the crowd was much more frightened. I can't figure it out."

"Keep your eye on the beaker," Robert said. "I overheard someone in Tony's office talking about it yesterday."

At four I was in the back of the theater, once again flanked by Tony and the director. The sleeve hit the beaker and sent it flying.

"Damn!" the actress said on screen.

"Fuck," Tony snarled under his breath.

"Madre de dios," the director whispered.

None of us breathed as the beaker began its silent plunge. It rotated six times in slow motion before smashing. The actress leaned down, much more quickly in this version, and then—2:43 and the place exploded in terror. We had another near-unanimous scream. The director grinned and gave Tony the finger before the two of them walked outside. I followed a couple of paces behind to eavesdrop.

"When it spins six times, it is much scarier, as I told you it would be," the director said. "Four spins, like you had it, and *nada*."

Tony grunted. Then he reached over, gently pulled the director's braid, and clapped him on the back as they exited the theater together, arms around each other's shoulders.

The next morning, Allegra had Dagney send around an office-wide e-mail announcing that she and I would now be in charge of the department's interns, owing to Robert's increased workload. I knew that Robert had asked for a promotion and hoped that e-mail would come soon.

Dagney and I were ecstatic; we'd both been dying for some additional responsibility, and immediately started making plans to kick the intern program up a notch or two, although Robert would be hard to match as a recruiter and trainer of interns. Under his leadership we'd had an army of kids who were ready, willing, and even able to do whatever was asked of them, and they always developed a ferocious loyalty to him. I thought it was a variation of Stockholm Syndrome—he sort of broke them down and rebuilt them. Certainly his example would be an inspiring, if also somewhat intimidating, act to follow.

The two of us were so excited about our new area of influence that we were getting along like a house on fire. We made lists, drew up charts, and created plans for an operation that would certainly let us bite off more than we could ever chew. Robert came over to our desk to drop off an enormous three-ring binder of notes and articles he'd collected and consulted from time to time. It was filled with everything from Dear Abby to Sun Tzu, each page carefully encased in a plastic sheet protector.

"You know, it's not going to be as easy as you think," he said.

"What's so hard about it?" Dagney asked. She generally didn't have much patience for Robert's "he who has it all figured out" routine. Today, he was getting under her skin like a sand flea. Robert, ever vigilant, decided it was a good time to leave us to our new responsibility. "You'll see," he said, nodding sagely before disappearing down the hall.

Aside from Oliver and Trisha, there were seven other interns in our department this summer. Three were connecteds, three were regulars, and one was on exchange from a Glorious producing partner in London. Robert had done a great job with this group, and I was impressed by how quickly they'd become accustomed to the various executives' quirks and peculiarities, which was key at Glorious. He had received almost no complaints about them, and the intern program was definitely a "no news is good news" operation: now it was up to Dagney and me to keep it that way. We were keenly aware that any disruption would be seen as our failure, and that we would be held accountable.

We decided that the best way to take up our new responsibilities was to speak with each intern individually to determine their interests and hear what they would like to accomplish in the remaining half of the summer. Of course, Oprah's impending phone call prevented both Dagney and me from leaving the desk at the same time, and neither of us trusted the other to fully ascertain the situation on her own. We agreed that on Friday afternoon we would alternate speaking with each intern for ten minutes apiece in Oliver's sure-to-be-empty cube, after which we'd compare notes. We didn't really need to interview Oliver, since his goal—to spend the least amount of time in the office possible—was more than obvious, but Dagney scheduled ten minutes with him anyway. I felt good about my interviews, but also a little bittersweet; after all, this was just the sort of conversation I'd so desperately wished someone would have with me about my own career direction at Glorious.

The consensus among the interns was that they were enjoying themselves so far, but every one of them wanted to feel more included in the department and what was happening within it. Most of all, the kids wanted to be acknowledged by the people they reported to once in a while. Our free labor force definitely heard about the things they did incorrectly—but what about the things they did right? Charlotte, the intern from London, put it best when she said, "They give you the bloody silent treatment unless you really balls it up. But do something right, and you don't get so much as a thank-you."

Dagney and I tried to be diplomatic, but we couldn't realistically envision their situations improving. Instead, we decided to go out of our way to thank the interns ourselves, and see if we could get some of the other junior publicity staff to follow suit. Unfortunately, all of Glorious Pictures worked on the Waxman Management Model—the brothers ran roughshod over everyone who reported to them directly, and the department heads, in turn, treated their own staff like dirt. When you got down to the assistant and intern level, things were pretty grim. It was the trickle-down theory, except at Glorious it actually worked. Nevertheless, in our small way, Dagney and I decided to buck the trend: we started off our Intern Appreciation Series by giving some deli flowers to Trisha, including a little note that said, "Hey Trisha, Thanks for doing such a great job! We appreciate you! Karen and Dagney."

Trisha had told us that she enjoyed Publicity, but that she really wanted to get into Development. As an aspiring screenwriter, she was anxious to learn about that part of the business. I told her that it sounded like an excellent plan and secretly, I envied her confidence. But Development was not an easy department to join; jobs there were scarce and fiercely guarded. To make matters worse, the development department at Glorious Pictures was run by a tigress of a woman named Yvonne Stapleton. Yvonne was something of a legend at our company: she'd scrambled up the corporate ladder with astonishing speed and at twenty-seven ran her department with an iron claw. A favorite of both Phil and Tony's, she had joined the company only two years earlier. Now she had a string of hit films to her credit, and some others to her credit that she'd had nothing to do with whatsoever.

While she'd always been difficult, Yvonne had been recently promoted to off-the-charts impossible. During a faux-smoking break, Sabrina, still holding down the fort in Phil's office, told me that Yvonne had attended her UCLA reunion a couple of months earlier and discovered that she was the last unmarried Tri-Delt from her year. Phil and Tony were furiously rifling through their Rolodexes for eligible bachelors and setting her up on a flurry of blind dates, but their efforts had yet to yield a viable candidate. To make matters worse, a lot of the setting-up was left to the assistants, who resented having to arrange dates for Yvonne on top of the million other things they had to do each day. So now Yvonne was suffering the double whammy of being the only single Tri-Delt *and* having everyone know that her bosses were trying to find a husband for her. When Trisha told us that she had her sights set on Development, Dagney and I knew that we couldn't be of much use; even Robert couldn't help her. We were all too junior to approach Yvonne, and, since it was such an unsavory prospect, none of us even wanted to try. I was confident, though, that Trisha would somehow figure it out on her own, and after conferring with Dagney, decided to leave it at that.

Tuesday threatened rain, and as I got ready for work, I had a sense of foreboding that I just couldn't shake. It was Dagney's morning to go in early, so I lingered at home for a while, not in any rush to get downtown and start my work day. When I finally stepped off the elevator I could hear Vivian on the phone, telling some poor soul that she needed an awning to cover the platform that had been erected on the street outside Planet Hollywood, and that there would be hell to pay if any of the world's most famous action stars felt even a single drop of rain. I was surprised she didn't know who to call to simply eliminate the possibility of precipitation.

As I slumped into my chair, Dagney gave me the rundown on what had already taken place this morning. Hang-up guy had called, there were plenty of Hits, and Allegra was in a meeting with her pillow.

Late in the afternoon, when I took a Town Car with Clark and Trisha to Planet Hollywood, it was obvious that Robert's plan had worked perfectly—if the ninety-seventh caller had won tickets to the party, numbers one through ninety-six had shown up to line the streets around Planet Hollywood in an attempt to see Fly and Ronald, as well as catch their first glimpse of Jimmy. The platform, with its very secure-looking awning, was completely surrounded by screaming fans who filled the street for a block in both directions. I was on "general crowd control," a perfect job for a five-foot-tall woman equipped with a cell phone and high heels. Perhaps I would be introduced as the newest superhero—SpinGirl.

Phil was at the microphone, blowing into it. When he was convinced that he could be heard he said, "We're here tonight to welcome the best export from China since dim sum. But first, I'm going to turn this over to a couple of fine gentlemen who you may already know."

I waded through the crowd, angling for a position where I could see the stage. Phil held out an arm in a gesture of welcome. First Fly came out and said a few words, then he introduced Ronald, who said many more words in the accent that everyone from stand-up comics to news anchors loved to imitate. The fans in the street screamed for their heroes, jumping up and down and craning their necks to get a better look. Then Fly and Ronald jointly introduced the guest of honor, who back-flipped from the street onto the stage. Jimmy, who was slight of build, took his place between Fly, who was taller than Jimmy but still not very tall, and Ronald, who was the size of a building. Crouching slightly, he leapt into the air, landing with his right foot on Fly's left shoulder and his left foot on Ronald's right one. The two of them looked up at Jimmy in amazement before he triple-flipped down again, landing just in front of them on the stage. Then all three waved to the crowd and went into the party.

Tonight's event was much more casual than usual, so we hadn't been given hard and fast assignments. The guests at the party were a mix of contest winners, people who were going to be involved in Jimmy's American career, several teenaged children of Glorious executives, and many of Fly's and Ronald's friends and relatives. Gloria was there, and Clark snapped a pin-up style photo of her, one hand placed coquettishly behind her head as she was held aloft across the arms of Fly, Jimmy, and Ronald. "Thank you, boys," she said, kissing each one on the cheek and giggling before Clark led her off in search of another cocktail.

Seeing that I didn't have anything particular to do, Allegra cornered me. "That's Fly's chair," she whispered, pointing to a vacant seat at the head of an empty table. "You need to make sure that no one else sits in it."

Fly was deep in animated conversation with Phil, at Tony's table.

"He's not there, and there's a RESERVED sign on it."

"You need to make sure no one else sits in it," she repeated, before walking away.

I found a spot from which I could keep an eye on both the chair and the party and stood there for a while, just looking around. Fly wasn't going anywhere near his seat, it was getting late, and this was a complete waste of my time. After taking a few careful looks around and determining that Allegra had already left, I slipped out and headed home.

The next morning, Oliver materialized, two hours late, looking a little haggard after a night of hard partying; he was still wearing the same clothes that he'd had on at Planet Hollywood the previous evening. Despite his fatigue, however, he was clearly bursting with news, and now that Dagney and I were running the intern program, we were the ones he chose to tell first. As Oliver approached our desk, I could see Dagney straighten up and instinctively run a hand through her hair. She smiled, a genuine, friendly smile.

"Hey babes," he said, ambling over. I could see why Dagney liked him so much—even on no sleep and not smelling particularly good, his charisma was completely intact. "I have to tell you guys something. I'm really sorry, but, today's going to be my last day."

Dagney eyes opened in shock. "But there's half the summer left," she said plaintively.

"Yeah, I know. But I really need to just kick back and take some time off. School just ended, and my dad's been talking about some kind of job for me in the fall."

Dagney was nodding, unable to speak.

"That's too bad for us," I said. "You'll certainly be missed."

I thanked him and then wrote the information on Allegra's phone sheet. She had Dagney order a cake from the Magnolia Bakery and at five that afternoon the entire department gathered in the conference room to toast Oliver. Allegra, who'd decided to use her voice a second time, said, "Oliver, we can't thank you enough for your incredible contribution and dedication this summer." Dagney found a spot right next to Oliver and busily helped cut the mocha-flavored layer cake, while mentioning that she might be spending a weekend on Nantucket before the end of the summer.

"Really?" Oliver said. "That's great. I'll tell you some cool places you can hang out."

Dagney's face fell for a second before she caught herself. "I'm going to take you up on that," she said, smiling flirtatiously.

The next afternoon I was frantically rereading *Entertainment Weekly* to find an item on *Imitator* that Allegra was positive had run. This was my third time through and I still couldn't find it, but I didn't relish reporting my apparent failure. Dagney's phone rang and she answered it and spoke briefly before hanging up. She turned to me with a puzzled look and said, "That was Marsha, Yvonne's assistant. She said that Yvonne is on her way over here and that she's furious. She wanted to know if I knew why."

A moment later, we heard someone kick open the door that separated Publicity from the rest of the floor—kick it so hard that the knob smashed into the wall and cracked the plaster. A pile of newspaper clippings from Robert's "To Be Filed" tray went flying into the air, and Yvonne appeared. She marched past Clark's desk, arms pinned to her sides, and came tearing through our maze so fast that we could almost see sparks coming off her calf-leather driving mocs. Then she came to a stop in front of Kimberly and Trisha's desk. Kimberly's face immediately drained of all color. Trisha had her phone headset on and didn't know anything was up until Yvonne reached over with a long-nailed finger and tapped her on the shoulder.

"Did you write me this letter?" she asked, brandishing a piece of cream-colored paper.

Trisha blinked. "Yes, I did," she answered, nervously.

"What makes you think you can just *write* me a letter?" Yvonne asked, her voice rising.

I looked at Dagney and shrugged. Eyes wide, she shrugged back. Unconsciously, I moved my chair closer to hers. Minute 2:43 of *Imitator* had nothing on what was happening right in front of me.

"So you think *you* can just write *me* a letter?" Yvonne said, even shriller now. She started reading aloud in a nasty, mocking voice, "'Dear Ms. Stapleton, I'm an intern in the publicity department but I'd really like to learn about development. Do you have any recommendations for how I might do this? Thank you, Trisha Sadowsky.'"

"*You* writing *me?*" Yvonne was leaning toward Trisha now, really getting in her face. "Do you think I'm your *friend*? Just because I'm incredibly successful and close to your age doesn't mean that *you* can just *pick up a pen* and *write me a letter*!"

I needed some air. I'd been trying to make a subtle exit but the damn phones just kept ringing and I had to answer them. I wanted to be anywhere else in the world but there, listening to Yvonne ripping Trisha, our perfectly nice intern, into a million tiny pieces. All of a sudden I was praying silently, "Please God, make this stop." But it wasn't nearly over. Yvonne had an audience and was making the most of it.

I tried to give Trisha a comforting look, but Yvonne, positively trembling with self-righteous rage, was blocking my line of sight. I could see only that Trisha's feet were up on her chair, as if she were trying to protect herself by curling into a ball. Maybe she was trying to play dead.

"Well, *Trisha*," Yvonne continued, "here's my advice about getting into Development. Don't *ever* write to someone who is *much more important than you'll ever be*!"

Yvonne gave a kind of withering half-smile to Vivian, who had come outside of her cube to watch the show, and then she took off down the hall, stopping only to give Robert's file cabinet a kick for good measure. He started to gasp but wisely converted it into a cough. The door slammed again, and we sat in stunned silence as her stomping faded into the distance.

I looked back over at Trisha. Her head was in her hands, and her back shook with uncontrollable sobs. Kimberly looked relieved and even a little smug that for once she wasn't the one in trouble. I really wanted to go and talk to Trisha, just to see if I could help her calm down, but I knew from my wealth of Glorious experience that now was not the time to do anything. The all-clear had not yet been sounded. I turned my attention back to my desk and asked Dagney to coordinate the incoming phone calls of the last ten minutes with me so that we could be on time with Allegra's new call sheet. The whole episode had me seriously shaken and I needed to settle down and try to get back on course.

Then I heard, "Trisha. Trisha. Trisha. Come in here right now," from the next cube. I'm not sure why Vivian bothered taking Trisha behind closed doors—it wasn't as if we all weren't going to hear every word, anyway.

"I don't know why you did something like that. Can you tell me why, Trisha?" Vivian sounded like a stern kindergarten teacher speaking to a child who had drawn on the wall. I heard Trisha sniffling.

"I was reading a career book that said that you should write a polite note to someone if you were interested in what they did," she explained.

Oh, shit. Glorious wasn't a *What Color Is Your Parachute?* type of place. It was more likely that they had packed you the old, ripped one for your jump. This was the one thing neither Dagney nor I had thought to explain to the interns; they were here in the service of the department, and if they learned something during their stay it was just a happy accident. Had we misled them into thinking that the executives actually gave a damn about their futures or their interests? "Trisha," Vivian said, "I know you meant well, but that was just so stupid. Yvonne was right. You can't just write her a letter. You're an intern, you don't just go around writing letters whenever you feel like it. How can we trust you if you're going to go around writing letters?"

Not only did she say everyone's name three times, Vivian had to make her point at least seven times. After an excruciating five minutes of this, Vivian finally uttered the words we'd all been dreading: "Get your things and go." Tricia got fired for writing a letter—for "embarrassing the publicity department," as Vivian put it.

Kimberly had already decided to be unfriendly toward this presumptuous outsider who had done us all such a gross injustice. Brusquely she helped Trisha pack, tossing her things into an empty toilet paper box, including the now exhausted-looking flowers. I was touched that Tricia had held onto them, but also stricken. Dagney and I had been so excited about working with the interns; now it just seemed like another thing I'd gotten wrong—only this time at tremendous expense to someone else.

Trisha was sobbing again, gulping great lungfuls of air as she collected the last of her things and stumbled through the rickety maze of cubes. Everyone in the department was back at their desks, acting busy, and no one raised his or her head to say goodbye. "Wait up," I said softly. "At least come and splash some water on your face."

Trisha followed me into the bathroom, and I held the box while she was at the sink. Then I rode the elevator down with her, hailed a cab, and helped her inside. I told her not to worry. But I was the worried one. I'd believed Clark when he'd said that my early run-in with Vivian had been just a ritualistic hazing. Now, five months later, I understood how easily I could have lost my job, and how precarious my position actually was.

I got back into the elevator, took it to the top floor, climbed the staircase to the roof, and sat down, leaning on the parapet. I hadn't been back up there since my visit with Clark, in the dead of winter; now the air was heavy and close. From where I was perched, I could see part of the Statue of Liberty through TriBeCa's old factory buildings and new high-rise apartment towers. I could see the side of her torch and a couple of the prongs on her crown. I thought about countries where people were sent to jail for writing letters, and I thought about what I had just seen—two ugly, abusive displays of power, guaranteed to poison anyone who witnessed them with a paralyzing fear. Tricia had been assaulted by a monster right before our eyes, and not a single person had screamed. In the following months I'd revisit that day in my memory again and again.

CELEBRITY

At six in the morning, I carried my recyclables to the curb, already wearing my black silk dress and a pair of sling-backs. In deference to the cooling weather I'd added a black sweater, which I tied around my shoulders. It was hard to find evening clothes that worked from dawn into day into evening into late night, so over the past eight months I'd amassed a collection of wraps, sparkly cardigans, and a velvet cloak to use as layering pieces.

As I stood next to a stack of bound newspapers for a moment, trying to remember which color bin was the one for glass and plastics, I made a mental note to put an extra pair of stockings in my handbag, just in case. I had a long day ahead of me—first the Hits, then setting up for the *Anyone Can Sing* premiere screening, and finally over to the East Side townhouse where the benefit gala was being held. As I reentered the lobby, I ran through a checklist in my mind, trying to make sure I'd thought of everything I'd need for the day and night ahead.

While I was waiting for the elevator a tenant came up behind me, back from the dog run; I recognized her as the middle-aged nurse who'd moved in shortly after I had. When I bent down to pat her sweet-looking cocker spaniel, she suddenly tugged his leash so I couldn't reach him. "Does he bite?" I asked. "No," she replied curtly, pulling the dog away when the elevator door opened. "We'll wait for the next one," she said, to no one in particular. Did she think I was just coming back from an illicit encounter? If only. Outside of the footsie I'd played with Elliott, I hadn't had anything resembling a real date in months. Although that was about to change, I hoped. Elliott had called yesterday and asked if I'd be at the premiere. Perhaps we'd get a drink together afterward.

As my colleagues arrived in the office, each one of them looked ready for a glamorous evening out, although it was still hours before lunch. Dagney was wearing a clingy knit wrap dress, and Robert looked dashing in a charcoal double-breasted suit. It would have seemed more sensible to wear our regular clothes and get dressed up later on, but we'd learned from experience that we couldn't count on having a chance to transform ourselves. Too many unexpected things came up on premiere days, and no one wanted to have to change in a taxi. To a casual observer, the scene would have appeared bizarre—a group of people who looked far more suited to a cocktail party making photocopies and sending faxes, all speaking into headsets. For us, though, it was completely normal—Glorious's slate of films was so large that we often did this once or twice a week.

By ten thirty, our phones were ringing off the hook. It seemed that the collective unconscious of the uninvited had just awoken and been psychically directed to call Allegra Orecchi's office and make their last appeals to be included in the festivities. I apologized as politely as I could to the offended and transferred anyone I thought was a possibility to Vivian, so that she could make the final decision. *Anyone Can Sing* was "her" film, and she was in charge of the evening.

Gulping down my first coffee of the morning, I grabbed another ringing phone. "Allegra Orecchi's office," I said briskly.

"Hello, my name is Deirdre Williams," a woman said. "I'm calling on behalf of the Person." The Person was an eccentric and reclusive musician who changed his name every few years. Lately he'd taken to using a kind of petroglyph to represent himself and insisted that there was no way to pronounce it. The kinder media started referring to him as "the Person" and the name stuck, even with the people around him. I had a vision of him standing in a burning building. Everyone called out to him by his former name while he stubbornly shook his head and refused to leave.

"Right," I said. "How can I help you?" I was sure it was a prank.

"Well," she continued, "the Person is in New York City today, and he just called me because he was watching *Live with Regis*—"

"Okay, who is this?" I interrupted, positive now that it was Abby, Ellen, or maybe even Elliott. "If you'd picked some other show, I might have believed you. You're funny, but I'm really busy here."

The woman sighed. "No, I really do work with the Person, and he saw Emily Downes on *Live* this morning and assumed she must be in New York."

Maybe this woman was for real. I knew that Emily Downes, most recently seen in *The Foreign Pilot*, was in town touting a film she'd made for Paramount. Because of her close affiliation with Glorious, we got phone calls about her all the time, even when she was working for another studio. "Yes, Emily is in New York," I said cautiously. "She's doing some media for a film."

"Well, I called because I figured someone at Glorious would know how to get in touch with her," Deirdre said. "The Person would really like to see her while he's here." I was still recovering from the image of the Person, perhaps reclining in his famous orange paisley pajamas with a cup of tea, watching the show that enthralled millions of American housewives each morning. The chirpy, canary-like banter of *Live*'s cohosts reminded me of that weird medical anomaly in which exposure to a certain vocal pitch causes a seizure.

But then a lightbulb blinked on in my brain. The Person rarely attended public events—if it really *was* him, this would be a tremendous coup for the premiere. "You know, I'm not sure that we'd be able to track her down today, but Emily's definitely going to be at the premiere of *Anyone Can Sing* tonight," I offered, emboldened by my quick thinking. "If the Person would like to come, we'd love to have him."

"Oh, right, the new Buddy Friedman musical," she said. "The Person doesn't really like Buddy's films, and he's not usually interested in parties. But I'll find out. He's not what you'd call predictable," she said, without a trace of irony.

We hung up and I immediately turned to Dagney and told her that I'd just invited the Person to the premiere. Dagney, who was always pretty tough to impress, looked awestruck for about fifteen seconds before she reassembled her features into their usual blasé expression. "Is he definitely coming?" she asked.

"She's calling me back," I said. "Can you believe he was watching *Regis*?" I was still enjoying the image of the smoldering rock star channel-surfing, halting his search as he became mesmerized by a segment on quick and easy no-bake desserts, when my phone rang again. It was Deirdre. "The Person would like to attend," she said. "Can he bring his bodyguard?"

"No problem, but that's got to be it. We're packed tonight." My heart was beating a mile a minute, but I tried to act casual. The Person was a great get, and he'd landed right in my lap. "The screening is at the Paris Theatre at eight, and the after-party is at Dr. Rich's townhouse immediately following, probably around ten," I told her. "Where should I send the tickets?"

"You can send them to the concierge at the Four Seasons and put them under the name Michael Mitchell. He'll take it from there, but you need to put the exact addresses and cross streets in a note for him. He'll use it to coordinate his security plan." When I asked for Michael's cell phone to confirm the delivery, she let out a little sigh. "I'm afraid we have certain communication issues here. Michael doesn't let anyone have his cell phone number. I'll have him call you, all right?" I took her number also, just in case there were problems. I hoped to God there wouldn't be.

Hanging up, I leapt out of my chair and sprinted into Vivian's office, unable to contain myself. "Vivian, the Person is coming tonight!" I babbled. "I invited him, and his person said he's coming!"

This, of course, was a total lapse in judgment. Vivian was at her desk, comparing the list of invitees to the list of RSVPs. Deciding to ignore my breach in etiquette in favor of the decidedly more pleasurable opportunity to ignore me altogether, she asterisked a couple of names, put slashes through a few others, and wrote a note to herself in the margin before finally addressing me without raising her eyes.

"He never comes. We've done this a dozen times before, and it's always the same." She adjusted her glasses and frowned down at her lists. "They put us through an annoying process about where to send the tickets and how he has to have a bodyguard, and then he doesn't show." She finally looked up at me, her face full of pity. This was her "some people never learn" look, and she was seizing the first real opportunity I'd given her to show it to me in a while.

I returned to my desk, trying my best not to feel deflated. Maybe they'd invited him before and he hadn't shown, but this time the Person had had *his* person call *us*. Why couldn't she see that after more than eight months on the job, I had a reasonable handle on what it was we did? I looked over at Kimberly, who was fully absorbed in meticulously decorating paper signs for the back of the celebs' seats. She had a knack for turning even the most basic task into a colossal art project, but perhaps that was what happened when your only major responsibility was the soup list. I was surprised that she hadn't died of boredom over the summer, when every single restaurant had offered either gazpacho or cold fruit consommé. I picked up a Sharpie and made a sign for the Person, trying my best to approximate his petroglyph. It looked like a bear with an extra pair of arms. Then I made another that said "GUEST OF" and managed a slightly better version. Posted on the outside of Vivian's cube was the latest tip sheet so that whoever needed it could fax it around. It was being updated nearly every ten minutes and was loaded with A-listers. "Hey, Kim, I've got another one for you." I couldn't help myself.

Vivian, with her bionic hearing, heard me from across the hallway, where she was badgering Robert about something. "Don't add the Person, Kimberly," she shouted. "He's not going to come."

I glared in the direction of Vivian's cubicle. It was clear that she would rather not have a major name like the Person at her premiere than risk seeing me rewarded. She was the kind of executive who clung to the status quo like a mountain climber to a finger hold. Distracted from her task, Kimberly was now eyeing me impatiently, a glitter pen halted about three inches above her current work. "Karen, this is important. What if we all look stupid?" I noticed that she was cocking her head in exactly the same way Vivian did, and I wanted to stuff that pen, along with her beloved silver marker, right up her button nose. Kimberly had two distinct modes—forlorn serf or enthusiastic lieutenant in Vivian's army. I'd obviously missed reveille this morning.

Miserably, I grabbed my bag and headed to the elevator. Somewhere between the phone call from Deirdre and Vivian's insults I'd run my hose, and I'd forgotten to pack a spare pair after my early encounter with Nurse Ratchett. I thought I'd multitask by replacing them and rearranging my attitude before going uptown, since I was going to have to spend the rest of the day and most of the night with these people. Not to mention that I wanted to be in a reasonably good mood for Elliott. When the elevator door slid open and I saw Eddie Di Silva inside, I started to feel positively cursed. As usual, he just held his hand up in the "Stop" position as the door slid closed.

I jabbed the down button again and waited. This time, the door opened to reveal Tony Waxman, who *did* let people share the elevator with him, but strictly at their own peril. Looking offended that his ride down had been delayed, he reached across me and started punching the DOOR CLOSE button over and over with his fist. The first time I'd been in an elevator with Tony, he'd nearly knocked me flat in his hurry to be the first one out, even though he was standing way in the back. This time I preemptively pinned myself to the side of the car as we approached the lobby; as soon as the door opened, he bolted like a rodeo bull who'd just been shocked with a prod.

I walked around Glorious's neighborhood, looking for a place to buy a pair of pantyhose. After a few blocks I gave up. This was one of the problems with TriBeCa—you could easily find five different types of Gruyère, but if you were looking for something an average person might need—like a birthday card, or new hose—it was nowhere to be found. Deciding I'd have better luck closer to the theater, I hailed a taxi.

I got out of the cab at Fifty-Ninth and Fifth, and for a moment I just stood, enjoying the surroundings. This part of the city always cheered me up. It was a gorgeous day and the hansom carriages were lined up at the south entrance to Central Park, which was showing the very first hints that autumn was on its way. The flags flying from the Plaza snapped in the breeze and droplets of water from the fountain in front caught the sun, looking like tiny gems before they disappeared into the pool below. This was the very same corner where at the end of *The Way We Were* Barbra Streisand had told Robert Redford that her life had turned out just great without him, and then the music had surged. I lingered for a little while longer before scurrying into Bergdorf's, where I grabbed a pair of pantyhose, winced at the price, and got in line to pay.

While waiting for my charge slip the cashier frowned for a moment before saying, "I'm sorry, but your American Express card has been declined." I felt my cheeks burn, and heard titters from the Park Avenue Princesses in line behind me; it took all my self-restraint not to blurt out: "But that's impossible! There must be some mistake!" Instead, I meekly paid in cash. As soon as I was outside, I called AmEx to see what had happened. The customer service representative told me that "my recent charges had put me over my acceptable spending limit." That didn't make any sense. I hadn't used my card since I bought Ellen's birthday present last month, and that had been a $150 cappuccino machine from Macy's Cellar.

"Hey, isn't this the card without a limit?" I asked. "Technically, yes, Ms. Jacobs," the representative replied, a hint of disapproval in his voice. "But when a cardmember spends more money than is available in their checking and savings accounts combined, we have no choice but to freeze the card. You don't have seventeen thousand dollars," he finished.

I certainly didn't. "I really don't understand. Is it possible there's some kind of error?"

"Well, it could be a case of fraud. Did you give your card to the Pierre Hotel in New York City for any reason?"

Instantly, I realized what had happened. "There's a mistake, but it's not yours," I said, hanging up. Last week I'd gotten a call from the harried assistant to Erica Hall, an actress and former Buddy Friedman muse who had come to New York for a meeting with Phil. When they'd arrived at the Pierre, at two A.M., there was no record of Glorious's having paid for their rooms. Unwilling to use their own credit cards to check in, they'd phoned me, the "emergency contact" listed on their itinerary. I'd given the hotel clerk my card number over the phone, asking him to hold it until the Glorious travel desk contacted him. The next morning I'd called our travel person and been assured that the situation would be corrected.

I couldn't imagine what two women in town for three days had charged to their rooms that could have approached that total, but it wasn't important right now. I'd straighten it out tomorrow.

By the time I got to the Paris, most of the others had arrived. Dagney and Kimberly lost no time asking me for cigarettes: I now had a pack-a-day faux-smoking habit, thanks to the constant bumming of my coworkers. While the two of them puffed away, Clark and I started setting up. I'd just taped the first sign to a seatback when my phone rang. A terse voice greeted me. "This is Michael Mitchell. Deirdre said you were sending the tickets for tonight's premiere to the Person. They're not here yet."

I started to tell Michael that we were thrilled the Person was coming and that I'd find out where his tickets were, but before I could get the words out he'd already hung up. Praying that they weren't lost in transit, I called the messenger service and was assured that delivery had already been made to the Four Seasons. Ringing the hotel's operator, I asked to speak with Michael Mitchell. "I'm sorry," he replied. "Mr. Mitchell's room is strictly 'do not disturb,' and he specifically asked us not to take messages." Wonderful. I asked to be transferred to the concierge, who told me that he had the tickets at his desk, but that he'd been forbidden to phone the Person or to knock on his door.

I couldn't believe what I was hearing. All that was preventing the Person from coming to the premiere was the fact that his staff didn't allow anyone to speak with them and they hadn't thought to call the concierge for their tickets. There was something extremely comical about the whole situation, and had I been in a better mood I might have appreciated it. As it was, my bruised ego could be salved only by the presence of the Person. I needed to see the look on Vivian's face when he exited his car and coolly sashayed down the red carpet before taking the seat designated by his symbol.

Taking a deep breath, I phoned Deirdre, hoping that somehow we could sort out the confusion. "Deirdre, I need you to just do me one favor. If the Person's not coming tonight, will you please call and let me know?" I asked.

"That's a little tough," she replied. "The way it works here is that only four people are allowed to speak to the Person, and I'm not one of them. I'm not even sure who the four are exactly, but Michael Mitchell has contact with one." And here I'd been thinking that Glorious Pictures was the most dysfunctional organization on the planet.

"Can you *please* just ask someone to call and let me know that the Person or his people have received the tickets? We really need to know on this end." Exasperation was making my voice squeak.

"I'll try," Deirdre said, "but you won't know for sure until you see him, or you don't."

She hung up.

I watched as Vivian inspected the pile of headsets for tonight, quizzing Clark about the freshness of the batteries. I knew that she and Marlene thought the whole idea that I'd invited the Person to the premiere was extremely hilarious. Vivian kept asking me if I'd heard from him, making me feel like the last kid in second grade who still believed in Santa Claus.

"I sent the tickets, and they say he's coming," I answered, trying to be offhand. At that moment I found the two of them so utterly loathsome that I began to wish for torrential rain, the only thing that truly spelled disaster at a premiere.

I spent the next couple of hours taping names to the backs of seats per Vivian's meticulously designed seating chart. It was of utmost importance that the celebrities be seated correctly—near others that they liked and away from those whom they were feuding with or no longer married to. The highest-ranking stars present would be seated nearest to Phil and Tony in a kind of symbiotic acknowledgment of achievement. It was also important that the film's cast be seated on the aisle, so they could exit quickly as soon as the lights went down: no one actually watched their own movie at a premiere.

As showtime drew near, a large crush of photographers were milling around in the press pen, and another twenty or so television and radio outlets were set up along the carpet, along with some "select" media that were allowed inside the theater's lobby. We'd distributed a new, revised tip sheet to the press listing the names of those who would be attending. Late RSVPs were noted in bold, and those who had let us know that they were not coming had been quietly deleted. Tonight's list had the media rapturously excited. *Anyone Can Sing*'s cast could have filled an entire issue of the *Star*, loaded with actors from film and television, many of whom had been involved in various excesses, scandals, and affairs. All of them would be here tonight, along with anyone else in town we had deemed worthy of an invitation. Vivian had left the Person off the tip sheet.

The biggest buzz tonight was that Buddy Friedman, the film's famously neurotic director, would be bringing his new bride, Mindy. Besides being much younger, Mindy was also his step-niece via his brother's second marriage. It was their first public appearance as man and wife, and the press was positively champing at the bit. Even tonight's limited access had them wriggling with anticipation, and we had issued twice the usual number of press credentials. Before marrying Buddy, Mindy had been a fixture on the New York debutante–party girl scene and had apprenticed in Malcolm Leonard's design studio. She'd left Malcolm's to be an assistant costume designer on *Anyone Can Sing* and moved in with Buddy two weeks after fittings began.

Buddy and Mindy's relationship was the subject of endless speculation. Even though they weren't blood relatives, their coupling had an ick factor that fascinated the public. E! had gotten hold of a home video of Mindy's tenth birthday party and had broadcast it over and over all week. It showed Buddy making monkey faces to cheer up a petulant little Mindy. Apparently the pony she'd been given was not the right color. Mindy's mother was cooing, "Darling, sweetheart, everyone knows that palomino is the new black," but Mindy wasn't buying it. You got the distinct feeling it was the last time Mindy didn't get exactly what she wanted.

I was hoping for the chance to sprint to the bathroom when the Friedmans' limo glided to the curb and Mindy jumped out, flinging her arms wide as if to embrace all the photographers in the pen. They went nuts. She was twirling so they could photograph her gown, a dark emerald green silk with a ridiculously long train, which she was holding up so as not to trip while twirling. She gained a little too much momentum and teetered on her heels for a moment, but Clark jumped forward and took her elbow to steady her.

"It's Malcolm Leonard Couture," she said, before anyone had even asked her. Then she blew kisses with both hands toward the press pen. Her makeup was a modern take on a forties film siren—blood-red lips, high-arched eyebrows, false eyelashes, and even a fake beauty mark strategically placed above the upper-left corner of her mouth. Her shiny mahogany hair was done in a towering updo fastened with twinkling barrettes. The photographers clearly adored her.

Buddy blinked from all the flashes before starting to move rapidly down the carpet. In place of his usually rumpled tux was a stylish suit with pegged pants, making him look like an old Beatle. "Buddy! Buddy! Don't go!" came the shouts from the press people. Mindy reined him in, and together they walked the carpet slowly, making sure to stop and chat with every reporter. If Buddy didn't want to speak, that was fine with his wife; she was happy to do it for both of them. "Yes, Buddy especially enjoyed making this movie because it was filmed in Milan, one of our favorite cities," she told *Extra*. "Well, of course Buddy's not really known for romantic films, or even for musicals, but we started seeing each other just as the film went into production, and I guess some of our romance just seeped in," she told *Access Hollywood*. "We've been *so* happy." Buddy started walking briskly again, this time toward the door of the theater. He made it.

Mindy had just noticed his absence when I heard a new shout from the press pen. The three teenage actresses who played squabbling sisters in *Anyone Can Sing* were making their grand entrance. Each was wearing blinding, whiter-than-white Gucci; the overall effect was stunning. They were each beautiful, but Francesca Davis, the fourteen-year-old who played the middle sister, still managed to out-dazzle the others. This was due partly to luck and bone structure, and partly to the $7,500 hair and makeup job that was performed in her home that afternoon, courtesy of Glorious Pictures. Allegra was furious about the extra expense and was still blaming me for it.

The makeup mess had started early the day before when I answered Allegra's line. "Hello, Gladys Mermelstein for Allegra," a shrill voice said. I was on strictest orders to always put Francesca Davis's mother through, so I patched her over to Allegra's cell. Allegra was occupied at Dr. Rich's, trying to decide where to put the VIP room for the after-party. I hit the mute button to listen in.

"Allegra? Gladys Mermelstein. We need a small favor for tomorrow night."

"Oh, Gladys, of course we'll help you out. What do you need?" I could already hear the worry creeping into Allegra's voice. Francesca was Phil's new favorite, and the Davis-Mermelsteins were milking it for all it was worth. Their demands were becoming more frequent and increasingly expensive, a trend Allegra was trying her best to stem.

"Well, you know that Francesca always wants to look her best for Glorious, and with all the work she's been doing on behalf of this film—I mean, she spent *two hours* with that *People* reporter." Gladys spoke as if being the subject of a fawning *People* cover story was akin to having a root canal.

"Gladys, we're thrilled that Francesca did *People*. What do you need?" Allegra's tone now had a distinct edge.

"I need hair and makeup at the house tomorrow afternoon for Francesca before she leaves for the premiere."

"Okay, no problem, we'll take care of that. Is three o'clock a good time?"

"Actually, Francesca wants Loosey Long for her hair and Randy Bennett for her makeup. Sarah Jessica Parker told us that they're just incredible."

Ouch. Those two cost a fortune.

"Gladys, I doubt that Loosey and Randy are available on such short notice, so why don't I just send someone over who I know is great. We'll get Loosey and Randy for Francesca for the *Pretty Face* junket next month." Allegra was tap dancing fast, but Gladys was holding the big cane.

"Fantastic idea! We'd love to have them for the junket. I hadn't even thought that far ahead, so, wonderful—set that up." Gladys continued, "But the good news is that they're both definitely available for tomorrow. I called their agency and put them on hold."

A short silence.

"Okay, Gladys, I'll have my office make the arrangements. Is three okay?" Allegra's tone had plummeted into the range that only dogs could hear.

"Actually, four is fine. You know my daughter doesn't really need that much work," Gladys said, clicking off.

Allegra phoned me immediately. I focused all my concentration on pretending that I hadn't heard the conversation.

"Karen, how could you put Gladys Mermelstein through to me on the day before a premiere?" she whispered fiercely. "Now I'm going to have to pay a fortune to have Loosey Long and Randy Bennett go to Fort Lee tomorrow afternoon to put lip gloss on Francesca Davis. Why didn't you tell her I was unreachable?"

"Allegra, you told me to make sure you were always 'here' for Francesca's mother," I pleaded, trying hopelessly to defend myself.

"On the day before a premiere, people call us. Because. They. *Want*. Things," she said, enunciating each word. "Give me to Dagney," she whispered through clenched teeth. I put the call on hold, motioned to Dagney and then at the phone. I was too angry to speak.

Now, watching Francesca and the two other actresses glide down the carpet, I realized that while Gladys Mermelstein was a huge pain in the ass, she was an absolutely brilliant manager. The three girls posed together briefly, and then a photographer yelled, "Francesca, can I get one of you alone?" Francesca put on a "Who, me?" expression before quickly taking a step forward from the other girls, who looked rather shocked. "Francesca, let's see your dress!" shouted another photographer, and soon they were all shouting again and clicking away. Clark saw what was going on and whisked the two abandoned young women into the theater.

My designated task for the next part of the evening was to stand near the curb with a headset and announce the arrivals to my colleagues, who would then escort the VIPs to their reserved seats. On our official "Premiere Directives" memo, the job was listed as "spotter." I often had this job at events because, as Allegra once pronounced, "You have a background in news." This was marginally true, so I got the benefit of being left outside in all seasons. The fact was that Phil and Tony were becoming major players in the world of political fund-raisers, lobbying, and philanthropy. Politicians and all types of moguls and scions were invited to Glorious events, and the brothers wanted to ensure that they were treated with respect. There was also the terrifying legend of the publicity assistant at Fox who had denied Rupert Murdoch entrance to a party because she didn't recognize him, even after he'd identified himself. I could be counted on to recognize noncelebrities like the secretary of defense, the former governor of Connecticut, or the CEO of Intel. Tonight we were pretty light on CNN types, and other than spotting the film's cast, I had little to do besides watch and wait. It was 7:58 when I saw a bulletproof limo pull up and heard the shouts.

"Hey, the Person! Over here, the Person! Person, just one!"

The assembled press seemed about to spontaneously combust. My prince had come, after all. Centering my mouthpiece, I triumphantly announced, "The Person has arrived."

The Person, resplendent in skin-tight orange leather, did a quick jog up the length of the carpet. He didn't stop for the photographers, who began to boo him when they realized he wasn't going to hang around. With him was a man with the largest neck I'd ever seen, dressed in black from head to toe and wearing a black knitted hat. He looked like a cat burglar on steroids. He surveyed the press and the fans on the sidewalk and then craned his neck so he could see if there were any snipers atop the marquee. "Are you Michael Mitchell?" I asked him excitedly. "Where are our seats?" came the reply, just as Robert arrived and whisked them both off into the theater.

A few minutes after the film started, most of the cast left quietly so they could primp for the party. Clark and I had planned to grab a quick bite in between, but the film was so short that we had barely put the last celebs in their cars when it was time to head over to the town house, which was in the Seventies, between Madison and Fifth.

Once at the party, I was supposed to spot arrivals again until Elliott showed up, at which point Dagney would take my place so that I could be "on" Elliott. Being on a columnist meant accompanying him during the party and allowing him access only to the celebrities who had told us beforehand that they were willing to speak. If a topic got touchy or the columnist spent more than three minutes or so with any given celeb, we would gently end the conversation. Then, at a previously determined time, the gossip columnist would be escorted "ALL THE WAY TO THE CURB," as stated in bold on our memo. Once I'd asked Clark what the story was with the "all the way to the curb" ritual.

"Well," he said, "one time when Robert was new, he took the guy from *New York* magazine only as far as the door, and Robert assumed that he'd left. The guy came back in and started pestering Uma about some secret tattoo he'd heard she had. The next day, the president of OMG, who's also Uma's personal publicist, called Tony and tried to rip him a new one." Clark gave me one of his signature grins. "Now they need an official 'Elvis has left the building' announcement to be satisfied."

That explained Robert's zealous enforcement of the "to the curb" rule at every premiere. Last week he'd said to me, "I think from now on I'm going to walk my columnist to the corner. You can't be too careful with these people."

Spotting arrivals at a premiere after-party usually went quickly, because most guests arrived at the same time and there was no red carpet or outside press. One of the first arrivals was the Person—or, rather, the bodyguard possibly known as Michael Mitchell. The Person, my person, waited in the limo while the black-clad behemoth went inside. I tiptoed in behind him, and from the enormous foyer of Dr. Rich's townhouse, I watched him perform his security check. He tapped on a couple of the windows and knocked on one of the walls of the first-floor ballroom. He opened a closet door. He picked up a telephone receiver. He walked into the restaurant-sized kitchen, came back outside, and said to me, "Not safe enough."

"Wait," I said. "Are you Michael Mitchell?" He got back into the limo. Then Emily Downes got out of the backseat and bent down to say a final farewell to the Person, before shutting the door and waving him off. But I still had my victory, and the night had taken on a special glow for me. It was one of the rare occasions in my entire Glorious career when I felt able to relax.

A few minutes later Clark was standing next to me, smoking and waiting for Joanna Molloy, half of the husband and wife gossip-columnist team from the *New York Daily News*.

"I know who's happy tonight," he said.

"Who?"

"Come on, Karen. You're on Elliott Solnick. I know you're into him."

"Yeah, maybe, but he's going to hate me after this. You know that almost no one's talking."

"Then that'll give you more time with Elliott. Besides, Francesca, Mindy, and Phil are talking. It's only the major players in the *film* who aren't."

How did Clark know that I was interested in Elliott? I was positive I hadn't told him, or anyone else in the office. Had Dagney noticed my goofy expression when Elliott called? I wasn't going to let on, though, and opted to just stand there and wait.

"Hey, Karen." Elliott was suddenly in front of me. He leaned over and gave me a chaste kiss on the cheek. "Nice shoes," he said, although he didn't sound too convincing. "Let me guess—you're on me tonight, and no one's talking."

Elliott's ability to figure out the situation on the spot impressed me, and in that instant I understood why women fell for James Bond—there's a certain sex appeal in a man who knows exactly what's happening without needing an explanation.

"Well, you're only half right," I told him. "I am on you, but some people are talking,"

"Oh, don't tell me. Mindy Friedman's talking. Francesca Davis is talking. And Tony or Phil."

"Phil," I said. "Correct on the rest. Sorry."

Elliott shook his head, smiling. "Your bosses are such control freaks. What's next for me, a leash?" I could live with that, I thought. I still felt light and a little manic from my victory with the Person. Maybe some of the anxiety that had been hounding me since Trisha's firing was finally lifting.

"Do you think I enjoy my role as official sanctimonious bitch?"

"I think you like it a little," he said, winking as he lit a cigarette.

"How does it work at other studios?" I asked, realizing that I had no idea. My entire view of "normal" had been colored by Glorious. "What are their premieres like?"

"It's the same idea, basically—a movie, a party, stars. But they're not trying to control us so much. I walk around, I talk to a few people, and then I leave. All on my own."

"But then you wouldn't get to hang around with me," I said.

"Maybe, but then I could *choose* to hang around with you. And not feel like Big Brother was looking over my shoulder."

"Brothers," I corrected.

Elliott shook his head and changed the subject. "Karen, I heard a story about Tony's son."

I didn't even know if Tony had a son, but I motioned for him to continue. "Someone told me that the kid was supposed to start college last week, and Tony sent two thugs ahead of time to go into the dorm and guard the better bed and closet, just so Waxman junior's roommate didn't get any ideas about taking them."

"I wouldn't put it past him," I said. "But honestly, I didn't even know that Tony had children."

"Apparently, he keeps it pretty quiet—security and all," Elliott said, before stamping out his cigarette. "Okay, let's go."

I was happy to finally enter the light and the warmth of the party at Elliott's side. Dr. Rich's townhouse had been in her family for three generations and was decorated in a European landed-gentry fantasy of sweeping staircases, glowing chandeliers, old master paintings, and stunning Persian rugs; the various stars huddling in every corner and draped in every doorway only added to the setting's opulence. The Louis XIV furniture had been pushed to the sides of the room to make more space for the guests to mingle, and mingle they did. Three of the film's actresses were loudly telling anyone who would listen that they weren't wearing any underwear and were thinking about never wearing any again. The rock star–actress girlfriend of Norman Harris, one of the male leads, was trying to corner Phil about possible roles in upcoming Glorious films. Buddy, who definitely didn't like crowds, surveyed the party from the second floor landing, leaning his thin frame awkwardly against an ornate iron railing. Behind him, a string quartet was playing with measured dignity but the conversation level in the room effectively drowned out its efforts.

I was starving, but food, as usual, was in short supply. The bar was well stocked, however, and the guests indulged without hesitation. Mindy was holding court in front of a little circle with a few columnists, so Elliott and I headed over to where Francesca was standing with her parents and I introduced them. "Francesca Davis, this is Elliott Solnick from Page Six." She kissed his cheek and demurely said that she hoped he'd liked the movie. I could see that Elliott was charmed, and he asked her about her love scene with Norman Harris in the film. When she began to speak, I noticed Elliott's eyes drift down to the floor. I followed his gaze. Francesca Davis's teeny, tiny feet were in stiletto sandals and her toes had been polished a deep crimson red.

"I was *so* nervous," she replied. "Norman didn't, like, know where to put his hands, and then we both kept, like, leaning the same way for the kiss and Norman was totally sweaty."

"Sweaty?" Elliott said, still staring at her pretty red toes. I yearned to kick off my slingbacks and stand barefoot before him.

"Did you lose something, Elliott?" Mrs. Mermelstein interrupted.

"No, I was just admiring this exquisite parquet floor," Elliott answered, smooth as cream. "Francesca, you were telling me about kissing Norman," he prompted.

"Well, I think we were both really nervous. But I made this movie last year. If I had to kiss Norman today, I wouldn't be nervous at all."

She raised one eyebrow at Elliott. Smacking the talent would get me fired, I knew, but it seemed almost worth it at the moment. Instead I forced a chuckle at her comment about Norman. Elliott was trying to be casual, but he knew he'd just gotten a great quote. I was sure it would run under a headline that said something like "FRANCESCA DAVIS IS WAITING TO BE KISSED." Francesca then launched into a story about the film she was currently shooting for Warner, in which she costarred with Sarah Jessica Parker, she of the expensive makeup artist recommendations.

"Francesca, I heard a story that you, Casey, and Corinne actually ad-libbed a lot of your lines so that they would sound more natural," I interjected, trying to steer the conversation back to *Anyone Can Sing.*

"Yeah, we did," she said hastily, before reverting to her worshipful monologue about wonderful Sarah. "You know, she so, like, intimidated me at first, but she's so cool. I was really nervous, but she really got me to believe in myself. And then she turned me on to her stylist, and now I have the best shoes." I had to agree on that point. This was hopeless. I couldn't get her to talk about the film, and she was babbling on about some other movie while looking absolutely gorgeous. Finally, after what seemed to me like three hours, Elliott thanked the teenage starlet, and gave her a quick good-night kiss. Then Elliott asked to talk to Phil.

"Are you sure you don't want Mindy first?" I asked.

"You're not scared of Phil, are you?" he said.

"Of course not."

Over the past few days I'd been avoiding Phil more than usual. On Monday Matt had phoned Allegra to tell her that there were a pair of advertising executives he needed to have invited to the *Anyone Can Sing* premiere, but Vivian had refused his request. I'd been listening in when Matt told Allegra about a bizarre scenario he'd witnessed while flying from Los Angeles to New York on Phil's jet. "Well, you know he smokes like a chimney, and on that little plane you can't get away from it. And, of course, it's not as if you can ask him to stop." Matt said that about midway through the flight, the attendant brought Phil a half-gallon container of vanilla ice cream and a spoon. Phil continued to smoke while he ate, and then when he was tired of the ice cream, started flicking his ashes into it, eventually planting the butts in there, too.

Allegra, true to form, hadn't responded. "Allegra?" Matt had said, making sure she was on the line.

"Go ahead."

"Well, the next thing I knew, he'd taken off his shoes and socks and taken out a toenail clipper, and just started clipping away, letting his nails fall into the ashy ice cream. It was all I could do not to vomit."

Allegra had responded by informing Matt that his media buyers could attend the premiere, but that they couldn't have a "plus one."

I'd been so disgusted that I'd had to hang up and go tell Robert immediately, as a sort of exorcism, but it had only half-worked; I was afraid that I wouldn't be able to look at ice cream for a good five years.

I told Elliott that I'd see what I could do, and headed over to Phil's lair. Two of his assistants were positioned like watchdogs between the entrance to the VIP room and his personal table so they could ward off intruders. I approached Sabrina and asked if I could bring Elliott over. The reply came back affirmative, but with a three-minute limit.

When I began to introduce them, Phil interrupted me and barked, "I don't need you to tell me who Elliott Solnick is. Elliott, sit down. Thanks for coming." He didn't look at me but flicked his wrist in my direction. "You can just leave us alone," he grumbled. "Elliott, how about that Francesca? Is she a piece of ass or what?" The two of them shared a dirty-old-man laugh as I began to slink away. "But seriously, the girl is a major talent, a young Audrey Hepburn. She's got that natural something that just leaps off the screen"—here he reached over and grabbed Elliott's shoulder— "and right into your lap." More guffaws. I slipped off to the side of the room where I could keep an eye on Phil and Elliott but be spared their conversation.

From my vantage point near the entrance to the ballroom, I could see that Robert, who was "on" Cindy Adams, was in a deep discussion with the Mermelsteins while Francesca spoke with Cindy, who I could see from here had put on her little eyeglasses to have a better look at Francesca's magnificent shoes. Most of the party was spread out, glittering before me. The flow and swirl of people, accompanied by the silent string quartet, resembled a dance in which people chatted, switched partners, admired each other's clothes, and then switched again in an elaborate pattern. Everyone seemed to be enjoying themselves, but I knew that they wouldn't really cut loose until they were sure that the press had been removed from the room.

After a few minutes, a voice on my headset announced that the moment had come. I waved to Sabrina and pointed to my watch, and she leaned down to whisper to Phil. He and Elliott shook hands and I walked up to claim my columnist.

"Elliott, I'm sorry, but I've got to do that thing now."

"I'll see myself out." He opened his mouth and held his hands up in mock horror. "Only joking, Karen. I know how it works." I walked him out of the townhouse, and following Robert's caution, headed slowly toward the corner. It was a beautiful evening and the real stars were out in force. The September night air was crisp and liberating and I remembered from the memo that after kicking Elliott out, I was finished for the evening. I was meditating on how to subtly let him know this when he squeezed me on the shoulder, before saying, "Thanks, Karen. I've gotta run." A flood of disappointment washed over me. I was hoping that I'd at least get to have a drink with him, now that I was an off-duty official sanctimonious bitch. Instead, he had already found a cab and was tucking himself inside. I had a renewed flash of hope when he leaned out toward me as if he'd forgotten to ask me something. "Karen! Do you have to make sure I close the door, too?" He laughed, closed it, and the cab pulled away.

I leaned against the bus shelter, surveying the smart boutiques of Madison Avenue while I tried to figure out why Elliott had been so cold. I knew that it was hard to look attractive in a room full of celebs, but certainly Elliott knew the difference—he'd been doing this kind of work for years. Interrupting my train of thought, Robert materialized next to me and asked for a cigarette. He lit up and inhaled deeply, rocking back on his heels. "That was great, Karen. You put Elliott Solnick all the way into the cab. I'm going to have to remember that for next time."

"It wasn't exactly the strategy I was hoping for," I said, glumly.

"Tough night?" he said. I nodded and he suggested a stop at a nearby bar, but I told him I'd rather just go home. He got into a cab and I stood there, trying to piece together what I'd done to make Elliott run away.

"Hello." I was startled to hear a voice from out of the shadows behind me.

"Hello?" I called out, looking to see who was there. Midnight was midnight, even in the most affluent zip code, and I was a bit unsettled. A figure stepped out in front of me. In a flash I recognized him as the man from the top of the red carpet in L.A.

"Well, if it isn't my little friend from Hollywood," he said, and something in his manner made me uncomfortable. He looked exactly the same—I was pretty sure he was even in the same well-pressed suit from that night so many months earlier.

"Are you, are you, George, um, Mr. Hanratty?" I stammered.

"Why would you think that?"

"Just a hunch."

"Don't tell me—Phil and Tony have probably given all of you my picture. Public enemy number one," he said bitterly.

"Not exactly," I said. "I don't have a picture. They really don't talk about you much."

"Because they think I'm not a threat," he said, his mouth a firm line. His hands were shaking a little less than they'd been in L.A. "Tell me the truth—they say I'm a drunk, washed-up, can't write anymore—that kind of thing."

I stood frozen in my spot.

"It's nothing I haven't heard before. You might as well tell me."

I dipped my chin and raised it slightly, just once.

He sighed, and all of the anger left his body, replaced by a palpable sadness. He stood there, head hanging forward, shoulders slumped.

"Mr. Hanratty? Are you okay?" He looked almost ill.

"I'm fine," he said, standing up straight once again. "Just fine. And I'm going to be better, once I finish this book. Can you imagine how many people want to know the truth about the Waxmans? How it wasn't all Gloria cutting hair in her sink and Phil and Tony pulling themselves out of the Bronx by their bootstraps?" I didn't answer, so he continued. "The real story is a lot less charming."

I desperately wanted to leave so I made a move for the curb to get a taxi, but he touched my arm, and I froze. "I didn't mean to frighten you, dear," he said softly. "I would never hurt anyone."

"Mr. Hanratty, I understand. But I can't help you."

"You don't need to. I have eyes and ears all over the place."

"So why are you talking to me?"

"You just seemed different from them. When I saw you at the Oscars, and you told me about Ted Roddy—I could see that you were upset. And you're so earnest, it nearly breaks my heart."

"What are you talking about?"

"You take it all so seriously. The early mornings, reading newspapers in the Town Car, going to the *Times* in the middle of the night."

Hanratty knew way too much about me—maybe even my address. I was terrified. A taxi came around the corner and I waved wildly to it, sprinting across two lanes of traffic to the safety of its locked interior. Giving the driver my address, I peered out the window at Hanratty, a small, sad figure standing alone in the dark.

In the morning I came in to collect and distribute press generated by the premiere. The majority of the papers had photos of the Person—or, rather, the back of the Person—going into the screening. Most of them had captions with a variation on "Anyone Won't Sing."

As soon as she spotted me, Allegra called me into her office and had me sit down. "I know you're excited about the Person showing up last night, and I'll admit I didn't think he was going to," she whispered, rifling through the Hits. She was in what I thought of as her "morning after" dress, a loose-fitting black velvet garment that she frequently wore on the day following a premiere, and it fit her as flatteringly as a hospital gown. I assumed it was her version of hangover sweats and a T-shirt. "But it's not like we need that kind of publicity for the film. Now all of the papers have his photo instead of Buddy Friedman or Francesca Davis or any of the film's *talent*," she said, enunciating the word to make me understand that I didn't have any, before swinging her chair around to face the file cabinet so that her back was to me. I left her office.

Unbelievably tired and reeling from a pounding headache, I didn't know what to do or say about Hanratty. We were supposed to report any sightings, but no one ever had, at least as long as I'd been here. When he'd said that he had eyes and ears all over the place, I understood that if anyone at Glorious knew that I'd met him, I might somehow be implicated in whatever eventually happened with his book. It dawned on me that maybe I wasn't the only one who'd met him; perhaps many of us had, all choosing to keep quiet about it. Hanratty was familiar with Glorious—familiar enough to use the company's inherent mistrust of its own employees as a convenient cloak under which to conduct his investigation.

After my encounter with Hanratty, I'd gone home and found Ellen awake, waiting up to tell me that one of the neighbors had asked her if I worked for an escort service. Apparently more than a few tenants had their suspicions, which probably explained the spaniel incident from what seemed like last year, but was in fact only hours earlier. When Ellen told him that I worked at Glorious, the man had the nerve to ask her if I could get him a *Perp Friction* poster.

Was everyone in my life going to use me or insult me? It was getting to be a fucking epidemic.

EXECUTIVE DECISION

Lately I hadn't been sleeping well, so when the phone rang at 4:30 in the morning I was awake and online, taking one of those Enneagram tests. I thought it might provide some clues about the personality types of my coworkers, and why my basically stable character didn't seem to be helping me win friends and influence people at Glorious.

"You need to get to your office, love." It was Belinda from the magazine store. I'd given her my number in case of an emergency, and this was the first time she'd ever used it. "There's a front page story in the *New York Observer* called 'Cash, Lies and Videorape—How I Swindled Phil Waxman out of $15 Million.'"

I thanked Belinda, retrieved yesterday's clothes from the floor, jumped into a cab, and headed downtown. It was still dark outside when I reached the store. Belinda was waiting for me with four copies of the pinkish paper and a double espresso; before I'd even finished scanning the first two paragraphs, it was clear to me that this article would wreak tremendous havoc on my immediate future.

Two weeks ago, Phil had acquired a film called *HackSaw*,

about the friendship between a mentally retarded ex-con and a little boy from an abusive family. It had been written and directed by a relatively unknown actor-screenwriter named Jimmy-Dale Hawthorne, who had poured his blood and guts into this film during the nearly ten years that had elapsed between inspiration and completion. Hawthorne also starred in *HackSaw*, in a real scenery-chewing role as the film's exceptionally odd protagonist. I knew this much from reading a few posts that I'd seen online, although I hadn't paid much attention to them. Tony thought that the movie was a piece of crap and had been riding his brother mercilessly as a result, screaming that he'd overpaid for it and that this was "just another one of your really fucking stupid ideas."

Part of the deal with Gary Masters, the producer from whom Phil had bought the picture, was that the financial arrangements would remain confidential. Now that the check had cleared, Masters had given an exclusive to the *Observer*. In the piece he claimed that he'd staged a false auction to get Phil to overpay for *HackSaw*, described the film as "materially flawed," and predicted *HackSaw*'s bloody massacre at the box office. Mentioning some poor reviews that it had already received from festival critics, Masters declared, "Mercifully, *HackSaw* is now off my plate—thanks to Phil Waxman's far less discriminating palate." He concluded with an enthusiastic description of his new motor yacht, "your basic 85-footer."

I phoned Allegra while sending the fax through to her home. It was just after five, but I knew she'd want to see this as soon as possible. "Allegra, I'm sorry for calling so early," I said, obviously understanding that I'd woken her up. "I'm faxing through an *Observer* piece that I'm sure you'll want to see right away."

"I hope this isn't another one of your overreactions." The woman could go from dead asleep to full-on bitch in less time than it took most people to sneeze.

"I think you'll find it worth waking up for," I replied curtly, trying to control my anger.

Inside of three minutes Allegra called back. "Find Phil." At this hour, the best way to get hold of him was through Mahmoud, his driver, who was always aware of Phil's movements. When I reached him, he was fifteen minutes away from Phil's Old Westbury home, picking him up to go to the airport. Phil and his wife maintained several residences in the New York area, including this one, a large apartment on the East Side, and a farm upstate in Millbrook.

I faxed the article through to Mahmoud, who promised to bring it right to Phil's door when he arrived. The car, a Mercedes S600, was tricked out with two fax machines, flip-down monitors to watch DVDs or tapes, and several phone lines, including one that was absolutely secure. The car's communications system had been designed by the Secret Service as a favor to Phil after a particularly profitable fund-raiser for the Democratic senator from New Jersey. The car also had a mini-fridge stocked with Diet Dr Pepper and every type of condiment imaginable so that Phil could properly garnish whatever he was eating. This went way past Grey Poupon, although there were a couple of varieties of that aboard. There were dozens of bottles and jars that held wasabi, mango chutney, red horseradish, Tabasco, Heinz 57 Sauce, A1, ketchup, hoisin, kosher dill pickles, tahini, Miracle Whip, salsa in five levels of heat, sweet relish, jalapeño peppers, balsamic vinegar, duck sauce, raspberry jam, and two containers of Phil's beloved spicy deli mustard. In the event of a nuclear war, Phil wouldn't necessarily have more food than anyone else, but his share would certainly be much tastier.

After faxing Mahmoud, I patched Allegra in to Phil at home, staying on the line to listen. Allegra tried to break it to him gently but Phil wanted to see the article for himself, so Allegra had me patch Phil in to Mahmoud. Phil told him to hit the gas pedal. There was a fax machine in the office-screening room on Phil's sprawling property, but when Mahmoud offered to send it there Phil said that if he could simply drive fast enough, it would take the same amount of time.

After a few more minutes Phil called and I put him through to Allegra. He was conjugating and combining expletives in ways that I'd never heard before. Allegra tried to whisper him down but had no success—an unprecedented event, as far as I knew. After a while, Phil finally stopped shouting long enough to let Allegra speak. She told him that the best course of action at this moment would be to completely ignore the allegations in the *Observer*. Instead, they would chart their own offensive.

They agreed, of course, that the newspaper would have to be dealt with, and I knew it would be a long time before anyone from the *Observer* would get into a Glorious screening or premiere or be allowed to interview any Glorious talent. Their phone calls would go unreturned and all questions would be answered with a terse "No comment." But Allegra and Phil had not yet begun to fight.

Phil told Allegra that he would fly to Chicago a bit later than planned—what he needed right now was a series of meetings with Publicity, Marketing, Acquisitions, and the legal team. Mahmoud would drive him to the office, and they were all to be ready and waiting in Town Cars within the hour. They would follow him to Teterboro Airport in New Jersey, where his jet was fueled and ready, and each group would meet with him on the way.

Allegra phoned me back with a long list of people to call at home. I was also to order five Town Cars and have them at Glorious right away, and I needed to try to collect all the copies of the *Observer* that I could get my hands on.

Belinda was happy to hide all of her *Observer*s in the back of the store, and I promised to send an intern over with money later on. "I can see why Phil doesn't want every tongue in TriBeCa wagging over this," she said.

I'd heard about Phil's "moving meetings" before, but this was the first one that I'd gotten to be part of, if only as an organizer. After ordering the cars I began to call the soon-to-be occupants. The three lawyers each tried to argue with me, until I pointed out that they were wasting valuable shower and shave-time. Matt Vincent understood immediately, and even offered to call Cheryl and Kenny, whom Phil also wanted present. I took him up on it and moved on to the Acquisitions people, who quickly acquiesced. I called Clark and told him that he needed to show up and he thanked me for calling. I'd saved my favorite person for last, and when I reached Marlene, she was as pleasant as I'd imagined. "Karen, it's not as if you've been particularly good at communication—are you sure this is what Phil wants?" I invited her to not show up and find out for herself.

I'd surprised myself by how calm and firm I could be. There was an incredible sense of power in invoking Phil's name—"Phil wants, Phil needs, Phil says . . ."

I photocopied the article and ran outside to where the Town Cars idled, placing several copies in each one before dashing back in. I phoned Allegra to tell her that the *Observer* was out of Belinda's store, the executives were all on their way, and the cars were at the curb. She told me to make sure that the article didn't go in this morning's Hits, and that I was to play dumb to any media calls about it and just take down call-back information. Allegra added that she'd like me to "manage the information flow" around the department—people who were directly involved in this knew who they were, everyone else was to be told that the situation was under control. If any members of the media called them, they were to be directed to her office.

By six, journalists from all over the world had called to get more information on the *Observer's* story. I logged calls from the *Wall Street Journal*, the *New York Times*, Reuters, Sky News, CNN, the BBC, and dozens of others. Allegra's e-mail in-box looked alive—the screen literally pulsed with the arrival of new queries. Some of them had already spoken to Gary Masters and were now looking for an official word from Phil. For the entertainment press, many of whom had long been looking for a crack in the walled fortress of Glorious Pictures, the story sounded too good to be true. Had Phil Waxman, the master deal-maker, the guy who never got duped, actually been swindled by a C-list producer who was now snickering all the way to the bank?

By 6:30, the five cars were loaded and waiting for Phil's arrival. The legal team, acquisitions people, and marketing department each had their own car; Marlene and Clark shared the fourth, and Allegra rode alone. Mahmoud called and had me line up the cars with Allegra first, Legal second, Marketing third, Marlene and Clark fourth, and Acquisitions last. He said he was about five minutes away and that they would need to be ready to fall in behind him. I jogged outside once more to give directions to the passengers and their drivers, making sure they would be ready to go the moment they spied Phil's car coming around the corner. The other directive was that the cars remain in this order as they followed Phil to the airport.

Mahmoud asked me to keep a phone line open so that he and I could be in constant communication. Right before he arrived at the office, he told me that Phil wanted to see the lawyers first. I called one of them and as soon as Phil's car came into view they jumped out. Mahmoud stopped for about two seconds to let them in, and then the motorcade to Teterboro began.

Once they were through the Holland Tunnel, Mahmoud told me that Marketing was needed next. All six cars pulled over, the lawyers left Phil's car through the right-side door as Matt, Cheryl, and Kenny entered through the left, legal got back into their Town Car, and all six started again. This was repeated right before US1 in New Jersey, with Marketing exiting and Acquisitions getting in. Teterboro's convenient location meant that Phil had to conduct these meetings quickly—even with traffic, the airport was seldom as much as an hour away. Right before the entrance to Route 17, Acquisitions got out and Marlene, Clark, and Allegra got in and remained there for the rest of the trip. Mahmoud had me tell Marketing, Acquisitions, and Legal they could return to the office.

I'd been on the phone with Mahmoud and the members of the different departments for the whole trip, and I felt like an air traffic controller who had brought everyone down for a smooth, safe landing. Finally, Mahmoud told me that Phil's plane had taken off. We thanked each other and I took a deep breath. It was 7:45. Allegra would be calling at any moment, and as I was on my own I couldn't leave the desk, so I busied myself with the morning's Hits, all the while grabbing ringing phones and trying to stay on top of the e-mail, which was arriving in staggering quantities. I was so busy that even the hang-up guy hadn't rattled me when he'd phoned at 7:22, although I'd still made a note of his call.

The phone rang for the millionth time. "Allegra Orecchi's office," I said, while adding more paper to the printer to keep up with the e-mails.

"Having a busy day, Karen? The *Observer* article has everyone in quite a state, hasn't it?" It was Hanratty.

"How would you know?"

"I read it myself. That kind of thing doesn't sit well with Phil, I'm sure of it."

I wondered if he knew about the cars. "Actually, I think he's taken it in stride."

"Really? Then there was some other reason that all the poor little troops had to march in the Phil parade this morning?"

This was way too weird for me. He was close enough to see what I was doing—watching like a sniper.

"Don't ever call me again," I said, slamming down the phone. It took me a few minutes to regain my composure, and, just as after my encounter with him at the premiere, I didn't add this to Allegra's phone list. By not talking about it I was joining the conspiracy of my colleagues, and saving my ass.

At around 9:30 Clark and Marlene showed up, having taken a detour to eat a leisurely breakfast on their way back. "Where's Allegra?" I asked.

"She's not here yet?" Clark said.

"No, and I haven't heard from her. She isn't answering her cell phone."

"Maybe she's 'it,'" Clark said.

"It?" I repeated.

"Sometimes when Phil does these road trip meetings, if he's not finished he'll make whomever he needs to talk to get on the flight with him. Then he'll leave them to find their way back. Once Marlene got stranded in Las Vegas overnight with no clothes and no wallet. My guess is that Allegra is 'it' today."

E-mails and phone calls were still pouring in when Dagney showed up at ten, looking pretty and well-rested—as she did most of the time, now that her Juliet fixation was most decidedly a thing of the past. She had also been e-mailing with Oliver regularly, even meeting him for drinks a couple of times now that summer was over and he was back in the city, working at one of his father's companies.

"Do I have déjà vu?" she asked, critically eyeing my repeat ensemble. I ignored her. "Karen, you look horrible. Are you feeling okay?"

"I've been here since five, dealing with a huge Phil issue." I knew that this would get her attention. Tomorrow she would probably come in at four. She pressed me for details.

"An article in the *Observer* claims that he was completely tricked into buying *HackSaw*. They all had a moving meeting on the way to Teterboro that started at around 6:30, and now they're on their way back, except Allegra, who we think flew to Chicago with Phil." I left out the part about Belinda's early warning call—I wanted to make sure that she remained my source only.

Dagney reached for a copy of the Hits and flipped through it. "There's nothing in here."

"All copies of the article have been destroyed."

"Are you telling me that I can't see it?"

"Here." I thrust the only remaining copy in TriBeCa across our desk.

"Can you believe the nerve of this guy?" Dagney asked, scanning it eagerly. "Basically calling Phil a loser in the paper. I wonder if the movie's really that bad." She picked up the phone and began to dial. I reached over and pressed the disconnect button. "Do not call your little pals and spread this around. It's a much bigger deal than that nonsense with Juliet, and I guarantee you right now that we'll both fry if it gets out. You need to lay off."

My aggressiveness startled her into silence, so I continued. "A million media people are calling and they want details. Pretend you don't know anything, and get their information. Same with the e-mail—just print it out." I pointed to the stack already in the printer. "I need to use the bathroom. Can I trust you while I'm gone?" She nodded meekly. "Great. Why don't you order us both some breakfast? A couple of coffees and a blueberry muffin are exactly what I need right now." She picked up the phone, and I lingered just long enough to confirm that she was speaking with no one more dangerous than a deli clerk.

When I returned to my desk the stack of e-mail printouts had grown fatter and I could see that the phone log open on Dagney's PC was loaded with dozens of additional names and numbers for Allegra to call back.

At around eleven, the gossip columnists woke up and started calling. I gave Elliott the standard line.

"Karen, you can do better than that. It's me."

"I don't know any more than what you've read," I insisted, which was the truth: before this morning, I had read only a brief description of *HackSaw* in an e-mail that Matt had sent to Allegra, and I'd heard Tony's shouts about it. I promised Elliott that someone would get back to him with information later.

"Well, what do you think? You must have some kind of opinion," he insisted.

"My opinion is that it's going to be a very long day and this Masters guy must have a death wish, or at least a gross underestimation of Phil."

"There you go. At last, an answer."

Shit. "You're not going to quote me, are you?"

"Karen, of course not. Would I want to get those little feet in trouble? Or make their owner angry with me?"

"I'll call you as soon as I know something." I couldn't deal with Elliott's foot thing right now. The task at hand required all of my concentration.

It was 2 P.M. and we still hadn't heard from Allegra. The phone rang and I picked it up. "Allegra Orecchi's office." Hearing nothing but static, I repeated myself, then heard a far-off voice say, "Would you care for a beverage?" A pause. "Ice in that?"

Loudly, I said, "Allegra, this is Karen. I can't hear you, the plane must be in a bad spot. You need to call back." Dagney looked over. "I could hear the flight attendant, but not our charming boss." Her eyeballs did three complete revolutions.

Half an hour later, Allegra rang again to say that she would need a car to meet her at LaGuardia, that we could expect her back at around 4 P.M., and that we should both plan on a late night at the office. Allegra called again the moment the landing gear made contact with the runway, and was still on the phone with us when she walked into her office and shut the door, passing Dagney and me without a glance. During the call, she outlined the plan that she and Phil had designed. When I heard what they were up to, it became immediately apparent that Gary Masters's cap-gun offensive was about to be answered with an onslaught of mortar fire. Allegra had made her reputation on this kind of work, but the Masters debacle would require the delicacy of a landmine removal technician. Watching Glorious attempt to spin itself out of this would be a crash course in crisis communications.

As it turned out, their entire battle plan hinged on one incredibly coincidental, yet critical fact—both Jimmy-Dale Hawthorne and the president hailed from Louisiana.

While still in flight, Phil had spoken with the president of the United States and asked him to screen *HackSaw*—providing an opportunity to support another boy from the bayou. The president agreed, adding that he'd set some time aside the following evening to spend with his mother, always an ardent fan of anything from their home state.

Phil, Tony, Allegra, and Gloria would fly to D.C. together the following afternoon so that they could watch the president and his mother watch *HackSaw* in the White House screening room. If his response was favorable, which they assumed it would be, *HackSaw* would fly on the wings of a presidential endorsement.

Allegra had Dagney and me put together the details for the presidential screening. Just FedExing the reels of film took on an added excitement and urgency—Attn: Projectionist, 1600 Pennsylvania Avenue!

Elliott called again. "What's the story? Did Masters rip Phil off or what? Why are you guys so quiet?"

I knew this couldn't leak. If something changed and the screening didn't happen, it would be a disaster. "You'll know soon, I promise, but I can't tell you anything now."

"Can't you just give me a hint? Please, Karen?"

Elliott in begging mode was especially appealing, but I'd said too much already. Not to mention how I'd felt when he'd ditched me after the premiere. I'd give him an early heads-up, but not before I had the official go-ahead.

The phones kept ringing and the e-mails kept pinging their way in. By the end of the day we had received more than five hundred calls and four hundred e-mails, some of them forwarded from all different areas of the company. Even Geraldine had gotten some queries: When it became apparent that the publicity department wasn't being particularly forthcoming, inquiring minds tried their luck elsewhere, but we'd really battened down—nobody was talking. Dagney and I were double-checking that we'd logged everything when Clark ambled over and asked if we knew what time the plane for D.C. was leaving the following day.

"At this point, it's set up for two o'clock," I said.

"That's reasonable."

"You're going?" I couldn't believe it. "You're going to watch *HackSaw* with the president of the United States?"

"Allegra asked me to come along and supervise the photographers—they're doing a series of shots of the president and his mother with Phil and Tony and Gloria. You know, just your average family portrait." He grinned. "Besides, Gloria wants me there. I beat her badly at pinochle last week and she's challenged me to a double or nothing rematch."

Typical. I chased newspapers in the middle of the night while Clark posed Tony and Phil with the First Family.

"I'll let you know if anything changes."

Meanwhile, Marlene was in charge of Phase Two: booking hotels for a *HackSaw* junket that was to take place the following weekend—although she wasn't telling the press what film they would be seeing, or who they would be interviewing. This way she wouldn't have to confirm or deny any rumors—if she cancelled the junket, no one would know which film they weren't seeing. Marlene cautioned each journalist that it would be in their best interest to accept this invitation; in a day's time she had two hundred confirmed attendees from broadcast, print, radio, and Internet outlets across the country.

The following evening at around eight, Dagney and I were waiting for Allegra's call. The press release I'd written earlier in the day was up on my screen, ready to be completed. Allegra had instructed me to leave it full of blank spaces where information could be added later. It looked like a page of Mad-Libs. "PRESIDENT ELECTS *HACKSAW*" was the headline. "After screening *Hacksaw*, a soon-to-be released film from Glorious Pictures, the President remarked, [*insert glowing accolade.*] He was tremendously impressed by Hawthorne's ability to [*insert verb and adjectives,*] saying that it reminded him of the work of [*insert name of author, filmmaker, or rock musician.*]" The two of us were preparing e-mail blasts and fax cover sheets for the nearly twelve hundred journalists who had contacted our office over the past two days.

At 8:13 Allegra called, still in the White House screening room. I could hear the president's familiar drawl in the background, and Gloria's girlish giggle in response to something he'd just told her. My heart started pounding loudly. Allegra whispered excitedly that the president had pronounced *HackSaw* "a master-piece" and declared Jimmy-Dale "a national treasure" and "a storyteller in the tradition of Faulkner." He believed that every American should see *HackSaw*! Dagney and I high-fived as we hung up the phone. It was undeniably cool to have the president on our team.

We filled in the release and began e-mailing and faxing it. Before I called anyone else, though, I dialed Elliott, thinking he might have a shot at getting this in tomorrow's paper, an advantage I wasn't giving the others. "It's Karen. I have the official word on *HackSaw*. Do you think you can get them to hold the page?"

"I'll try." He gave me his fax number and I stayed on the line while he received it.

"Thanks, Karen. I really appreciate it. Can you tell me who went to the screening with the president?"

"Phil, Tony, Gloria, and the president's mother."

"Great, that's my angle then—a family affair."

"I'll have Clark wire you a photo—he's with the White House photographer."

"Thanks. And Karen, I'm sorry for being such a jerk after the *Anyone Can Sing* party. I didn't mean to leave you standing there."

"Elliott, I'm under water. Can we talk about this some other time?"

"Sure. But just know that it's not what you think."

Meanwhile, Clark, in D.C., fed photos of Phil, Tony, and the president to the newswires directly from the White House press office so that they could appear around the globe in the days to come—a valuable bonus, since Glorious owned *HackSaw*'s international distribution rights as well. I called and asked him to make sure he sent one to the *Post* right away.

"I smell an Elliott Solnick exclusive," Clark said.

"Just doing my part to be media-friendly."

I called Ellen, wanting to tell her about my near-presidential encounter. She listened as I told her about how much he loved *HackSaw* before saying, "I don't know, Karen. Don't you think the president should have something better to do with his time than sell movie tickets for Phil and Tony Waxman?"

"You know, Ellen, motion pictures are one of the most valuable American exports, so of course the president will do everything he can to support the industry," I answered coolly, repeating a line I'd heard Allegra use on someone with a similar complaint.

A SIMPLE PLAN

Shortly after the *HackSaw* junket I began chanting. Not chanting exactly; it was closer to silently meditating in my head. I found a mantra that seemed to work: *This can't be real.* I said it over and over to calm myself whenever things seemed strange. This can't be real. This can't be real. I played with it, mixed it up. Can't be real, this. Real this can't be. This be real? Can't! It made sense no matter which way the words went; some arrangements even sounded poetic. This was evidence that it must be the Truth. With my mantra safely tucked inside my brain, I dealt with the events of the next few weeks better than I would have without it. At least I thought I did. I wasn't about to do it all over again and compare.

The junket itself had been a thoroughly exhausting, completely maddening exercise in mind control. For people who hosted segments on their local affiliates with names like "Marylou's Movie Minute," *HackSaw* was completely different from the romances, action films, and star vehicles they were used to seeing. When many of them were, in fact, only lukewarm on the film, we had to repeatedly point out its merits, as many times as it took, until they finally saw it our way.

Not that their less-than-enthusiastic reception of *HackSaw* stopped them from wanting to provide quotes to be used in our ads. When the junket broke for lunch on Saturday, I'd been literally surrounded by press people eager to add their two cents to the list I was compiling, at Marlene's behest: "One of the year's most important films"; "*HackSaw* is an important lesson for our times"; "Jimmy-Dale Hawthorne has the gift"—and that from a woman who'd snored next to me during the second half of the movie. But a quote was a quote, and I recorded them all and gave them to Marlene, who could proudly hand them off to Allegra, who would then present them as evidence of her hard work to Matt, Phil, and Tony.

To top it all off, Clark, Robert, and I had returned to the office on Sunday night to drop off boxes of leftover press kits to find that Robert's office had been vandalized, or so we first thought.

I'd gone over to my desk to find an issue of *Rolling Stone* that I wanted to give Ellen. "Can you two come in here for a second?" Robert had called out, clearly distressed. Fearing hang-up guy, rodents, or even a soused Hanratty, I peeked into the opening of his cube while Clark joined him inside it. "It looks like you've been robbed," I said.

"No, just trashed. Look more closely," Robert said. "Can't you see? Someone shrank my cube." He was right—the space was significantly smaller than it had been originally. Robert was able to put his hands on one wall and his feet on the other, so that he was in an above-ground push-up.

Clark ran into Marlene's space, which shared a wall with Robert's. They were really just partitions on tracks, meant to be temporary. "Here's your answer," he said. "I can't believe that woman."

Following him in, I saw that Marlene's wall had been shoved back into Robert's space, creating more room for her, while he now had a cube so small that he couldn't pull the chair away from the desk.

Robert ran from his cube to Marlene's and back, twice, as if to double-check what had happened.

"When could they have done this?" he said.

"Must have been on Friday, after we left for the junket," I said, vaguely remembering an e-mail exchange that had taken place between Marlene and Allegra that morning. Marlene was demanding a larger space to accommodate her "significantly increased responsibility" and Allegra had e-mailed back that she would try to work out a solution.

I turned on my computer, entered "LLOYDISDEAD" and logged into Allegra's e-mail. "Here it is," I said to Robert, pointing at the screen. There was a long thread of correspondence between the two women, ending with Allegra's finally caving in to a suggestion about moving the wall.

"But no one mentioned this to me!" Robert said. "I worked my ass off for this company all weekend and this is my reward?" I'd never seen him so angry. As a matter of fact, I'd never seen him angry at all.

Not knowing what else to do, but understanding that some kind of statement was necessary, the three of us had marched over to the Bubble Lounge, where Clark promptly expensed a thousand-dollar bottle of champagne.

Now, it was early December and the office was chaotic—there were several films opening before year's end, and a lot to accomplish before any jingle bells could be rung. Phil had just received word of a ruling by the Venezuelan Ministry of Film that *El Lechero*

(The Milkman), the film we'd all assumed had a virtual lock on the Best Foreign Language Film Oscar, had been deemed ineligible to receive a nomination, as the director was Australian. The ministry had a rule stating that any film representing Venezuela in an international awards competition had to be directed by one of their countrymen. Phil had applied for an appeal, and was expecting an answer any day. For now, he paced the halls and calmed himself by consuming large quantities of Italian pastry that Sabrina ordered for him from Veniero's.

Tony had long ago figured out that although the holiday season was chock-full of high-minded art films and serious Academy contenders, the millions of vacationing American teenagers were being completely left out of the film loop; they'd come to the theater in droves if only there was something for them to see. Therefore every year, as a holiday gift to the nation's youth, Tony released a genre movie, either horror/comedy, rock/comedy, hip-hop/comedy or straight-ahead blood and guts, and every year Tony's Christmas was merrier than the last. This year's plan was to release a sequel to the cult-smash Gothic thriller *The Raven.*

To make things even more stimulating, Allegra, Marlene, and Geraldine had embarked on a new diet plan to lose some extra pounds before the holidays; apparently dialing, insulting, and finger-pointing hadn't burned as many calories as they'd hoped. Safe and effective, Thin-Then provided its users with the same results as balanced nutrition and exercise, without any of the hassle. They all went to the same Upper East Side doctor, who was happy to write them identical prescriptions. Marlene and Geraldine visited him together, sharing a cab, while Allegra went on her own, keeping her appointments a secret. When the doctor's office called to confirm, Dagney and I just left a note on her phone log, pretending not to know a thing.

Phil was also working on his health. Focused on giving up his three-pack-a-day smoking habit, he'd started using a nicotine patch—patches, to be precise, one on each arm—to try to control his cravings. Soon, though, he discovered that smoking while wearing the patches produced a buzz preferable to either of them alone.

The diet drugs and nicotine overdoses resulted in an amped-up and often cranky senior staff with a nearly superhuman ability to work tirelessly around the clock. The rest of us, who valiantly tried to keep up with coffee and various herbal energy boosters, were run ragged, with only our dreams of holiday vacations giving us the will to continue.

I didn't have anything special planned, but was really looking forward to going home to Providence to see my parents, where I knew I'd be fussed over and allowed to sleep late. Dagney would be rendezvousing in Ibiza with some of her sorority sisters. Clark had planned his annual jaunt to Canyon Ranch. Gloria had urged him to try it a couple of years ago and now he was hooked. The two of them had lengthy discussions about the pros and cons of algae masques and full mud immersion. As Gloria had earned "multiple massage miles" there, she always gave him the names of the spa's best facialists, herbalists, and aromatherapists. "Only the crème de la crème de la Canyon," she liked to say. Robert was intent on creating a mosaic of the periodic table of the elements on the bathtub wall in his Lower East Side walk-up, something he'd wanted to do for a long time. Since I'd be away, he'd asked if he could stay at my place while the grout dried. Knowing that he would leave my apartment in much better shape than he found it, I was happy to agree.

Then, on the Tuesday two weeks before Christmas, Phil's appeal to the Venezuelans was turned down. *El Lechero*, the story of a gentle dairy farmer who read poetry to his herd in the belief that it would inspire them to give more milk, was no longer in the hunt for the Best Foreign Language Film Oscar. Phil called Allegra for an all-day strategy session, during which she was in his office for three and a half hours. After that Vivian was summoned and the three of them huddled for five more hours. By the time Allegra returned to her office Dagney and I had left for the day. The next morning Dagney grimly informed me of what had been decided.

"Phil's cancelled Christmas," she said, her eyes red-rimmed. "None of us are allowed to take vacation because we have to get *El Lechero* nominated for regular Best Picture," she said, breaking into tears. "I've been planning this trip to Ibiza since February," she said, carefully pronouncing the "z" in Ibiza with a Castilian "th" sound, even through her sobs.

"This completely sucks," I said, sitting down hard in my chair, raking my hands through my hair. *Can't be real, this,* went my mantra.

"Yeah, well, you were only going to Rhode Island. Robert was tiling his shower. Only Clark and I had real plans," she said.

I hadn't seen this side of Dagney in a while, and decided to ignore her. It was very possible that she was exaggerating. Dag was often given to hyperbole, especially in matters pertaining to herself.

"In Here NOW," buzzed on both sides of our desk. Dagney stood up and kicked her chair as we both got up. Allegra was sitting with her back to us as we walked in, and she didn't bother to turn around after we'd entered the room. From what I could make out, straining my ear drums to listen, Glorious was launching a full-scale Academy campaign on behalf of *El Lechero.* It would involve dozens of events and a media onslaught kicked off by a press conference this very afternoon, during which Phil and the director would throw themselves at the mercy of the Academy members, explaining that the film must be nominated for Best Picture, if it was to be recognized at all.

Since our boss still hadn't turned around to face us, we weren't sure which one of us was supposed to do what. We'd split it up later, I figured, steeling myself for an unpleasant confrontation with Dagney. She wouldn't be in a particularly helpful mood, but, to be fair, neither would I. After fifteen minutes of mumbling, Allegra swiveled around to face us. "The first thing you have to do is draft a press release to explain what's happening, highlighting the fact that Phil and his family are cancelling their vacation on behalf of the film." This time I rolled my eyes. Phil could vacation anywhere he liked, whenever he wanted. It was the rest of us who were getting ripped off.

Dagney and I went back to our desk, where she started to make arrangements for the film's female lead, Ana Maria Verdades, to arrive in New York the day after tomorrow. Ana Maria portrayed the milkman's wife, a shy, sweet young woman who constantly defends her husband to the other farmers in their village. His poetry readings to audiences comprised of cows had made him a laughingstock. While she was a thoroughly convincing actress as well as a head-turning beauty, Ana Maria spoke very little English. Dagney enrolled her in a Berlitz immersion program that she would attend daily until she was fluent enough to be interviewed by the American press. Then she booked Ana Maria a one-way ticket from Caracas and a junior suite at the Hilton Towers.

I began to draft the press release, giving Phil a quote that read, "In the interest of giving *El Lechero* the best possible chance of receiving its due from the Academy, I, along with my loyal employees, have decided to forgo our holiday vacations. I have an extremely dedicated team, and have no doubt that due to their efforts, *El Lechero* will be nominated for Best Picture."

After adding in some language explaining the Venezuelan ruling about the film and affirming that *El Lechero* was indeed worthy of a Best Picture nomination, I put the draft in Allegra's in-box, grabbed my cigarettes, and headed outside. By now I'd learned to hold and light a cigarette convincingly enough to join the rest of the Glorious smokers in the area they'd staked out near the building's back entrance. Once there I saw Robert, Sabrina, and Yvonne Stapleton's new assistant—the seventh since I'd joined the company. This one, Janet, had started about two months ago and seemed as if she might stick. On her first day Robert and I had asked her to intercept any seemingly innocuous queries from upwardly mobile interns.

It was warmer than usual for this time of year so no one was in a hurry to go back inside. Sidling up next to Robert, I leaned against the building's brick. Everyone was quiet for a while; we were all just slumped dejectedly against the wall. Robert spoke first.

"We could start this whole *El Lechero* thing right after the holidays and still have plenty of time to get it nominated," he said.

"Yeah, but Phil wants to impress the Academy members with his sacrifice," Sabrina answered.

"I don't think they're going to care. I don't even think they're going to be home when we call them," Robert said.

I thought back to last year's mad phone frenzy for *The Foreign Pilot* and couldn't imagine doing it again for *El Lechero*. We'd have to stop and explain on every call that, yes, you would think it belongs in Best Foreign, but there was a technicality that meant it was in the general race only, and it's up to you, esteemed Academy member, to nominate it in the general Best Picture category. I wasn't the same person I had been last year, excited and enthusiastic and happy to be calling Academy voters at all hours to shout about Glorious Pictures. Too much and yet not enough had happened since then. I'd looked at our kitchen calendar last night, and confirmed that in just over two months I would have to decide whether to stay or leave. No matter what my choice was, I would have held up my end of the bargain with my cousin, and lasted the year at Glorious.

"Where was Phil going, anyway?" I asked Sabrina.

"Phil? He never goes away at Christmas—or at least he hasn't in the three years I've been here. But usually everyone else gets to leave, except for one of Phil's assistants, one of Tony's, and a couple of others in the middle of production, or something. If you have to stay, they usually try to give you enough money to make up for it."

"Right, but this year, with everyone sticking around, it's not going to look like much of a hardship, is it?" Robert said.

"Nope," Sabrina said. "Easy as pie." She ground out her cigarette by slamming her boot heel with a force that could have cracked pavement.

"Is Yvonne going to be around?" I asked Janet.

"She says it's just in case," Janet said, nodding, "but she won't say in case of what."

"What else happens around here at Christmas?"

"Well, there are the people who choose to stay," Robert said.

"Don't tell me. Marlene?"

He nodded and made a "keep going" motion with his hand.

"Vivian?"

"Yup, her too."

"And I'm sure Allegra can't allow any of them to be in the office without her supervision," I said, and Robert quickly confirmed it. *Real this can't be,* I thought.

I shook my head and went back inside to find Dagney, makeup perfectly reapplied, smiling and practically bustling around. My stomach flipped over. Nothing that made Dagney this happy wasn't going to affect me, I was sure.

"You'll never believe it," she said, her eyes shining.

"I might."

"I told Allegra about how important this Ibiza trip is, and how it's been arranged for almost a year, and she said that I could go!"

"I'm happy for you."

"You don't sound happy."

"If you're away, I'll be lucky just to get Christmas Day off. I wished you had said something to me and then maybe we could have worked it out so that we'd *each* get some time off."

She pouted for a second and then said, "But you didn't even have any real plans."

"So, that's the reason you think I don't deserve a vacation as well?"

"No, it's because I'm going to Ibiza." She walked away, head held high.

I wasn't surprised when Clark e-mailed a couple of hours later to say that he'd gotten special permission to go ahead with his Canyon Ranch trip. Golden Children: 2, Work Horses: 0.

Back in the underworld, Tony was having difficulties keeping his sequel to *The Raven* on course. Known as *The Raven II: Nevermore*, on paper the film had everything going for it—a rabid fan base, a moody sensibility sure to appeal to angst-ridden teens, and Erich Klostenheimer, a German pop star with smoldering looks stepping into the role of The Raven. Not yet known in the United States, Erich was a huge sensation in Europe, where he was hailed as Germany's answer to the Backstreet Boys, even though there was only one of him. The actor who portrayed The Raven in the first film was not available due to a scheduling conflict and Tony couldn't risk the possibility of delaying *The Raven II: Nevermore*'s holiday opening.

Unfortunately, Erich's English, though very good, was heavily accented. His agent had promised Tony that Erich would work with a dialect coach in order to sound like a Midwesterner, which is what The Raven had been before he became undead. During the film's shooting, however, it had become clear that despite Erich's best efforts he was unable to shake his pronounced Teutonic inflection. Instead of the avenging angel he was portraying, Erich sounded exactly like one of Mike Myers's wacky German characters from *Saturday Night Live*. Tony had insisted he would deliver *The Raven II: Nevermore* on time and under budget. The problem, he told anyone who dared ask, would be fixed in post-production.

The next morning Clark and I went to the sound studio where Erich was looping his dialogue for the film. A writer from *People* was meeting us there to interview Erich. He was to be included in their annual "Most Intriguing People" list, a major coup for us. Intriguing was a good way to describe Erich, as we knew very little about him besides the fact that his song "Ich Habe Fieber" had teenage girls swooning all over Europe, and that his green eyes, angular features, and soot-black hair translated into "hunk" in every language. It wasn't necessary for me to come along, but I'd lobbied Allegra with the argument that it would be good practice in case I was needed to monitor an interview on my own, perhaps over the holiday break that I wasn't getting.

We arrived at the studio and were directed to wait in a lounge area full of low-slung, ultra-hip looking furniture that proved as uncomfortable to sit in as it was nice to look at. Gold and platinum records covered the walls from floor to ceiling—artists ranging from Elvis to Enya to Eric Clapton had recorded here. Little glass tables were scattered around the room and each one had some kind of candy on it. Clark grabbed a couple of Tootsie Rolls from a huge bowl while I helped myself to Peanut M&M's from a dispenser that poured out a generous handful each time you pressed the button. "What's with all the candy?" I asked, refilling my palm with M&M's.

"I think it's left over from the days when all the rock stars were on heroin," Clark said, moving on to a tray of individually wrapped Reese's Peanut Butter Cups. "Now it's hard to find people who are even doing sugar."

Erich's looping session was supposed to end at noon, giving him time to relax before the *People* reporter, Patrick Braithwaite, arrived at one. Clark and I planned to meet with Erich to go over some talking points specifically designed to bring readers flocking to see *The Raven II: Nevermore*.

At 12:30, Clark and I hadn't yet seen Erich, so we asked the receptionist if she could locate him in the building. She made a couple of calls, then said that Erich was still looping with Tony. At 12:45, when the session still hadn't ended, Clark decided that he'd go in and remind Tony of the commitment to *People*. The receptionist directed us to Studio C. We walked down a hallway and slowly pushed open a door that had an IN SESSION light glowing outside of it. We stood just inside, trying to be invisible. The room had a screen on one end on which *The Raven II* was running. Opposite the screen was a glassed-in booth, which held a shaken-looking Erich Klostenheimer, his six-two frame crumpled over a microphone stand, which he was gripping with white-knuckled hands. Between the screen and the booth was a mixing board covered with at least a thousand dials, buttons, and things that slid up and down.

Standing in front of the board was Tony Waxman, who was shaking his fist at Erich. "Is the sound on in there?" he barked at one of the two recording engineers. The man made an "okay" signal with his hand.

"Listen to me, Klostenheimer. I don't care how long this takes. You are going to sound like an American Raven if you have to do it again and again until you drop dead."

Erich's only response was a nervous nod.

"Rewind!" Tony shouted at the engineers, his index finger pointing toward the ceiling.

They pressed a couple of buttons and the film started to run again. Erich was in the booth, speaking along with his Raven-self on the screen. "I am the Raven. Nevermore will you worry about these evil forces" was the line that he was trying to loop. Erich synched it up perfectly, but his "v" sounds were a little soft.

"What the fuck is this? Rafen? Nefer? Efil?" Tony pounded the mixing board with his fist at every word.

Erich cowered inside the booth. "I will try again."

"Rewind!"

This take was a little better, but no one would ever believe that this guy was from Kansas. Tony's face grew red and a sound like a strangled cat escaped from him. He picked up a chair, swung it around his head twice, and released it in the direction of the booth. It bounced off the heavy, soundproof panes. Erich's eyes widened in terror. He didn't look at all intriguing. He looked as if he were about to wet his leather pants.

Tony had the mike switched on and ordered Erich out of the booth. Slowly, Erich opened the door and walked down the two steps separating the booth from the rest of the room. Tony walked right up to Erich so that his bulbous nose was almost against Erich's delicately contoured one.

"Am I going to have to kick the fucking Kraut out of you?" Tony demanded. "Am I? Because I have a fucking movie to make here and I'll do it. By fuck, I'll do it."

My mantra kicked in, evidently on the same repeater loop as *The Raven II*. This can't be real. This can't be real. This can't be real.

"I am sorry. I will keep trying," Erich said, looking at his feet.

"You bet your fucking bratwurst you'll keep trying. I don't care how long this takes."

Erich climbed back into the booth, his handsome face sunken and worn. Clark tapped me on the shoulder and we left.

Once outside the room he said, "No *People* today, although I'm sure they'd find this quite intriguing. I'll figure out what to tell the reporter."

Patrick Braithwaite was seated in the lounge, munching on Hershey's Kisses. Judging from the pile of balled-up silver wrappers next to him, he'd been waiting for a while. Clark apologized to Patrick, telling him that Erich was feeling ill and needed to reschedule the interview for the following afternoon. Patrick was unhappy, reminding Clark that Vivian had twisted his editor's arm to include Erich in the issue. Clark continued to apologize, and repeated that it was unavoidable. Patrick grabbed a couple of Kisses for the road and we all froze at the unmistakable sound of shattering glass.

"What was that?" asked Patrick, suddenly overtaken by a fit of investigative journalism.

"Oh, it's just some Foley guys messing around in one of the studios. They spent all morning trying to imitate the sound of a piano falling out of a building. I guess they've moved on," Clark said, shaking his head at the folly of the silly sound men.

Patrick nodded but then we heard a string of curse words followed by, "I'm going to pound you into a fucking schnitzel!"

Patrick's eyes widened. "That's no Foley team, unless they're trying to imitate the sound of Tony Waxman in full-on screaming mode. What the hell is going on here?"

I decided to play good cop. "Look Patrick, we'll level with you. It's not sound effects guys, you're right. Phil and Tony have been arguing on the phone about something all morning and it interrupted Erich's looping session. This has to be finished today so that the dialogue can be added to the print. We're only two weeks away from the movie's opening day."

Patrick nodded.

Clark picked up where I'd left off. "If we can just reschedule Erich's interview for tomorrow you'll have plenty of time with him. And I'll make sure you get to see the first screening of *The Raven II*."

Patrick seemed okay with that explanation and picked up his briefcase to leave. Two inches before he got to the door he turned around and said, "So what are they fighting about?"

Clark and I looked at each other. My mind went completely blank.

Patrick was insistent. "Why are the Waxmans screaming at each other?"

"It's about . . . ," Clark started.

"It's just . . . ," I said.

"Phil and Tony can't agree about a holiday gift for their mother," Clark said. "Phil wants to give her a luxury cruise, and Tony wants to give her a home gym with a personal trainer."

"Can't they just give her both?" Patrick asked.

"Yes, but that's not the point. Every year they give her a gift together. Otherwise she worries that her boys might not be getting along," I said.

Patrick didn't look convinced, especially as the shouting had started again, and was nearly earsplitting. "Right. That makes perfect sense. Can you please come up with a better lie next time? That one was insulting," he said, slamming the door as he left.

"Not the greatest save," I said to Clark, who appeared maddeningly calm and collected. I felt as if my hair were standing on end. My mouth was uncomfortably dry. The sight of Tony terrorizing Erich had upset me deeply, and I went into my embarrassing default mode of dreaming up "what if" scenarios.

"I'll bet Hanratty would love to know what just went on in there. That was vintage Tony—live and uncensored."

"Karen, you've really got to get off this whole Hanratty thing. No one's seen him in years, he's too much of a mess to write a grocery list, let alone a full-length book. Allegra keeps that thing on her phone sheet as a reminder, nothing else. Will you please just drop it already?"

Clark had never spoken to me so sharply before. Hurt and angry, I said, "You know Clark, sometimes I don't think you appreciate that some of us really care about what happens here. You flit in and out, working when and if you want, but I don't have that luxury. Of course you're not worried about Hanratty, because you don't worry about anything," I turned away from him.

"Karen, I'm so sorry. I didn't mean to upset you." Clark made a move to hug me, but I shrugged him off. "Please, don't be like that. I just don't want to see you all worked up over nothing. Honestly, Karen, I feel terrible."

"Okay, it's fine. I overreacted. It's just been a crazy day." I didn't want to continue this conversation.

"Really, sweetie, I am sorry."

"Apology accepted. Can we go now? Please?"

We left the studio. I learned later that week that Erich's looping session went on for a total of thirty straight hours, after which Tony decided that he would just make edits to the film and The Raven would have less dialogue than originally planned. Erich could brood convincingly and Tony would work around that.

When we got back to the office I found the draft of the press release on my chair. Allegra had edited it and left instructions that it was to be distributed to all major news outlets with a cover note explaining that Phil was not available for comment, "as he is completely focused on the Academy campaign for *El Lechero*." The quote from Phil had been altered dramatically. Gone were the references to the loyal staff and dedicated team whose efforts would help the film get its recognition. Instead, it was only about Phil's decision to cancel his holiday and remain in the city. The rest of us would remain a platoon of automatons programmed to get Phil whatever he wanted.

Recently, I'd been finding Allegra's behavior even stranger than usual. In the past month she'd lost more weight than anyone else in the office, yet she steadfastly refused to admit that her new figure had been pharmacologically assisted. When asked how she'd managed to lose so many pounds so quickly, she gave highly improbable answers, like "basketball" and "roller skating." This morning I'd heard her ascribe her downsizing to a recent infatuation with billiards, which she claimed was "great for the waistline."

A major portion of the *El Lechero* campaign would involve poetry readings of the work of Walt Whitman, whose poetry the film's title character believed to increase bovine fecundity. Juliet Bartlett, Jimmy-Dale Hawthorne, Bob Metuchen, Harry Spindler, Francesca Davis, and Ivan-Melissa Pell, as well as some other Glorious regulars, had already agreed to read at gatherings to be held in the lavish homes of Academy members in New York, Beverly Hills, and London, with sumptuous catering supplied by the studio. The hosts were allowed to invite whomever they wanted as long as Academy members comprised at least 75 percent of their guest list.

Dagney had become a one-woman flurry of phone calls and e-mails, as it was her job to coordinate this series of literary events. She was also in charge of the stylists, advising them on appropriate clothing selections for their clients. For the men, the look was right out of *Dead Poets Society*—khaki trousers, navy blue blazers, and a striped red tie over a white shirt accompanied by loafers, the more worn the better. The women were going strictly librarian chic, although their labels were out of the reach of most actual librarians. Tailored designer skirt-suits worn with silk blouses and stiletto-heeled black pumps were the order of the day. Hair would be pulled into a smooth French twist or a low ponytail. Most important was the eyewear. Dagney had succeeded in getting a chic SoHo optician to lend eyeglasses to the celebrity readers; the lenses were made of clear glass. Overall, these ensembles whispered "I am a well-read intellectual who shall enjoy sharing this poetry with you."

This fit exactly into the plan drafted by Phil, Allegra, and Vivian, who understood that *El Lechero* could be an important weapon in Hollywood's ongoing war against insecurity. Glorious would start an epidemic of intellectual anxiety, then offer a quick and easy cure for it.

"*Sí, sí, claro.* Actors know a lot of things," Vivian was saying into the phone. Her voice was a couple of notches above even its usual volume, so it was impossible not to eavesdrop. "They know they're adored. They know they're rich. They know they're talented, even if they're not." I wasn't sure to whom she was speaking, but I was riveted. "But the one thing that has them in knots is whether or not they're actually smart. So, Phil figured out this amazing plan to use *El Lechero* as a way of tapping into that and getting everyone excited about the movie at the same time." She went on to outline the strategy, which, if successful, would bag the nomination for *El Lechero*. "*Sí, sí.* How dare we call ourselves *artistas* if we don't even know how to appreciate poetry? *Es perfecto,*" she finished, loudly.

The first reading was held in the Beverly Hills mansion of a prominent producer. Juliet Bartlett and Jimmy-Dale Hawthorne read poetry from the film to the assembled guests. Within a week, there was poetry echoing from the Hollywood Hills to Wall Street, from Tower Bridge to TriBeCa and back. Dusty, leather-bound volumes became the new must-have accessory, and paparazzi shots in

People, Us, and *The Star* caught bespectacled celebrities in the act—in bookstores and libraries and even at a first-editions auction at Sotheby's, where the prices broke records. Allegra's phones rang off the hook with calls from Academy members who wanted to host readings and publicists who wanted their clients to orate. Dagney and I could barely keep up with the requests and the confirmations. We began to worry that there might not be enough poetry to go around.

Even Clark was swamped, as he'd been put in charge of the catering for each event. Phil appeared on all the morning shows, expounding on the virtues of poetry and mourning its loss in our busy culture. He sat in the living room-like set of each show, his ungainly shape slumped in sorrow during the interview portion. Then, to the delight of the hosts, he stood, threw his shoulders back, clasped his hands in front of him, and dramatically recited "O Captain! My Captain!" Suddenly *El Lechero* was the remedy for what ailed our souls and it was selling out at theaters across the country. Poetry was hot.

When one of the New York readings was held in the apartment of an Academy member who lived in the Dakota, I begged to go— the only time I'd gotten a glimpse of the inside of that building was when I'd seen *Rosemary's Baby.* I gave my name to the guard in the little booth on West Seventy-second Street, who made a phone call, then let me inside. Once in the apartment, which had a marvelous view of Central Park, I noticed several actors and actresses whom I knew lived in this building among the group of about forty elegantly dressed people; I also spotted Miranda Priestly, the editor of the world's most famous fashion magazine. Dressed in Prada and wearing huge sunglasses, she was standing alone by the window. Phil and Allegra were huddled together in a corner and Phil beckoned me over. "Make her take off her sunglasses. It looks like she's not paying attention."

I was rooted to the intricately patterned Persian rug on which I was standing. Asking Miranda Priestly to remove her sunglasses was number one on the list of things in New York that were Just Not Done. I tentatively took a couple of steps toward her, already imagining the columnists' gleeful scribblings at my expense. I glanced back over my shoulder in desperation and saw Allegra whispering in Phil's ear. "Karen," I heard, so softly it might have been imagined. I turned again, and saw my boss shaking her head from side to side. Even though she was doing it to protect Phil, I felt an unusual rush of gratitude.

After taking our seats in a large library with a fireplace, our host introduced the first of the two readers, Ivan-Melissa Pell. She wore a navy blue suit with a short yet tasteful skirt, and matching tall boots. There was nary a puka bead in sight—instead she'd chosen a matching pearl choker, bracelet, and earrings. She cleared her throat while putting on a pair of large, horn-rimmed eyeglasses, then launched into "Mannahatta," which she'd memorized, at several points gesturing dramatically behind her toward the park. She'd modulated her voice somehow, and it sounded less squeaky. Her transformation into an intelligent reader of poetry was astonishing. When she finished, Ana Maria Verdades stepped up and read "A Clear Midnight" in Spanish, as it had been read in the film. Then, in a tremulous voice, she read it again in English—Ana Maria's Berlitz classes had been coming along so well that she was now able to call Allegra every day to ask if she could return to Caracas for Christmas.

The crowd was moved by her sensitive performance and applauded enthusiastically before adjourning to another room for dessert wines and tiny pastries. I thanked Ana Maria and Ivan-Melissa on behalf of Glorious before leaving.

* * *

Ana Maria's pure loveliness and her near-mastery of English had begun to get her noticed within the American film community. She now had a Los Angeles–based agent eagerly sniffing out "situations" for her, and we had compiled a long list of interview requests, which she would sit for within the next couple of weeks. Phil felt that between Ana Maria, the director, and the platoon of celebrity poetry readers, *El Lechero* had as much visibility as was necessary to earn the nomination.

There was progress on *The Raven II* front as well. Erich had recorded an English language version of "Ich Habe Fieber (I Have a Fever)." In the tradition of ABBA, and to Tony's loud chagrin, his accent disappeared when he sang. The video was in regular rotation on MTV and Erich had become romantically involved with a Lithuanian supermodel. The couple seemed intent on attending every event to which they were invited while remaining joined at the face. They loved having their picture taken, and their photos appeared in numerous party round-ups.

Meanwhile, the film was complete, and there was every indication that fans of the original were unbelievably excited to see it. They filled Web sites with theories and suppositions about the film's plot, and loitered in the hotel lobby where Erich was staying in New York, genuflecting with a sort of swooping and bowing motion whenever he passed them. Each morning, when I arrived at work, there was a man dressed and made up to look exactly like The Raven standing like a sentry on the corner closest to our building. Except for being kind of creepy, he was harmless, and on one of the colder days I noticed that he'd switched to a pile-lined cape. Leaving the metaphysical home of The Raven unguarded due to the cold was not an option for this guy, whose name I never learned. Tony even stopped and took a picture with him one day.

The Glorious promotions department, run by an actually raven-haired woman named Delilah Billings, had coordinated a fifty-state radio promotion for *The Raven II* and the morning-show DJs on each of the participating stations were amping it up, playing the organ chords that signaled The Raven's imminent appearance on screen. The twenty-seventh caller (twenty-seven was an important number in Ravenology) would be entered into a drawing to win a trip to L.A. One lucky winner and a guest from each station would be flown to Los Angeles for a sneak-preview viewing of the film the night before it opened. They would then go on to an after-party, devoid of celebrities but full of Raven gifts and memorabilia. There would even be a raffle with a grand prize of an actual cape worn by Erich during the film's shooting.

But there was a significant problem with *The Raven II* that we were working hard to keep quiet. Simply put, *The Raven II: Nevermore* was awful. While the first film had been a huge hit, turning many people who'd never even heard of the comic book series into Raven devotees, this film was going to disappoint them. Badly. But by the time Tony, Phil, and the senior executives at Glorious realized that they had a real disaster on their hands, rather than just a thriller, the plans were too far gone to cancel or change.

The focus-group participants who'd seen the film had been unanimous in their poor reaction to it. At the conclusion of our department screening, we'd filed out silently, not knowing what to make of *The Raven II*, or what could be done to save it. Up until now it had always been The Raven who did the saving.

Absorbed in *El Lechero* as he was, Phil wasn't going to leave Tony holding the whole Raven bag by himself, so he took some time out to work on the problem. The film had a solid fan base and it was possible that the first weekend's box office might be saved, but only if they played their cards right. They couldn't use *The Gravedigger*'s playbook and have a celebrity-packed premiere, because with the exception of Erich, a nascent star at best, *The Raven II* had no real names attached to it. It was easy to eliminate the critics' screenings—the glut of year-end important, Academy-type films was taking up most of the reviewers' time and attention right now. The only sticking point in the plan to move *The Raven II: Nevermore* silently into theaters was the radio contest.

Tony wanted to call it off, but plane tickets and hotel arrangements had already been made for the one hundred people who would be attending. To kill it would mean that the same radio stations who had been promoting the contest for a month would undoubtedly spend a lot of on-air time speculating about why the screening had been cancelled. It would be a coast-to-coast question mark that Glorious could not afford to have asked.

Allegra and Tony made dozens of phone calls to each other, in which they tried to figure out what to do. Today was Monday, the film opened this Friday, and the contest-winners' screening was set for Thursday evening.

They came up with a plan and decided that Vivian would go to Los Angeles on Wednesday morning to oversee it. Vivian argued that she would be able to do more by remaining in New York and working on *El Lechero*. Allegra explained that this matter required Vivian's mix of precision, discipline, and diplomacy. Marlene offered to go instead, and that, coupled with Allegra's compliment, caused Vivian to throw herself into organizing the entire thing. Every few minutes she'd call orders over her cubicle wall to Dagney and me.

"I need two deluxe—*deluxe*—touring buses chartered for all day Friday; tell them you're not sure of the destination but that it's in-state: the pick-up is at the Los Angeles Holiday Inn on South Figueroa at 6 A.M., and the return will be to the same place at about 8 P.M."

"Make a sign that says, 'Place your cell phones in this basket—you will receive them on the way out.'"

"Get me a basket large enough to hold one hundred cell phones."

"Vivian, is there anything I can do?" Kimberly asked.

"Yes. Get me a large split pea with extra pepper and make sure it's vegetarian, not like the one with ham you ordered last week." With Kimberly occupied, Viv turned her attention back to us.

"Call Accounting and tell them I need twenty-five thousand in hundred-dollar bills. Tell them to call Tony if they need approval."

"Bring me fifty envelopes."

"Put five hundreds in each envelope."

"Seal each envelope using a glue stick *and* Scotch tape."

"Here's a list of the contest winners—make a label with each name on it."

"Stick one label on each envelope."

As Vivian was a determined nondelegator, when she absolutely had to share the workload she broke everything down into grain-of-sand-sized steps. Still, she frequently looked over our shoulders to make sure her instructions were being carried out to the letter. I'd just sealed the last envelope of cash (one swipe with the glue stick, tape covering the entire seam) when Vivian came over and asked me, "Are you sure that there are five hundred-dollar bills in each envelope?" I nodded and mentioned that Dagney and I had counted several times. Plus, we'd had exactly fifty envelopes and fifty name labels and it had all matched up, so we were confident we'd gotten it right. I nearly blurted, "It's not rocket science," but I knew that if I said that I'd surely be chastised for my underestimation of the seriousness of this operation.

Once we'd pulled together the items Vivian asked for, we packed them into a small black road case, the kind that rock bands use to carry equipment between cities. Vivian checked each item as it went in, then had us dump the case and do it again. When she was satisfied she had everything she needed, we secured the case with a heavy chain that went through the handles and ended in a large padlock. Vivian was planning to take the case on the plane as a carry-on. Having heard tales of her "Do you know who I am?" scenes in airports, there was no doubt she would succeed, whether or not the case fit in the overhead or comfortably under the seat in front of her. After we'd given her two extra copies of the padlock key, Vivian finally left the office. What was she up to? Even after Dagney and I had pooled all our clues together, we couldn't fathom what was about to take place.

BAD SANTA

On Wednesday morning, after I'd confirmed for Allegra that Vivian's flight had left New York and would arrive in Los Angeles on time, an e-mail was sent to everyone below the VP level. It said: "Santa has something for you—come to my office and see what's in your stocking!" The message was from Lowell Berglund, Glorious's acting CFO. Lowell had been in this position for close to three years but Phil and Tony were still unwilling to make his promotion official.

Lowell's office was located in a small room two floors above the rest of the company, almost as if having a CFO had been an afterthought. Of course, Lowell begged to differ. He told whomever he could get to listen that the reason his office was separate from ours was because of the "extremely sensitive nature of his work." It didn't matter. Lowell was a particularly unpleasant individual and it was a relief that we didn't see him too often. The e-mail puzzled me—it just didn't sound like something that Lowell's fingers could have typed. With six days left before Christmas, perhaps he'd gotten a visit from the Ghost of Christmas Yet to Come. Dagney told me that I should go first, as I "needed it more than she did." Eagerly anticipating whatever bonus I would be receiving, I trotted upstairs.

There were about seventy-five Glorious employees there already, in a line that started at Lowell's closed door and wound around the floor. People continued arriving from the elevator and stairwell. Most chattered excitedly, anticipating the holidays and the much-needed extra cash they were getting. The door to Lowell's office flew open and Lowell stepped out, holding a finger to his lips. I wondered if he was about to deliver some type of homily, or simply say, "God bless you each and every one." The crowd went silent. Lowell waited a few moments, just because he could, and then said, "You people disgust me. You're all squeezed into this hallway like pigs at the trough. And for what? A little money? I feel sorry for all of you." Then he took the box holding our bonus envelopes and tossed it high in the air. The envelopes fluttered down before scattering all over the floor. Lowell watched until the last one landed, then shook his head and returned to his office, slamming the door behind him.

Robert was closest to the spot where most of the envelopes had fallen. He scooped them up and handed them out, wishing each person a good holiday and a happy new year, in lieu of our acting CFO's acting like a human being. I got my envelope and went back downstairs, not bothering to see what was inside. "This can't be real," I accidentally said aloud to Dagney, who was trying not to look as if she was eager to pick up her bonus.

"What can't be?"

"Nothing," I said, startled that I'd spoken my mantra out loud. "I think Robert has your check," I told her, and then described what had happened upstairs.

"What's with this place? Tomorrow I'll be in Ibiza—far away from Lowell and the rest of this crap."

"Thanks, Dag," I said, sarcasm creeping into my voice, but obviously not enough for her to notice.

"Oh, you're welcome," she said, distractedly. "I'd better go see Robert now. I want to deposit that check and exchange some money before the bank closes."

If she rubs my face in it any more, I'll taste paella, I thought, while tossing the unopened envelope into my bag. Whatever meager amount they'd elected to give me couldn't begin to make up for this latest humiliation.

In the early afternoon, another e-mail came around. This one was from Geraldine, inviting everyone to a preholiday celebration, courtesy of Gloria. We were scheduled according to the first letter of our last name and would attend for half-hour intervals. The A–Fs were going now, but Dagney was out attending to her currency exchange. The G–M group was slated for the following half hour, so Clark, Robert, and I would go together.

Dagney came back just in time for the changeover and I let her know where I was headed as Clark stopped by the desk and gallantly offered me his arm. We picked up Robert and continued on to the conference room.

The moment we walked in, Gloria came dashing over to squeeze and pinch Clark, and to quiz him about the spa treatments he'd signed up for next week. She looked like a fancy present, her smart crimson pantsuit liberally trimmed with tinsel and topped off with what looked like a tribal headdress.

Robert and I left them in favor of a long table loaded with all types of goodies—chocolate Santas, caramel reindeer, and marshmallow Christmas trees; chocolate coins, caramel Hanukkah candles, and marshmallow menorahs; and then an assortment of plain chocolates, caramels, and marshmallows. At the end of the table was a sundae bar with assorted flavors of ice cream, hot fudge and other toppings, whipped cream, and three bowls of sprinkles—red and green, blue and white, and multicolored. Robert and I helped ourselves and quickly found the marshmallow menorahs to be our favorite before moving over to the ice cream area, where we concocted a pair of extremely creative desserts. Our goal was to use everything available. Gloria came over and kissed each of us. "What do you think of this spread?" she asked.

Robert and I nodded, and after I'd swallowed another mouthful of ice cream laced with menorah I told her that it was delicious.

"You see, I have things for people who celebrate Christmas, things for people who celebrate Hanukkah, and then things for our friends from other faiths," she said, pointing at the plain candies. "My girl, Roxanne"—she pointed to her long-time social secretary, an African-American woman currently nibbling on a reindeer— "told me that it's not PC to just have treats for Christmas and Hanukkah. 'You have to include everyone Mrs. W.,' she told me."

Robert nodded.

"I would feel terrible, but what do I know?" Gloria answered. "To me, a holiday's a holiday. Who knew it could all get so complicated?" she said, smiling.

"It's always good not to leave anyone out," Robert said, biting the head off a Santa.

"I would never forgive myself," Gloria said. Then she did a spin for us. "What do you think of my outfit? I figured I could be Christmas and Kwanzaa on the outside. Inside I'm Hanukkah, as you know."

Just then Geraldine showed up to let all us G–Ms know that our party was over and she needed the room cleared before the N–Rs could come in.

"Such a sour puss on that one," Gloria said, shaking her head. "Maybe she'll find a husband in the new year." She gave us each a squashing hug before we left.

Back at our desk Dagney was in a snit. Geraldine had told her that anyone who'd missed their letter couldn't attend the festivities with another group. "She's such a pain in the ass," Dagney said. Part of me wanted to tell her that it had been like a third-grade birthday party, but I decided against it. It wasn't likely that she'd let on if it rained in Spain. As if she could read my mind she said, "I can't wait to get out of this place and get to Ibiza. Maybe I'll never come back."

Clark stopped by the desk to show us the gift Gloria had given him. It was a sterling silver money clip from Tiffany, engraved with the initials "CRG." Each letter was punctuated with a tiny diamond.

"Very *Goodfellas*," I said. "And what's the 'R' for?"

"Gloria said I need this for when we're playing cards. She said she'll feel better taking my money if I have a decent clip to hold it in."

"How much did she take from you this year?" I asked.

"Counting the canasta, pinochle, and Texas Hold'em, not to mention an out-of-control game of Go Fish that nearly bankrupted me, it was about thirty-five hundred. But it doesn't matter, I get to expense it."

"You get to expense the money you lose to Gloria?" I was incredulous.

"Gloria Waxman is a card-counting, double-dealing shark. Sure, she pretends we're buddies, but I'm more like her victim."

"So, what's the 'R' stand for, Clark?"

"My middle name."

"Yeah. I figured that. What is it?" I said, playfully grabbing his wrist.

"Crap. It's Rufus." He held up his hand. "Before you make fun of it, be aware that it's the same name as my mother's dear, departed West Highland Terrier."

"You're named after a dog?" Dagney popped into the conversation.

"Rufus was no ordinary dog. He was an AKC champion, and his puppies and grandpuppies are funding my parents' retirement."

"Of course he wasn't. You wouldn't name your firstborn son after some mutt," I said.

Robert, who had been standing silently nearby, could no longer help himself. "Clark!" He said it so that it sounded like a bark. "Rufus," he said, lengthening the "Roo" part so that it resembled a howl. Pretty soon we were all barking and howling until Marlene came out and yelled at us about the migraine we'd given her.

Vivian called and told me that she'd arrived in Los Angeles and was on her way to have a look at the venues where the screening and after-party would take place tomorrow night. "Let Allegra know I've secured everything," she said. I typed her message onto the call sheet, unsure of what she meant.

Then I started getting dressed for the next party. Glorious had purchased a $10,000 table at the annual Young Democrats in Entertainment Holiday Gala, but no one in the higher ranks wanted to go, so Clark, Robert, Dagney, and I, along with some other Young Glorious Staffers with Asses had been pressed into service to fill the seats. Dress was "festive," and the event was being held in the ballroom of one of those two midtown Sheratons that face each other—I wasn't sure which one, but was confident that Robert would know.

The place was packed, but the four of us mixed and mingled only with one another during the cocktail hour, having decided to do away with the name tags issued upon arrival. Systems Alejandro was there, along with Kimberly and Sabrina, who joined us. Kimberly waved to a guy who came over and introduced himself as "Trevor from Stan Coburn's." His boss had purchased a table as well, and ordered his minions to fill its seats. According to Trevor, this was a rare night out of the office for them; Stan tended to keep his staff quite late.

Stan was an independent producer who had teamed up with Phil a couple of times in the past, although not since I'd been at Glorious. Most of his films were distributed by other studios, and it seemed logical that Phil would want to partner with him again in the future. Stan was known for having a fantastic knack for producing films that were winners with the critics, the Academy voters, and the box office, and he could work his magic in nearly any genre. In the trades, which chronicled his voracious purchases of the rights to theatrical properties, novels, and biographies—anything that he thought had cinematic value—he was often quoted as being "all about the script." Stan was also known to be as difficult as he was successful, going through assistants the way other people did chewing gum.

Trevor left for a moment and returned with five colleagues, all of whom were in their late twenties, impeccably dressed, and extremely handsome. We introduced ourselves.

"You work for Allegra Orecchi?" one of them said, after he'd asked me what I did at Glorious.

"Yes, Dagney and I are her assistants."

"That's so funny," he said. "I know you guys. You're the ones whose damn boss is always in."

"What are you talking about?" I said. I knew that I'd never logged a message from Stan Coburn. I looked at Dagney quizzically, who raised her eyebrows back.

"Every morning, Stan has us call about nine hundred people," Trevor explained. "There are six of us, so we make one hundred fifty calls apiece. He has us call really early, before anyone is in, so that when that person gets to their office, they know Stan's already working—even though of course he's not in yet."

"And what happens if you call someone and they actually answer?" I said, everything suddenly clicking into place.

"We have to hang up, because we can't actually patch him in," Trevor said.

"Dagney, meet the hang-up men," I said.

"What? Oh shit! You have no idea how badly you frightened us," she said.

"We thought we were being stalked, or that some lunatic was in the building with us," I added.

"I'm sorry," Trevor said. "It's just that Allegra comes in so early; we never manage to leave word before she's there."

"But that's the whole point," I said, immeasurably relieved. "She's not in. She's at home, in bed. We just put whoever calls on hold for a few seconds, then pick up and say she's in a meeting." So Clark had been correct—the hang-ups were not the work of George Hanratty or a serial murderer.

Just then all six of Stan's assistants reached into their pockets and answered their cell phones in unison.

"I'm sorry," one said.

"Trevor's going to find one," another said.

"No, we didn't mean to leave you there," the only blond one said.

"You're absolutely right, it's not acceptable," said another.

Then they all hung up, except for Trevor, who had moved away to place another call. "Stan's in London and he's having trouble finding a cab," one of them explained.

"So he called you in New York?" Dagney said, looking at her watch. "It's nearly one in the morning there."

He nodded. "Stan doesn't really care. No matter what happens, it's someone's fault. Now Trevor will call a car service and Stan will hail a cab on his own and be gone before it gets there. Happens all the time."

Trevor returned to our group.

"Trevor, the next time one of you calls our office, just leave a message. Do you realize that this has been going on for the past nine months and they've never actually spoken?" I said. "Allegra doesn't even know that Stan wants to reach her."

"There's a fable in here somewhere," Trevor said. "The tale of what happened when the man who's never in called the woman who never leaves."

"And scares her assistants out of their minds," I added. "We nearly called the police."

I turned to Dagney for confirmation, but she had vanished. Systems Alejandro, I noted, was also missing; perhaps he was giving her a private lesson in his native tongue, to help her get ready for Ibiza. I'd have to remember to quiz her closely when she came back from her vacation.

The next morning Belinda gifted me with an early copy of *Us Weekly*. I'd been trying to get my hands on it before it hit the news-stands. This was the holiday double issue with its annual "Stalking Stars' Stockings" feature; it described what all the household names were giving and getting for Christmas. According to *Us*, everyone you'd ever heard of would find some poetry stashed under their tree this year. The tone of the article was a little disappointed, as if the writer yearned for a return to years past, when outrageously priced baubles and ultra-sleek gadgets had been the only gifts worth getting. It also had a handy sidebar about specific poets whose work would make excellent gifts, along with a helpful shopping guide showing where *Us* readers could emulate their favorite stars and actually purchase books.

I ordered enough copies of the magazine so that it could be handed out at the *El Lechero* mini-junket taking place tomorrow. The press would arrive tonight, screen the film, and have an audience with Ana Maria, who would read poetry in English and Spanish. On Friday they would interview the director and Ana Maria, who would work with an interpreter. Owing to its small size, I didn't have to work on the junket—although I'd been told to consider myself "on notice."

This morning, Liz Smith's column had noted that the president's holiday gift to his wife would be a first edition of *Leaves of Grass*. The columnist further suggested that in these materialistic times a volume of poetry would be the best gift for anyone on your list. Along with being a leading tastemaker, Liz Smith was widely syndicated, so when Allegra finally arrived for work at three, she immediately had me find Phil so that she could feed him the good news. She also told me to bring the copy of *Us* to his office right away.

"Don't just give it to one of his assistants. Hand it to him directly," she muttered.

Once at Phil's, I saw Sabrina and gave her the magazine. "I'm handing this to Phil directly," I said.

"He always flips right to the 'Stars—They're Just Like Us!' pages," she snickered, tossing the magazine on top of a pile of scripts, unopened mail, and a week's worth of the Hits.

"That smells amazing," I said, inhaling the scent of New York delicatessen and realizing that I was famished from having not eaten all day. I glanced over and there on the table were the generous remains of Phil's lunch meeting. "Help yourself," Sabrina said, handing me a paper plate. I took half a corned beef sandwich from the platter, painted the top piece of rye bread with mustard, then added some fries and cole slaw. As I was leaving, Sabrina put a huge dill pickle on my plate—"for the road."

With Dagney on vacation, a temp was guarding the phones, so I needed to get back quickly. "Thanks!" I called over my shoulder, sprinting with my loaded plate in front of me. The temp was nervously taking down a message from Vivian when I returned. I motioned for him to hand me the phone and Vivian immediately launched into a criticism of my decision to let an "outsider" answer Allegra's phones. She told me that she would be performing some highly delicate maneuvers regarding *The Raven II* over the next few hours and that I would need to be exceptionally careful about any information I gave out regarding the film. As I'd been completely left out of the discussions regarding what it was that Vivian was doing in L.A., there was nothing I could say, anyway. During this conversation Robert appeared and grabbed a couple of fries from my plate. I shook my fist at him and he left, only to return a couple of minutes later with a packet of ketchup that he drizzled on the rest of them.

"What's up with Viv?" he said, wiping some ketchup from the corner of his mouth.

"I can't believe you did that," I said, pulling my plate closer to me.

"Relax, it's just a few fries. What's up with Viv?"

"Just a few of *my* fries. Something about 'delicate maneuvers' around *The Raven II.*"

"At least you don't have to go to the *New York Times* tonight. There's no review."

"Small favors," I said. "The movie's so bad that it wasn't shown to critics."

"That's good, you'll get to go out or go home or do something else for once," he said.

"Not exactly. I'm supposed to stay here and wait for Vivian to call. Doesn't this feel somehow wrong to you?"

"Wrong?" he said, reaching for my pickle. I grabbed his wrist.

"That all a bad movie means is that I don't have to stay up late on Thursday? That it's not disappointing or upsetting? We don't celebrate the good ones, either, Robert."

"You've been here almost a year and you just figured that out?"

"It just never seemed so apparent until now," I said, biting into my sandwich even though my appetite had disappeared. The phone rang. "Allegra Orecchi's office," I said, glumly.

"Get me Allegra now! This is an emergency!" Marlene screamed into the receiver. For once she sounded as if she were telling the truth, and I walked into Allegra's office with a Post-it that said, "Marlene—real emergency." I had underlined the "real." Allegra finished her call and then picked up Marlene. Two minutes later, Allegra buzzed me to come into her office.

"There's been an error. A serious error. The hotel doesn't have the reservations for any of the junket press—they say they were cancelled yesterday and that now they don't have any rooms. I need you to get someone in Travel to find seventy-five rooms at any hotel—or more than one, if you have to." She swiveled her chair away, my cue to get started.

My first call was to Robert, who rushed over. "Has anything like this ever happened before?"

"Never, ever," he said, looking oddly amused. "For a minute there, I thought you said we had to find seventy-five hotel rooms in New York City during high tourist season."

Then I dialed the executive vice president of the travel department, and left a detailed message with her assistant.

"At least we have trained professionals on the case," I muttered to Robert, recalling the Erica Hall incident. It had actually taken two weeks for me to have a working American Express card again, during which time I'd received an itemized accounting of the not-so-very incidentals Erica had charged to her room during her three day stay at the Pierre. Why anyone would need two manicures a day escaped me, but the expense of those didn't compare with that of the floral arrangements, in-room spa services, and enough room service meals to feed an army—all of which Glorious was expected to cover. But there was an upside in that I'd gotten to keep the seventeen thousand mileage points; almost enough for a free ticket. Now I just needed permission to take some time off.

After a while the travel person called back to let us know that the best they could do was a place out near JFK that she described as "not exactly a flophouse, but not Howard Johnson's, either. They have hourly rates, if you need them," she said, which seemed to be her idea of putting some positive spin on it. She was definitely telling it to the wrong people. I relayed this to Allegra, who had me conference her in with Marlene. As expected, Marlene threw a fit but really had no other choice than to book the motel. "At least there are no real stars attending this junket," she finished, hanging up.

For the first time in weeks I was truly in an excellent mood: The thought of Marlene managing a junket in Queens was the best corporate holiday gift I could have received. And for once, I hadn't taken the blame for something I hadn't broken. But given Marlene's preternatural ability in the area of junket management I couldn't help but wonder—who had? Could it have been Hanratty? That didn't make sense. Now he'd have to go all the way to a horrible joint in Queens to spy on us. If only Abby were here so that we could have dinner together the way we used to. We would have ordered some pizza, opened a bottle of Merlot, and soon we would have been laughing at the insanity of it all.

I finished up what I was doing and left a message for Vivian, telling her that I was leaving and that I'd be on my cell if she needed me. Then I called Allegra and told her the same thing. Had I thought of it earlier, I could have called Elliott and seen if he was around. It would be simply lovely to have my feet expertly attended to, while having a drink, phone firmly switched off.

When I arrived at 7 the next morning, Allegra's voice mail already had five messages from Delilah in Promotions. I called her back. "Karen, what's going on with the screening? I've had calls from more than twenty disc jockeys from the stations that held this contest. The deal was that this morning the winners were going to be interviewed live on air to talk about the movie. No one can find them. It's as if they've fallen into in a black hole."

I told her that I'd try to find out what was going on. It was too early on the West Coast to call Vivian, so I worked on the Hits and when Allegra called promptly at 7:45, I relayed Delilah's message.

"Karen, I hope you didn't tell her anything."

"I don't have anything to tell."

"You're not supposed to. Call Delilah and let her know that I'll speak with her later."

After calling, I started printing out Allegra's e-mails. Christmas was Wednesday, just five days away, and not much was going on. Allegra had only a couple of e-mails and the phone hadn't rung once.

At nine, Vivian called and asked to be patched through to Allegra. I put them together and muted my phone to listen in.

"Okay, we're on the bus, I've given out the money, and the phones are back in my hotel room safe," Vivian said, somehow whispering stridently.

"Are they angry?"

"No. How could they be angry when I told them their phones were stolen by a man who held a knife to my throat? Then they all had so much to drink at the after-party. I don't think any of them could have dialed if they tried."

"And this morning?" Allegra asked.

"After they'd left for the screening last night, I insisted that the hotel disable their outgoing calls for the rest of their stay. I had the hotel make personal wake-up calls to all fifty rooms, telling them to come downstairs for breakfast immediately. I took attendance and handed out the envelopes as they boarded the bus. After we were rolling, I told them where we were going."

"And?"

"*Todo es bueno.* Aside from the fact that I have to spend a day in Disneyland with one hundred *Raven* fanatics, everything's going to be fine. Five hundred dollars is more than most of these people earn in a week. They were thrilled."

"I'm going to make sure that Tony knows just how instrumental you've been in this whole process. I don't know anyone else who could have handled this so perfectly."

"He already knows. I just spoke with him."

Allegra was silent. She wouldn't be able to make it look as if it had been her own save. Vivian had practically grown up at Glorious—did Allegra really think she could put one over on her?

"Allegra? Are you there?" Vivian said.

"Yes. Just make sure you give those phones back later. It's not in our budget to replace them. Are you sure they're safe?"

"I'm absolutely certain."

That was what passed for an argument between Allegra and Vivian.

Allegra called back and had me put her through to Delilah, who sounded frantic when she answered. "Allegra, what's going on? Where are the contest winners?"

"We decided to have them spend the day at Disneyland. Vivian's with them, and we gave them plenty of spending money."

"But they were each supposed to call their radio stations and tell them about the movie. It was part of the deal we promised the DJs in exchange for running the contest."

"Well, Delilah, all of their cell phones were stolen during the screening. What can I tell you?"

"I can't believe this. One hundred phones were stolen?"

"Yes, it's unfortunate. We're hoping the LAPD can find them so we don't have to deal with all of the insurance claims."

"Are you sure they were stolen? How could someone take every single person's phone?"

It's not hard when they're all in one basket, I thought.

"It's unfortunate," Allegra repeated, dismissively. Allegra's presidency trumped Delilah's directorship. There was nothing else to be said.

When Robert showed up a half hour later, I filled him in on what was going on in L.A. with the screening of *The Raven*.

"I love it!" he said. "They kidnapped the audience so that they couldn't tell anyone from the radio stations how bad the movie is. By the time they get their phones back, the film will be open all over the country. They've saved the opening weekend! It's brilliant!"

"I think it's really sneaky."

"Yes, but there's nothing like a truly clever scheme, well executed. This is the best one I've seen since I started here. I love it! I love it!" I could hear a trail of "I love it"s as Robert went back to his cube, which we'd all started referring to as "the Cub."

I understood that it was an excellent plan, which had come off without a hitch. No one was going to be hurt by a day at Disneyland, or by an extra $500, not to mention the fact that they'd all get their phones back that evening. The "LAPD" would have recovered them by then. But what I understood even more deeply was that I would never be capable of dreaming up this sort of conspiracy. My brain just didn't work that way, nor did I want it to. And if that was the kind of thinking that was respected here, I'd never make it. This much was crystal clear, even though the rest of the day went by in a fog, as if I were sleepwalking. *This can't be real this can't be real this can't be real* ran through my head in all of its variations, but it did nothing to calm me. I passed Delilah in the hallway in the afternoon and felt ashamed at the face she made in my direction. She'd always been nice to me—a notable distinction at Glorious. Although I'd had nothing to do with *The Raven II* contest, there was no way she would believe me, so I didn't even try to explain or apologize.

I got home that night and dreamed that Erich, as The Raven, was chasing me. He kept telling me that I needed to go somewhere, but when I asked him where I should go, his accent made it impossible for me to understand what he was saying. I woke up feeling awful. My head ached, my throat hurt, and it took all my energy just to get out of bed and to my medicine cabinet. A couple of minutes later, the thermometer confirmed it: I had a fever.

THE GREAT ESCAPE

t was the first weekend in months that I didn't have to work at a junket, a premiere, or some other Glorious happening and I managed to get sick. I spent both days napping and generally moping around. In a way it was exactly what I needed—an excuse to do nothing more labor-intensive than click the remote. On Sunday night I watched *A Charlie Brown Christmas,* and when Linus put his blanket around Charlie Brown's little tree I suddenly started crying. It was the most tender moment I'd experienced in months.

I called Abby in Baltimore, but got her voice mail and hung up. She was probably studying for exams or carving up poor old Lloyd, if there was anything left of him. It was better not to leave some teary, fever-enhanced message, which would only lead Abby to want to diagnose me over the phone, probably scaring me half to death.

I'd thought a lot about that last conversation with Robert, and how impressed he'd been with Viv's deceitful behavior toward the *Raven* fans, applauded by all because in the end it benefited the company's coffers. When I'd joined the company, I'd known it had a reputation for being harsh, but I could handle that. I could handle harshness and hard work and nasty comments and unpleasant coworkers and nearly everything else that had been thrown at me during the past year. But "handling" and "succeeding" were two different things entirely, and it had become unnervingly apparent that I was going nowhere at Glorious. At best, I was treading water; at worst, my head was being held under the surface. There was no single moment that I could pinpoint as the beginning of the decline, but I had a sneaking suspicion that it had probably been during my interview. I made a premature New Year's resolution to find my way out of this morass.

The next morning, fever gone, I went into work.

Things were pretty quiet throughout most of the company, but the publicity department was in session, even with Christmas two days away. The front page of *Variety* read: "MILKMAN DELIVERS SWEET MOOSIC TO BOX OFFICE." Over the weekend *El Lechero* had broken a record and become the highest-grossing foreign film in U.S. history. While we wouldn't learn if it was nominated for Best Picture until announcements were made in mid-February, we knew that the film was at least reaping its financial reward.

The take for *The Raven II: Nevermore* had dropped off precipitously after its opening night. The newspapers that had chosen to review it at all were unanimous in their panning. Every single headline had incorporated the word "Nevermore," and the critics took it from there.

In an advantageous coincidence for Glorious, PBS had scheduled a Walt Whitman documentary to air this week. Produced several years earlier, it had now been updated to include some clips from *El Lechero*. To express its gratitude, Glorious made a large cash grant, earning the underwriter spot that preceded each airing. Glorious also donated a large amount of merchandise to the network. PBS incorporated the documentary and the film into their holiday fund-raising effort: Viewers who pledged more than $1,000 would receive a "theater lobby quality" *El Lechero* poster, along with a copy of the screenplay. Allegra ordered a videotape of the hosts enthusiastically chattering about *El Lechero* and asked me to bring it directly to Phil.

On the way over, I bumped into Matt Vincent, on his way out of the conference room. Matt and I e-mailed regularly, but I rarely saw him. He'd had nothing but praise for the film summaries and news bits I'd written for the site and had sent along several complimentary notes about my work. Those printouts were stashed in my desk drawer and on particularly bad days I'd reread them, reminding myself that I wasn't as inept and untalented as Viv, Allegra, and Marlene led me to believe.

"Hey Karen, nice to see you. I didn't know if you'd already left for the holiday."

"Allegra asked us to stay and work on *El Lechero*," I said, trying to be diplomatic. "I'm here for the duration."

He grimaced. "Well, I was going to ask you to come speak with me after the New Year, but since we're both here now, we can get started sooner. I've got some ideas for the site that I'd like to run by you—we're all really impressed with what you've done so far, and frankly, if you can take it on, there's some more we'd like you to do."

"Thanks. I'm around."

"I'll call you later and give you the download—I'm leaving for a week's vacation tomorrow night, so I'd like to try to get together tomorrow."

"That's great, Matt. Just let me know when," I said, as I continued on to Phil's office, feeling almost giddy about the exchange. I'd love to do more with the marketing department—Publicity was just looking like a lot more of the same. In just over a month I'd be laying my cards on the table, deciding what to do. A plum assignment from Matt Vincent would certainly tip the scales.

"Here's the PBS tape," I waved the box at Sabrina.

"*Masterpiece Theatre?*"

"Not exactly. The *El Lechero* holiday pledge drive."

She took the tape from me. "I'll put this right in Phil's hands," she said, adding it to a stack of videos on the floor.

Five feet from my desk, I realized that there was no way I could possibly have a meeting with Matt, what with Dagney in Ibiza and Allegra still clinging to the hope that Oprah would return her call. Even my trips to Phil's office had to be kept brief so that my temp wouldn't be on his own for too long. It would have made more sense to send him to Phil's office with the tape, except that Geraldine had enacted a strict rule that no one who wasn't a full-time employee of Glorious was permitted within a twenty-foot radius of the brothers' offices. The edict had been issued about a month after I'd started, when a freelancer from the art department had been caught lingering around their suite. Tony had had a fit and ordered Geraldine to remove the wayward lurker from the premises immediately. She'd frog-marched the guy out, just short of holding him by the scruff of the neck. "I was only trying to *look* at them," he'd said, in his unsuccessful bid to keep his temporary position a bit longer. Geraldine's memo on the topic had been distributed the same afternoon and was refreshed on a quarterly basis.

As I composed an e-mail to Matt explaining my need to speak on the phone instead of meeting with him in person, I grew angrier with each draft. I wasn't even getting the opportunity to get an opportunity. Didn't NAFTA guarantee me something like that? The glass ceiling in this place seemed to be at shoulder height, and I was tired of hunching over. My musings were interrupted by the message box beeping. "In Here NOW."

I entered Allegra's office and she motioned for me to sit down on her couch. "Karen, I have something important to tell you. In case you haven't noticed, I've needed a break for quite some time."

Actually, I hadn't, strangely preoccupied with my own problems, as it were. Besides, Allegra wasn't really one to share.

She continued, "Phil and Tony have agreed to my taking a leave of absence. Vivian will be the acting head of this department. You and Dagney will run my office as usual, but you'll give Vivian a hand if she asks. While I'm away, please continue to do things as per usual with regard to my telephone calls and e-mails."

"You'd like us to tell people that you're in but not available?"

"Basically, but by now I expect that you'll know who's important enough to hand over to Vivian. You'll tell them that I can't answer their call, and then Vivian will get back to them."

"How do we reach you?"

"You don't. I'm going to be traveling in Europe and I won't be available for anyone. I may call in, but that's still up in the air."

"That sounds wonderful."

"It really isn't any of your concern."

"When are you leaving?" I asked, figuring this was all just in the planning stages.

"Today is my last day in the office, and my flight leaves on Wednesday evening. I'll be announcing this later in a meeting, which I need you to organize, but I wanted to make sure you were very clear about what was going on."

I tried not to let my facial expression belie my inner bliss. She swiveled her chair so her back was to me. I dashed out and saw that I had an e-mail from Matt, asking if I could go over there at eleven tomorrow, and I quickly replied that I could. It looked as if Allegra's break just might lead to my big break out. In the hastily called Publicity staff meeting, Allegra's announcement was met by questions from all corners of the room.

"Which cities are you visiting?"

"When will you be back?"

"Will you be here for the Oscars?"

"What if Vivian is not responsive to our needs?" This was from Marlene, clearly vexed at the idea of having to answer to Viv.

Allegra didn't answer any of these, choosing instead to look truly enigmatic, a Mona Lisa smile on her face. Was this a clue that she would be in France? Italy? The whole thing was just so weird. She spent the rest of the afternoon cleaning up her office, passing me huge piles of memos and correspondence that she wanted destroyed. As I fed a year's worth of Marlene's moanings into the shredder, watching as it turned her angry ranting into innocuous little ribbons of trash, I recalled how upset I'd been the first time she'd included me in one of her missives; now I was mildly insulted when she left me out. There were also phone logs, including the ones from the first hours of the *HackSaw* incident, those hundreds of calls; Dagney and I gave Allegra a new log every hour and she'd kept every one. The small bits of type that caught my eye before they were eradicated brought back the entire year that had passed: the calls from Francesca Davis' mother; a frantic back-and-forth with Ivan-Melissa's manager about the importance of her hyphen; Harry Spindler's mother complaining about me; Juliet Bartlett, followed by her publicist, her agent, then her assistant—a kind of *A Star is Born* played out in several weeks' worth of phone messages; message-less messages from Marlene; Clark calling from JFK, requesting permission to expense Jimmy Chin's new wardrobe at Barneys; journalists, gossip columnists, and TV-newsmagazine producers by the dozen; the devastating news of Oliver's early departure;

and Ana Maria Verdades's multiple requests, still unanswered, to return to Caracas for Christmas. On every first page was the specter of George Hanratty, in the space designated for sightings of him. Nothing had ever been written there, but I was positive that he was well known to many of my Glorious colleagues. Having met or spoken with Hanratty was a shameful secret that many of us undoubtedly shared. And that was another resolution I was going to make—next year, I wasn't going to worry about Hanratty or his book. Shredding the mountainous pile of papers felt good, cleansing, like a restful night's sleep after a hard day of physical labor. It seemed like the planets might be lining up just right for me. Allegra would be away for a while, I would be meeting with Matt in the morning, and the New Year was a little more than a week away.

The last thing Allegra had me do before she left was install her message box on Vivian's desk. And then, in a final flurry of tote bags and goose down, she was gone. My footsteps echoed as I entered her completely bare office. Apparently all that paper had absorbed a great deal of sound; the acoustics were now so good that Allegra's voice would have been downright thunderous. The room was empty, save for a few pieces of furniture and the desk, on which her cell phone lay—a symbol of her unreachable status. Allegra was completely and officially unplugged. I waited around for a while, just in case she came back to retrieve some forgotten item, but she didn't.

Vivian had also left, so I headed home to do a little research about our competitors' sites. I wanted to have some good information and suggestions for tomorrow's meeting with Matt. As I rode down in the elevator I felt an unfamiliar yet pleasurable sensation. It stayed with me through the subway ride home, and grew while I worked online, pulling together facts about how other companies were using the Internet to market their films. As I printed out my findings, I realized that it was simply a sense of purpose—something that had been absent from my life for a long time.

The next morning, I gave the temp lengthy phone-call-handling instructions and my own cell number before walking over to Matt's office. My head brimmed with ideas and my manila folder bulged with information—if only I could just achieve the right look, the right overall presentation, to make Matt want to work with me. Suddenly I flashed on Juliet Bartlett in her Timberland boots and giant jewelry. I felt precisely as if I were in costume for a role that I desperately wanted.

The meeting went well. Matt told me that he was pleased with the research I'd done and thought it might even help him get some additional funds out of Phil and Tony. It was clear that the other studios had really invested in their online marketing; taking baby steps just wouldn't get Glorious up to speed quickly enough to compete. In addition to continuing with my synopses of the upcoming films, Matt wanted me to start a kind of gossip column, to be updated weekly. It wasn't real dish, since all the items would be Glorious-approved and most probably already reported in newspapers and magazines, but we would spice it up with on-set photographs and "first looks" at the stars in their costumes. Matt said that the project was mine, and I was thrilled to have his vote of confidence. The meeting ended, and he asked me to come see him again at the same time next week. This was the lightest I'd felt in a year, and I hoped that it was the beginning of a much-needed uptick in my career.

For the rest of the day Robert and I camped out in Allegra's office, pulling together the huge, year-end compilation of Top Ten

Lists. We were trying to get through them quickly; it was Christmas Eve. Robert was in charge of this every year, and he showed me his system for making the annual ritual as fast and accurate as possible. Nearly every media outlet released a list of their top ten films. Our goal was to find out how many of them had listed *El Lechero* in their top ten, and of those, how many had listed it as their number one choice.

This laborious procedure had started right after Thanksgiving, when the top tens started appearing. I'd saved each one after it went around in the Hits, and Marlene had requested that each junket reporter send their own picks to her. Dagney had been in charge of getting the television and radio lists from the broadcast monitoring company, and Clark had diligently worked the Web, unearthing some Spanish-language film lists that gave *El Lechero* a significant boost, as well as many self-appointed critics who'd posted lists on their own pages. It was all fair game.

Without Allegra's physical presence, the place took on a different vibe—not one of anxiety but of possibility and industriousness. I sat on the couch with stacks of paper all around me while Robert sat at the desk, entering information into the computer; he typed as I read them aloud.

"*Orlando Sentinel,* one list, has it in fifth place."

"Got it. Next."

"*San Jose Mercury News,* two critics, one doesn't have it, one has it in second, but it's alphabetical."

"Got it."

"KKYX-AM San Antonio, 'Franny on Film' has it in first."

"Wait a second, okay, got it."

I noticed that Robert was exceptionally quiet. We'd been in Allegra's office for hours and he hadn't made one cynical comment, or even commented on Allegra's disappearing act. He seemed distracted and a few times I had to call his name repeatedly to get his attention.

"Robert, are you okay?"

"Yeah, I really want to get through this and get out of here, that's all." I wasn't convinced, but didn't want to pry. By the end of the day, we knew that 659 critics had ranked *El Lechero* in their top ten, and of those, 148 had named it the year's best. It was six o'clock, and Robert was late to his uncle's, where he was due for Christmas Eve dinner. He was reluctant to leave me alone, but all I had to do was e-mail the lists to Vivian, Marlene, Matt, Phil, and Tony, so I made him go ahead. Ten minutes later, as I was putting on my coat, the phone rang. It was Phil. "Where's Vivian?"

"She left for the night."

"Marlene?"

"Also left."

"Fuck. Is anyone there?"

"Can I help you, Phil? It's Karen, Allegra's assistant."

"Yeah, you can help me. Find two more lists with the picture on top. What the fuck am I supposed to do with one hundred forty-eight?"

I understood exactly what he meant. He wanted ads that read "150 Critics Agree—*El Lechero* is *Numero Uno!*"

"I'll see if I can find them."

"When you do, get them to Mahmoud." He hung up.

I got online and started to search for any publication, Web site or pop-up ad that had *El Lechero* in first place. After looking for a while, I found a site for the Century Village Cinema Club in Boynton Beach. The list was embedded inside an article that started, "In the most contentious voting ever seen by the Century Village Cinemaniacs, *El Lechero* won our top honors by a nose." Yes! One more to go. I Googled, Nexised, Yahoo'd, and Alta Vista'd and nearly gave up before pinning my last hope on Terra Lycos. All of a sudden it was there: Cine Montevideo Online had it as number one. "Thank you Uruguay and good night!" I shouted, rock star style, to the empty cubes around me.

After adding in these two new entries, I phoned Mahmoud and e-mailed the new lists to all concerned parties. Mahmoud had me send the fax to Phil's car and assured me that he'd receive it within the hour. It was 8 P.M. and I had promised Ellen that I'd be home in time to help her serve the eggnog at our building's annual lobby party. It had started at six-thirty.

"Thanks, Mahmoud. And please tell Phil that I got it up to one fifty."

"My pleasure, Karen. Merry Christmas."

On Wednesday, Ellen and I celebrated a New York City Christmas together, complete with takeout Chinese food and a day at the Angelika, where we watched three movies from other studios—movies that didn't give me stomachaches or headaches, movies that I could just sit and enjoy. After we got home, I called Abby to tell her about the online nongossip column I'd be writing, and also to refine our plans for New Year's Eve. She made me swear to e-mail her every column. "I'm so out of the loop on movies—I can't believe how far I've slid!" she said. I assured her that I'd bring her a bunch of tapes at New Year's. I called my parents just to chat and get caught up. They wanted me to promise that I would come home over President's weekend, and I told them that I would do my best. They were a bit taken aback by how many hours I seemed to be working—Ellen had apparently told her mother who, of course, had passed it on—but happy to hear that I had a new opportunity with Matt.

I decided to call Robert and wish him a Merry Christmas. He was my closest friend at Glorious, but was extremely guarded about his personal life. Still, I had a feeling that something was wrong. Maybe, outside of the office, he'd talk to me about it.

"It's Karen. I just wanted to say hello and see how your Christmas was."

"Horrible. And yours?"

"Just dull. What happened?"

"I didn't want anyone to know about it, but my fiancé and I have decided to become unengaged. Or disengaged. Or whatever it's called when you realize that the person you want to spend the rest of your life with doesn't feel quite the same way about you," he said softly.

"I'm so sorry. When did this happen?" I'd fly to Pago Pago and find that girl if she'd dumped Robert over Christmas, I thought, shocked by my own vehemence.

"It started a couple of months ago. She was supposed to come back and spend the holidays with me, but then she called and said she'd decided to stay because she wanted to experience a traditional Samoan Christmas. Maybe that would have been okay if I'd seen her sometime between now and last year, but she kept saying she couldn't leave. We've been having some long, drawn-out conversations about it and over this weekend I just realized it was over."

"Couldn't you visit her?"

"I asked, but she said that she was working constantly, and wouldn't get to spend any time with me. I didn't want to go to Pago Pago and be by myself. I do that here all the time," he said, his voice catching.

"Robert, I'm so sorry. Why didn't you tell me?"

"I didn't want to talk about it. Everyone thinks that I'm always in control, that I'm the guy who keeps it together all the time. But I don't know how to deal with this."

I wasn't sure what to tell him. I'd been trying hard not to think about last Christmas with Gabe, when he'd painted a picture of an ornate, overly decorated tree and hung it in my apartment. He, Ellen, Abby, and I had had a wonderful time.

"I don't know if there's anything you can do, Robert. I think maybe you just have to feel terrible for a while. And talk to your friends whenever you need to," I added hastily, afraid that I'd sounded too harsh.

"You're probably right. I have to go now. But thanks for calling, Karen. I really appreciate it."

Robert was a terrific guy, and while I hadn't said it to him, because it was too much of a cliché, I was sure his fiancé would come crawling back before too long. Would he let her, I wondered?

I was actually looking forward to going into work the next day: the office would be completely dead, and I could use the time to write some more synopses and get started on the column. Dagney was returning after the weekend and I wanted to be well into the additional Web site work I was doing while making sure she understood that there was no way this would become a shared assignment. Like me, she'd been looking for some additional responsibility. She'd have to find something else.

On Monday morning Dagney breezed in, looking wonderfully refreshed and with her hair subtly lightened to a shade that suited her complexion perfectly. She presented me with a pair of maracas that had "Shakin' it in Spain" painted on each of them. Clark, back today as well, got some castanets, and for Robert she had a T-shirt that said "OLÉ!" across the front. We could have been our own flamenco combo, if only someone knew how to play. Of course, Dagney and Clark had heard nothing about Allegra's leave of absence. The four of us convened in her empty office, Robert and I interrupting each other in our breathless rush to share the news. It took a while before Clark and Dagney understood what we were saying. And then Dagney said, "That's impossible."

"No, it's not. She's gone. Her flight left on Thursday evening," I said.

"She's outta here," Robert said, making a baseball umpire's "safe" motion.

"That's impossible," Dagney repeated. "I just saw Allegra in the coffee shop."

"You saw her where?" I said, looking at Robert to keep my world from collapsing.

"In that little coffee shop farther down Greenwich Street, the one that has the fresh beignets," she said.

"Are you sure?" Robert asked her. "What did she say?"

"Well, that was the strange part. She didn't say anything. She was next to me in line to pay and I know she saw me—she must've—but it was as if her eyes didn't focus." Dagney said.

"So what did you do?" Clark asked.

"I paid for my coffee and ignored her. I knew that I'd see her later, anyway."

"Are you sure it was her?" Robert said.

"Blond hair, puffy coat, about six tote bags—ring any bells?"

"Maybe she just didn't get on her flight on Wednesday. Maybe there was some kind of delay," I said, clinging to hope.

"What kind of delay would keep her here for five extra days?" Robert asked.

"I don't know, family stuff? Dagney, are you sure it was her?" I was in deep denial at this point.

"Karen." Dagney spoke slowly and used elaborate hand gestures so that it was clear how stupid she found me. "Allegra. Was. Getting. Coffee. In. TriBeCa. This. Morning."

"It sounds like it was her," Robert said. "But I still don't think she's coming in, Europe or no Europe."

I shrugged my shoulders and Robert and Clark left Allegra's office. I asked Dagney to stay because I wanted to tell her about how we'd be handling the office for now, and how we were in the unenviable position of giving Vivian some help from time to time.

"Well, that sucks," she said, getting right to the point. "If Allegra's away, why should we still be acting as if she's here?"

"How much has Allegra ever made sense? Twice a day we'll weed through the phone sheet and the e-mails and decide which ones to give to Viv."

"I'm not going to survive this," Dagney said. She and Vivian had a particularly rocky relationship, worsened by the fact that in many ways they were quite alike. Both insisted on getting their way, both would do anything they could to avoid doing something they deemed unworthy of their attention, and both were incredibly stubborn. Answering to Vivian was going to require all of Dagney's self-restraint. I tried to reassure her. "It's not as if Viv's ever asked very much of us. You know she likes to do everything herself. Even that whole thing with *The Raven II* screening took only about an hour." Then I realized that Dagney didn't even know what had happened with the assorted envelopes, signs, and cash we'd assembled for Vivian.

After a thorough explanation that started with the cell phone heist, continued through the Mickey Mouse hostage-taking, and ended with Delilah being forced to renege on her promise to the radio stations, Dagney was shaking her head. "Wow, that's just the coolest, most fucked-up thing I've ever heard." She whipped out her green notebook and had me repeat some of the main plot points to her while she transcribed them. "This is definitely one I want to remember."

"By the way, Dag, I didn't have a chance to ask you—what happened to you the night of the Young Democrats party? One minute we were talking to those guys from Stan Coburn's, and then you completely disappeared," I said, looking at her meaningfully.

Dagney squirmed and her voice dropped to a whisper. "Oh, Karen, I thought no one would notice. I went home with Systems Alejandro. You haven't mentioned it to anyone, have you?"

"Of course not. How was it?"

"Incredible. Unbelievable. Amazing," she said. "And I don't have to tell you how gorgeous he is."

"Sounds like a lovely way to start your vacation."

When Vivian showed up to work later, Dagney all but knelt in front of her, wishing her a belated Merry Christmas. Vivian actually looked pleased and said, "I'm glad you'll be working more closely with me now that Allegra's gone."

"Oh, you weren't here before," Dagney said. "She's not gone. I saw her in the coffee shop this morning."

Vivian's mouth dropped open. "Are you sure? What did she say?"

"I'm positive. She didn't say anything. She just looked at me as if she'd never seen me in her life."

Vivian quickly recovered her composure and said, "Obviously you mistook someone else for her."

Dagney didn't answer, not wanting to contradict her new idol.

"Listen, you two." Vivian fixed us both with her steely gaze, and I felt my insides tighten. "There's been something I would like to get straight right off the bat. Has Allegra now, or ever, to your knowledge, spoken to Oprah Winfrey?" She sounded like one of the members of the House Un-American Activities Committee that I'd seen on grainy old newsreels.

Dagney and I stared at our hands and said nothing. She wouldn't have dared ask us if Allegra were around, but if we lied, Vivian would see right through it, and we'd be paying for the next month. "I knew it," she said triumphantly, before striding back into her cube, having successfully outed her boss as a pseudo-Oprah confidante.

The afternoon was so quiet that I didn't care when Dagney went out for a three-hour cigarette break. It gave me some time and privacy to work on the column. Scouring some of the recent Hits packets for material, I wrote a breezy news report on all that was (semi) new and (perhaps) exciting at Glorious. There was a bit of gossip that most movie buffs would have known for a while, but linked to some new photos it might not appear so stale.

After making a few changes to the draft and reading it back a few times, I was satisfied that it was good to go. Halfway through giving it a final read, Dagney said, "Karen, what are you doing?"

I turned to see her reading over my shoulder. "Do you think there's anyone left who doesn't know that Juliet Bartlett is playing the hip-hop Jane Eyre?"

"Everyone knows, but this will have the first photos of Juliet in costume as Jane."

"What will?"

"The Web site."

"What do you have to do with the Web site?"

It was time to come clean. "I've been helping Matt Vincent's group out with it for months, but now they'd like me to do some more. And with Allegra gone, I'll be able to."

"Why didn't you tell me?" she demanded.

"I don't know."

"Then I guess you're not going to care that I've been watching tapes for the people in acquisitions. They really trust my judg-ment," she said.

"Good for you," I said.

"Well, good for you, too," she said, and just like that, all the tension left the air around that tiny little desk. I wondered if our goodwill might flourish in Allegra's absence.

I pulled my things together for a faux smoking break but in-stead went to Belinda's store to deliver her holiday gift. While Glorious had a long list of corporate gift recipients, Belinda hadn't made the cut. Marlene was the person who put together our de-partment's list. I'd lobbied for Belinda's inclusion, explaining how much she'd done for us over and above the call of duty.

"Don't we pay for the newspapers and magazines Belinda gives us?" Marlene had asked.

"Yes, but she gets them for us earlier and lets us know when there's something that's potentially problematic," I said. "You re-member how she helped us with the *New York Observer* when it ran that hatchet job on *HackSaw*?"

"Sure. And we bought about fifty copies from her. I'd say that's present enough," Marlene retorted.

It was hopeless but of no great consequence, especially when I learned what the Glorious corporate gift was this year. Belinda, who'd read classics at Cambridge, would not be excited by a leather-bound, special Glorious edition of *Leaves of Grass*, com-plete with photos from *El Lechero*. I surmised that a couple of bot-tles of Cabernet would put her in a much more festive mood—a hunch that paid off when I presented them to her. She thanked me profusely and then said, "Odd bird, that boss of yours. She was here a couple of hours ago and bought a few magazines. She's been coming here as long as I've been open, about seven years. This time, though, she looked at me as if she'd never seen me before."

"What did she buy?" I asked, hoping that she'd picked up a travel monthly or two.

"*Bon Appétit, The Washingtonian,* and *Architectural Digest.*"

"She's been acting a little strangely lately," I said, hurriedly wishing Belinda a happy new year. I needed to rush back to the office and relay this to Clark and Robert.

"It's official. She may not be here, but she's not far away." We were sitting in Clark's office, since the three of us no longer fit in Robert's.

"That's twice today," Clark said. "For some reason, I feel a need to keep track." He left for a moment and returned with a ragged piece of whiteboard and a couple of dry-erase pens. "In the *El Lechero* meeting last week, Tony said he couldn't stand listening to any more of that 'fancy-shmancy poetry shit' and then he tore this in half." In red calligraphy Clark wrote:

Allegra Sightings
1. *Coffee Shop on Greenwich (the one with the beignets)*
2. *Belinda's magazine store*

Robert got some double-sided tape and hung the board outside Clark's office. Dagney walked by. "I love it! She was in the magazine store, too?"

"Belinda saw her this afternoon. She didn't buy any travel magazines, though."

"I was right, after all."

The next morning, two more entries had been added to the list:

3. *The dry cleaner on Hudson Street*
4. *Nobu*

We didn't know who'd written them, but it proved that not only was Allegra in town, she wasn't trying to hide it. I wondered if this might be Page Six material, or just a good excuse to call Elliott. I also wondered what he was doing tonight for New Year's Eve, but since it didn't involve me, I didn't really want to know. I liked him, but it was hard to trust if his interest in me was personal or professional. True, he gave me far more information than I gave him—everything I told him he seemed to know already. But the longer I worked at Glorious, the greater my potential as a source. Perhaps Elliott was just keeping me warm for later, hoping that by the time I knew more about the inner workings of Glorious, I'd feel comfortable enough with him to share them. But the way he popped in and out of my life without warning always kept me slightly off balance when I did speak with him, making me somehow more excited each time.

I was determined to get out of the office, and for once I made it—catching a late train to Baltimore to see Abby. We went to a New Year's Eve party that was chock-full of good-looking med students. We drank more than was medicinally necessary and spent Wednesday hungover, barely stirring from the couch while working our way through a pile of Glorious videos that I'd snuck out of the office. On Thursday morning I took an early train back. It had been a short visit, but a good one, and I made another resolution to see more of Abby this year, no matter what.

Thursday morning Allegra called. Dagney answered and motioned for me to listen in with her. "Is everything okay? Does anyone need me?"

"It's fine, Allegra. It's really quiet," Dagney said. "By the way, where are you?"

"In Europe." Dagney and I looked at each other.

"Tell Vivian that I'll call her later," Allegra said, and hung up.

Later that day, Dagney, Robert, Clark, and I got an e-mail from Marlene. She'd copied Vivian, Geraldine, Phil, Tony, Allegra, and anyone else who made a habit of not listening to her. In it she referred to our "actions" as being "extremely disrespectful to someone who, if I may remind the four of you, is your boss."

Within fifteen minutes Sabrina from Phil's office showed up. "I just had to see this," she said. "And I have something to add." I handed her a green marker and followed her over to Clark's office, where she wrote:

5. Nail Nation

"You saw her at Nail Nation?" I asked.

"At around one. It's my day to go to lunch, so I decided to get a pedicure. She was in the chair right next to me, reading *Architectural Digest*."

"Are you sure it was her?" Dagney asked. "She called this morning and said she was in Europe."

"Positive. I said hello to her, and when she didn't answer I said her name. She turned and looked at me as if I were a stranger. Then she went back to her magazine. Weird," Sabrina said, shaking her head.

"If this is what gets her freak on, then I feel really sorry for her," Dagney said.

"Gets her freak on?" Robert said. "Did you become part of the famous Ibiza rap posse?"

"No, but at least I know that Ibiza doesn't rhyme with pizza," Dagney snapped.

"Please forgive me. Spanish is not one of the five languages that I speak," Robert said.

"You speak five languages?" Dagney asked.

"Da, ja, oui, ja, and hi. Plus English," he said.

"You said 'ja' twice."

"Yes, but the first was in German and the second was in Dutch."

Robert, who had once told me that he could say "yes" in thirty-seven languages, winked at me as I struggled to keep a straight face.

Back at my desk there was an e-mail from Matt asking me to meet with him tomorrow at noon. I had a sneaking suspicion that something good was about to happen.

Arriving at his office the next day, Matt ushered me in and closed the door behind us.

"Karen, we were all really impressed with your work for the site. You're a strong copywriter and you work quickly."

I thanked him for the compliment and he continued, "For a while, it's been just me with Cheryl and Kenny. But this place is getting busier and I've wanted to create another level, a sort of junior marketing executive role to help pick up some of the slack. We need to be able to simply hand some things off, and I want to expand the number of capable people in the department."

"Sounds good," I said, holding my breath.

"So, we talked about it and agreed that we'd like to offer you a position as marketing associate. I think you'll learn quickly and become a strong addition to our group."

"I'd love to come work for you, it sounds wonderful," I said.

"The only thing I'm not sure about is how to extricate myself from Publicity—especially since I can't ask Allegra's permission right now."

"I'll take care of it. I told Phil that I needed to enlarge the department and wanted to hire someone from inside. He told me to take my pick and he'd smooth it out."

I exhaled. "What are the next steps?"

"It will take about a week. This is a contract position, so the legal department will have to draw that up so I can make the formal offer. It will be a slight bump in pay, not a huge one, and Geraldine's going to have to work on logistics, like where your office will be."

I didn't say anything, just beamed and tried to make sure I didn't look too dopey.

"By the way," Matt said, "what's up with Allegra? I thought she was supposed to be taking a leave, traveling in Europe. But I swore I saw her this morning. I was walking my dog down near Battery Park and she passed right by me without saying anything."

"You probably did see her," I said, telling him about the rapidly filling whiteboard. "Well, chalk up another one," he said, shaking his head. "I have no idea what's going on with her."

"We're not sure either, but I'll add your sighting to the list."

"Happy to contribute to the cause. One other thing. Until this is absolutely, one hundred percent done, please don't tell anyone. If people know that we're hiring, I'm going to be deluged. Mostly by the folks in your department, I'd guess."

I thanked him and stood up. I had a difficult time staying calm and when I'd gotten outside I felt like dancing around, but there was a distinct possibility that the now-ubiquitous Allegra might see my impromptu boogie.

When I got back to the office, the place was in an uproar and Dagney looked panicked.

"You won't believe what's been going on here," she said, pulling me into Allegra's office, a copy of the Hits in her hand. She flipped to Cindy Adams's column. I read down a couple of paragraphs until I saw what had her so upset:

> *Heard that my favorite downtown sibling act have their holidays mixed up. Seems that Phil and Tony Waxman are playing Cupid to help one of their top lady executives find her one and only. Fellas, if you get the call, take them up on it and take her out. She's a classy, smart broad who's just gotten a little stuck in the starting gate.*

"Did you tell Vivian about this right away?" I was dreading a repeat performance by Yvonne.

"No, because it wasn't in the paper," She showed me the actual clipping, which had a different item in that space, one predicting "splitsville" for a long-estranged political couple. What was going on?

Squinting at the Xeroxed page, I could just make out a faint shadow running around the item. "An extremely careful cut-and-paste job," I said, pointing out the razor-thin line to Dagney. "Someone's sabotaged the Hits."

"But it's still gone around to the whole company. Yvonne has completely flipped. She's been on the phone with Marlene for the past hour, trying to find out who did this. Of course, the obvious suspect was me, but I think I've been cleared."

"They would have an easier time trying to figure who *didn't* have a motive," I said, thinking of our weeping former intern. "I'm only sorry it's not in the real paper." This was one of the most inspired acts of revenge I'd ever seen, and I was dying to know who was responsible.

"Why are you so happy?" Dagney asked.

"Oh, someone just e-mailed me another sighting for the board. This is the most fun I've had in a while."

"You need to get out more," she said. I ignored her and headed for Clark's office. In my absence, the list had grown. Now it had:

6. *At the ATM (corner of N. Moore)*
7. *In the Health Food Store*

Underneath those I added:

8. *Near Battery Park*

It was the second day of the new year. I was getting out of Publicity and into Marketing. Allegra was gone, it didn't matter how near or far, just having her out of the office was enough for me. It was Friday afternoon, and there was no junket this weekend. Things were so good I decided to tempt fate.

"Hey Elliott," I said when he answered the phone. "It's Karen. Happy New Year."

He sounded glad to hear from me. "What are you up to? I've been meaning to call you."

"Not much. Not much I can tell you from the office, anyway." I tried to sound mysterious.

"Could you tell me over a drink?"

"Probably."

"Could you tell me over a drink tonight?"

"It's likely." We arranged to meet at a bar in SoHo that had been the favorite hangout of Erich and the Lithuanian when they were in town. It had been a few months since I'd seen Elliott, but every time we'd spoken he'd dropped some rather unsubtle hints about what he'd like to do with my feet. My anticipation was compounded by the fact that right after I'd started dating Gabe, he'd had to suck my toes on a dare. I'd been beside myself with pleasure at the sensation, but he'd hated it, and no matter how much I'd pleaded, he'd refused a repeat performance. But my feet and the rest of me were entitled to some male attention—it really had been a while. And besides, I was moving into marketing—Elliott wouldn't be quite so off-limits when I was there. I'd finally have the opportunity to test my theories about him.

I was thinking about what to wear, and whether or not my toes were fit for public viewing, and if there was time to run out for a pedicure. After rummaging around to find the sandals that I'd left in the office after a summer event, I snapped out of planning my assignation when I heard my name repeated three times, followed by a triple-Dagney.

"On Monday we need to start making calls to the Academy members about *El Lechero*," Vivian said. "I want it to be more organized than last year. The names will be divided up among the department and everyone will be responsible for making their assigned calls, as well as providing notes on what each person said, double-checking that they received their screeners, and making sure that we note if they're not home and need to be called back."

It was incredible how quickly I'd stopped thinking about publicity whatsoever. Vivian continued. "We're going to make Excels for each person in the department that will have the names and phone numbers of the members they are to call, as well as space for them to type in the rest of the information. I'll need the two of you here with me all day tomorrow and maybe Sunday, depending on how much we get done."

There were nearly six thousand Academy members. Last year we'd just made a copy of the overall list, alphabetized by last name, and each of us had been assigned a couple of letters. Obviously, that system had worked, but of course Vivian wanted to put her mark on the process while out from under Allegra's thumb. I couldn't believe we were going to spend an entire weekend on this. "I can't do that," suddenly came out of my mouth. The minute the words hit the air I knew they were ex-actly right.

"You can't?"

"No."

"In Allegra's absence you report to me. And I need you to work on these lists."

"If you needed me so badly, you should have told me before the end of the day on Friday," I said, pumped up with defiance.

"This will be noted."

"Note it, then."

"I'll be here Vivian, is seven okay?" Dagney piped up, eager for some quality time with her new guru.

"Six-thirty. Now that it's just the two of us, we'll need to get an earlier start," she said, glaring at me.

Later, snuggled in a leather banquette with Elliott and working on my third cocktail, I told him about my upcoming move into marketing. Alcohol and a giddy sense of possibility loosened my tongue and all of a sudden I was telling him everything—the story of *The Raven II: Nevermore* contest-winner kidnapping in L.A., Allegra's phony trip abroad, the two extra first-place rank-ings I'd needed to find for *El Lechero*, the new and improved method Glorious would be using to call every Academy member over the next few weeks. Best of all, I confided, had been the practical joke played on Yvonne that morning, which I described in all its brilliant detail.

"Someone's chatty tonight," he said, placing his hand on my ankle, and beginning to knead it. "I don't think you really want to tell me all those things. They're awfully, you know, tempting," he added, as he slid my right foot out of its sandal. Elliott was a guy who started at the calf and worked down. Successful, he moved on to the left and quickly I was barefoot, which brought a whole new realm of insecurities. Were my feet sweaty? Did they smell? How did I rank in the toe cleavage department? Elliott's eyes were closed and he was massaging my left instep. I leaned back in the banquette, and boldly placed both of my feet in his lap. He gasped softly before bending his head down and very gently kissing my toes in order from little to big, first on the right foot and then on the left, before giving my right sole a good long lick from heel to toe. Then he started to suck on my right second toe, while gently circling his tongue around it, a move that had me nearly on the ceiling. Did this qualify as "canoodling"? I didn't think so—it was more like he was worshipping my feet, but that wasn't a word I'd ever seen used in a gossip column. It felt great, better than I'd ever imagined, and he lavished the same care on all nine other grateful little piggies. But what I really wanted was for him to kiss me.

Suddenly he looked up and said, "Karen, we've got to get out of here." I put my shoes back on and followed him outside. We walked for a while, him not saying anything and me having to half-jog to keep up. My feet, burning just a little while ago, were now absolutely freezing. And then Elliott took my hand, pulled me into a doorway and began to kiss me, hard, as though he were running out of time. I opened one eye and could see that even through the kiss, the corners of his mouth were turned up like he was smiling, like he was incredibly glad to be kissing me, and then he gently tilted my chin up with one hand while placing the other on the small of my back. I closed my eye and kept kissing back, kissing and sneaking a peek every now and then. Each time I looked, Elliot was still smiling.

When he stopped, we walked together for a few blocks and then, without saying a word, he hailed a cab and opened the door for me.

"Don't worry, Karen. All your secrets are safe with me." He kissed me again, on the cheek, and whispered in my ear, "Thank you," before slamming my door shut and heading in the opposite direction. I gave the driver my address and spent the ride home in a state of suspended animation, in which I could feel but not think. I slept more soundly than I had in months.

The week went by incredibly quickly. Aside from a few dozen dirty looks from Dagney and Vivian, who had become frighteningly chummy during their weekend ordeal, and the discovery that my list of Academy calls was twice as long as anyone else's, I was actually enjoying my work. Clark's whiteboard had bloomed into a montage of colors and handwritings, and some enterprising person had found the other half of the board and hung it next to the first one. Soon that was covered, too. Allegra had morphed into a type of *Zelig* character, appearing everywhere and blending in, never acknowledging anyone. I saw her a couple of times myself that week—once at the deli when I was buying cigarettes and another day on the Franklin Street subway platform. Both times she gave not a flicker of recognition.

On Thursday, Matt called and asked me to come to his office for a meeting with him and Cheryl and Kenny, the two marketing VPs. He told me that things were still hush-hush, but that progress was being made. Just as I was about to tell Dagney that I was stepping outside for a smoke, I decided instead to tell her I was going out for a walk.

"A *walk?*" she said, plainly disgusted.

"A walk."

"Are you quitting smoking?"

"Yeah, I'm on the patch," I said, knowing she couldn't see if I had one on my arm or not.

"Do you have any cigarettes left over? I mean, now that you're a former smoker and all?"

"Sure, Dag, have the whole pack." I pulled them out of my bag and tossed them onto the desk.

In Matt's office, Cheryl and Kenny were sitting at a long table. Matt wasn't there. I knew the two of them, but just barely. Except for Matt, who often had to deal with Allegra, the marketing department made it a point to steer clear of Publicity.

Cheryl Porter was a tiny wisp of a woman, a good few inches below five feet tall, with the smallest hands and feet I'd ever seen on an adult. She was nervous in a hummingbirdlike way, waving her spindly arms about when she wanted to make a point. She possessed a tic that caused her to constantly blink multiple times in quick succession. She also had a habit of running her hands through her hair; by this time of day about half of it was standing straight up.

Kenny Delano was slightly more relaxed, a tall, shaven-headed guy with a pointy nose and bushy eyebrows that gave him the appearance of a pudgy Mr. Clean. He was something of a chronic tapper, and when I entered the room he had his left foot on the floor and his pen on a legal pad, each going at a different rhythm.

I entered the room and held out my hand. "Karen Jacobs, it's nice to see you." I wasn't sure if they knew my whole name or not.

"Yes, very nice," Cheryl said. When I shook her hand I was

afraid I might hurt her. Clearly she'd never shaken hands with Geraldine.

"Glad you're joining us," Kenny said, waving at me. I took a seat opposite the two of them.

"Matt's going to be here in a couple of minutes," Cheryl said. "Phil called him and was yelling about the television spots for *El Lechero.*"

"You're okay with yelling right?" Kenny said. "I mean, you come from Publicity."

"Well, I don't enjoy it, but I can handle it, if that's what you mean."

"Kenny, don't scare her," Cheryl said, blinking. "I wouldn't really call it yelling. And if there is, it's yelling of a higher caliber than what you're used to. It's an intellectual type of shouting that goes on here—boisterous discourse, if you will."

"Things are much more . . . ," Kenny paused, "conceptual in this department. We don't sit around and talk about who's wearing what, or who not to invite, or if I think your assistant is a bitch. It's a much more businesslike environment."

"Right, businesslike environment," Matt walked into the room. "And in a businesslike environment, we offer employees a contract so that everyone knows what the terms are. And here"—he handed me a manila folder—"is your contract, Karen. Welcome to the marketing department."

"We need you so, so much." Cheryl blinked.

"It's like we've rescued you from the coven, and now you have to work for us to pay back the favor," Kenny said, and he and Matt laughed. Cheryl stood her hair up a little higher.

"Is everything all set? Does Allegra know?" I asked.

"Allegra knows," Matt said.

"You talked to her?"

"No, but I was in line behind her at the pharmacy and I said, 'Karen Jacobs is joining my department.' She didn't turn around, but she must have heard me. Geraldine's straightened out your office, and you start with us on Monday."

Once in the street I did a little end-zone-style dance, hoping that Allegra was somewhere nearby to see it.

BREAKING AWAY

Working in Publicity had been difficult, but leaving it required the stealth and patience of an undercover operative. It was as if my desire to do something else had crawled under everyone's skin and given them a collective itch that could be relieved only by scratching me.

"Do you ever think of anyone except yourself?" Vivian asked after she heard the news. "Did it ever occur to you that someone else has to do the work you're leaving behind?"

Shrugging, I continued to pack up the contents of my desk as Dagney watched. I'd dragged over a large cardboard box from the copy room but soon realized I wouldn't need it. Even though I'd spent a year in this space, very little of me was actually here. At CNN, my cube had been alive with photographs, doodles, funny headlines, and Gabe's drawings. Aside from a *New Yorker* cartoon that showed a little girl sitting in front of a television asking her mother, "Why does she want to go back to Kansas, where everything is in black-and-white?" and a photo of Abby and me taken on the Cape a few years ago, I had no personal effects.

Within five minutes it was as if I'd never sat at that horrible, crowded, L-shaped desk.

"You do realize that now Vivian and I are going to have to redo all the Excels that we made last weekend," Dagney said.

"Why don't you just hand out my pages to other people?"

"It's not that simple." Of course it wasn't. Any project of Vivian's was immediately sent to Stockholm for the Nobel Committee's most urgent consideration.

"Karen, I need you at the 86 junket this weekend," Marlene said from across the office, not bothering to get up or even dial the phone. 86 was a film about a fabled seventies disco where celebrities hustled, snorted, and screwed each other until the wee hours of the eighties.

"Can't do it, Marlene. I'm not in this department."

"You don't start in Marketing until Monday, so you're still part of this department until then."

"I don't think it works that way."

Marlene called Matt, speaking loudly so that I could hear her. In her sweetest, most wheedling tone she told him that she was shorthanded this weekend for the junket and needed me to be there. "It really would help us out. Thanks, Matt" was all I heard her say. She called over the wall to me again. "Matt says it's up to you." At the same time my e-mail, still connected at this desk, pinged: "Blow her off." It was from Matt.

"Sorry Marlene, I can't work on 86 this weekend."

"The cast is really big and we need you. Henry Hauser, the male lead, is going to take up all my time and energy because he insists that his interviews be closely monitored. *I will not let you ruin this for me!*" she shrieked.

"I don't work here anymore. I'm bringing these things to the other building and then I'm going home. On Monday morning, I'm starting in Marketing."

"Where will you be this weekend?" she challenged.

"Floating somewhere between Heaven and Hell," I said, opening up the file cabinet where I kept a toothbrush, toothpaste, deodorant, and a few other items. My phone rang and I picked it up reflexively. It was Geraldine. She seconded Marlene's notion that I still worked in Publicity until Monday morning at nine, mentioning pay periods, cost centers, transitional efficacy, and other HR-ish-sounding phrases she'd never used before.

The phone rang again and it was Matt. "Karen, I'm sorry. Geraldine called me and it looks like you're going to have to work this junket. If I had known, I would have pushed to have the whole thing done earlier."

"It's all right. You didn't think I was going to change departments the way people do in a normal company, did you?"

"Thanks for being a good sport."

Marlene called me into her office. "I expect you to behave like a professional this weekend, Karen," she said. Ignoring her, I went back to the desk to make sure I'd gotten everything.

I turned to Dagney. "Well, this was supposed to be good-bye," I said, "but now it's just see you tomorrow."

Monday morning, wide-eyed but junket-weary, I rode the subway to my new job, reading the *New York Times* on the way in an unhurried fashion, and picked up coffee and a muffin before reaching the building that housed the marketing department. Allegra was leaving the deli as I entered it but I didn't even bother trying to make eye contact.

As I stepped off the elevator onto the eleventh floor, where I'd be working, Cheryl breathlessly greeted me. "Let me show you your office and then we can get started. So much to do!" She reminded me of the White Rabbit from *Alice in Wonderland*.

Cheryl led me to a room that was a few doors down from hers. It was an actual office, with walls that went to the ceiling and a real door. I played with the doorknob, pressing and releasing the lock button.

"It's pretty bare, I know, but you can order some things for your desk as soon as you know what you need. There's a stack of movie posters in the closet near the elevator, and you're welcome to take whichever ones you want to hang up."

The office had a desk, a chair, and a bookcase. It also had a television and VCR with two decks, ostensibly so that I could flip back and forth between two films. "The cable people will be here by the end of the week to get you all set up with that," Cheryl added. "We'll need you to occasionally spend some time watching so that we have proof that the commercials we paid for actually run when they're supposed to."

Geraldine walked in, followed by Harvey, trotting along looking especially proud of himself. "I just wanted to remind you, Karen, your contract needs to be signed and returned in a timely fashion."

Not wanting to pay for an attorney, I'd asked Ellen to look it over for me. "You'll have it soon."

"Welcome!" Kenny tapped on my open door. We all shifted around so that he could come in and I accidentally stepped on Harvey's tail. He yelped and sunk what felt like a triple row of teeth into my calf.

"Goddammit!" I yelled, "He just bit me!" I bent down to look at the damage. My wool trousers had prevented him from breaking the skin, but they now had a small crescent of holes.

"Could you please be more careful next time, Karen?" Geraldine bent down to minister to Harvey, who was trying to get the lint out of his mouth. "Let me help you with that, sweetheart," she murmured, kneeling in front of him to pick invisible pieces of my bad-tasting pants off his tongue.

"Geraldine, your dog just bit me."

"It's always quid pro quo with Harvey, I'm afraid," she replied, scooping him up. "Don't forget your contract," she added on her way out. I could swear that freakish animal grinned at me over her shoulder.

"So much for the morning's excitement. Karen, are you okay?" Cheryl asked.

I nodded. "Harvey really needs to stay home until he learns how to behave."

"Did you show Karen what she's going to be working on yet?" Kenny asked.

"I was just about to before that walking sausage interrupted us." Cheryl picked up a shopping bag that had been stowed outside my door and poured the contents on my desk. There were about a dozen videotapes, along with press kits and festival programs. One tape, titled *Lip Balm,* fell off my desk and onto the floor.

"These are films that Glorious needs to release because we're contractually obligated to do so. They'll open in just two theaters, one in New York and one in L.A. Nobody is expecting them to do well, we just need to get them up, open, and over," Cheryl said.

"We call these Tony's Blockbuster Videos," Kenny said. "After his divorce, Tony spent a lot of time on the road visiting smaller film festivals. When he met a filmmaker he thought had a certain," he paused, "potential"—Kenny rubbed his hands together lasciviously at the last word—"he'd have the acquisitions people buy the film. Of course, she'd be indebted."

"All these films are by women directors Tony wanted to sleep with?"

"No. Sometimes it was the producer."

"It doesn't matter how or why they were bought, we just need them out of our hair," Cheryl said hurriedly. "Your job is to create a mini-marketing campaign for each of these. They're not going to have a trailer, or television commercials. Instead of printing up the thousands of one-sheets like we did for, say, *The Foreign Pilot*, we'll print about five, at Kinko's."

"Only five?"

"Maybe six. That's enough for one each in the theater lobbies, two for the filmmaker, and a couple of extras just in case. You'll be responsible for the concept, and some copy, and then the art department will help you with the design."

"The things the art department can do with type and graphics are just incredible," Kenny added. "So if there's no photography provided they'll still be able to come up with something. Just concentrate on the overall idea you want to convey and a line of copy. The main thing is that these get finished quickly so that we can have you work on more important things." Kenny said. "So get watching!"

He and Cheryl left my office. I surveyed my surroundings. Not bad, Karen, I thought to myself. This space was positively deluxe compared to what I'd had in Publicity. Just the idea of a desk to myself was almost too good to be true. But a bookcase? Cable? A door? I felt like Charlie at the end of *Willy Wonka & the Chocolate Factory*, when he learns that the factory and all the candy and even the Oompa Loompas are his to keep.

The videos were scattered all over my desk and I arranged them into two stacks of six, looking at the titles to try to get some sense of them. Besides *Lip Balm* there were *Pocket Protector, The Big Bleu, Carrion Sweet Vulture,* and *Sneezing by Numbers*, as well as seven more that sounded even less compelling. It was obvious from thumbing through the press materials and accompanying photos and bio pages that each of the filmmakers was the kind of woman for whom the only suitable boyfriend would be the head of a motion-picture studio. Later on, when watching the films, it became apparent that only a smitten mogul would have acquired any of them. The synergy was astonishing.

A while later, Systems Alejandro came by to get my computer set up. While he was working, he congratulated me on my promotion. I marveled at how good-looking he was, and wondered if he and Dagney had gotten together again since the Young Democrats fund-raiser. As soon as everything was up and running, I zipped an e-mail off to Abby, to let her know that if she really wanted to meet Tony Waxman, perhaps all she had to do was make a twenty-minute movie about her first year of medical school and send it in with one of her headshots. I suggested a title for it—*Lloyd's Grave Mistake.*

I popped *Lip Balm* into the VCR. The film followed a single tube of ChapStick from its initial purchase at a Mojave Desert truck stop to its untimely end on a dashboard parked outside of an upscale mall in Houston. Told completely from the ChapStick's point of view, the actors' faces were never seen. Chappy went from counter to glove compartment to Prada purse to Wrangler jeans, to nightclub bathroom floor, to a school bag, through a harrowing cycle in a washing machine, and on and on. But this was my first assignment and I was hell-bent on figuring out this film's redeeming qualities. Was it a keen social commentary about a product used by millionaires and welfare moms alike? A meditation on our disposable culture, where we attach an item's value to its cost and not its function? A ChapStick in the desert is worth its weight in platinum. Might it be symbolic? A balm for something else, perhaps? Were the filmmaker's parents divorced?

I riffled through the pages of *Lip Balm*'s press kit. Written, produced, and directed by twenty-four-year-old USC grad Reba

Koronis, *Lip Balm* had been financed by the Koronis family. Reba was also credited in the notes as the "star of *Lip Balm*," although this was a bit of a stretch as only a woman's left hand, shoes, and a shoulder from which a purse swings were visible in the film. It was clear that Reba had wielded an unusual amount of creative control for a first-time filmmaker: I wondered if she did her own stunts.

I was trying to come up with ideas about what a good poster would be when Matt called. "I'm sorry I'm not there this morning to greet you properly, but I'm in L.A."

We chatted a bit and I told him about *Lip Balm*, which made him laugh. He said that he'd be in Los Angeles for the next couple of weeks for meetings but would be available via phone and e-mail. Matt asked me to try and get through the Tony films as quickly as possible so that I could help Kenny and Cheryl with their projects.

Although the film was only going to have a poster to market it, I still wanted it to be really good, even though Cheryl said that I should concentrate more on speed than substance. I needed to come up with some tag lines so that we could try them on for size, and an idea for what kind of artwork the poster would have. So far I had none, but was working on the copy.

"It's 8 P.M. Do you know where your ChapStick is?"
"It goes further than you think."
"You've never seen it like this."
"These lips were made for walking."
"A journey of salve-ation."

These were horrible and I began to get panicky. Just then Cheryl stopped by and told me that she and Kenny were going to Phil's office, to show him the first *Policeville* poster looks. "Do you want to come along?"

I smiled, not wanting to give away how excited I was. *Policeville*, a hard-hitting drama about a town where all the cops are criminals, was slated for a spring release. Cheryl handed me a few foamcore-mounted posters to carry and we stopped by Kenny's office to pick him up. I was slightly unsettled to see that he had an entire bookcase filled with Beanie Babies, bears only—each one entombed in a plastic dome.

"Oh, um, you have so many . . ." I gestured at the wall of plush figures.

"These are highly collectible," Kenny said. "Investment quality, as a matter of fact, each one in mint condition with its original tag."

"Right," I said, nodding. Not certain how to proceed with this conversation, I changed the subject. "What's the story for this meeting?"

"When we get in there, we'll introduce you to Phil as the new marketing associate. Then you won't have to say anything after that," Kenny said.

"Phil knows me already."

"He does? How?"

I told Kenny about reading the reviews to Phil late on Thursday nights from the *New York Times* printing plant. He and Cheryl exchanged a look.

"You went to the *New York Times* on Thursday nights?" Kenny asked.

"Sure, to get the reviews to read to Allegra, Phil, and whoever else needed to hear them."

"But we get them on Wednesdays at about five from the *Times*'s ad department," Cheryl said.

"You do?" I was so shocked that I forgot to keep walking.

"Yes, of course. That way we can pull quotes from the *Times* review to use in Friday's ads," Cheryl said.

"The reviews get filed on Tuesday or Wednesday so the *Times*'s ad people can get them around to the studios," Kenny added. "You really didn't know that?" He shook his head and Cheryl sighed.

"Matt can't stand Allegra, and in all the areas where they could combine their efforts, they refuse. You can't imagine the amount of repetition that goes on between Marketing and Publicity. But it's not worth the effort to figure it all out and risk forgetting something."

"And then you'd have to believe that the two departments could trust each other to share information," Kenny added.

I was pondering this when we got off the elevator in the Glorious building, trying to calculate how many hours of my life had been wasted as a result of this particular feud. I felt an unfamiliar flash of anger toward my new boss, which I quickly suppressed; after all, Matt wouldn't have had any knowledge of our Thursday night routine. The three of us took a seat on the famous bench outside of Phil's office, leaned the posters against the wall, and waited. There was a steady snapping sound coming from the direction of Tony's office. "Tony's jumping rope again," Kenny said, drumming a pencil against his knee. "If we sit here long enough, he might open his door and let us see him do chin-ups."

"We really don't need Tony around right now," Cheryl said, blinking about fifty times. "He's already moderately irate that the one-sheet for 86 isn't finished yet."

"What happened to it?" The movie was opening a week from this Friday.

"Image approval," Kenny said. "Somehow, when the deals were being struck for the cast of 86, four of them were granted the right to sign off on the poster. It's been a circus ever since."

I'd seen 86 at the junket last weekend. The movie was only so-so, but the press had been enthusiastic about the film's soundtrack, which we'd handily made available to each of them.

Sabrina ushered us into Phil's office. I hadn't been in here since that near-fatal mistake in my first week. Phil's mouth was full of something and he motioned for us to sit on the couch. It was so small that I had Kenny's elbow in my ribs from the moment we sat down. "Phil, before we show you the new looks for *Policeville*, this is Karen Jacobs. She used to be Allegra's assistant, but we've brought her into our department."

Phil glanced at me for a split second and then went back to eating what I now saw was a huge assortment of sushi arrayed on beautiful pieces of Japanese ceramics. Apparently Phil was able to get takeout from Nobu, a privilege famously denied the Emperor of Japan during his last New York visit.

"So. We have six revisions, based on our last conversation," Cheryl started, blinking a bit to get her bearings. I helped her spread them out on a ledge that was at Phil's seated eye-level. He looked them over for a second. "They all suck," he said calmly, dipping a piece of eel sushi into a vat of soy sauce before putting it in his mouth.

"You don't like any of them?" Kenny asked.

"Did you hear me? They all suck." His voice was quiet and matter-of-fact, as if he were telling us the time.

"Is there anything in particular that you don't like about them?"

Phil looked up from a yellowtail and scallion hand roll. "What I don't like about them is that they suck." He was getting louder now, and the "suck" reverberated a little. Phil bit a large piece from the roll and took a long drink of Diet Dr Pepper.

Cheryl stammered. "We used all your suggestions from the last group we showed you. Can you tell us what's wrong with these?"

"What's wrong with them is. That. They. Suck!" Phil was shouting now. "They just suck!" He grabbed a handful of shrimp sushi, shoved them into a mountain of wasabi, splashed them into the soy sauce, and stuffed them into his mouth. With his face full of sushi, he picked up where he'd left off. "Why can't I get a poster that doesn't suck? Is it really asking too much of you people to have a poster that doesn't suck like all the other ones?" Kenny's glasses now had several grains of rice stuck to them.

The sound of Phil's raised voice brought Tony in at a dead run. He was covered in sweat and wearing a tank top and running tights. Large tufts of hair bristled from his shoulders like military epaulets. The smell of Tony's perspiration mixed with the sushi could have been the key element in some type of chemical weapon.

"What's the matter, Phil?" He peeled a piece of belly tuna away from its bed of rice and popped it in his mouth. "That soy sauce, man—enough sodium to kill a person." He turned and looked at the three of us, and then at the ledge holding the posters. "Oh, the *Policeville* looks." He shook his head. "These really suck."

Tony's confirmation of Phil's original diagnosis had a greater effect than if he'd sucker punched his brother in the stomach. Phil stood up, his impressive girth filling the room. "Don't you think I know they suck?" He slammed his fist on his desk and a tsunami of soy sauce rose up, curled over the edge of its dish, and splashed into my lap. I stared at it, not knowing what to do. "Since when do I need you to tell me what sucks?" he yelled through clenched teeth.

"Since always," Tony shouted back. "Since day fucking one." He put his middle finger so close to Phil's face it threatened to go up his nose.

Phil came out from behind his desk, picked up the six posters and snapped them in half over his knee. He held one at Tony's throat. "Get the hell out of my office," he said, menacing Tony with the broken piece of foamcore.

Tony grabbed another piece of poster and swatted Phil's

away with it. Soon the two of them were fencing with the smashed pieces of posters. The foamcore disintegrated into millions of tiny white balls that rained down on Kenny, Cheryl, and me. Kenny motioned to us and we quickly moved out of the office, dodging Phil and Tony's flailing parries and thrusts.

I patted my hair and then looked at my hand: it was covered with specks of foam. The soy sauce in my lap had made a large, embarrassing stain, and my pants had holes in them from my encounter with Geraldine's beast this morning. Cheryl and Kenny were looking at me; I think they were waiting to see if I would cry. Instead, I just stood there.

"Welcome to Marketing, Karen!" Kenny said. "Why don't you go home now. It's nearly six and you've definitely had enough for one day."

"Karen, what happened to you?" I turned and saw Delilah waiting on the bench.

"I just got in the way of Phil's soy sauce, the remains of the *Policeville* one-sheet looks, and Harvey's teeth," I said, beginning to laugh. Delilah looked at me quizzically, before laughing as well. "I'm going in for an 86 meeting with Phil," she said. "We're going to do a tie-in with the soundtrack and Tower Records."

"Sounds great," Kenny said.

"It's been a good week," Delilah said proudly. "I've also worked out a promotion for *Policeville* with the company that makes The Lock, that anti-car theft device that goes on the steering wheel. I showed them the script and they're really enthusiastic about partnering with us. It happens to figure prominently in the story."

"Yup. Well, see you later, Delilah," Kenny said, motioning that it was time for us to go.

As we rode down in the elevator together, Cheryl was clearly trying to catch Kenny's eye, but he stared resolutely ahead. "Delilah must have an early version of that script," she finally said nervously, but "Yup" was Kenny's only comment on the subject. I said my good-byes on the corner and walked over to the subway.

"Bad day, Karen?" my building's doorman said, as he whisked me inside.

"Actually, no." It really hadn't been, considering. Despite everything that had gone on, Marketing showed no evidence of the psychological warfare of my former department. Once inside, I tossed my pants in the trash and took a shower, carefully combing all the bits of foam out of my hair. I had just changed into jeans and a sweater when Ellen walked in.

"You're home early."

"It looks like this marketing job isn't going to have me working nearly as many nights and weekends as I did in Publicity."

"About that. I looked at the contract today and I can't let you sign it."

"Why not?"

"It's completely insane. It basically takes your rights away."

"I think they gave me the same contract they give everyone else."

"That's possible, but it's still way out of line. I even faxed it to a law school classmate of mine who specializes in labor contracts, and he said it was completely shocking."

"What's so shocking about it?" I figured it was going to be some Latin term that scared lawyers but not regular people.

"Well, basically, if you leave Glorious, even if they fire you, you can't work for any of their competitors."

"Ellen, none of our competitors are even based in New York. I'm not about to move to L.A. to work for some corporate studio. It's Glorious that I'm interested in."

"Maybe so, but this has more to do with how they've defined competitors. It's a long list that covers all of these businesses that they don't even compete with, but they justify it by noting that they intend to explore expansion into these areas."

"Like what?"

"Well, television for instance. You couldn't go back to CNN, even if they would take you. Or any other network, which is a shame because your résumé has several years of good broadcast experience on it."

"Uh-huh." Ellen still hadn't forgiven me for leaving CNN.

"You can't work in publishing—newspapers, magazines, or books. And you can't work in any business under the corporate umbrella of any of Glorious's parent company's competitors."

"English, please?"

"Most companies, including Glorious, are owned by some kind of large conglomerate. I can't think of any that don't have at least one business that competes with something owned by the one that owns Glorious."

This wasn't good. The company that had purchased Glorious Pictures from the Waxmans several years earlier was huge and had a multitude of tentacles reaching into virtually everything in the world that was seen, heard, eaten, purchased, or even thought about. They were a small world unto themselves. It was said that most Americans would find it difficult to get through a single day without doing something that rang the company's cash registers, like it or not.

"So basically, if I quit Glorious, the only thing I can do legally is flip burgers?"

"Not even that. They've actually noted that since Happy Meals and the like are often film-themed, the food franchises are out, too."

This was awful. I slid down, slumping against the back of the couch. "What could I do, then?"

"Make pottery? Teach nursery school? Get your Masters in something?"

None of those sounded interesting to me. "This competition clause lasts forever?"

"No, just for two years, but that's a really long time at this point in your career."

"Ellen, I had no idea."

"You wouldn't. There's a paragraph in here that prohibits anyone under contract at Glorious from discussing what's in it."

"Is there anything you think you can do? You lawyers like to negotiate."

"There's one thing that might work. You're not planning to quit Glorious any time soon, right?" I shook my head, although I'd been so caught up in my switch to Marketing, I hadn't really thought about how soon my self-imposed year would be ending. "Well, I've seen 'noncompete' clauses before, although they're usually for someone who is much higher up on the ladder than you. It protects the company so that someone doesn't go there, learn the business, and then jump ship and help one of their competitors. But I've never seen one where they said you couldn't compete if you got fired. I don't even think that's legal."

"Really? Because I'm definitely not going to quit, especially now that I've started in Marketing." I calmed down. As usual, Ellen was saving the day.

"I'll talk to someone in your legal department tomorrow about that clause. Hopefully they'll just take it out."

"What if they don't?"

"I would recommend that you don't sign it. If you choose to, though, they could sue you if you break the noncompete."

"But I thought you said it was illegal?"

"If you agree to it, you're accepting their terms. That's why it's called a contract."

To paraphrase Phil, this sucked. It seemed that just as I got a toehold into something that I really wanted to do, something else threatened to take it away.

The next morning I was back in my office, staring at the awful copy I'd written for *Lip Balm*. Kenny walked by with the latest 86 posters. "What's going on with those?" The posters that Kenny was holding showed the four main characters' faces inside a star-shaped, metallic border.

"Each time we make a change based on something one of the actors says, the other three need to approve it. So here's where we are with this round: Henry Hauser, the most famous actor in the film, said that in the first version his head was too big. Everyone else was fine with that one. So, we shrank Henry's head by about 2 millimeters all around. I can't even see the difference, to tell you the truth." Kenny strummed his fingers on my door. "Then, after we made that change, we had to send the new poster around to all four of them again. Henry signed off, and so did Frankie Braden and Brie LaDoux. But Tamara Traynor said that now her face looked too fat next to Henry's head."

"What are you going to do?"

"We'll have the art department thin her out a little, but that woman is emaciated as it is. And then we'll go around again, hopefully for the last time," he said, looking up at the ceiling as if asking for an assist from above.

I nodded sympathetically before telling him that I was stuck about what to do for the *Lip Balm* one-sheet. He suggested meeting with the designer from the art department who was assigned to it. "Those guys are usually good at jump-starting things," he said. He e-mailed me a list of all the upcoming Glorious films with the designer assigned to each one. Next to *Lip Balm* and the rest of what I'd been assigned was the name James Bartholomew.

The art department had recently moved to a building that was a couple of blocks on the other side of Glorious's primary office. The company was rapidly expanding around TriBeCa, with each new space completing a spokelike pattern around the hub of the main office. I walked in and was met by a woman whose hair was dyed pink and arranged in spiky projections around her head. "Hey. Are you looking for someone?"

"James Bartholomew?"

"J!" she yelled. A figure zoomed over on a tall, wheeled chair, putting a foot out and neatly braking just inches from me. James was an African American man of about twenty-two who had on the smallest eyeglasses I'd ever seen—his pupils were larger than the lenses. He looked over his glasses at me as I introduced myself. "Oh right, Kenny told me about you. The new marketing person who's going to work on all those Tony flicks. Why can't he find a woman who's hot *and* a good filmmaker? Have you watched any of them yet?"

"Just one. *Lip Balm*." I said. "It doesn't really have a lot going on. It's about a tube of ChapStick and the many owners it has over its life. One person loses it, another picks it up, someone borrows it and never returns it, that kind of thing."

"How does it end?"

"Someone leaves it on a dashboard in Houston and it melts in ultra slo-mo."

"You've got to be kidding."

"I wish I could make that up."

"Well, who's in it? Was there any art provided?"

"There's no one actually in it. It's completely from the Chap-Stick's POV."

James threw back his head and howled. "Please, please tell me that this is some kind of prank," he said, trying to catch his breath. "Do you think it might be some kind of allegory?"

I told him my theories about the film, adding that none of them felt exactly right.

"Sometimes, a movie about a tube of ChapStick is really just a movie about a tube of ChapStick," James said, in a Zen kind of way. "And it's up to us to get people interested in it."

"Apparently no one here has any expectation that the movie is going to sell any tickets. Kenny and Cheryl said that we just need to open it to fulfill the company's obligation."

"Right. But to you and me, this poster becomes part of our bodies of work." I hadn't thought of it that way, but he was absolutely right. James suggested that I look through some books of old movie posters while we brainstormed. "Have you figured out the tag line yet?"

I told him of some of my more woeful attempts.

"You're right, those won't work. Maybe having the design figured out will help you come up with something."

"James, look at this!" I said, pushing a book in front of him.

"You might just be on to something," he said, carefully inspecting the page.

I'd found a picture of the original *Rocky Horror Picture Show* poster, the iconic one with the mouth.

James started sketching and said, "The *Rocky Horror* color scheme was very goth—you know, really red lips, the whitest teeth, black background. We could go with a Southwestern palette and have the mouth look not so transvestite."

We talked a bit more about it, and James said he'd have some mockups by the next afternoon. I went back to my office to try to write a decent tag line. There was a message from Geraldine on my voice mail that I decided to ignore. I played the movie again for inspiration.

> **"These lips have a story to tell."**
> **"Shhhh. We have a secret for you."**
> **"Wait until you hear our point of view."**

I didn't love any of these, but thought they were sexier than what I'd come up with yesterday.

The phone rang, interrupting me. It was Geraldine. "Karen, you've got to get that contract signed and returned or you won't get a paycheck on Friday."

"My attorney"—I liked the sound of that—"had a couple of questions. She was going to speak to the legal department today."

Geraldine tittered as if I'd used the wrong fork at a society luncheon. "All Glorious contracts are completely and utterly non-negotiable, so if your attorney wants to waste her time and your money, she's welcome to do so." Geraldine laughed again, only this time it was more of a cackle, before hanging up.

"The balm's about to drop." That was it! My revenge fantasies about Geraldine had inspired the best tag line yet. I e-mailed it to James, who replied back, "I love it!"

It was nearly four and I'd forgotten to eat. Delilah was ahead of me on line at the deli and invited me to join her. After we sat down I said, "So how's it going with The Lock?"

"They're on board. I don't think they've ever been approached about a promotion before but this was such a great fit. Now we'll have displays in nearly every auto-parts and hardware store in the country. Just where the target audience for this film will see it."

"That sounds like a home run. Congratulations."

"Actually, congratulations to you Karen, on getting out of Publicity."

"Thanks. I really needed a change. It was getting harder every day just to get out of bed and go to work."

"Those women can be very difficult," she said. "You know how at summer camp there was always one cabin of nasty girls? Every year you'd go back, hoping that maybe this was the summer that they'd be nice to you. Well, this is where those girls wound up."

"Speak of the devil," I said, as Allegra walked in, bought a huge container of pasta salad, then left without acknowledging either of us.

"This is just so weird. She's walking around TriBeCa like a ghost. Not that she ever spoke to me in the first place, except for that whole *Raven II* mess she got me into," Delilah said.

"I felt awful about that."

"I knew it wasn't your fault. Allegra was unbelievably nasty, treating me as if my job didn't matter, and the agreements I made were hers to dissolve. It's going to cost us the next time we need to work with those radio stations and no one will even take my call."

I nodded sympathetically. "I had no idea what was going on, but it must have been terrible for you."

"Unfortunately, there are snakes everywhere at Glorious, not just in Publicity. I know that Matt loves being known as the resident nice guy, but don't let your guard down."

I walked back to my office, considering the conversation. Delilah was the first and only employee of the Glorious promotions department, and from scratch she'd created contests, retail tie-ins, product placements, and sponsorships on a level with those of the major studios. And yet many of our colleagues treated her as if she were just Tony's ex-girlfriend. She'd more than proved her worthiness, but it was as if the Glorious staff couldn't allow anyone the freedom to move outside of her previously assigned box. I'd seen how poorly the publicity department behaved toward her, and noticed in that brief exchange with Kenny that he'd been rather cold. I would be wise to heed her warning.

James had left a folder of *Lip Balm* looks for me to show to Kenny and Cheryl. Because the film was only receiving a cursory release, Phil and Tony didn't have to approve it. If Kenny and Cheryl liked the one-sheet, it would then go to Matt, who would give the final okay. Opening the folder, it was hard not to gape at what James had created. The lips, colored a deep plum, floated above a desert in which beautiful cactus bloomed, red rocks jutted in gorgeous formation, and multihued sand gave the impression that it was shifting. The Kodachrome blue sky made me wistful for long-ago summer vacations. Underneath it, the film's title was boldly spelled out, a tube of lip balm at the end of the "m," making it look as if it the title had been drawn by the tube. The type that spelled out "The balm's about to drop" matched the color of the lips. I flipped through the rest of the stack. James had made six in all, altering the title font and the lip color in each. The one-sheet was surreal, evocative, and visually arresting. I called Cheryl and asked if I could show them to her. Kenny helped me tape all six to Cheryl's wall. "Wow, that's really gorgeous," Cheryl said.

"The balm's about to drop—was that yours?" Kenny asked. "It really works." The three of us gazed at the posters, Kenny noting that one of the fonts was perhaps the cleanest and Cheryl suggesting that the lips that were more raspberry than plum "sent a more fertile message."

"It's such a waste," Kenny said. "A poster like that for a film no one's ever going to see."

I shrugged my shoulders, not sure how to answer.

"Really, Karen," Cheryl said. "I know that you want to do your best, and that this is your first try and all, but you really can't put this type of energy and effort into these films."

"I don't think it took any longer than another one would have," I said, explaining that James and I had met once about this yesterday and he'd sent them over today.

"I'm sure there was a simpler solution." Seeing how disappointed I looked she said, "Don't misunderstand. It's a *very good* start. It's just that I'd rather have seen you get through three of those by now, not just one."

I called James and told him about the feedback, complimenting him on the utter beauty of those posters. I didn't feel the need to tell him the rest of what was said.

My in-box pinged and there was a new missive from Geraldine asking about my contract. I deleted it and sent an e-mail to Ellen asking if she'd made any headway. I started to e-mail Clark about my latest Allegra sighting, but decided it wasn't worth my time. Instead, I sent an e-mail to him and to Robert, suggesting that we three pick a night to have drinks after work. I looked up and Cheryl was in the doorway. "We're going to an audience test screening of *Policeville* tonight. Do you want to come along?"

"Sure."

"It's at a multiplex in New Jersey. There's a car coming for Kenny and me at six, but we have a lot to discuss. Why don't you order your own car, and my assistant will print the directions for you."

"Okay then. I'll see you there."

Cheryl blinked, nodded, and left. I called the car company, the same one that used to drive me to the office when I worked for Allegra. The dispatcher recognized my voice and said, "Karen, what happened to you? I was worried." I told her about my job change and then reserved a car to take me to New Jersey. "Oh, yeah, you guys are testing *Policeville* again. This is the fourteenth time already. I wonder what's wrong with it?"

The dispatcher knew more about the testing process than I did.

I'd heard, however, that *Policeville* had a lot riding on it. The film featured a roster rich in A-list talent, including Eddie Di Silva, Fly Faccione, and Marvin Fischell, whose mammary predilections had helped me get hired. Phil had been cutting and recutting this film, hoping to improve the test scores. He'd even humored the director by allowing him to test his own cut. Phil had earned his "Philminator" nickname by editing so heavily that some directors claimed he used a scythe.

I stopped at Belinda's to say hello and pick up some newspapers and magazines for the ride to New Jersey. She asked me how I was enjoying Marketing. "I like it. It's like using a completely different part of my brain."

"Good on you, then," she said. "I'm glad to see you got out of there."

On the ride to New Jersey I spread out in the backseat, flipping through magazines and pondering my new area. I hoped that I was getting it right. Matt had sent an e-mail indicating that he wouldn't be returning from Los Angeles any time soon. He still hadn't answered my message, and I needed to talk to him about my contract. Cheryl and Kenny were nice enough, but they were so stressed I didn't feel comfortable asking questions. This morning Frankie Braden's agent called to say that Frankie had seen the new poster with Henry's smaller head and Tamara's thinner face and felt that with these changes Frankie's Adam's apple now "overwhelmed" the entire poster. "I don't really see how you can fix this one," the agent had added helpfully. Tony's suggestion was to "rip his fucking throat out," but instead he decided to go find "which one of my legal geniuses gave image approval to four goddamn no-talents in the same picture." I hoped it was the same attorney who was working on my contract—this meeting with Tony would undoubtedly soften him up.

At the theater, I picked up popcorn and a Diet Coke before

meeting Cheryl and Kenny in the lobby. The three of us settled in and then Phil and the director took seats right in front of us, Phil flanked by two of his assistants. Everyone else from Glorious had a clipboard with a gooseneck light attached. I made a mental note to order one in the morning. "I hope you don't have any ice in that," Kenny said, tapping on his knee.

"I do, why?"

"If Phil hears it rattling around in your cup, he's going to let you know about it. Loudly."

I slipped out of my seat and went back to the concession stand, exchanging my soda for a quieter one. When I returned, Kenny explained that after the film ended the audience members would each fill out a card with questions about the film—the ending, the various characters, and some other key elements. Then twenty or so preselected people would stay behind and have an in-depth discussion with a moderator. Overnight the scores would be tallied and the tape from the discussion transcribed. In the morning Phil, Cheryl, and Kenny would have a meeting with the director to discuss the results.

Even after the lights went out, Phil's assistants kept walking in and out of the theater, cell phones pressed against their faces. Three quarters of an hour after the film started, a Domino's delivery man walked down the side aisle, looking around until he saw one of the assistants beckoning to him. The assistant handed him some cash and gave Phil the whole pie, which he inhaled in about six minutes; then he folded the cardboard box up into a baton shape.

At one point in the film Marvin Fischell, playing a policeman, accosts two thugs who are attempting to steal a car. The thugs proceed to beat the living shit out of him. The final blows are delivered by a metal rod that I realize is . . . The Lock! Soon Marvin's lip is split open, he's missing most of his front teeth, and his jaw is obviously and badly broken. Meanwhile, Phil was sitting in front of us waving his pizza-box baton in exact synchronization with each thrust, showering crumbs over three rows of people, including Cheryl, Kenny, and me.

On the way back to the city, my thoughts kept returning to the gruesome scene with The Lock. How in the world did Delilah get the company to agree to a promotion? Then I remembered she hadn't seen the film, which meant that they hadn't, either. This couldn't be right.

The next day, James delivered the completed *Lip Balm* poster for Cheryl to approve. She and Kenny were meeting with Phil and the director of *Policeville* so I left it in Cheryl's in-box before starting to watch *Carrion Sweet Vulture*, which I quickly realized had less going for it than *Lip Balm*. I couldn't make head or tail out of it, but the press notes said that Valhalla Bounty, *Carrion*'s director-screenwriter, had been the Penthouse Pet for August 1985. So that was the plot.

Fast-forwarding through the other films and reading the notes, it was clear I'd have my work cut out for me. Each movie was less compelling than the previous one, and a few seemed to be unfinished, or just barely started. The notes that were included with each tape spoke of grandiose ideals like "triumph over adversity," "a search for life's higher meaning," and several mentioned that they were meant to be "an allegory for our troubled times." Whatever the filmmakers' intentions had been, the works were so hopelessly muddled it was hard to match the notes to the films. I put the videos, press kits, and photographs into a pile on my desk, hoping to make order out of the chaos.

Just then my phone rang. It was Ellen, completely up in arms.

"I can't believe that place," she started. "Just the nerve."

"What happened?"

"I spoke to the attorney at Glorious who drew up your contract.

He told me that if I didn't like the terms, he could find another Karen Jacobs by snapping his fingers."

"That's weird. I don't even know anyone in the legal department."

"I told him that you were in no way fungible, nor were you to be treated as such."

"Fungible?"

Ellen sighed. "Replaceable. Interchangeable. Things you certainly are not."

"That doesn't make any sense. I thought they wanted me to work here."

"That's the irony of these types of agreements. They offer you a job, but make it nearly impossible for you to agree to the terms and conditions."

"I'm going to ask Matt, my boss, if there's anything he can do to help."

"Please do. I'm out of ideas," she said, hanging up.

I left a message with Matt's assistant asking him to call me, closed my eyes, and reached into the pile, vowing to work on whichever film I pulled out next. *Pocket Protector.* I put the tape in my VCR and began to watch the film, making notes about images and themes that might be of use for the one-sheet.

Cheryl stopped by and told me that the *Lip Balm* poster had been approved by everyone who needed to okay it. The next order of business would be to have James oversee the actual "printing" at Kinko's and then I'd send the filmmaker her copies.

I called James and told him the good news. He said he'd have the posters done by the middle of next week, and we picked a time to meet and discuss the rest of the films.

Not having heard back from Clark or Robert, I called and left each one a voice mail. It wasn't like them not to communicate with me. I called Elliott but he wasn't in and I decided against leaving a message. I hadn't heard from him since our date a couple of weeks ago and I wasn't sure what was going on with him, or with us, or whatever this was. But the thought of how he'd looked when he kissed me was unbelievably distracting—enough so that each time I remembered, it took me quite some time to regain my concentration.

Methodically I went through the rest of the Tony films, coming up with a poster concept and tag line for each. The whole process took four days, and at the end of it I met with James and discussed the ideas for the eleven one-sheets. He promised to turn them around quickly and then presented me with the finished *Lip Balm* posters. Even printed at Kinko's, instead of a real press, they were stunning.

I logged on to e-mail Matt that the one-sheets were done and was surprised to see that I had an e-mail from Vivian. I read it twice, not believing what I saw. It was, of all things, an apology.

> I would like to apologize for the unconscionable way I have sometimes treated you. While we all labor in an extremely stressful environment, that is no excuse for my poor behavior in the past. My only hope is that going forward you will allow me to treat you with the respect and courtesy you deserve.
>
> Sincerely,
> Vivian Henry

I grabbed the phone and dialed Clark. "What in the hell has gotten into Vivian? I just got the most bizarre, heartfelt apology from her."

"More like who's gotten into her e-mail?" Clark answered. "Everyone in the company got it, including Phil and Tony, and Vivian's in a complete freak-out. She said she didn't send it.

What's worse is that half the company is writing her back, telling her that they're happy to forgive and forget."

Just then I heard Vivian's voice, clear as a bell, coming through Clark's phone. "The nerve of these people, to think that I'd apologize to them. Why? For what? They think I *owe* them something? I'm going to find who did this and . . ." Clark started to speak again and I couldn't hear the rest of Vivian's diatribe.

"It's funny," Clark was saying, "but a little eerie, too. If she didn't send it, who did?"

I hung up, tried to think of a list of possible suspects, and came up absolutely blank.

I walked over to Kenny and Cheryl to show them the *Lip Balm* posters. They were discussing Vivian's e-mail. "Maybe she had a near-death experience," Kenny was saying as I entered his office. "That can sometimes spark this kind of a transformation." I decided to let him enjoy his fantasy. After showing them the posters, I assured them that I'd have looks for the rest of the films within the next few days.

The two of them seemed preoccupied, even listless. At first I chalked it up to Matt's absence, as he often acted as a buffer between them and the brothers. Without him, they were facing the full force of the Waxmans' wrath, currently stoked by the still-unsatisfactory scores for *Policeville* and the ongoing Academy campaign for *El Lechero*, which had escalated once more to its pre-Christmas mania. At least the 86 one-sheet was finally finished, thanks to a Photoshop shortening of Frankie's neck that put his chin just slightly above his sternum. After seeing Harry's little head, Tamara's pinched face, and Frankie's squat build, Brie saw that she was the only normal-looking one in the group, and gave her approval without further ado.

Even so, I felt that Cheryl's and Kenny's interest in me had dwindled: now that I was in the process of finishing my initial assignment, they didn't seem to know what to do with me. The last time I'd spoken with Cheryl she'd told me to remind her to add me to the "cc list" for meetings, but I'd asked a couple of times, to no avail.

I'd left Matt another message about the contract, as Ellen had given up on getting any changes made to it. All I wanted was to speak with Matt and explain my concerns before signing it. Geraldine was now calling me three times a day on average and true to her threat, I hadn't received a paycheck. In Publicity I had always felt beleaguered; here I felt invisible. If I closed my new door and locked it, would Cheryl and Kenny even notice that I was missing?

THE LAST PICTURE SHOW

M arketing is to publicity as psychiatry is to psychology, I thought, patting myself on the back for creating such an SAT-worthy analogy. I was studying the scores for the most recent test screening of *Policeville*, which showed that a few well-placed edits had raised the audience's "I would recommend this film to a friend" percentage to 80, up from 72 percent at the screening I'd attended a week ago. I knew that Phil would be pleased, particularly as yesterday I'd seen a memo in the trash noting that these specific cuts had been his idea. The document I was now holding had been left on the copier—I still wasn't receiving much information from my new colleagues, and needed to rely on whatever methods I could to keep myself up on what was going on in the department.

Recalling the machinations we'd gone through in Publicity, trying to figure out how many stars a reviewer meant to give a film if their paper awarded stars, or debating whether granting "inside access" to a premiere would be better or worse for the film's box office, I knew that marketing was hard science. It was as clear as the difference between the women I knew in college who'd majored in sociology and the ones who'd chosen applied mathematics. You could postulate, guess, and theorize for hours, or you could confirm the actual answer, of which there existed only one. The idea of this satisfied me, although my own major, political science, seemed to have done nothing to advance my Glorious career thus far. But in the unlikely event that Phil or Tony needed to seek an amendment to the Constitution, they could count on me to tell them how to go about it.

It was good to see that *Policeville* was getting better scores— it had already received so much advance press that no one could afford for it to fail. *Lip Balm*, though, was decidedly lower on the Glorious radar screen. The one-sheet was ready, and the only things left for me to do was find out the film's release date as well as the names of the theaters where it would be opening, so that I could prepare a form letter to Reba Koronis.

This was standard operating procedure when a film was getting ready to open. For a movie like 86, the filmmakers, cast, and all of their representatives would already have received the poster, and then they'd be sent a long list of theaters where the film would be shown on its opening night, a list that could number in the thousands. In the case of *Lip Balm*, which would open only in one theater each in New York and Los Angeles, I still needed to confirm exactly which venues had been selected. While I didn't know Reba, I was sure she'd want to tell her friends and family where they could finally see the film she'd made some seven years earlier. Each time I'd asked Kenny, however, I'd gotten the brush-off.

"Why are you so stuck on that stupid movie?" he'd exclaimed impatiently. "It's going to open and close in a week; what difference does it make where it flops?"

I'd e-mailed Matt twice, but received no response. Where *was* he? I wanted to talk to him about my contract.

With all the posters and tag lines for Tony's Blockbuster Videos finished and approved, I'd asked Cheryl and Kenny for some direction about what to do next, but they'd told me they were "too busy" to give me anything to work on, so I'd spent the last few days watching my newly installed cable. I flipped through the channels and saw Oprah who was thin again. I dialed Dag's extension.

"I just saw Oprah on TV and I thought of you. Has she called?"

"Very funny. And, no, she hasn't. Although I have heard from Allegra."

"And?"

"She phoned yesterday to give me instructions on how to reach her at the hotel where she says she's staying in Germany, but then about four fire trucks came screaming down the street and I could hear them through the windows and the phone."

"That's too funny."

"I know. I didn't know what to say, so I asked, 'Allegra, is the Black Forest on fire?' And then she hung up on me."

"That is beyond abnormal."

"Above and beyond," Dag agreed. "You know, I really miss you Karen, and not just because Geraldine hasn't found another assistant yet and I have to do everything by myself. We really worked well together."

"I know. I miss working with you and Robert and Clark, although there are a few people in Publicity I'd be happy never to see again."

"Do you like what you're doing now?"

"It's a funny question. I think I could like it, but Matt's nowhere to be found—he's been in L.A. since before I started, and Cheryl and Kenny can't take a break from telling everyone how busy they are to actually involve me in anything. Hence my Oprah-watching."

"Well, stop by some time. At least you can leave your desk," she pointed out.

I hung up and rechecked my e-mail, hoping that I'd have at least one or two new messages. The nonstop pinging I'd experienced in Publicity had slowed to a trickle—I'd even asked Systems Alejandro to see if my e-mail was working properly. He'd come around, run a check, and assured me that everything was in order. It was late January and Abby had finished her research project at 2 A.M. last week—on the same day that her new semester had begun. It would be a waste of her time to tell her how bored I was. I put on my coat and hat in preparation for a walk around TriBeCa. I felt almost regretful that I didn't have to faux smoke any longer—the need to pretend had been obliterated by the lack of anyone needing me to do anything in particular.

Planning on visiting Belinda for some conversation and a hot chocolate, I ran into a stricken Delilah in the elevator. "Can you talk for a minute?" she asked me.

I followed her out of the building and we headed about four blocks south, where there were some benches. Delilah looked at me. "I know I've told you this before, but please, promise me that you'll be careful," she said, before bursting into tears.

"Delilah, what's wrong?"

"Remember when I bumped into you, Kenny, and Cheryl outside Phil's office, and he asked me how the promotion for The Lock was going?"

"Yes. What happened?"

"Well, you know I put the whole thing together—it was going to be the largest tie-in we've ever done."

I bit my lip, remembering the bloody head-bashing for which The Lock had been used in the film.

"I screened *Policeville* for their CEO yesterday and he was absolutely furious. It was so embarrassing—it was the first time I was seeing the movie, and I wanted to yell up to the projectionist to stop the film. Instead of a promotional tie-in, we have a lawsuit. If they can't get that part of the movie cut, they're going to sue Glorious for misrepresentation."

Something was missing from the story. "Delilah, what made you approach them in the first place?"

"I read the script months ago, when it first went into production. In my copy, thieves try to steal a car, but they can't because it's got The Lock on the steering wheel, and then Marvin's character apprehends them. A textbook use of their product."

"So when you saw us that day in front of Phil's office, Kenny had to know that it was a bad idea," I said, as Delilah nodded emphatically. "And he decided not to mention it. What a bastard."

"Phil has been asking me to do more promotions and product placement deals, and this seemed like a terrific pairing. Male demographic, cops, car-gadgets—I thought it was a perfect fit."

"On paper it was," I said. "But none of this is your fault."

"We were even going to be in Wal-Mart with this," she said wistfully. "Phil screamed at me for fifteen minutes and told me he's thinking of firing me."

This was news. Wasn't Delilah a Tony Tryout with a guaranteed job for life? "Oh, he'd never do that," I said quickly, even though I had absolutely no idea.

"I know, everyone thinks that because I used to be Tony's girlfriend I can't be fired."

"Yeah, that's the rumor about you," I said guiltily. Enough people had been lying to her lately; I didn't feel right continuing the trend.

"It's not true. We were together for a while, maybe a year or so, but I was already working here. And I've had to do my share to stay, believe me."

"I wish I knew what to tell you. This is just horrible. And here I was, thinking that I was in a better group."

"It depends how you look at it. Those Publicity bitches will yell and carry on right to your face. Kenny and Cheryl, on the other hand, smile while stabbing you in the back."

"I'll be careful," I said, getting up to leave. "And let me know how this turns out. It's ridiculous for you to take the fall for something so stupid."

Back in my office, there was an e-mail from Geraldine, asking for the ninetieth time about my contract. It was ready for my signature; I just wanted to speak with Matt about it before turning it in. When he'd invited me to join the department, I'd had no idea that I would be asked to sign something so significant. A conversation with him would assuage my discomfort, not to mention that signing the contract would allow me to finally collect my now three weeks' overdue paycheck.

My eye fell on the *Lip Balm* posters. There wasn't any Publicity being done in support of its opening, so no one in my old department would have any information, either. I didn't understand why Kenny couldn't just tell me what I needed to know, so I could send the damn letter to Reba, but after my conversation with Delilah, I didn't want to push him. And where in the hell was Matt, and why didn't he call back or e-mail me?

Frustrated, I phoned Elliott. Page Six had become my most reliable source for Glorious information these days, and I was at the end of my rope.

"Karen, this is a nice surprise. It's been a little while."

"Since I moved into Marketing and there isn't any dish you can try to extract from me," I said, laughing, "I guess you've lost all interest."

"Not at all. What's on your feet?"

"Sneakers, Elliott. Adidas Rod Lavers to be precise. And sweat socks."

"You really know how to turn a guy on."

"Seriously, I didn't call you to talk about my feet. I just thought you might have some information that could help me."

"Try me."

"What do you know about Matt Vincent? He's supposed to be my new boss, but he's been in L.A. since I started, and I can't get him to return a phone call or an e-mail."

"So you think maybe he's in L.A. the way Allegra's in Europe?"

"You know about that, too?"

"Everyone does. We're not even bothering to put it in the page."

"No, I think Matt's really in L.A. It's just created a huge mess for me."

"Okay, Karen. Here's the deal. I've been following this story for a few days but don't have enough solid information yet to confirm it. So, you didn't hear it from me."

"Promise."

"Matt Vincent is in Los Angeles because he's trying to force Phil and Tony into renegotiating his contract. He wants out of Marketing and into Production, and he says he's staying on the West Coast until they agree to move him into the production department and hire someone else to oversee Marketing. Essentially, he's holding himself hostage, in a way that can happen only at your crazy company."

"That explains his mysterious disappearance, then. I really can't believe this place."

"And what do I get for supplying this off-the-record information?"

"My heartfelt gratitude."

"I would be much happier with some time alone with your left pinkie toe."

"Glad to arrange," I said, but thinking how much more I'd

enjoy a nice Chardonnay and some conversation. And then I thought again about that kiss, and how it had stayed with me for about three days afterward.

I hung up, meditating on what to do next. Was someone going to tell me what was going on? Were Cheryl and Kenny my new bosses? Now I was extremely glad that I hadn't signed the contract, although my last trip to the ATM revealed that I was in dire need of that check. I was surprised when the receipt didn't say, "Feed me."

I wrote Kenny a fifth e-mail asking about Reba's opening dates. I knew it would annoy him, but I wanted a paper trail showing that I'd been trying to do the right thing. Kenny might have some ulterior motive for keeping this information from Reba, or from me, and I wasn't going to leave myself open to whatever he was cooking up.

I'd just hit "Send" when Cheryl called. She was leaving to go test movie trailers on unsuspecting mall patrons in suburban Philadelphia.

"Karen, I'm so glad you're still here," she'd started. "Tony asked me to put something together for him, and I've been too busy to get it done. I thought he'd forget all about it, but his assistant just called to remind me that it's due tomorrow. Can you help me?"

"Sure," I said.

Cheryl explained that Tony wanted a list of five hundred movie titles created to stockpile for the future. He might use them to re-title films, to create English-language names for foreign pictures, or, if the title was particularly evocative, he might even create a movie around it.

"Karen, I promise. If you can just do these for me, I'll make sure that everyone understands it was your work. You'll be getting me out of a huge jam; Matt, Kenny, and even Tony will really appreciate it." She sounded so forlorn, and I really wanted to put my name on something besides *Lip Balm* in the marketing department, so I agreed, even though I'd be pulling an all-nighter.

"Here's the deal. Tony likes to look at titles and imagine the way they'd look on a theater marquee," she said. "So you need to type them in twenty-six-point text in the Helvetica font, and you should bold and center each one. E-mail me the file when you're through," she added, before I overheard Kenny tell her that their car was downstairs. I got started right away. Finding it hard to feel any kind of spark, I stared at my fingers on the keyboard for a while. Finally, I had an idea:

THE HAND
RETURN OF THE HAND
THE HAND 3: PINKY'S REVENGE

Those looked good, and I knew that Tony liked films that easily lent themselves to sequels and more. I imagined *The Hand* as sort of a comedy-horror film, in which an amputated hand terrorizes a beautiful woman, who, coincidentally, earns her living as a ring and bracelet model.

I turned on the evening news, hoping that it might bring more inspiration, which it didn't. I ordered dinner, which did.

JUST WHAT SHE ORDERED
SIDE OF FRIES
OFF THE MENU

I thought of these as a "girl in the big city" series—all of which would feature a plucky young heroine who gets swept off her feet by a guy who is definitely not her type. Or so she thought!

This was difficult. No wonder Cheryl had allowed me to do it. I looked around my office, rejecting the possibility of *Palm Pilot* as being too close to *Pocket Protector* and realized that this was far from uncharted territory. *Desk Set, The Odessa File,* and *Dial M for Murder* had already locked the best office supply titles.

As it got later, I grew tired, and a bit melancholy.

TALES OF THE BLANKET
THE PILLOW
MORNING BECOMES TRIBECA

When I'd finished the list, now operating on the time-honored doctrine of CYA, I added a footer, "Karen Jacobs/Marketing," along with the date. It was 4 A.M. when I e-mailed it to Cheryl.

In the morning a photocopy of the list, no longer bearing the footer, was lying on my chair. It had a cover note to Tony from Cheryl reading, "Here are some ideas my assistant and I put together."

I walked into her office. "You know, the only reason I worked on those titles for you is because you said that my work would go directly to Tony, and that everyone would know I'd written it."

"I never said that," she said, as calmly as if she were ordering breakfast. "And besides, it's not as if you delivered something I could just send to him. Several of your titles had to be edited."

Disgusted, I walked back into my office, shut the door, and tried to think of what to do next. I sent an e-mail to Matt, and one to Kenny, more out of routine than any belief that I'd get a response. Still tired from my title-writing marathon of the night before, not to mention irate, I called Dagney.

"I never thought I'd ask you this, but can I read some of your magazines? Even if I have to rip them up for you?"

"Yeah, come on over, I've got a stack," she said.

After I got off the elevator on my old floor, I knocked on the open door of Robert's cube. He looked up, and when he saw me, he stood on his chair and walked over the top of the desk to greet me—it was the only way he could operate in the tiny space Marlene had left him. He gave me a huge hug.

"What are you up to?" I said.

"Working hard, trying to get my equilibrium back." He'd reorganized the cube so that everything hung from the walls in neat rows. His desk was stacked with three boxes of file folders and he was using a little electronic gadget to neatly label each one.

"Where's Clark?"

"He's running some errand for Gloria, or something. I barely see him these days."

"What's this project?"

"The next five years' of the Glorious release schedule. I wanted to prepare. It all happens before you know what hits you," he said, and I was painfully aware of the double-meaning.

"Let's talk soon," I said. "I don't want to get in your way here."

I was planning to sneak up on Dagney, but Vivian saw me first. "Karen. Karen. Karen. You don't work here anymore. We have sensitive documents all around. Please make it brief."

I looked at Dag and rolled my eyes. She rolled hers back and I said, "Vivian, I swear, I didn't see a thing." Dag handed me a pile of magazines and I managed not to laugh until I'd passed through the doors that separated the publicity department from the others. Or maybe it protected the others; I couldn't be sure. On the way to the elevator, I was stopped by the sight of a heaping platter of sandwiches on the table in the conference room, which was empty. Grabbing a pastrami sandwich and liberally slathering mustard on the rye bread, I added a dill pickle and some potato salad to my plate before continuing to the elevator bank, where I hit the button and waited, already three-quarters of the way through my pickle.

From where I was standing I could hear a woman with a crisp English accent shouting, "Phil, you don't know anything about how to run a goddamn magazine and I'd appreciate it if you'd leave it to those of us who do. Otherwise I simply can't be bothered to . . ."

Who in the world was yelling at Phil like that? I'd have to remember to zip off an e-mail to Robert and find out. The elevator door opened and I got inside.

All the other doors on the floor were closed when I arrived—it looked as if Kenny, Cheryl, and Delilah weren't around, and naturally, there was little activity in Matt's area, although his assistant glanced up at me as I came in. Placing the sandwich on my desk, I turned on my PC and logged on, keying in "LLOYDISDEAD" and thinking how much I wanted to talk to Abby.

Nothing happened, so I tried another couple of times. "LLOYDISDEAD" "LLOYDISDEAD." I called Systems Alejandro, and for the first time in the dozens of times I'd called him for IT assistance, his voice mail picked up. I'd begun to assume that he didn't have voice mail. I left a message and continued to eat my sandwich.

The phone rang and I swallowed before answering. It was Matt.

"How are things?" I said, not wanting him to know that I knew he was in a standoff with the Waxmans.

"Karen, I'm really sorry to tell you this, but I have to let you go. It's not your fault, but it's not open for discussion."

"What?" I shouted. "What are you talking about? Why in the world are you firing me?" This had to be some kind of practical joke, or just a terrible mistake.

"I'm sorry Karen, but you no longer work here."

"Matt, what happened? What happened? Whatever it is, I'm sure I can explain!" My heart was pounding and I had the phone in a white-knuckle grip. "I'm sure I can fix it." My mind rewound, spinning through the past couple of weeks, frantically searching for whatever error I'd made.

"There's nothing to explain or fix. You're through," he said, completely without emotion.

"I've done everything around here that I've been asked. Everything!"

"I know you have. But sometimes you have to take one for the team."

"Matt, you don't understand. I've been trying to get on the team but no one lets me. I'm doing handsprings here, just trying to find out what it is I'm supposed to do, and no one will talk to me. I'm excluded from everything, getting my information from memos that I pull out of the trash, and *now* you're telling me I'm taking one for the team? Can you at least explain that?"

My hands were shaking, and I was perspiring from the effort it took not to cry.

"It's about Reba Koronis, you know, from *Lip Balm*?"

"Yes, I know all about *Lip Balm*. I'm the *only* one who knows about *Lip Balm*."

"Well, she was driving in Los Angeles and she went past the

Nuart Theatre on Santa Monica and absolutely freaked out when she saw *Lip Balm* on the marquee."

"Matt, I've been trying to send her that information for weeks. I can even show you all the e-mails I sent Kenny asking for it, so that I could send Reba her posters and the names of the theaters where her film was opening. He refused to answer me."

"I understand, and I've had a conversation with him about that. No one thinks this is your fault."

"So why am I getting fired?" I asked, the tears finally spilling out.

"Reba's gotten hot. She's at P&Q now, with the same agent who represents the director of *Perp Friction*, and a lot of other good people. He's insisting that we roll a head to show that we understand how serious this is. He told Phil and Tony that if we didn't do this, Glorious won't be able to hire any of his talent."

"And in your new role as producer, you no doubt want a good relationship with this agent," I said, bitterness seeping into every syllable.

Matt waited a second before answering. At least I'd surprised him. "Well, Karen, obviously I do."

"That's just great. I really fucking appreciate this. You know that I was trying to reach you for days. You know that this was precisely the problem that I was trying to fix. And you're keeping Kenny? He's the one who decided Reba wasn't important enough to bother with in the first place!"

"Kenny's more experienced. I'm not going to be leading this department any longer, and we can't afford to lose one of the most senior people. Karen, I'm sorry, and I have to go."

I slammed the phone down at the same moment Geraldine appeared at my door. "I assume Matt's told you," she said. I nodded, and continued to cry. "Can we please not have any of that? I need to get your exit paperwork finished," she said, as Harvey jumped on my now-former chair, put his two stubby front legs on the desk, and sniffed the sandwich. "Oh, let me fix that for you, darling," she said, lifting off the rye bread and dabbing the mustard away with one of my napkins. After removing the offending condiment, she put the plate back in front of Harvey, who gulped it down. I hoped that he'd choke as it traveled through his extra-long dachshund alimentary canal.

Geraldine told me to pack my personal belongings and to make sure that I didn't take anything that wasn't mine—which wasn't even an option as she was standing over me, watching everything I did. "Honestly, Karen, I don't know why you're crying so hard."

"You know," I tried to compose myself so that I could speak. "It's just that I've enjoyed this job, even though it's hard, and I'm really going to miss working with the friends I've made." I was thinking of Robert, and Clark, of Dagney and Sabrina.

"You don't have as many friends as you think," she said. "You're really more of an acquired taste."

This remark had the uncanny effect of drying my eyes immediately. I stood for a moment, then said, "While we're being honest here, Geraldine, I thought I'd tell you that that fucking overstretched rat is not a substitute for a husband. After all, you deserve to know what people say behind your back."

I was completely calm and rational now. "Let's get to that paperwork you say you need. I really don't want to spend any extra time here. And I'm sure you want this," I said, sliding my cell phone hard across the desk toward her. It fell on the floor and smashed. "Oops, you didn't think fast," I said, laughing manically.

"Well, you never signed your contract, so there's no severance," she began. "That makes my life a bit easier."

"Yes, I suppose it does," I said. "Not to mention mine. I don't have to abide by the completely illegal noncompete clause, or the part that says that I can't bring suit against Glorious Pictures."

"No, I suppose you don't," she said.

"And, you know, that confidentiality agreement doesn't apply to me, either," I said, looking her right in the eyes so she could see how deadly serious I was. "Because as you said yourself, I didn't sign my contract."

"Really Karen, you're going to want to think about that. You don't want to make enemies in this industry." My comment had had the desired effect; Geraldine clearly looked shaken.

"Me? Enemies?" I laughed. "I'm not really concerned." I picked up my small box of belongings and left the room. Geraldine rode down in the elevator with me and, in true Glorious fashion, escorted me all the way to the curb.

THE EMPIRE STRIKES BACK

Out on the street, I tried to calm down, shifting the box from hand to hand as I wiped my eyes. I didn't want anyone from Glorious to see me like this. I looked back and saw that Geraldine was standing there, arms crossed over her chest, actually tapping her foot. I hailed a cab, smiled at her, and slammed the door, willing myself not to cry again until I was above 14th Street. I looked up to see if I could weep yet, and was startled to see the back of a familiar overpuffed down coat. "Stop!" I shouted to the driver, who almost gave me whiplash with his eagerness to comply.

Tossing about twice the fare in his direction, I jumped out of the cab and shouted. "Allegra! Allegra Orecchi!" She didn't turn around. "Allegra! Allegra! I don't work there anymore. Turn around!" The puffy coat kept moving away from me. I got closer and then said, "I have Oprah Winfrey for you, Allegra," in my best snooty-assistant voice.

She spun around, almost knocking me over with her tote bag, which was swinging wildly from the centrifugal force. "I suppose you think that's funny, Karen," she said, loudly and clearly, the way regular people spoke.

"Funny? No, that's not funny. It's pathetic. Pretending to be in Europe is pathetic. Your whispering and hiding is pathetic." I was once again experiencing that strange calmness that I'd had with Geraldine. "You, Allegra, are a sad excuse for a human being."

"You think you know so much," she said, her face full of rage. "All of you assistants, you think you know so goddamn much. You know nothing!" she shouted, starting to walk away from me again.

"Tell me," I said. "Tell me what I don't know. You might as well. Matt fired me today, for no reason."

"Maybe I was trying to have some piece of a life that didn't involve Phil and Tony and their movies. Or Vivian and Marlene and the rest of you. Not to mention George Hanratty—and yes, of course I know that you've met him."

How could she know that? She was either bluffing or just confident that he'd met all of us, just as I was.

"I just wanted to have ten minutes to myself—to try to have a relationship, or to talk to my mother, or deal with something other than this goddamn company. If I said I was talking to Oprah, they *had* to leave me alone." She suddenly sat down, parking herself on the crumbling sidewalk next to the West Side Highway. I sat down opposite her, keeping a safe distance.

"Why didn't you just ask?"

"I'm glad you think it was so simple. Do you think I wanted to spend every day listening to Vivian and Marlene whine and bitch about everything, and then deal with Phil and Tony and all their crap?" She stopped for a moment and leaned forward, pulling her knees against her body.

"You were supposed to be running the department; it's why you're the president."

"What I *wanted*," she said, "what I wanted, was to publicize films, to have something to do with the outcome, not to be some kind of mediator."

"So why did you pretend you were in Europe?"

"I was trying to get things back under control. I thought the rest of them would see that they could either figure out what they needed to do, or kill each other trying, but that they could do it without me."

"And that was the best you could come up with? I mean, Allegra, why didn't you at least take the damn trip?"

"I was afraid that Phil and Tony might need me, so I stayed nearby."

I stood up, my need to tell Allegra off any further suddenly disappearing. She looked like a street person, sitting there on the curb with her tote bag collection. I raised my arm and hailed another cab. "Good luck," I called out, not bothering to turn around before I got in.

Once at home I waited for Ellen and the moment she was through the door the whole story tumbled out. She listened patiently until I had finished and then asked, "You didn't sign the contract, did you?"

I shook my head. "No, that's the one thing I did right."

"That's good news. And I do think they owe you severance regardless—I'm going to make a couple of calls tomorrow. People are entitled to be paid for the work that they've done."

I thanked her and slipped into my room to call Abby. She was shocked, and sounded even more upset than I was. After my encounters with Geraldine and Allegra, and having explained everything to Ellen, I was finally at the point where I could explain the story to her without crying. At the same time, I was incredibly tired, and just wanted to go to bed. After chatting with Abby for a while, I told her I'd call her the next day.

"You'll get something new, something better," she said, before hanging up. Truthfully, I hadn't even thought that far ahead.

It was only eight, but I fell into a deep, thoroughly exhausted sleep and was completely surprised by the ringing phone. I looked at the clock and answered at the same time. It was 10 A.M. and it was Kenny. Maybe he was calling to apologize, or to offer me my job back, I thought.

"Karen, do you have Reba Koronis's home number?"

"What?"

"Reba's home number. You have it, right? I have to set up a meeting with her—Phil wants to release *Lip Balm* in twenty-five cities now, as a show of good faith."

"Kenny, why didn't you answer me all the times that I needed that information?"

"I was busy; it didn't seem important."

"But wouldn't it have been just common courtesy to answer me, and let me do my job?"

"I suppose, but I was involved in much bigger projects and that stupid little movie wasn't worth my time."

"But now the director of that stupid little movie is, and you don't know how to get in touch with her but I do, so you call me. That's amazing," I said.

"Karen, will you cut out the dramatics and just give me the number?"

"I'm sorry, Kenny, for being upset because I got fired over something that was completely your fault. Will you do me just one favor? I think you owe me that, at least."

"What do you need?" he asked, guardedly.

"I need you to go fuck yourself," I said, before slamming down the phone. These people were unbelievable. I toyed with the idea of calling Reba myself—her number was in my Palm Pilot, along with every other number I'd dialed while at Glorious. She deserved to know what her new pals really thought of her film, didn't she? After thinking about it some more, however, I changed my mind. Now that I was no longer a Glorious person, I didn't have to act like one.

The conversation with Kenny had woken me up completely. Ellen had been at work for hours; I was alone in the apartment and not sure what to do. I wasn't ready to call my parents just yet—they'd be sure to hop in the car and head down here, and I knew I didn't want that. I even thought about calling Elliott, but I needed my wounds licked, not my feet.

The phone rang again. It was Dagney and Clark, calling together. "We're so sorry," Clark said. "What can we do to make you feel better?"

"Actually, I think I'm okay. I just need to kind of decompress."

"Do you think you might want to come back to this department?" Dagney asked. "Geraldine still hasn't found another assistant to work with me."

"No, thanks," I said, choosing not to tell her what I'd found out from Allegra. "I don't want anything to do with that place."

"I understand," she said.

"You have to tell me one thing," Clark said. "Please?"

"Sure, anything."

"Is it true that you told Geraldine that her dog wasn't a substitute for a husband? The rumor's all over—I have to know."

"Absolutely," I said, laughing at the memory of her shocked face after I'd said it.

"Someone needed to tell her," he said.

"Where's Robert?" I asked, realizing that it didn't seem right not to have him on this call.

"I think he's in a screening," Dagney said, "but I haven't seen him all morning."

"Tell him to call me," I said, an idea forming in my mind. "And I'll talk to you both soon."

I called Robert on his cell and he picked up. "Can you meet me at your apartment at about three? I really want to talk to you," I said.

"I'm so sorry about this whole mess. I'll see you at three and you can tell me everything."

"Thanks," I said, before hanging up.

Ellen called. "Okay, I've got a little good news. I've had a couple of conversations with one of the attorneys at Glorious. You're getting the money you're owed, and you're also getting a couple weeks' severance. Additionally, they've agreed not to contest your unemployment claim, if you decide you want to collect it. And you're entitled, by the way."

"Thank you. You're a real life saver. I can't believe you did this so quickly, and that you were able to get what you wanted out of those morons."

"Well, actually," she said, hesitating, "it's this new guy I've been dating. He specializes in employer-employee issues and he took care of it."

"You're dating someone new?" I was thrilled for her. "How come you didn't tell me?"

"I haven't really seen you that much, and I was trying to keep it kind of quiet, until I had a better idea of where it was going. But the way he stepped up to the plate to help you—well, he's golden now, as far as I'm concerned."

"And I'm sure he thinks the same about you," I said, really meaning it. I was so glad for her. "I can't wait to meet him," I said, before hanging up.

I showered, dressed, and took the subway down to Janovic

Plaza, a paint and decorating store in SoHo. Seeing all the paint chips and wallpaper swatches made me feel like things could be new and fresh, as if people started again every day, maybe even every fifteen minutes. Besides, I needed to be busy with a project. Walking down an aisle lined with brushes, I heard a familiar voice.

"I said that the color needed to be the Tunisian sky at twilight in April. Clearly you have no idea! This is how it looks in May." It was Mackie Moran, chewing out some unsuspecting paint clerk. I wasn't even curious to see what she looked like.

I picked out some ceramic tiles, adhesive, grout, a bucket, and a special tiling sponge. It had been nearly ten years since I'd helped my father retile our kitchen, but I remembered exactly how we'd done it. Then I went to Pearl Paint on Canal Street and picked up several packages of adhesive letters and numbers in various sizes. I lugged everything into a cab and went to Robert's. He was standing outside his building when I got there, even though it was only sixteen degrees.

He hugged me tightly and held on for a moment. "I'm so sorry," he said. "I don't know the whole story, but I can't imagine what you could have done to get fired."

"Can we go inside?" He picked up a couple of the packages and we climbed the three floors to his apartment.

"I know this is going to sound absolutely insane, but remember that periodic table you wanted to make on your bathtub wall?" I said. "The one you were going to do before Phil cancelled Christmas?" Robert nodded, still not saying a word.

"Could I make it for you? I mean, I know what I'm doing—I helped my dad retile our kitchen a while ago, and you've been such a good friend, and a teacher, really, and I just kind of want to do this." I was babbling and Robert just stood there, smiling, understanding that I needed to concentrate on something besides losing my job.

"I'd love for you to do that. I'm so touched that you even want to."

"Here, let me show you." I poured out the contents of my various bags and boxes. "I got these tiles. I thought, this sort of light steel gray for the metals, and this lime green for the nonmetals and here's this ice blue that I thought would work well for the semimetals, even though there are just a few of them." Robert was nodding approvingly at the colors. "And then a nice, clean white for the background." I unfolded a copy of the periodic table that I'd printed out before I left home, then showed him the letters and numbers I'd bought at Pearl. "For the symbols and atomic numbers and weights," I said.

"Are you sure you want to do this?"

"Absolutely."

"Because it's a really big job."

"Honestly, that's exactly what I need right now. You'd be doing me a favor."

"Since you put it that way, how can I refuse?" He smiled. "I'm going back to the office now—Academy campaigning," he said with a grimace. "But I'll see you later. And I can shower at my gym in the mornings so that everything can stay nice and dry while you're working."

Robert left and I was alone again. I turned on the television, flipped to CNN, and turned the volume up loud enough that I could hear it in the bathroom. I studied the area around the bathtub; the wall was smooth and would take the ceramic adhesive well. Instinctively knowing that Robert would have a well-stocked toolbox, and that it would be stored under his kitchen sink, I opened it up and pulled out a tape measure. On a blank piece of paper I roughed out how the table would look on the wall. Then I took a few of the white tiles and used the adhesive to place them on the opposite wall, down near the bottom, so that tomorrow morning I would be able to tell if they had adhered sufficiently.

I methodically laid out the supplies in the order I would need them—tiles and adhesive first, then grout and the sponge and finally the letters and numbers, which would be last, after the grout had dried. Before I knew it, Robert had come home. "You're still here?" he said. "It's nine thirty."

I showed him the test tiles and told him that I'd be back in the morning. He gave me his extra set of keys so that I could let myself in the next day. "I brought you something," he said, pulling out a package of nonslip bathtub stick-ons. "So you don't fall in my bathtub. Blood's not an element," he said. They were shaped like little stars.

"Thanks," I said, before heading into the night.

The next morning I got up bright and early, and dressed in some old jeans and a tattered UMass sweatshirt. After getting off the subway near Robert's apartment, I stopped at a deli and bought a couple of Diet Cokes and a sandwich for lunch. In the apartment was a note: "Look in the refrigerator." It was stocked with juices, sparkling water, fresh fruit, and a bag of Milano cookies. I turned the television on to CNN, as I had the day before, and began to work.

Robert had put the stars in the bathtub and they gripped my feet nicely. The tiles from last night had held fast, a sign that the project was off to a good start. I taped the periodic table and my hand-sketched diagram to the wall next to me, and began to apply the tiles, row by row, from the bottom up. The news drifted in around me, as if a group of serious people were speaking in the next room. Without fully concentrating, I heard bits and pieces of political discussions, foreign affairs, news on the economy—all things that used to concern me in the days before I worked at Glorious. The entertainment segment came on and I heard a lead-in for an interview with Juliet Bartlett, and smiled to myself, thinking of her *Air Jane* costume. At two I broke for lunch, the tiles more than a third done at this point. I stepped back and looked at it with satisfaction. Robert was really going to like this.

Around seven Robert came in to check on my progress—by now the tile work was about three-quarters finished. "Karen, this is amazing. It's just how I imagined it would look. This calls for a celebration."

Citing my messy attire, I didn't want to go out, so Robert ordered in some Mexican food. After taking a bite of my grilled chicken burrito, I said, "So, what is it about the periodic table for you? Why do you like it so much?"

Robert bit into his steak taco before answering. "I've always loved it. Chemistry was my favorite subject because it was the one place where everything made sense, and behaved consistently."

I laughed. "I know that having things in order makes you happy."

"It's more than that. The elements have relationships with each other in a dependable way. Bromine is always going to melt at $-7.2°C$, and boil at $58.78°C$, no matter what. And it will always live right between selenium and krypton."

I didn't completely understand him, but I wanted to hear more. "And then I think about the world that we live in, how part of the beauty of it is that we don't know what's going to happen next, but it's important to have things that are reliable, too."

Working at Glorious could definitely make someone yearn for predictability. I imagined Phil and Tony, Allegra, Marlene, Vivian, Kenny, Matt, and Cheryl as elements, all fighting with one another about who got to do what, and when. The elements didn't have egos, I thought, and then mentioned this to Robert.

"Exactly. They can't afford to. They're the building blocks of matter—if any of them failed, the entire world would stop—no kidding."

"Do you have a favorite?" I asked, eating some more of my burrito. "Element, I mean?"

"The ones that we use every day—hydrogen, oxygen, sodium, nitrogen. And then there's argon, which is classified as a noble gas," he continued. "It's colorless, odorless, tasteless, but it can prevent other chemicals from exploding. And it's used in Geiger counters, too."

"So, basically, if argon's around, you won't notice it, but if you don't, that's bad news."

"Exactly," Robert said. "You get it. It's there to help, but not harm."

It was getting late, so I decided to leave. Robert walked me downstairs and helped me into a cab, then insisted on paying for it.

At six the next morning, my phone rang, waking me from a sound sleep.

"Karen, it's me."

"Hello?"

"It's Elliott. Have you seen the paper yet?"

"I'm still in bed. I think I'm still asleep."

"Good. I wanted to tell you myself. I wrote the book."

"The book?"

"Yes, the Waxman biography. I've been collaborating with George Hanratty, and last week we finished it and sold it to HarperCollins. They're putting a rush on to publish it in the spring. It's called *The Twins of TriBeCa*."

"Wow. That's great. I'm really happy for you. But how did you fall in with George Hanratty? I thought he was a drunk, a has-been. No one thought he could pull it off."

"It's a long story, but I'd love to tell it to you in person. Meet me for a drink tonight?"

I almost said "yes" automatically. I felt a wave of gratitude toward Elliott, who'd had me drunk and upside down and completely pliant with my feet in his mouth, and never once tried to get me to betray anyone, when it would have been so simple. I wished him a life full of beautiful women with pillow-soft feet that smelled like roses, who could walk on their hands so that he could enjoy them all the more. But at the same time, I knew that I couldn't be one of them.

"Actually, I'm trying to lay low right now. It's been an upsetting few days."

"I heard what happened—another Glorious mistake, in my opinion."

"Thanks, Elliott. I appreciate it. I'll call you," I said, knowing that I wouldn't, and knowing there would be many times in the years to come that I'd think about how he'd looked when he'd kissed me—when he'd kissed me and smiled at the same time.

I fell asleep for a couple of hours and then got ready to go to Robert's. Before I left I put on just the faintest touch of mascara and lipstick. Being unemployed didn't give me the right to look like a mess, I reasoned. I wanted to talk to Robert about Hanratty, and the book, but by now he'd be at the office and I was sure he couldn't speak freely there.

At the apartment, things were pretty much the same, except today's cookies were Entenmann's chocolate chip, and I had much less work to do. Confidently tiling away, I was able to pay more attention to the news. What had I been thinking, when I let *The Raven II: Nevermore* or *Anyone Can Sing* become more important than the latest Supreme Court decision, or what was going on in the countries that didn't have film festivals? I used to be so passionate about these things—but I'd let myself get swept up into this completely artificial life. And to make matters worse, that same make-believe world had chewed me up and spit me out. I concentrated on the tiles and pretty soon had the last one in place.

I was admiring my work, and trying to calibrate how much grout I would need to mix when the phone rang three times before the answering machine beeped. "Karen, pick up! Pick up!" Robert was saying urgently. I grabbed the receiver in the living room and heard the screech from the answering machine. "Hit the off switch. It's in my bedroom," Robert instructed me.

"That's better," I said.

"You're not going to believe this. I'm calling from Belinda's store. I had to leave the office to tell you."

"What?"

"So you didn't read Page Six today?"

"No, but I heard about the book that Hanratty and Elliott Solnick wrote."

"I know you had a couple of dates with that guy," Robert said.

"Well, I never told him anything," I said, defensively.

"No," Robert said. "He didn't need you to. He had Clark for that."

"Clark?"

"Yeah, apparently Clark was feeding all the information he could get from Gloria right to Elliott and Hanratty. He got fired an hour ago—Geraldine called the police to take him out of the building."

"And all the way to the curb, I'd imagine."

"But of course."

"It's horrible that Clark would be so two-faced. Gloria adored him."

"Oh, not that much. Gloria set the trap that caught him in the end."

"How did she do it?"

"She told Clark a story about Phil and Tony's father, that he'd run away because of gambling debts that had gotten out of control. When Elliott started calling around to confirm the story, they knew where it started."

"This is all just too much."

"It's absolutely insane around here. Allegra even came back from Europe to manage the crisis."

I imagined Robert standing there making finger quotes around "Europe."

"Anyway, Karen, I have to go back inside. Will you be there when I get back?"

"I think so—I just finished the tiles and I'm getting into the grout."

"Good, because I'm bringing home a surprise."

My head was spinning from all of this news. Clark, everyone's favorite Golden Child, had sold out Gloria Waxman, the beloved Glorious matriarch. Hanratty had actually managed to pull off what no one thought he could, and Elliott was probably out right now, using his advance to treat himself to the best scotch money could buy.

I turned it over and over again in my mind while continuing to work in the bathroom. A lot of things made sense now. Elliott had ditched me at the *Anyone Can Sing* premiere because his accomplice, Hanratty, was close by. Clark knew that I'd liked Elliott because they'd been working together. And, I guessed, Elliott had told him that we'd had a couple of dates, which is how Robert had found out.

A little while later, Robert walked in, carrying an oddly shaped bundle.

"What is that?"

"You'll see," he said mysteriously. "Are you hungry?"

"Starving. I've had only a few cookies and an apple today. Let me see what's in there!" I said, trying to pry it out of his hands.

"Okay. Close your eyes."

I closed them.

"Open them."

When I did, I couldn't believe what was in front of me. Robert had stolen Gloria's entire brisket, along with the precious Royal Doulton serving tray.

"You see, it's got the well-done half for Phil, and the rare for Tony," he said, pointing. "No matter what, Thursday is brisket day, but in the hullabaloo it wasn't hard to sneak it out of reception. The police were way too busy with Clark," Robert said. Then he got some silverware and we sat down to eat the brisket that until now had been enjoyed only by people named Waxman. It was delicious—marvelously seasoned and wonderfully cooked. If Le Bernardin ever did brisket, this is how it would taste, I was sure. I only regretted that I would never be able to tell Gloria how good it was.

A wild thought popped into my head. "Can I ask you something?"

"Sure."

"Do you know anything about those cancelled hotel reservations for Marlene's junket?"

"Perhaps," he said, smiling.

"The fake Cindy Adams column? The apology e-mail from Vivian?"

Now he was grinning like the Cheshire Cat. "No one thinks I'm there to do anything except break my back for them, so they'd never suspect me," he said. "I did everything pretty much in plain sight."

"Are you some kind of avenging angel?"

"More like an avenging Work Horse," he said.

"I just can't believe it. Those little tricks were all so unbelievably clever. And everyone got exactly what they deserved."

"That was the idea. The people at Glorious are so completely divorced from reality that it's not as if you can have a conversation with them and say something like, 'Hey, I didn't appreciate it when you screamed at me in front of everyone' or 'You know, that person made an honest mistake—you might have been a bit harsh with the punishment.' But they do register anger and embarrassment, at least on some kind of primal level."

This was a lot to take in all at once. Robert—quiet, organized, anal-retentive Robert, had dealt some severe blows to some mighty dragons. He'd eaten them for lunch, in fact.

"Robert, that's incredible. What a day. Hanratty's getting published and Elliott is his coauthor. Clark's been a mole—no, more of a rat—all along. And we've dined on the Waxmans' brisket!"

"Can I interest you in some more information?"

"Is there any more?"

"Well, there's the small matter of Hanratty, and why he was ejected from the kingdom in the first place."

"That's right. I almost forgot. They used to really like him, or at least that's how the story goes," I said, realizing that I'd heard it from Clark.

"Hanratty is only a couple of years older than Phil and Tony."

"He looks twenty years older than them."

"Yeah, well, a life on the bottle . . . ," Robert trailed off. "When Gloria and her husband, whose name was Irving, by the way, first got married there was a couple down the hall in their building in the Bronx. The husband's sister was living with them—she'd just gotten divorced and was having a hard time of it. She was staying with them until she got back on her feet.

"Sounds reasonable."

"Well, it was. And the sister, her name was Betsy Kincaid, became really good friends with Gloria. Betsy worked part-time at the butcher shop, and she used to trade Gloria lambchops in exchange for getting her hair done. This was while Irving was still around, and Gloria was just a talented housewife, not an entrepreneur."

"Okay, so what happened?"

"Well, Betsy's brother and sister-in-law had a little boy. And after the twins were born, Betsy would baby-sit the three kids while the two couples went out. And then one day, Betsy asked Gloria to do her hair in a really big bouffant, as big as she could get it. Gloria teased and combed for two hours, until Betsy's head was tremendous. She gave Gloria a whole rack of lamb in exchange, then ran off with Irving that same night."

"Poor Gloria. That's awful."

"Well, Gloria recovered pretty well, as you know, except that she never ate lamb again. As a matter of fact, that's when the brisket tradition started. And Betsy's brother and sister-in-law were so embarrassed that they moved away, and Gloria lost touch with them completely."

"So what does all this have to do with Hanratty?"

Robert held up his hand. "I was getting there. Gloria never really told the twins much, simply that their father left. They just figured he was a horrible bastard for leaving her, so they wanted nothing to do with him."

"That's sensible. I wouldn't cross Gloria Waxman, either."

"So imagine Gloria's surprise when, ten years ago at a premiere, she was seated next to George Hanratty. She nearly fainted."

"Why would she faint?"

"Because George Hanratty was the little boy whose wayward auntie ran away with Irving! At first, she didn't know who he was, but then they got to talking, and you know how Gloria likes to know everything about everyone, so she figured it out. Well, she was really shocked at first, but Gloria's a tough lady. And after she calmed down, she told Phil and Tony that she bore no grudges. 'It wasn't his fault that his aunt was a floozy and your father ran away with her. My only regret is that I wasted three cans of hair spray on that rotten head of hers,'" she said.

Robert's impression of Gloria had me in hysterics.

"So what happened?"

"They told Gloria that they wanted nothing to do with it, and then they told Hanratty in no uncertain terms that he was banned."

"And it destroyed his career, and then he destroyed himself," I said. "But at least he had a second act!"

"Exactly. I think it's going to be a great book," Robert said. "There are going to be all kinds of secrets in there. Between what Gloria's inadvertently told Clark, what Hanratty knows from the family, and what Elliott's been able to find out with all of his connections, it could be pretty damaging to the Waxmans."

"Yeah," I said, thinking it over for a moment. "It could also be really dull."

"Dull? I don't think so."

"I can't be positive, but I don't think there's really some big secret. They're twins. And one likes artsy stuff that wins Academy Awards, and one likes horror and comedy films that make a ton of money. They fight a lot, and they scream and they curse and they're miserable to work for," I said, thinking about my own year at Glorious. "But I don't know what else there is, really. Their movies are much more interesting than either of them, in my opinion."

"You might be right. We'll just have to wait and see," Robert said.

"And speaking of seeing"—I waved a hand toward the bathroom—"I might as well show you."

We got up and walked inside. Robert sucked in his breath.

"Karen, it's perfect. It's more than perfect. I can't believe you did this for me."

"I'm glad you like it. I just have one question," I said. "Do you see these spaces, where I've put white tiles?" I pointed to the bottom. "The spaces between ununbium and ununhexium and ununoctium? I don't know what to do with those."

"That's the best part. That's the beauty of the whole periodic table," he said, and suddenly he was holding my hand, and just as suddenly I realized that I wanted him to hold my hand.

"Those are the spaces left for the things that we know will be discovered, but we don't know exactly what they are," he said, turning toward me. "It's an acknowledgment of the unknown, and of not needing to know everything before it happens, but trusting that it will."

And at that moment, nothing in the entire world made more sense than what Robert had just told me.

ACKNOWLEDGEMENTS

I am surrounded by many wonderful, kind people who share their gifts with me every day. Each of you has made me feel truly blessed, and incredibly lucky. But I did want to single out just a few.

Steve Krupa, whose generosity and creative passion were key ingredients in this book—I will never be able to thank you enough, but I won't stop trying. Alice Truax, whose extraordinary mind is rivaled only by the benevolence of her heart; and to whom I owe a tremendous debt for helping me "use my words." Ian Spiegelman, for teaching me patience, and being the loveliest friend ever. Lynn Harris, *the* Lynn Harris—for finding the "on" button. Sue Feldman, my real Other Mother. Camille Colon, for always being in my corner. Tom Clavin, for having been there and done that, and willing to share his considerable wisdom at every turn. My cousin and best friend, the esteemed Dr. Maya Kravitz, for always being near by, no matter how many miles apart (too many!) we actually are. The irrepressible Mary Parvin, who graces TriBeCa with an abundance of warmth and opinions, which, of course, are always right. Kathy Diamant, who somehow always has enough to go around. The extremely intelligent and very beautiful Carina Wong, who is honest, no matter what. Stephanie Azzarone, for always knowing just what to say. Rebeca Schiller for telling great dog stories that make me smile.

Everyone at Psilos/Miles High—Jeff Krauss, Dr. Albert Waxman, Valerie Dudley, Leslie Hoeflich, Warren van der Waag, LaTanya Dial, Dave Eichler, Joe Riley, Lisa Suennen and Diane Gentile—you may never know how much letting me share your days, your pizza, and your lives has meant to me, but your contributions are on every page.

My distinguished panel of experts—no question was too tough, no detail too small for any of you to help me obsess over: Caroline Bitkower, Britt Bensen, Dahlia Smith, Dr. Glenn "The Great Gadoo" Muraca, Sigrun Hill, Hillery Borton, Stephanie from Bubble Lounge, Leonard Parker of Blue Star Jets. And Hillary Herskowitz, who knows *everything!*

The Pet Buffaloes—Sissy Block, Sabrina Paradis, Rachel (Sklar), Leslie Kaplan, Annemarie Conte, Alix Light, and Don Seaman—you are a superb herd and I am honored to have shared your table.

At Miramax Books, Jonathan Burnham, calm of manner and possessed of extraordinary diplomacy—many thanks for your patient guidance; Caroline Upcher for not putting up with any of my s***; Kristin Powers, who somehow makes everything come out right; Caroline Clayton, the best person to have on the end of the phone when I was sure I'd screwed up completely; Kathy Schneider and Claire McKinney, who talked me down from the ledge more than once; JillEllyn Riley and Jen Sanger—for always being helpful and compassionate.

And on the business side of things—Katherine "Braveheart" Boyle, my agent, who never once faltered.